THE PEACH STONE

BY PAUL HORGAN

NOVELS

The Fault of Angels   Far From Cibola

No Quarter Given   The Habit of Empire

Main Line West   The Common Heart

A Lamp on the Plains   Give Me Possession

A Distant Trumpet   Memories of the Future

Mountain Standard Time (*a collected volume containing* MAIN LINE WEST, FAR FROM CIBOLA, *and* THE COMMON HEART)

OTHER FICTION

The Return of the Weed   The Saintmaker's Christmas Eve

Figures in a Landscape   Humble Powers

The Devil in the Desert   Toby and the Nighttime (*juvenile*)

One Red Rose For Christmas   Things As They Are

The Peach Stone: *Stories from Four Decades*

HISTORY AND BELLES-LETTRES

Men of Arms (*juvenile*)

From the Royal City

New Mexico's Own Chronicle (*with Maurice Garland Fulton*)

Great River: The Rio Grande in North American History

The Centuries of Santa Fe

Rome Eternal

Citizen of New Salem

Conquistadors in North American History

Peter Hurd: *A Portrait Sketch from Life*

Songs After Lincoln

THE PEACH STONE

Stories from Four Decades

by Paul Horgan

NEW YORK ❈ FARRAR, STRAUS AND GIROUX

for
Rouben Mamoulian

NOTE

A word about the plan of this book.

These stories from the varied backgrounds and experiences of my life— East and West, the historical past and the legendary present—are drawn from different periods of work between 1930 and 1966. They are grouped here in four parts. Part One brings together stories that speak primarily of childhood, Part Two of youth, Part Three of maturity, and Part Four of age.

P.H.

Contents

[vii]

PART THREE ❧

PART FOUR ❧

PART
ONE

To the Mountains

Julio lay as quietly as he could, only his eyes kept moving, turning toward the open door that led into the other room, as if by looking there he could hear better what the women were saying. His brother Luis was asleep beside him. The same blanket of catskins covered them both. Luis could sleep no matter what. The firelight on the walls and the ceiling was enough to keep Julio awake, even if his mother were not weeping in the next room. It was a silent night outside, like all the other nights in this place of home.

"When the fire goes out I will go to sleep," thought Julio; his legs ached from holding them still. But he slept before the coals began to breathe their rosy lives to ash. And he dreamed of his world with much sorrow and love. The dream was a kind of memory that pursued him as if to be told again, a legend like one of the saints' lives, and thus worshiped.

Four nights ago his mother had given birth to a baby girl. Josefina Martinez came nine miles from Bernalillo to assist. The father was in Mexico on a wagon train. The trade in the summer and autumn of 1800 was promising, and the weather very fortunate. Rosa's baby came with no one there but her two sons and Josefina, the midwife.

They made a huge fire in the front room and left the door open so the heat would wave silently through. The boys stayed outdoors, shuddering like horses under the November moon. From within came the wafting firelight and the nimble sounds of repeated sufferings.

The great river lay beyond in the groves of cottonwoods. In the chill night the boys fancied they could hear river sounds . . . lappets of wave and shift of sand and suck of mud and the airy clamber of the huge heron as it heavied itself upward on bony wings. The chimney behind them blew fragrant sparks. Each boy felt like the deputy of his father. Luis was sixteen and Julio was thirteen. Luis was a stout boy, legs and arms like cottonwood branch, round and wieldy. He had pale eyes, and his glance never erred from guilt, the boy's guilt of accidental knowledge of the world. Julio was slender and something like a half-grown cat in his physical ways. He was wary and respectful of life's dangers. His eyes were black and so was his hair, and his face was dark. He had grown with caution, because fear slowly told him more as he grew up. Everything Luis did easily because he was older, Julio had to learn to do because he was younger, and thus everything was harder for him. The boys had no one but each other for companions, mostly; for they lived in the Rio Grande valley a ways out from the village of Bernalillo. They sometimes went there on horseback, when their father could spare the animals from work in the fields. Once, riding to town, Julio's horse had stamped and run wild, because a hunter in the tall saplings by the field near the river had shot his musket at a rising goose. Julio often dreamed of it, and the triumph of regaining the horse's head.

The brothers slept and the firelight faded down.

In the back room Rosa presently slept too, and Josefina sat watching her and the new baby.

Josefina was greatly girthed, with two circles of fat at her middle.

She was heavy-faced and her eyes were kind, even when her tongue was sharp and filthy. Thus her character: good heart, from instinct; wicked mind, from dealings in the hard world.

The baby lay by its mother's side.

"The face of a piñon," thought Josefina, staring at the tiny brown head and the little open mouth that breathed so roundly.

The house was thick as a fortress, with adobe walls. It stood on a little green flat of land above the fields, beyond which lay the Rio Grande. Over it went two mighty cottonwoods planted a long time ago by the grandfather of this house, who himself had left the service of the Viceroy of New Spain to scratch his own land and yield it to his own sons. To the east the fields faded into mesa country, rising face of gravelly sand that held dusty bushes. The mesa rolled away and lifted hills where little pine trees grew. In morning, distant under the early sun, the pine trees seemed to exhale a blue air; and from the blue air rose the mountains, whose trees looked far away like scratches upon the face of blue rock. The mountains were miles away from the house of the family, and sometimes they were altogether hidden by weather: cloud, or rain, or wind alive with dust. At other times the mountains were momentously close, as if moved in golden light by the hand of God, and every canyon, every wind course and water hollow in the rock, stood clear to the eyes of the wondering brothers. Hardly a day of their lives failed to be somehow influenced by the mountains off there to the east. In the lush river valley, life seemed spontaneous, from black earth; and bedded woman. The boys would one day own the earth and know woman; and perhaps, as some men did, know something of the mystery of the mountains at the world's rim.

Josefina came into the front room to kick some more wood on the dying fire; for cold was quick to get through her petulant flesh.

[5]

She woke Julio; but he lay with his eyes shut, identifying the noises she made and the profane rumble of her musing. When she went back, he heard his mother speak sleepily; then the baby squeaked and began to cry, what sounded to him like a mortal utterance and farewell of that alien little life in his mother's bed.

"Yes, if you all four of you get through the winter, that will be one of God's little jokes," said Josefina, slapping her hands on her cold belly. "This house never gets warm; and nothing to cover with, those boys out there, freezing on the dirt floor with a dirty old catskin." . . .

"My husband will bring back plenty of money and furs and clothes from Mexico," said Rosa. But she began to cry again, and mumble little sad doubts against the baby's hot temple.

"So, I will stay as long as I can," said Josefina. "But you know that can't be forever. . . . Be quiet now. You will choke the baby. Here, I'll take her, though God knows she may freeze to death. Get back to sleep. I will warm her."

Josefina took the baby.

Julio leaned and crouched from his bed to see what they did. There was a coldly steady candle burning by the wooden saint in the corner of the bedroom. Josefina held the baby with one arm and with her other hand pulled her tight dress away in front, and her huge bosom lay open and cavernous with shadow. There at her warmest and most copious being, she laid the baby and folded her breasts to it, and drew her dress together and held her arms like a cradle. Her cheeks quivered at the striving touch of the baby, some pleasure deepened in her being; and for no reason that she could recognize, out of her assortment of past lives—midwife, servant, thief, and harlot—she began to blush.

Her eyes watered and she smiled and sighed.

Julio backed into his bed again. His brother Luis flinched and jerked like a dog that is tickled when it dozes. Julio held his breath for fear he wake Luis. Yet he wanted to talk to him. He wanted to stir his brother into a fury of doing: to save this family; to prove that it was not a world for women, that it was their own little tiny sister who so blindly threatened their mother's life and will and who opened the disgusting bosom of a fat witch to lie there for warmth!

So his thoughts were confused and furious.

His boyishness misjudged the stuff of the complaining fat woman, just as his heart was jealous for his mother.

The fire was alive again in little flames like autumn leaves. He could not sleep. He could not forget. He hated his fears. They were with him, vaguely enlivened by Josefina's talk.

It was not long before winter.

In the broken darkness of firelight, Julio lay awake and prayed until he was answered by the same thing that always answered prayers, the earliest voice he had been taught to recognize, which no one else had to hear, the voice of God Himself in his own heart. Father Antonio made him know when he was a very little boy that the stronger a man was the more he needed the guidance of God. So when he felt afraid and feeble alongside his mild strong brother, he had only to pray, and shut his eyes, and remember Jesus, Who would presently come to him and say, "I see you, Julio Garcia; it is all right. What is it?"

"The mountains, to the mountains," thought Julio in answer to his own prayer.

"Blessed is the fruit of thy womb, Jesus."

"What is in the mountains?"

". . . now and at the hour of our death."

"There is much that my brother and I can do in the mountains, and as soon as he awakens I will tell him; we will take my father's musket and go hunting; we will bring home skins to keep our little sister warm, and show our mother that this is a house of men, who do what is right, no matter how hard it is to do." . . .

"*Amen.*"

Against the mica panes of the small deep window the early daylight showed like fog, silvery and chill. Luis jumped alive from sleep and went like a pale shadow to the dead fireplace, where he blew ashes off a few remote coals and, shivering in his bare skin, coaxed a fire alive. Then he found his clothes and got into them. He began to laugh at Julio, curled like a cat under the mountain catskins, waiting for warmth to get up to. Then he thought with pleasure of the work to be done outside; in the marching dawn; cold mist over the river; the horses stirring; animals to feed and release. He went out, already owner of the day.

Julio was awake all that time; and he squinted at the fire, judging nicely just when it would need more wood, lest it go out; and just when the room would be comfortable to arise into. He was soon up, listening for sounds in the other room. Presently Josefina came to make breakfast. She felt tragic in the cold morning, and her face drooped with pity for her heart which was abused.

"I am going home," said she.

"No, you can't do that," said the boy.

She looked at him with sad delight in his concern.

"Why can't I? —What do I get around here for my pains? —I was freezing all night."

"When my father comes home he will pay you plenty. —Luis and I can —We will bring you a glorious piece of fur."

"Oh, indeed: and where from."

"We are going to the mountains."

"—A pair of fool children like you?"

"Where is Luis? I must speak to him."

"He is out by the shed. —Yes, and another thing for your poor

[8]

mama to worry about. —If she lives through the winter it will be very surprising."

"What do you mean!"

She had nothing to mean, and so she made it more impressive by quivering her great throat, a ridiculous gesture of melancholy.

Julio ran outside and found his brother. They did not greet each other but fell into tasks together.

The sky was coming pale blue over the river, and pale gold edges of light began to show around the far mountain rims. The house looked like a lovely toy in the defining light, its edges gilded, its shadows dancing.

"Luis."

"What."

"I have an idea."

"Well."

"—Did you feel cold at night?"

"No, but you would not lie still."

"I am sorry.—I heard Josefina talking to Mama."

"The poor old cow."

"Do you realize that we are so poor that we haven't got enough things to keep us warm, especially with the new baby here? And an extra woman in the house—she ought to stay with us until Mama is well again."

"What are you going to do about it?"

"You and I should take the musket and go to hunt cats in the mountains, and bring home enough furs to satisfy everybody."

"Yes," said Luis, without any surprise, "I have thought of that too."

"Then I can go?"

"I suppose so. —If you behave yourself. It's no child's errand, you know."

"Of course not. —Then you will tell Mama?"

"Why don't you?"

"—She wouldn't think I *knew*."

"All right."

Now the smoke was thick and sweet above the house.

The light spread grandly over the whole valley.

Luis went to his mother's bedside and leaned down. The baby was awake and obscurely busy against her mother's side.

"Mama."

"My little Luis."

"Julio and I are going to the mountains for a few days, to get some furs."

"No, no, you are both too young, that little Julio is just a baby, now, Luis, don't break my heart with any more troubles!"

"What troubles: we have no troubles!"

"Your father is gone, we have no money, my children shiver all night long, that Josefina is a fat crow. Father Antonio hasn't been near us since the baby was born." . . .

She wept easily and weakly. Luis was full of guilt, and ideas of flight. He leaned and kissed her cool forehead and laughed like a big man.

"—You'll see. My brother and I will come back like merchant princes."

"Then you are going?"

"Yes, Mummie, we'll go."

She stared at him in a religious indignation. This was her son! So even sons grew up and went away and did what they wanted to do, in spite of all the things women could think of to keep them back?

Later Julio came to say goodbye and she shamelessly wooed him to stay, with the name of God, and her love, and his pure dearness, and various coquetries; he felt a lump in his throat but he coughed over it, and kissed her, while she said:

"My poor little darling Julio, already running off from home!"

"But I tell you!" he said, and then he began to smart in the eyes, so he shrugged, like his father, and went to the other room, where he paused and said:

"Thank you, Josefina, for staying until my brother and I get back."

"—The devil takes many odd forms," she said with a pout.

The little house was full of shadows in the daytime, for the windows were deep and small, and this suggested how narrow, how cloudy the world was to those who lived there. There were facts within eyesight, and farther away than that there were rumors only, and in the heart there were convictions learned of life and ordered by heaven. But through earnings of their bodies and their spirits, they owned life, and loved it, as it used them.

They had two horses and the musket which their father had left at home before his last departure for Mexico, from Albuquerque, where the wagon trains set out. They had a rawhide pouch containing things to eat, loaves and chilis and dried meat. As soon as they were free of the little fields of home, Julio began to gallop; and Luis overtook him and, saying nothing, reached out for the halter and brought him down to a walk. Julio felt very much rebuked; he sat erect on his horse and squinted his eyes at the mountain rising so far ahead of them, and thought of himself as a relentless hunter, the snake of the sand hills, who is hungry only once or twice a year, and comes forth then with slow tremendous appetite to take whatever he desires from resistless owners.

The boys toiled over the land all morning.

They paused and looked back several times, touched by the change in the look of their farm, which lay now like a box or two on the floor of the valley; and they thought respectively, "When I have my farm, I shall want it to be on higher ground," and "What if something dreadful has happened since we left home, if the baby choked to death, or a robber came, I should never forgive myself."

But they turned again to the mountains, letting their dreams of personality fade.

The mountains looked strangely smaller as they advanced. The foothills raised the riders up, and from various slopes the mountain crowns seemed to lean back and diminish. The blue air in canyons and on the far faces of rock slides and broken mighty shoulders was like a breath of mystery over the familiar facts of memory.

"Let me carry the musket now for a while."

"No, we might as well decide that now. I am to have it all the time."

"Why, that isn't right!"

"No, I have had more experience with it. It is our only arm. Now be sensible."

"Just because I am the younger, you always do this way. —I tell you, I am an excellent shot."

"You may be. But I am nearly four years older, and—I just think it better this way."

"I wish I'd known before we started."

"Why don't you go back, then?"

"I will."

But they rode on together. Easily triumphant, Luis could afford to be indulgent; later on he rode close to Julio and knocked him on the back and winked.

"You think I am not as much of a man as you are," said Julio bitterly.

"Well, you're not."

"You'll see! I can show you!"

"A man always agrees to do the thing that is best for others."

"Well, whose idea was it, coming to the mountains to hunt skins for our family?"

"Sure. Yours."

The brothers' love for each other was equally warm, but derived from different wells of feeling.

Sometimes they felt only the love; at other times only the difference.

Now in afternoon, riding on the windy November plain, and knowing that before nightfall they would be in the very shadow of the nearest mountain reach, they felt their littleness on that world; and so they made their feelings and their thoughts big, and owned those wild rocks and that crown-cut skyline in their souls; and their spirits rose; and in the wilderness, with none but themselves to use and know, they had a certain giddiness. The air was lighter so high up above the river valley. They looked back. An empire of sand-colored earth; and there, in the far light, the river herself, furred with trees. They looked ahead; but, in doing that, had to look up, now.

It was a crazy giant land; a rock that looked like a pebble from here was higher than a tree when they got to it.

"We must find a place to leave the horses."

"What?"

"You idiot, we can't expect horses to climb straight up cliffs like that over there!"

"Sure, we'll find a place to leave them."

"—It must be nearly too late to go into the mountains tonight."

"We'll make a fire here."

"If it is clear enough tonight, they could see our fire from home."

"They could?"

The thought made Julio shiver. But then it was already getting chill. The sun was going down. Great colorful energies from its last heat began to shift and brood on the mountains, until a veil of rosy mist covered it all; and then slowly earth's own shadow climbed with vast measure up the mountain faces and left them the night.

They awoke the next morning under the cold mountains, and in their rested souls there was a mood of gods. They caught their horses and rode along the last little flat before the great rise; and before the sun was up over the rocky shoulder, they had found a little box canyon where there was a growth of straw-colored grass and through which there washed a small creek. Leading the horses, they walked far into the narrow shadowy canyon and at last Luis said:

"There."

"What."

"Here is the place to leave the animals. We can make a little fence down here, and then be safe when we go off to hunt."

"What will you build your fence with?"

"Some big rocks and then a lot of branches that will seem high to the horses."

"Where does that river come from, do you suppose?"

"If you'll stop talking long enough to get to work, we'll go and find out."

The light of builders came into their eyes, measuring, devising; after a few trials, they had a system for their work; they moved harmoniously. Given need, materials and imagination, nothing wanted. They grew warm, and threw down their coats. The sun quivered in watery brilliance high beyond the rocky crown and then came into view, spilling such warmth and glory down the ragged slopes that the brothers hurried harder, enchanted by the job of life.

When they were done, they untethered the horses and took up their most valuable possessions—the food, the musket, the powder, balls, their knives, their tinder—and went up the canyon, following the creek. It led them into shadow; they had to wade; the rocks widened; sunlight ahead; then a miniature marsh with moss and creatures' tracks; then a little fall, which they heard, a whisper in diamond sunlight before they saw it, and under it a black pool plumbed by the sun to its still sandy floor.

The fall came down from a rocky ledge halfway up the face of a gray stone cliff.

The forest shadows beyond it, which they saw looking up, were hazy with sunlight and noon blue.

It was the shelf of still another world; the mountains seemed to be made of terraces leading up, and up, each into a new state of being; until to the brothers' souls, born of the obscure little farm in the river valley, far from cities and reliant upon God and priest for all further knowledge, it seemed that the last terrace of all must end at the very step to heaven.

"We'll swim!"

The fall drifted into the canyon and was wavered by the warm air reflected off the rocks about.

The boys took off their clothes and fell into the water; for a moment they hated the cold shock, and then they were happily claimed by the animal world. They were away from everything. They were let to their senses. They dived and splashed and bellowed, awakening the silences to echo, which only tempest and beast had awakened before them. This was a bath of a superman; not the idle, slow, muddy, warm current of the Rio Grande, which suggested cows and babies paddling and hot mud drugging boys who swam in summer.

They came out into the warmer air and slapped until they were dry; then they dressed.

"Up there, we've got to get up there some way."

Luis pointed up to the higher world beyond the fall. There were gigantic pines standing in light-failing ranks; and behind them a great plane of rock shaggy with its own breakage.

So they retreated from the waterfall and went around it, climbing and clawing until they had gained the upper level. They stood to listen. Enormous and pressing, the quiet of the mountains surrounded them. Their eyes, so long limited to a tame river world, hunted ahead. They were explorers, so far as they knew. What no man has ever seen before! There was a mysterious sense of awe in the first eye that owned it.

As they passed in and out of shadow, they felt alternately cold and warm.

As they went, they were often forced by the huge silence to stop and let their own sounds die away.

They would laugh at each other at such moments, and then go on.

In midafternoon they thought they must plan to go back, since it took them so long to come. The horses would need company and perhaps protection against beasts.

The sun was yellower and cooler.

The way they had come no longer looked the same; coming, they had watched another face of it; now retreating, they had to look back often to recognize their course. They lost it, or thought they had, when they came to a bench of gray stone in a spill of light through branches. Then they looked aside, and saw the ledge curve and vanish in a stout hillside, and emerge a little farther on and there become the rocky shelf over which rustled their waterfall of the sunny noon.

"It is made by heaven for our purposes!" said Luis.

"Yes, it certainly is. —How do you mean?"

"Well, the cats probably come and drink and lie here, and other animals. We could be here on this shelf, you see."

"And fire down on them?"

"Sure."

"Jesus!"

"Come on."

They started along the ledge and then shagged back and nearly fell down to the canyon floor below when a boom of air and shock arose and smote them from a few feet ahead. It was the thunder of a great bald eagle who beat his way off the rocks and straight up over them, his claws hanging down, his hot red eyes sparkling for one tiny second in the light of the sky. Then he wheeled and raised his claws and extended his head and drifted off in a long slanting line like the descent of the mountain edge over which he vanished.

The boys were breathless.

It scared them.

It also hushed them; the grandeur of that heavy bird leaving earth for air.

"How I would love to get a bird like that!"

"To kill him?"

"Or at least get some of his feathers."

Julio moved forward and then crouched and called for his brother.

"Luis, look, hurry, here is what he had!"

They were looking at a partially picked mountain lion cub, off which the eagle had been feeding.

"Julio, you see now? Here is where the big cats will come. They will roam until they find it, and they will watch. The eagle carried off the baby cat. He'll come back, too!"

Julio did a thing like a very small boy. He kicked the carcass of the cub off the ledge into the shaly slide below.

"What did you do that for?"

"I don't know."

"It was wonderful bait! Now it's gone!"

"Well . . ."

"Oh, come on!"

The godlike temper and power of the day was gone for them both; Luis exasperated; Julio tired and guilty.

As they went down to the canyon where the waterfall seemed to stand, not fall, in a mist of blue shadow now that the sun was sinking, they looked up and saw the eagle so high that he seemed like a spiraling leaf. Luis shrugged and said:

"Oh, cheer up, I suppose he would have come back anyway and carried his supper off!"

But Luis, though he was again friendly, could not offset the chilling of the whole day; and the rocky clear cold cupping of night in those walled places closed over Julio and confirmed his hunger, his bitterness, his youthful rue at the turn of happiness into misery, like the turn of day into dusk.

All right, if everybody was older than he was, let them parade and give orders.

Time was his enemy, just as much as mountains, and needed conquering.

He could dream of pushing them all back, and making his mortal little grant to the world.

If Luis felt so superior, Julio would show him some day.

They scampered down the canyon as fast as they could, for where they had left the horses was like a station of home to them, and thus desirable; man's claim endowing the earth with his own virtue and responsibility.

To the boys, the mountains seemed to create the weather, to give it off like a part of mountainhood.

When it was dark enough, they looked for stars, and saw some; but clouds had come, and a damp, warmish wind, and the canyon talked in wind, trees keening, and now and then an almost silent thunder of a wind-blow when it met a high rock side of a hill.

By the last light of their fire, Luis examined his musket, to see that the day's toil over hard ground hadn't damaged it any.

"Let me see it," said Julio.

"What for?"

"Oh, can't I just *see* it?"

Luis handed it over.

Julio sighted along the barrel.

"She's a lovely one," he murmured. Then he gave it back, ready to go to sleep, chuckling with affection for Luis, who would be so surprised.

Straight above the canyon, but so high above, the wind went by all night long.

The campfire hardly felt the breath of it.

But the high places of the whole mountain system did, and there was a gather of some moist, soft, warmish air over the peaks; the stars blurred; the highest timber exhalant; the top naked rocks misted.

Dawn came with a ghostly diffusion of misty light; the slow march of shapes.

Julio was ready.

He rolled with almost infinite slowness to the ground, free of the blankets, and left Luis slumbering like a mummy who knew the cold of Mexican centuries.

He crouched and slowly went around the bed, and took up the musket and ammunition from his brother's side.

He sniffed the air and it was bittersweet with cold and some drifting new flavor.

He didn't know, in his excitement and caution, that it was the presage of snow.

He went up the canyon chewing on a hank of jerked meat from his pocket. He was abroad in his own wilderness, with his own gun; in effect, with his own destiny. He remembered yesterday's trail very well; and he toiled while the light grew; yet, there being no sun, everything had a new look, though he had seen it before. He came after a long time to the pool and the waterfall. There he stopped and looked back. Now he realized how far it was; how many hours divided him from Luis, who must have been awake and wondering hours ago.

What would Luis do?

Would he kick the hard ground in fury, and halloo for him?

Or would he set out in pursuit?

But which way would Luis decide to go?

Or perhaps he was weeping at the conviction that his beautiful young brother Julio had been carried off in the night by beasts of prey.

Then the image of a devouring lion shouldering a musket was too odd, and Julio laughed; then he smartly turned to see where another's laugh came from; then he laughed again, at his echo in the rocky room with the sky roof.

The waterfall was like a wraith made of heavier air than the gray essence that filled the intimate little canyon.

"The cats will come to the ledge," thought Julio, faithful to his brother's wisdom even though he outraged it.

He went around the long way, slowly going across the roll of the rocky hillside, and found himself then in the tall forest up there. There the air hung among the trees like heavy cloths among dark dripping pillars.

He knew that a hunter must wait; so he settled himself to do so on a tilted shelf of moss, between two big boulders, lacy with fern and dark with shadow.

His stomach was clutched by doubts and partly whetted hunger, and the enchantment of folly, and the burlesque of courage.

Hardest of all was to keep the silence of the mountains, lest he startle his game.

Many times he was ready to get up, relieve the ache of his set legs, and go back to Luis, and pretend that he had only wandered a few feet away from home but had oddly managed to get lost.

But he was afraid now.

He was afraid of the way the sky looked, dark, and soft, and wind very high up which pulled the clouds past the peaks as if tearing gray cloth on the sharp edges.

He was lost, really.

The musket was a heavy sin across his lap. It was loaded. Perhaps he should unload it and scamper back.

But then if a mountain cat came to the ledge, he would be helpless.

Then he remembered for the first time that he might be in danger from the animals.

It sent blood back through him, and he grew angry at such menace.

"If they think they can hurt me, they are crazy, those wildcats!"

So he spent the early day and noon in thoughts of himself and his furies, while the peace of the forest was held, and the sky now came down in darkness and again blew upward in windy lets of silvery light.

And he stayed, watching.

He was so alone and silent that the first touch on his cheek out of the air startled him, and he faced his head quickly to look: but what had touched his cheek was the snow, shortly after noon.

It came down, dandled by the odd currents of airy wind in the irregular mountains, like white dust sifting through the ancient stand of trees up the mountainside.

Julio blinked at the spotty snow falling before his eyes, and he licked the delicious flakes that starred his lips.

The rocks were beginning to look white.

The distance was reduced. When he tried to peer as far as he would, his sight seemed to go so far and then turn back.

All suddenly, a most childish wave of lonesomeness broke over him, and he knew how far away he was, and how solitary; how subject to the mountains and to his own mortality, which was so dear to him now.

He got up.

Something else moved too, in the whitening world.

He saw it, obscurely dark against the white stone shelf below him in line of sight. It was a mountain lion coming down the ledge with beautiful stillness and almost the touch of snow in its own paws.

Its heart-shaped nose was along the ground, smelling the fresh snow and whatever it covered.

Julio lifted the gun, which was as light as he wanted it in this moment, and watched, and licked the snow off his upper lip. Then with his eyes wide open and his cheeks blown up, he fired.

He couldn't hear the lion cry, or the echo of the amazing blast through the canyons and the aisles. He was deaf from it. But he sat down behind his rock and watched while he reloaded, and saw the cat spilling its blood on the snow; and then gradually he could hear it moaning as his head cleared; and it cried and sounded like a huge kitten, which made his eyes water. Then it suddenly died. The snow continued on it passively, cooling the blood, and making it pale, and finally thickening over it entirely.

After a long time Julio came down from his rock and touched his game.

He glanced around to see if any more cats happened to be there. There were none. He was exalted and indifferent. He rolled the heavy lion off the ledge down to the sloping hillside below it. There the snow was thinner. There he set to work to skin the cat, as he had watched his father skin animals at home, for fur, for rawhide.

His knife was so wet and cold that it tried to stick to his hands.

He was late in finishing.

He felt proud.

[22]

Maybe Luis would be annoyed, but not for long. To bring home the first fur? He had a loving warm tender heart for all animals, now that he had conquered one of the greatest. He felt that animals must love men in return, and serve them humbly.

Done, then, he returned to thoughts of others, and then he could have groaned aloud when he really imagined what Luis might feel.

Now with the heavying snow and the night beginning to fall in the middle of the afternoon, Julio stared and said:

"Do you suppose my brother is in danger because I took away his gun? What if he has been attacked? What if I had not had the gun when the lion came? It would be the same with him, without any protection! —Oh, my Jesus and my God, help me to get back in a hurry, and have him safe when I get there!"

Now the hunter could not scramble fast enough to undo what his day had done.

He shouldered his new skin which was freezing and heavy, and his gun and his supplies, and went down off the rocky hill. In the bottom of the chasm where the waterfall entered the stream, it was dark. The black water of the creek alone was clearly visible. The snow lay against him in the air when he went.

He stopped and called out, then turned to listen; but the spiraling flaky darkness was vastly quiet.

He hurried on and sobbed a few times but he said to himself that it was simply that he was cold; not that he was sorely afraid and sorry.

"Certainly I can see!"

But he paid for this lie when he struck a rock that cut his cheek and threw him down to the ground, where the soft copious snowfall went on secretly to change the mountains, to enrich stony hollows with soft concavities, to stand the bare ridges barer above snowy articulations.

[23]

He struggled to make a small fire, scratching twigs and needles and branches from the lee side of rocks, having to feel for his wants. At last he produced a flame, and his heart leaped up farther than it had fallen. The firelight on the snow was so lovely, so like a blessing, that he felt like a young child, yet not afraid any more. In the light he saw where he was and collected more branches, building craftily, to bring up his flames, until the canyon was roaring with light and heat at that spot.

He sat, then lay on his new fur, with the raw side down.

The snowflakes made a tiny, fascinating little hiss of death when they fell into the fire.

"Luis will be all right. I will get to him early in the morning, as soon as it is light, I shall start out."

He dozed and awoke; at last to see his fire gone. Then he knew he must stay awake.

What he knew next was so strange that he felt humble. In spite of trying not to, he had fallen asleep, and was then awakened afterward by wave after wave of sound, through the falling, falling snow which hushed everything but this clamor that had awakened him, the ringing of a bell. The bell clanged and stammered and changed with the wind; like the bell of the church at home, miles up the valley on a still hot summer Sunday morning, speaking to him, and everyone faithful within its sound.

"But this is not—there can be no church in these mountains!" he said in the blackest density of the snowfall that night.

And he listened again, but now heard nothing, nothing beyond the faint sense of hushing in the air made by the falling snow.

The bell was gone; it had served to awaken him; somewhere beyond this cold separating fall, it had rung out for him; true, even if it came to him as a dream of security and the dear refuges of the suffering.

[24]

He did not lie down again; but sat; marveling; sick for home and fervid with secret vows and wonder at the obstinacy of the world.

The snow continued with daybreak.

He set out again as soon as he could see a few feet in front of him. As the light grew, so did his sense of folly.

It was as if he had dreamed of the things that might happen to his brother Luis.

All this greatness of accomplishment disappeared. What good was this smelling and frozen catskin now? He threw it down by an icy rock and found that he could now run, trotting, without the awkward burden of the cat hide, which was stiff and slippery with its frozen leggings of fur which stuck out, ragged and indignant, the congealed ghost of the cat.

The snow died away as Julio hurried.

The wind became capricious and bitter. It scratched in long sweeps down the canyon and bore out over the open plains, which Julio could begin to see as the day grew and he toiled farther down the shadowy chasm.

He kept staring ahead for sight of the spare pines which stood by their camp.

He remembered seeing the pines against open sky the first night there, which meant that they were nearly out of the mountain's fold.

He thought he saw the sentinel trees once; broke into a hard run; and then stopped panting when he saw that the gray light on a wall of rock had looked for a moment like a misty sky out there over the plain.

His heart came into his mouth; and he trudged on, confused by the fashion in which a child's devices ended in nothing.

The musket was heavy and cold in his grasp. He had it still loaded. Perhaps he ought to shoot it off, a signal for his brother?

But he would call first.

He cried out, and stood to listen, his whole body turned sideways to hear an answer.

There was none.

The sound of his own voice seemed mournful.

Now he knew that the bell he had heard last night, waking him up during the snowstorm, was a miracle, sent to keep him from freezing to death in his sleep.

So he began to run again, and his heart nearly burst, he thought, with burdens of hope.

Perhaps there would be another miracle, to keep Luis safe and bring Julio back to him right away.

Julio crawled over the rocks that seemed cold enough to crack in the weather; he waded where he had to in the glazed creek; suddenly it was lighter; the sky lay before him as well as above him; and at last he looked down on the miniature meadow of the canyon mouth where the horses were fenced. There! Yes, there were the guardian pine trees.

"Luis, Luis, I am back!" he cried, but he choked and made only a sobbing sound. There was no fire burning at the camp; and Julio was thumped in the breast by fear again, as if Luis had gone back home with the two horses and left him as he deserved to be left, alone in the mountains where he had been such a fool.

He hurried and then saw the horses, far down the way.

Then he heard a voice, talking to him from a distance; no words; level, careful sounds; it sounded like Luis.

"Luis, where are you!"

Julio came down farther.

He squinted around, and then upward.

"I am glad to see you back. Stop where you are!"

"Luis!"

"Be careful."

At the same moment Julio heard how Luis spoke from the tree where he was hanging, and he saw, at the base of the tree, the wolf which sat staring upward perfectly quiet and ready.

The wolf was huge and looked like a dog, except that he was gray, the color of rock, which was why Julio didn't see him for the first little while.

The wolf must have heard him, for his ears were standing up and the fur on his spine was silvery and alive. Julio stood shocking-still and was perfectly sure that the wolf's eyes were straining toward him as far as they could without the turn of the head, and that the animal was ready to turn and attack him if necessary.

So there was a grotesque interval of calm and silence in the canyon.

Luis was hanging to the pine tree, which had a few tough fragments of branch about sixteen feet above the ground.

The sun tried to shine through the bitter and cloudy day.

Luis looked white and sick, half-frozen; his eyes were burning black in new hollow shadows.

"Julio," said Luis, as lightly as possible, never taking his eyes off the wolf; indeed, as if he were addressing the wolf.

"Yes, Luis," whispered Julio.

"You have the gun there with you, haven't you?" asked the older brother, in an ingratiating and mollifying tone, to keep the wolf below him still intent upon his first design.

"Yes, Luis."

"Well, Julio," said his brother with desperate charm, velvet-voiced and easy, "see if you can load it without making much disturbance, will you?"

"It is loaded, Luis."

"Oh, that is fine. Then, Julio, pray Jesus you can manage to shoot the wolf. Julio, be easy and steady now . . . don't.move.fast.or. make.any.noise. Julio, for.the.love.of.God . . ."

It was like coming back to the reward of his folly to Julio.

He held his breath, to be quiet.

He thought Luis was going to fall from the tree: his face was so white and starving; his hands so bony and desperate where they clutched.

"Why, of course I can shoot the terrible wolf," said Julio to himself, slowly, slowly bringing the musket around to the aim.

Luis from his tree against the gray pale sky went on talking in tones of enchantment and courtesy to the wolf, to keep alive the concentration, until Julio fancied the wolf might answer, as animals did in the tale of early childhood, "A Dialogue between Saint Philip and the Wicked Fox."

"We shall see, my friend Wolf, just sit there.one.more.minute.if you please until.my.brother gets the thing ready . . . it.is.better, Wolf, for you.to.want.to.eat.me.than.my.horses . . . Are.you.ready. Julio . . ."

The answer was the shot.

The wolf lashed his hindquarters around so that he faced Julio, whence the sound had come.

He roared and spat; but he could not move. His back was broken. He sat and barked and snapped his teeth.

Julio ran a little way forward, then was cautious. He stopped and began to reload.

Luis fell to the ground.

He had his knife ready.

But he could not move as quickly as he would. He was cold and stiff and cramped. He hacked his knife into the animal's breast, but the stab was shy and glancing. The wolf made a crying effort and scrabbled its shattered body forward and took Luis by the leg.

"Now Julio! Your knife!"

Julio dropped the musket and came down to them.

"Where? Luis!"

"Under his left forearm!"

"Wolf!" said Julio, and drove his knife.

It was all.

For a moment they all stayed where they were; panting, the brothers; the animal, dead, and slowly relaxing thus.

The flavor of danger was common to all three while it lasted undecided.

Now there was victory; and the brothers sweated and couldn't speak, but hung their heads and spat dry spit and coughed and panted.

"Well," said Luis, at last.

"Did he bite you bad?" asked Julio.

"No, he couldn't bite very hard, not even like a dog; he was too hurt."

"Let me see."

They peeled the cloth away from the leg just above the knee. The teeth had torn the cloth and the flesh. It did not hurt. It was numb. It bled very little. The skin was blue.

There was nothing to do to the leg except cover it again, they thought.

They took as long as possible at it, but they had presently to come to the story of the young brother's folly; and as soon as that was done, they felt elated: the one penitent and grave; the other pardoning and aware that the terrors of the experience were more useful to his young brother than any words of rebuke.

"—And I know right where I left the lion skin; we'll get it later! —We can get many more!"

Julio was ballooning with relief, now that it was all over and done with. He felt as he always felt after confession in church, airy and tall.

The physical misery in snow and wind and rocky mountain

temper—this was their outer penalty. But the boys knew an inner joy at the further range of their doing. Simply being where they were, at odds with what menaced them—this was achievement; it was man's doing done, confirming the love for their family and bringing animal craft to protect it.

Late that day the sun did break through and a little while of golden light seemed to relieve the cold. It didn't snow again that night. They kept their fire high. Luis was oddly too lame to walk. But he was glad to lie and watch the flames; and to smile at Julio's serious bearing, full of thoughtful play in his face which meant plans and intentions.

The day after the snowstorm the valley itself came back in a kind of golden resurge of autumn. The house at the little farm was soaked with melting snow; running lines of dark muddy thaw streaked from the round-worn edges of the roof to the walls and the ground.

The temper of the river was warmer than the mountain weather. The willows and cottonwoods lost their snow by noon. The mountains were visible again, after the day of the blind white blowing curtain over the plain.

Not many travelers were abroad; but Father Antonio came down the road shortly after noon, and Josefina saw him, his fat white mare, his robe tucked above his waist, his wool-colored homespun trousers, and his Mexican boots. She went to tell Rosa that the priest was coming at last, and to stop crying, if that was all she was crying for.

The priest dismounted in the yard and let his horse move.

Josefina tidied herself in honor of the visit; and he came in, catching her at wetting her eyebrows. She immediately felt like a fool, from the way he looked at her; and she bowed for his blessing, furious at his kind of power over and against women.

"I didn't get your message about the baby until two days ago, and then I said nothing could keep me from coming as soon as I could. Isn't it fine! Where is he? Or is it a girl? —I hope you have a girl, already those bad boys of yours, where are they?"

Rosa felt as if authority had walked into her house and that she need have no further vague wonders and fears about surviving this life on behalf of her baby and her boys.

Father Antonio was a tall, very spare, bony man nearly fifty, with straw-colored hair, a pale wind-pinked face, and little blue eyes that shone speculatively as he gazed. He was awkward; he couldn't talk without slowly waving his great-knuckled hands in illustration of his mood; and he loved to talk, putting into words the great interest of his days. Everything suggested something else to him; he debated with himself as if he were two Jesuits, they said in Santa Fe, where he was not popular with the clergy because he preferred working in the open land among the scattered families of the river basin.

"Where are the boys?" he asked.

Rosa was at peace. Her cheeks dried and her heart seemed to grow strong. She felt a surge of calm strong breath in her breast. She was proud.

"They have gone hunting, they have been gone several days now. In the mountains."

Josefina lingered on the outside of a kind of sanctuary which the priest and the mother made, a spiritual confine which she could not enter, a profane and resentful woman. But she could toss her opinions into it.

"They are little fools, a pair of chicken-boned infants, crazy, going to the mountains. It snowed there for two days. They will never come back."

Rosa watched the priest's face, ready to be frightened or not, by his expression.

He glanced at Josefina, a mild blue fire.

"They are probably all right."

Josefina mumbled.

"How will a man ever know what goes on," asked Father Antonio, "unless he goes out and looks at it?"

"How long can you stay, Father?" asked Rosa.

"Till we christen the baby."

"But—"

"I'll wait till the brothers come back, so the baby will have a godfather."

"I—godmother," simpered Josefina on her outskirts, making a fat and radiant gesture of coquetry.

"Why not?" said the priest mildly, taking the sting out of her scandalous contempt.

It sobered her. She blushed.

"When your husband comes back in the spring with the wagon train," said Father Antonio, "you can send some money to my church."

"Gladly," said Rosa.

"Those must be big boys by now; I haven't seen them for months. Luis? Julio? That's right. —When I was a boy I had all the desires to go and look at what was over the mountains. Then when I was away, there, in Mexico, at the seminary, the world on this side of the mountains was just as inviting and mysterious. Eh? When I came back to go to work, everybody bowed to me and behaved properly as to a priest. But I always felt a little guilty for that, and went fishing or hunting. The animals had no respect for me, which was a relief, for they knew not of God, whose weight is something to carry, I can tell you!"

This was strange talk to the women.

"Next to catching a sinner and taking away his sin, I like best to fetch a trout, or play a long game of war with a beaver in the river pools. —So now I know why your two big brown babies went off to the mountains."

"Oh," thought the women. "That explains it."

Father Antonio stayed more than a week. The boys were missing. The priest would go and look at the mountains in all times of day, to see if he could see anything, even in his mind, which might be played with as news for the distracted mother.

But all he saw were the momentous faces of the mountains: light or the absence of light; at dawn, a chalky black atmosphere quivering with quiet air; at noon, silvered by the sun, the great rock wrinkles shining and constant; at evening, the glow of rose, as if there were furnaces within the tumbled stone which heated the surface, until it came to glow for a few moments and then, cooling to ashy black from the base upward, joined the darkening sky like a low heavy cloud.

"I have promised to stay for them, and I will," said the priest.

He spent the days making Rosa agree to get strong, until she finally arose from her bed and ordered her house again. He did the tasks of the outdoors. There was no need for Josefina to stay now; but stay she did, touched in her vanity by the godmotherhood which had been mentioned once.

She came in one day, still holding her arm over her eyes, as if staring into the distance, the golden chill of the open winter.

"I think I see them coming!" she cried.

They all went outdoors.

"You are crazy," said the priest.

They looked and looked.

The plain and the slow rise into the mountain lift was swimming with sunlight. They searched with long looks until they had to blink for vision.

"See! Like a couple of sheep, just barely moving," insisted Josefina, pointing vaguely at the mountains.

"Where!"

"Yes. I do see! She is right! —She must have Indian blood."

The mother was the last to see and agree.

There was an infinitesimal movement far on the plain, hardly perceptible as movement; some energy of presence, a dot of light and cast of shadow, just alive enough to be convincing. It was the hunters, coming on their horses on the second day's journey out of the mountains.

Late in the afternoon they arrived.

The marks of their toil were all over them.

To go and come back! This being the common mystery of all journeying, the mother could hardly wait for them to speak, to tell her everything.

She brought the baby, and the boys kissed her tiny furred head.

The priest gave them his blessing, and they bent their shaggy necks under it.

Josefina stared and then squinted at them, whispering something.

"Luis, you are hurt!"

"—Not any more."

"But you *were!*"

"I will tell you sometime."

"Now, now!"

"How long have we been away?"

"Ten days!"

The boys talked, confirming each other with looks.

Luis and the wolf; the bite; the fever; the body as the residence of the devil, and the raving nights. Julio and his amazing skill as a marksman; his reckless courage; the two of them together, after Luis's recovery, shagging up and down rocky barriers, mountain sprites, and their bag of skins.

"Look at that!"

They got and opened out their two packs of furs; and there were cats, the wolf, a little deer, and a middle-sized brown bear.

"Who got the bear!"

"*Luis,* it was wonderful; the bear was in a tree, watching us, and what made him, nobody knows, but Luis looked up, and whang! and boo! down fell the bear, and all it took was the one shot!"

"—But you should have seen Julio the time he saved my life, when the wolf was waiting for me to fall down; I was so cold and weak! Up in my tree!"

The silence was full of worried love: what had they not done! —But safe. —Yes, but what if!

The brothers looked at each other.

Nothing would ever be said about the other thing. Nobody ever managed to grow up without being foolish at some time or other.

"The nights were hardest, it was so cold!"

"We kept a fire going; we had to wake up every so often to fix it."

"The horses had a fight one day when we were gone hunting; they killed a small mountain cat that came down."

There were marvels to rehearse for many a time to come.

The priest thought,

"The boy Julio looks taller; I suppose it is only natural. Last time I was here he was . . ."

Luis took the baby sister to hold.

There was plenty of fur to keep her warm.

Julio sighed. It was a curiously contented and old man's comment.

Father Antonio felt like laughing; and he would have, but there was some nobility of bearing in Julio's little mighty shoulders that didn't deserve patronizing.

The priest glanced at Josefina.

He knew his materials like a craftsman.

He thought,

"Josefina sees—she even smells as a female—what has taken place in Julio. She stares at him and then squints and whispers to herself. It isn't *hers,* except in mind, and stir of flesh. —How little is secret! How much makes a life!"

The mother's arms were free of her infant. She went and hugged Julio, because, though she hardly thought it so clearly, she knew that he had gone and conquered the wilderness which was his brother's by birth. She knew that—and what lay behind it—as only a child's mother could know it; with defensive and pitying and pardoning love, so long as it might be needed.

"I wish I could write, now," said Luis.

"Why?"

"Then I would write to my father about it."

"But he could not read it."

"No, but he could get somebody to read it to him."

"Should I write and tell him about it for you?" asked Father Antonio.

"Oh, if you would, Father!"

"I'll be glad to. The minute I get back to my house where I have pens and paper. You have told me the whole adventure."

But when the priest did return home, and sit down, to keep his promise to the delighted brothers, what they had told him seemed to him man's story, and all he finally wrote was:

Dear Garcia,

Your wife has had a dear baby girl; and both are well and happy, with God's grace. Your two sons are proud of their family; and when you return, before hearing from their lips anything of their adventures during your absence, you will see that they are already proper men, for which God be praised in the perfection of His design for our mortal life.

[36]

The One Who Wouldn't Dance

Martin O'Malley was never sure that all three of his children would come with Frances, their mother, to meet his usual evening train. Sometimes one was missing—Lina, the middle one, who was five. In her own way she had an odd kind of strength unknown to Eugenia, her sister, who was nine, and to her three-year-old brother, Neddie. It was the strength of privacy.

Tonight only Eugenia and Neddie had come with Frances to meet the train. Martin found them quickly and took the wheel of the station wagon, leaning over to kiss Frances as she moved to make room for him. The two children climbed into the back seat. Neddie had to see the train leave, so they all sat and watched.

"No Lina?" Martin asked.

"No Lina," Frances said. "She's *gone.*"

Everyone laughed at this, for they knew what the word meant in a particular family sense.

"She all right?"

"Oh, yes—otherwise."

"All right, Brother," Martin said to Ned. "Train gone. We go please?"

"We go."

"Daddy," Eugenia said reprovingly, "you're talking baby talk, and we're not supposed to, any of us, to Neddie."

"You're right, my fat little pigeon. Don't ever let me do it again. Kiss me."

He leaned back so she could reach his cheek. A wisp of her hair got into his mouth and he blew it out loudly. She hugged him. The car swerved suddenly.

"Hey, let go," he cried. "Let go. Do you want to kill us all?"

Neddie beat on Eugenia to make her let go. The car went on through the town, out to the seashore, and turned in to the long graveled drive to the house.

"Here we are," Eugenia said importantly at their front door. She turned to help Ned out of the car. He let her lift him, relaxed and confident, a small king who granted his helplessness as favor.

"Upstairs, everybody," Frances said to the children.

"If we can't give our surprise, then I want to stay and talk to Daddy," Eugenia said.

"Surprise? What surprise, pigeon?"

"Lina and I have been working on a surprise and we were supposed to give it this evening. But now she won't play, or anything."

"Yes, we'll see," Frances said. "Upstairs now, right away, and then when you're ready for bed, you may all come down, Lina too—you must ask her—and if she is ready to be in the surprise, then you can give it. But if she isn't you can say good night in the library where Daddy and I will be."

Eugenia had a respect for contracts and accepted this one at once. Not Ned. He clung to his father's leg, his head back, his presence a claim. He understood nicely the power of limpness.

"Neddie, let go! You heard Mummy. Come on now, go upstairs like a big boy, you hear? Stand up."

They finally went and were received at the top of the stairs by their nurse, Dorla, a large, elderly Negress, who considered all white children insane but lovable. She wore spectacles, much bent and straightened from having been snatched off her face by baby hands. Nothing that a child might do surprised her, and she believed that the first duty of life was to forgive.

Settling down in his chair with a drink, Martin said, "This is nice." The pale daylight lingered above the ocean which he could see through the open French doors. Frances sat opposite him, pretty and cool. "How was Lina all day?" he asked.

"Simply fine. Until about an hour or so ago. I wondered if it was the cellar."

"What do you mean, the cellar? Is that where she is?"

"Oh, no, dear. She's been upstairs all along. You remember when we talked about making a playroom down in the cellar for the children? I thought I'd see about it today. I went down—we really must have more lights, it is so dark—and Lina went as far as the third step, and then got scared and sat down with the kitchen door open behind her. Neddie, of course, had to go all the way down with me. It *is* scary, but I held Ned by the hand, and turned on all the dim little lights. It *would* make a wonderful play place for rainy days. I had lots of ideas. I want to show you."

"I think we'll be able to manage it before winter. I agree it would be nice. Did Lina just sit on the step and wait for you?"

"Yes, just sat and waited. She was fine until just a while ago; then she wouldn't come to the train with us and just stayed in the nursery. Martin, it does hurt to see her; she seems absolutely *gone* under something so sad."

"I know. I thought she'd got better about that." He sighed. "What's the surprise?"

"A song they've been practicing. Eugenia learned it at school, and she's been teaching it to Lina. They do it together. I'm not supposed to know."

"Oh, of course not. Maybe I'll go up and see if I can—"

But he was interrupted by a company of players—Eugenia and Ned—who plainly believed themselves to constitute a great procession. Lina was not with them.

Martin and Frances exchanged a glance over that, but politeness required that they sit still and watch the entertainment that was about to begin. Eugenia was bulging out of a fairy-princess costume she had grossly outgrown, but she made up for her fatness by being more graceful than necessary in her gestures with a wrecked scepter that had lost its star. Neddie wore an Indian headdress with broken feathers and Indian pants decorated with flaking paint, and he carried a rubber-headed drum which supplied the music.

"Ladies and gentlemen," Eugenia said, motioning to Ned to stop his drumming, "we will dance the Dance of the Fairy Princess and the Indian Prince. Thank you."

She turned to Ned and made him a grand, unsteady bow. He squatted halfway in return, and then began to whale his drum and jump up and down. Eugenia heaved herself with panting delicacy through one position after another of her elementary ballet lessons. Her ardent face and half-closed eyes expressed the spirit of her dance, and her little brother's assertive co-operation on the drum greatly enlarged the dream.

Martin and Frances leaned forward, watching with an ache of pride under their expressions of comic solemnity. Yet without Lina the performance was not what it was trying to be. One wouldn't dance. One was absent. The family was incomplete.

The dance ended with uncertain bows from the stage. The audience applauded with wild enthusiasm so that the dancers would know the illusion of triumph before a vast throng.

"Oh, beautiful!" cried Frances. "Won't you do another dance for us, Fairy Princess and Indian Prince?"

Instantly and with gravity the actors resumed their performance.

"I'm going up to get Lina," Martin said softly. "She ought to be in this."

He started to tiptoe out. The dancers knew from the way he went that he would come back, and so they continued, but Ned called out over the erratic beats of his drum. "The kitty, the kitty."

Martin stopped and turned around. "What kitty, Ned?"

Eugenia scowled at all these distractions, and the Indian Prince renewed his caperings and beat his drum with penitent fury. The Fairy Princess floated off panting, again restored to her illusion. Martin shrugged and went upstairs.

The nursery was a large, square, corner room at the back of the house, overlooking lawn and trees and a flagstone terrace. Martin went in whistling, with his hands in his pockets, pretending to look all around for someone in hiding. He could see her all the time, though, and she knew it. She was in a dim corner of the room, as far from the window and the light as she could be, and on her face was an expression of contempt for her father's wistful game. She sat on a little hassock of washable imitation leather, her hands pushing up her cheeks, her elbows on her knees.

"Lina! There you are!" he cried, pretending that she needed only to be found to be restored to them all.

She did not answer, and looked away from him, and when he went to pick her up to hug and kiss her, she held herself rigid.

He put her down. He got nothing from her but a sense of fear and woe, as though there were some awful secret she could not tell.

"Will you come and dance with everybody else, Lina?"

She barely shook her head.

"We miss you," Martin said. "We want you with us."

[41]

She let her eyes fill with tears at the pity of this. The tears rolled out and down her cheeks but she made no move to stand up and go with him.

"Is something the matter, Lina?"

She nodded slowly.

"Won't you tell Daddy what it is?" Martin urged.

She opened her mouth in a faint meow and turned away from him, crumpling into herself. She was unable to speak. But Martin felt in her so much pity and sorrow that it made his eyes sting. He knew that he couldn't reach her now and that he could only wait until she came running and climbing on him, so full of love that she could eat him up.

The other door to the nursery opened, and Dorla looked in.

"Evening, Dorla. No."

"Just let her be, let her be, she be all right. I be here."

Martin nodded. He put his knuckles for a moment to Lina's face so that she could feel how little she was alone, how much strength awaited her return to the world. Then he went downstairs again where the formless dance went on. . . .

Later, in the last moment of the summer dusk, Martin went outdoors to look around. He walked down to the rocky point of land that reached into the sea, and then came back to the house to sit and have a cigarette on the terrace while upstairs Frances was playing the evening game of being reasonable about unreasonable requests that were made only to defeat bedtime. The nursery window was open, and through it he could hear the voices of two of his children. He supposed Lina was silent.

Or was that she overhead? He sat up and listened.

Again it came, a small noise in the still, warm twilight. He glanced at the branch of a tree that almost touched the second story of the house on the nursery side. There amid the dark shining leaves was a white kitten, now and then opening its rose-pink mouth to make a faint cry that was half breath and half sound. Abandoned and desolate, it blinked slowly. It had no idea how to get down, and it made its faint yawning cry without hope.

"Hey, poor little kitty," he said, and went over to coax it down, snapping his fingers and whistling. But the kitten only dug its claws into the bark of the tree and quivered.

Martin went to the outside cellar doors and laid them back with a mild crash. In the furnace room he found a tall ladder. He dragged it out to the big beech tree and leaned it against the trunk. The children had heard the ladder bumping along the ground, and as he mounted the rungs, he saw their faces in the nursery window.

Then he heard the missing voice. It was Lina. She clapped her hands and screamed in a voice so high and tight that it pierced his hearing like the song of a locust.

"Daddy! Daddy! Daddy!" she cried in happiness and love.

"The kitty! The kitty!" cried Ned, beside her, and Martin remembered his having said it before. This was what he had meant.

Martin reached the branch and carefully took hold of the kitten. It tried to cling to the tree. "Let go, you little fool," Martin said fondly and, pulling it loose, held it in his hand. The kitten trembled wildly.

The children in the window shrieked and clapped as he started down the ladder. Then their faces vanished and he knew they were all rushing downstairs to meet him. Lina was the first to reach him as he crossed the terrace. He put his free arm around her and picked her up, and he saw with relief that she had returned.

"Kitty," she said, and then hugged Martin.

"Where did this kitty come from?" he asked.

"I don't know."

"Did you see it before?"

"Yes."

"When?"

"Today."

"Did you play with it?"

"Yes."

"Then what?"

"It went in the tree."

"Oh. You saw it go into the tree?"

"Yes." She shuddered.

"What did the kitty do?"

"It cried and cried."

"Why?"

"Because it couldn't get down."

"Oh. And what did you do?"

She put her face against his cheek and shook her head.

"Was that when you went upstairs and wouldn't come down again?"

She nodded, rubbing her cheek against his ear. He tightened his arm about her. It was all plain now.

The other children came, reaching for the cat. Martin held it high above them in his hand. "Mine, mine, I want the cat," they both cried.

"Now wait," Martin said. He put Lina down. "The poor kitty is tired and frightened. We have to be very gentle with it." He knelt down and let the kitten go. It trembled, alert for new terrors.

"The kitty, the kitty," Ned said.

"Did you see it in the tree?" Martin asked.

"Saw it in the tree," confirmed Ned.

"Did *you*, Eugenia?"

"No, I never saw it before."

Lina reached out with her fingers spread tensely and took up the cat.

"I want it," she said.

"Yes," Martin said, deciding suddenly, "I think this will be Lina's kitty. But everyone may play with it."

"I don't see why it has to be her cat," Eugenia said. "I'm the one who likes animals the most. Why can't it be my cat?"

"We'll have a pet for you next time," Martin said. "Come on, now. We must make a house for the cat."

They went down through the cellar doors, Martin carrying Lina, and Eugenia guarding Neddie. Into the damp darkness they went, turning on the dim lights that only made greater underground mysteries than ever out of the winding cellar, with its fat overhead pipes, its triangles of shadow darker than coal dust, its wooden echoes of voices and steps, and the room where the furnace sat like a dusty, fat spider.

"Now. Here's a nice box," Martin said, hauling an orange crate from the caverns of shadow beside the furnace. "We'll make a house for the cat." He gave the kitten to Lina while he took up and shook free of dust a burlap sack that had been idly saved a long time ago. Of this he made a cushion and set it into the crate, which lying on its side revealed two compartments.

"He can sleep in one room, and he can sit in the other," Eugenia said. "Or maybe it's his dining room."

"Eugenia," Martin said, "would you like to go up and get a saucer of milk?"

She glanced over her shoulder at the dark passage with its formless threats on either side of the pale lane of electric light. Then she took a deep breath and went to do her duty.

Until she came back, walking so carefully that she left a trail of pearl-like drops, the others watched the kitten, which had been thrust into its bedroom, where it stood, staring and wild with apprehension.

"How old is he?" asked Lina.

"I should say he is about four weeks old."

[45]

"Where did he come from?"

"That's one thing nobody can ever say about a cat."

They fed the cat, and then he was put to bed strenuously several times with admonitions and pats and strokes.

"Can we leave a light on for him all night, like mine upstairs?" asked Lina. "He'll be scared in the dark."

"Oh yes, we can do that," Martin said.

So they left the light on in the furnace room and turned off all the others on the way to the stairs leading up to the kitchen. Looking back, just before Martin shut the kitchen door, they saw a faint glow in the heavy underground air about the furnace room entrance. Once again the children went upstairs to bed, and Martin and Frances went in to their dinner.

"It was that, all the time," he told her. "She was grief-stricken over that mangy little cat stuck in the tree."

"Yes, she could see it from her window. I wonder why nobody told us?"

"Neddie tried. I didn't get his point. And she did, too, when I went up, but I didn't understand. Why, what's this? Look, here come the dancers!"

It was a joy, but not to be openly noticed, that Lina was among them.

Frances groaned, for once again the children had escaped from bedtime. They came down the winding stairs—Eugenia and Ned in new costumes—accompanied by music that followed them from the nursery phonograph. The dining room was dimly lighted by candles. The little girls dragged rags of finery on the floor, and Ned wore a paper hat left over from a birthday party and a cloak made of his bathrobe tied around his neck by its sleeves. All three twirled independently but with zeal to the tune that rasped out of the

[46]

phonograph. Lina danced entirely by inspiration, for she had not yet begun to take lessons.

The record ended. Eugenia made a bow and whispered a reminder to Lina, who faced her and waited. Ned was impressed and stared from one to the other. Something was coming. Martin glanced at Frances and whispered. "The surprise?" She nodded. Impersonating a cavalier, Eugenia began to sing with pedantic firmness and clarity, addressing Lina, who stood suddenly abashed at what she had agreed to do:

> *I will give you a golden crown,*
> *To be the fine lady of the town,*
> *Madam will you walk,*
> *Madam will you talk,*
> *Madam will you walk and talk with me?*

Lina made her response, barely audible, in a breathy voice, with a lifetime's remove between her and the fine lady she was impersonating:

> *I do not want any golden crown,*
> *To be the fine lady of the town,*
> *Sir I will not walk,*
> *Sir I will not talk,*
> *Sir I will not walk and talk with you.*

Ned began to dance by himself to attract attention. Eugenia scowled at him but did not interrupt her performance as the attentive cavalier. With an accompaniment of sweeping gestures, she sang:

> *I will give you a coach-and-four*
> *With your name in gold upon the door,*

Madam will you walk,
Madam will you talk,
Madam will you walk and talk with me?

And perfectly expressionless but dutiful, the fine lady replied:

I do not wait for a coach-and-four
With my name in gold upon the door,
Sir I will not walk,
Sir I will not talk,
Sir I will not walk and talk with you.

A sudden awareness of her parents made her turn and look at them. Their faces were so full of protective love and understanding that she became self-conscious, and when the cavalier began his last verse, Lina stamped her foot and said, "I hate the old silly words."

But Eugenia coldly held the performance together by continuing:

I will give you the key to my heart,
That we may never, never be apart,
Madam will you walk,
Madam will you talk,
Madam will you walk and talk with me?

And so, near the end, Lina turned her back to her parents and sang her last response:

I will take the key to your heart
That we may never, never be apart—

Her pipy voice, barely a thread of tune, touched her parents so that even they could not look at each other, but allowed the little girl the privacy of her self-consciousness. Her neck was so thin, her jaws moved so bonily, she was so rigid with emotion that Martin felt a sudden sense of mortality, the sharper because it came to him from a life so barely begun. Seeing her turned away from him, the line of her cheek, the long lashes, the shadowy movement of her throat as she spoke her words, he blessed her in his mind and begged for her safety.

As she finished the song, she found her gaiety again, and ran to throw herself on her father's lap, while applause rang out, even from the stairs, where Dorla had come to watch the play. . . .

Early the next morning screams brought Martin to the upstairs hall where he found Eugenia clutching at something that Dorla held away from her.

"Eugenia!" he called. "Be quiet, what is it?"

"The poor, darling kitty!" Eugenia shrieked.

Lina and Ned ran out of the nursery, fascinated by Eugenia's noise.

"Dorla, what is all this?" Martin asked.

Dorla showed him the kitten, holding it high above the heads of the children.

"Kitty, he's dead," she said.

"Give me my darling cat," Eugenia sobbed.

"It's not yours. It's mine," said Lina loudly.

"What happened, Dorla? Hush, children."

"I found the cat in Lina's bed little while ago, I figured get it out of there before anybody wake. Eugenia cotched me. It died of smothering, I figure."

Martin looked at the children.

Death was a thing Eugenia had had explained to her, but this was her first experience with it. The other two children had no real notion of what it meant.

"In Lina's bed?" he said, astounded. "But how did it get there? We put it in the cellar, and closed the kitchen door."

"I went and got him," Lina said.

"When?"

"Last night."

Martin knelt and held her.

"No, now, sweetie, you didn't go all the way down to the cellar during the night and up again, with the kitty, did you?"

"I did so, I did, I did. I carried the kitty and I took him to bed with me, because I thought he would be so cold and scared in the cellar all by himself."

"But how did you find your way alone? Wasn't it dark?"

She nodded, suddenly shy over the terrors he reminded her of. Martin thought of the awful journey—down the stairs, the lonely first floor of the house, with everything unfamiliar-seeming in the dark, and the cold kitchen she must have gone through to reach the cellar doors; and then the descent into the underworld, a step at a time, guided by the dim glow of the furnace room where the light had been left on, and where in daytime with her mother at hand she had been too frightened to go.

"Lina!" he said and hugged her.

"I put on the kitchen light. I can reach it."

"Yes," said Dorla, "I found it on this morning, early."

He tried to conceal his amazement, and let go of Lina. "All right, Dorla," he said, "we'll dispose of it. Take it downstairs."

Eugenia cried out again with a new idea, turning on Lina. "You killed it!" she screamed.

"Hush, Eugenia!" Martin said sharply. "It was an accident. The kitten smothered because it wasn't used to being in bed with anybody. Never let me hear you say that again to Lina."

He watched Lina, fearing the effect upon her of her sister's words and their truth.

But Lina was unpredictable in her strength. She simply took Neddie by the hand and led him back to the nursery. Eugenia, wringing her hands and trying to weep, went downstairs after Dorla and the dead kitten. Martin went back to Frances.

With many speculative moments of silence, they talked of what had happened.

"I keep wondering why she didn't tell us yesterday, when she saw the kitten in the tree?"

"Perhaps she thought there was nothing to be done about it, no way to help the kitten out of the tree, and so she could only suffer. Who knows?"

"But why didn't the kitten's death bother her, if it bothered her so dreadfully to see it stuck in the tree?"

"You can only guess. But maybe it was because she could see herself lost in a big tree branch, high above the ground, and forgotten; but she couldn't see herself dead. Maybe that was why."

"Poor little thing," Martin said.

Winners and Losers

Wearing a look of avid curiosity, Eleanor came to see Myra late one summer morning, in the country, in California. "Well, Ellie, I'm glad to see you," Myra said to her visitor, at the same time saying to herself: Do you suppose she has heard?

Ellie, as she took a seat on the shaded terrace, made many movements but she never shifted her gaze from Myra's face. It was clear, though it was not supposed to be, that Ellie had motives and opinions which she believed to be secret. "I was just going out to Mr Krindl's to see some new roses he has for me," she said, "and I thought I'd pop in on you."

"Yes," Myra said, "he has some new beauties this year. We set out some two dozen, I think."

"You did? By yourself?"

"Oh, no. I had help."

"Who helped you?"

Myra smiled until Ellie looked down. "Barbara helped me."

"Oh. Is she old enough?"

"Oh, yes. She's twelve, you know. Not that I didn't have a time getting her away from the horses long enough to help me."

"She does ride?"

"Oh, if riding were all. No," Myra said, and laughed, "I don't know what has got into all the nice little girls of the land. They are all infatuated with horses."

"Imagine," murmured Ellie, clearly wishing the conversation would be left to her own guidance.

"Yes," Myra went on, "Barbara is down at the corral right now, with her colt Chico; and probably Ed Rumson is there with her. He's a dear."

"Who?"

"Colonel Rumson. He's taken the place next to this, toward the mountains. He's a retired cavalry officer, and he and Barbara have hit it off."

"What's he look like? Do I know him?"

"I don't know. He's rather small, but nice and thin and tough in a nice way."

"My dear."

"His wife, Amy, lives with him, of course."

"Is she horsy?" Ellie asked disagreeably.

"She rides, but she doesn't fit the definition as my child does, for example. For example, Ellie, you won't believe this, but a few evenings ago I gave a little party for Barbara; we had the thing out here in the garden, and the moon was full—they all looked so sweet in their party dresses and their gabardine pants and enormous sport shoes and loud jackets—and we had lanterns, and more food—one boy ate two pints of ice cream—and there was music, and they danced and played games, and everybody tried to pretend that nobody cared about prizes, but poor darlings, they knew better, and the winners were better than the losers—and both knew it, and you could hardly bear it. Anyway, at one point during the proceedings I missed Barbara, and looked everywhere, until finally I went down the lane to the corral. What do you think I saw?"

[53]

Ellie's face was so ready for scandal that Myra hurried on to the ridiculous truth. "The colt was reclining in the moonlight, and there she was, wearing her party dress, lying down with her face on the colt's cheek and her arm around his neck."

"Oh, Myra, how really too— Funny as it may seem at first, I'm not at all sure I would laugh at it."

"You don't quite see it, Ellie," Myra said, kindly pretending to be stupid. "The little girls don't just *like* horses, they *are* horses. Barbara nickers or whickers, or whatever it is. She prances and rolls her eyes. When she passes familiar objects, she often shies at them. Her equine psychology is sound, too. She'll get past the piano all right unless I've left the top up, but then, if I have, so that it looks strange, she will hump a little. You've no idea."

Ellie saw no reason to postpone talking about what she'd come to find out. Turning her face a trifle away and down from Myra, but still looking at her, she said. "Yes, well, her father was always a great rider, wasn't he?"

"Was?" Myra said lightly. "Was? Tom is still in the land of the living, Ellie." But she knew now that Ellie was here because of what she had heard.

"Oh, yes, of course, I mean— He's not been— I haven't seen him in so long."

"For that matter, neither have we."

"Even Barbara hasn't seen her father?"

"Not lately."

"Oh, my poor darling Myra," said Ellie, like a huntress now certain of closing with her prey.

"Now, Ellie, don't *understand* me right out of my wits. What are you trying to tell me?"

"I'm not exactly a fool, Myra, and neither is anyone else close to you."

"So you all know."

"I think so. It *is* true, isn't it?"

Myra was shocked. Her heart beat fast. Why did the truth seem truer if someone else knew it too?

Ellie took a deep draught of her cigarette, and spoke through the smoke from her lungs. A shred of tobacco clung to her mouth, and some desire to appear cool and reasonable made her pick delicately at the shred while she spoke. "Won't it help to tell someone? Tom is divorcing you, isn't he?"

"Yes, he is," said Myra.

With a rush of joyous sympathy, Ellie came to embrace Myra.

"Thank you, Ellie. Please—"

"And Barbara?" asked Ellie, unconsciously assuming the expression she always thought of at the words "lovely young girl." "What does Barbara think?"

"She doesn't know."

"Oh! My dear, you haven't told her?"

"No. Tom wants to tell her himself. I thought it only fair to him to let him, so he could make it seem, oh, sort of *natural,* I suppose."

"But he hasn't?"

"No. He hasn't."

"Oh, Myra." Ellie shook her head.

"Ellie, does everyone know?"

"Well," Ellie said, putting out her cigarette with unnecessary care, "I'll tell you how *I* heard it, and you can judge for yourself. The Fenways' maid told my Calla, and the Fenways got it in the first place from their boy, Hubert, who brought it home from school, where one of his little friends is the son of Judge Pierce. That's how *I* heard it. We've all been waiting for you to speak out, Myra. All your friends. Not that you owe us anything," she said, but her tone made it clear that she meant the opposite.

"I didn't care to," said Myra. "I don't know. I want as little as

[55]

possible to do with the whole thing. But if everyone knows—" She hesitated, with her eyes clouded in perplexity and pain.

"If everyone knows," Ellie said, plausibly mimicking the way Myra had said it, "then Barbara must be told, and told at once, mustn't she? To protect her? Think of her hearing it by accident! Maybe at school. You know how cruel children are; they never leave people's feelings alone."

And do you ever? Myra asked silently, then added aloud, "Yes, I know."

"Myra," Ellie continued, with an ambitious glitter in her eye, "do you want me to tell her for you? It will be too difficult for you. I'm not a complete stranger here," she said, smiling with hazy sweetness, "but it ought to be done by someone not actually in the family. Surgery is most merciful when it is impersonal. Shall I? You know I'll be gentle and very understanding."

"Of course you would be, Ellie, but I suppose I must take care of this myself."

"But right away, Myra. Really, I wouldn't wait a minute." She stood up and gave Myra an encouraging smile. "I'll run along," Ellie said, "but you must call me if you need me. Any time. Any place."

"Thank you, thank you," Myra said aloud. And go, go, she cried silently.

But Eleanor asked a question with such a hungry look in her face that Myra turned to her with pity instead of with resentment. "It is that woman, then, isn't it, Myra? Is Tom going to marry her?"

"That is my understanding."

"Of course," said Ellie, "perhaps I shouldn't speak of it. But why wouldn't he let you divorce him?"

"He offered to."

"But you wouldn't?"

"No. I wouldn't."

"But, Myra, your pride—"

"My pride is quite stout, thank you. I do not believe in divorce."

"I see. But this way, it looks as though you had no choice!"

"Oh yes, I had. I chose."

"Yes, I see," said Ellie, with a puzzled pursing of her lips. "Well, I think you're being simply—" She shrugged.

"Oh no, I'm not, Ellie. If you have any real feeling for somebody, things look different to you than they might to somebody else."

"Well, all I know is, *I* could never—" Ellie broke off, abandoning the comforts of indignation in defense of her imaginary self, and said with a warm, practical air, "Why don't I drive along to the corral, so I can tell Barbara to come right up because you want to see her? And then I can go on to Mr Krindl's by the back road."

Myra had no words, so she just nodded; and Eleanor, with long strides that indicated purposeful kindness, went to her car and drove down toward the corral.

As soon as she was alone, Myra clasped her hands and saw herself actually wring them with anguish. She saw bright pictures in her mind of Barbara's face that so much resembled her father's. She saw how it would change in shock, and she felt the pain she would cause. Barbara adored her father. Now Myra felt her heart come into her mouth at how comforting to her it would be to feel Barbara's sympathy and love in the lonesomeness ahead. Perhaps the news would mature Barbara suddenly. Or possibly Barbara would be able to feel nothing but her own desolating loss of an unquestioned enclosure of love. Myra reminded herself that children in their grief could feel for nobody else, and must not be expected to. She felt a momentary anger and she said, "That fool Ellie," as though Ellie were the cause of all her trouble.

"I won't tell Barbara," she said half aloud, and looked about the terrace for some task to give her if she came. The plants could be watered. But in her distress she took up a half-filled watering pot and began to sprinkle the plants herself. In a few minutes she heard a musical tinkle behind her and turned to see Barbara running toward her. The child carried a bridle and bit that chimed as she ran.

In a breathless voice, Barbara called out, "What is it, Mother? What's the matter?"

"What do you mean, what's the matter?" Myra asked in the humorously flat voice she often used with her daughter.

"That woman said you needed me, and she said I must be very tender with you. What does she mean, very tender, Mother?"

Barbara was a blazing power of energy and perspiring beauty. Her flax-like hair was loose, and her dark eyes scowled. She was at the height of her childish animal charm, in her boy's shirt and blue work pants.

"You are not to refer to my friends as 'that woman,' Barbara. She sent you to me because I asked her to. Sit down."

Barbara impatiently sat down, laying her bit and bridle lovingly across her lap. She put her head on one side and squinted at the metal to make it shine again.

Myra's love was so strong and protective in the next moment or two that it turned to anger. Feeling the power of the world, she knew she would have to obey it. "Barbara, put down those things and listen to me. Can't you forget horses for one minute?"

"Well, gosh, Mother, you haven't *said* anything yet."

Trembling inside and yet sure she looked entirely calm, Myra said, "You know, don't you, Barbara, how much Daddy and I both love you?"

"Well, gosh, yes."

"You must always believe we do, no matter what might happen."

"What? Is something going to happen?"

"Yes, something is going to happen, but you are always going to have each of us as long as you need us."

[58]

"Who? You mean you and Daddy?"

"Yes. Barbara, he is not going to live with us any more."

"He isn't?" Barbara asked simply, twisting and squinting again for an entranced look at her bit and bridle.

"No, he isn't. But you will see him often, and he will always love you as much as ever. Do you know what this means, Barbara?"

"I suppose it means you're having a divorce."

"Yes. It does."

"When?"

"It has already started. It is something they do in court. For all practical purposes, it is already done."

"Oh." Barbara drew her fingers along the satiny surface of the saddle-soaped straps over her thighs. She hunched her shoulders as if to control her desire to be gone to the corral again. Myra could not believe her eyes.

"Do you understand what I have told you, Barbara?"

"Yes, Mummy," Barbara replied, looking up with no expression, and then she added, "Is that all, now, Mummy?" She could not help glancing around down the lane.

Myra turned white and felt cold.

She found to her dismay that she could not speak. She waved Barbara away. Barbara jumped up, ran from the terrace and down the lane, making music with her bit and bridle.

Myra got up from the chair she had been sitting on and went across the terrace to another one, and half knelt on it, putting her head down against the back of it. Hungry for comfort, she saw Barbara lost to her. "Very tender . . ." Yes, she longed for the very thing she despised Eleanor for thinking of. To lose both Tom and Barbara—it was a double failure for which she was not prepared. She was sick, as though something sacred had been outraged. She had grown, married, conceived and borne a child, whom she had nursed and guarded and trained to be increasingly self-sufficient. Soon, soon the child, in her turn, would fulfill the same common purpose. May she be spared what I feel now, Myra thought, mourning for her child.

How long she did not know, but it was not long until she heard Barbara running toward the house, calling loudly, "Mummy, Mummy, hurry, help me!"

She sat up. Barbara was wild, white and sick under her deep summer tan. Her voice was quivering, and, as she came to the terrace and tried to talk, her mouth was dry. There were tears on her cheeks. There was blood on her shirt. Myra took her shoulders and held her.

"Hush. What is it, now? Slowly, Barbara."

"It's Chico. He's hurt, he's terribly cut by the barbed wire to the gate. Oh, the poor little colt, he's bleeding. Come on!" She pulled Myra not toward the lane but toward the kitchen.

"What are we to do, Barbara?"

"Colonel Rumson is down there with him. He sent me for some boiling water. He has to bathe the cut. He says Chico must not get screwworm!"

They went to work capably, putting two large pans of water on the stove to boil, and heating a bucket to take the water in.

"But how did it happen, Barbara?"

"I don't know!"

"You said it was the barbed wire."

"It was, Mummy," Barbara said. "The gate. I was taking him out the gate to the pasture."

"Didn't he see the wire?"

"I don't know. I don't know."

"But he's been in and out of the gate many times!"

"I *know* it! Oh, poor Chico. Can't we make the water hurry, Mummy?" She was dancing with terror and sympathy for her pet.

"It will boil in a minute or so. Was Colonel Rumson there?"

"He rode up right then."

"What's he doing now?"

"We tied Chico, and he rode back to his place to get his kit. Mummy, he may have to cut Chico, or hurt him."

"Well, darling, we are all going to be sensible if he has to. Now, watch out. I'm going to pour this pan first, and then the other one. Do we need anything else?"

"No, no, Mummy. Colonel Rumson is bringing everything else. Can we go now? Oh, please, dear God," she said in a soft, high voice as she held the door open for her mother to carry the steaming bucket through.

They both held the bucket handle and walked with rapid, level smoothness, like Indian women, to the corral where, near the row of eucalyptus trees, Chico lay on his side, with Colonel Rumson kneeling by him. In the bay velvet of the colt's exposed flank was a shuddering cut a foot long, deep, edged with suety white, and bleeding from dark red, almost black, depths.

"Oh, my poor darling beauty," said Barbara, as they set the bucket down near the colonel.

"Good," he said. "Set it there. Hello, Myra. Now—" He turned to his work.

In his calm brown eyes there was a tolerance for all creatures, dumb or human, as they were. He knew that what happened to them happened to them each alone. In a lifetime with horses, he had devoted himself to overcoming their fear. To people, he granted the dignity, and the duty, of overcoming their own fears. He liked gardening and once said that a thought worth keeping ought to come slowly, the way a plant comes to flower. In most relationships, he merely gave his presence and, when they were needed, his honest abilities with animals, machinery and the vegetable world. Now, as he went to work, he asked a powerful, silent question of Myra, gave Barbara a blink of encouragement, and laid a hot, wet, clean cloth on the wound in the young horse's quivering flank.

He worked steadily—irrigating, cleaning, cutting. He gave an injection. He sewed stitches. Barbara held Chico's head in her lap and watched everything. Her face was like that of a small woman, haggard with the double sufferings of sympathy. When she saw the colonel getting ready to commit some healing hurt, she murmured to her animal and held its head more tenderly. She anticipated every move. Colonel Rumson glanced at her now and then, and knew more about why she suffered than she did herself.

To Myra, the spectacle of the hurt animal, the kind neighbor and the pale child was sickening—not because of the wound, the blood, and the idea of pain, but because of its whole simplicity. There—you could see it plainly, you could touch it—there was a situation about which something could be done, was being done. But which of her troubles could be reached by any healing touch? Who could do anything with boiling water to the trembling rent in her life? What would you put on the ache caused by the innocent and icy heart of your twelve-year-old child who showed embarrassed impatience at the loss of her father and at her mother's hard grief, and only turned into a creature of feeling when her colt was hurt? If she had made a success of her marriage, she thought painfully, then her child would know the difference between losing her father and having a wounded colt. While the colonel probed and stitched in the shining well of scarlet that filled and filled as he worked, she probed deeper and deeper into her own hidden wounds.

"Now, boy, now, boy," the colonel said softly, gently stroking the colt's neck, "that's all we can do for now. All we could do in any

[62]

case was clean it up and get rid of the ragged bits and leave it to nature. I think he'll be all right. We'll watch him, though. I've seen lots of these cuts."

"Do they get well?" asked Barbara. Her voice sounded as though her throat were swollen inside.

"The majority of them, yes," he replied, looking at her with such earnestness in his hard, brown eyes that Myra was startled. What was he looking at in the child? she wondered. "All right," he said, turning to Myra, "I'll walk up to the house with you. There's nothing we can do here for the moment."

"Barbara, are you coming?" asked Myra.

"Oh, Mummy!" said Barbara, amazed at the heartlessness of the question. "And leave Chico? I couldn't."

The colonel saw to his horse, which was tethered to a post of the corral. Then he and Myra walked slowly and in agreed silence up the lane to the terrace. There they sat down and let their feelings settle for a few more silent minutes.

Finally, Colonel Rumson shook his head and said quietly, "I don't understand it."

"Understand what, Ed?"

"How it happened." He gave Myra the same earnest gaze that she had seen him use on Barbara.

"I suppose," she said, "anything can happen with a fool horse; they seem to me so clumsy."

"No," he said mildly, "I don't think horses are bright, but they do become creatures of habit. No, this is something different. Has anything happened lately, today, this morning, to upset Barbara?"

"Why do you ask?"

"Because of the way she was handling Chico. I was riding over from my place just as she was bringing him out of the corral. I actually stood up in my stirrups for a moment, to be sure it was she.

I thought someone was trespassing. Then I rode ahead, and saw the whole thing happen."

"How *did* it happen? Such an odd accident."

"It wasn't really an accident."

"But what else?"

He shook his head gravely. "Barbara," he said, "started to lead him in the corral toward the barbed-wire gate. He was arching his neck and dancing a little. She slapped him. He shied. She slapped him again, and he reared. She took the ends of the reins and cut him over the face with them. Ahead of him, she pulled on the bridle. He was quite frightened by then. As they neared the gate, she yanked him sharply toward it and he resisted. She pulled him again and, letting out the reins, she opened the gate and held on to the end post. All that barbed wire was sticking out loosely. She pulled sharply at the reins and the colt went through and reared just as he passed the post. She pulled him down and he turned and she slapped him with the leather, and he threw himself against the wire. He fell on the wire and cut himself trying to regain his footing.

"Just at that point, I rode up to make sure it really was Barbara, and it was, and she was crying. When she saw the horse was hurt, she threw herself on him and tried to hug his neck. I got her away, and helped Chico up, and led him over to the grove, and sent her for hot water. She never handled a horse—any horse, much less her beloved colt—that way before. There must be a reason. It must be a great big one—to a child, anyway. I just wondered."

He looked at her and waited. She felt her heart stop for a moment of pain, and there followed an odd lightness like joy. It was joy.

"Why, no," Myra said, as calmly as possible, "I can't think of anything that might have upset her."

Colonel Rumson saw that Myra was lying, and respected whatever made her lie. He believed that friends should be taken at their own evaluation of themselves. He began to speak of other things.

[64]

Myra was grateful. She wished the world would leave sorry secrets untroubled as he did.

It was a vain wish. A familiar car drove up the gravel driveway, and Eleanor was at the wheel. She rolled up as close to the terrace as she could; then, leaving her car, she walked across the lawn, talking as she came. She was carrying a little tree, planted in a rough green box. It was a rose tree, covered with white blossoms.

"Myra, my dear," she said, looking at Colonel Rumson, who stood up as she approached, "I saw this at Mr Krindl's, and I told him I had to have it, but he said it was already spoken for. But I made him give it to me. It spoke to me of you so strongly."

"Ellie, this is Colonel Rumson, our neighbor," Myra said, and in the face of Ellie's possessive air of consolation, completed the introduction with difficulty.

"Oh, the man who is so clever with horses," said Ellie. "Do sit down. I can't stay a minute, but I just had to bring this one lovely thing to Myra." She set the rose tree in its box down on the terrace floor, where it seemed to make a white light in the air.

"Thank you, Ellie. Isn't it beautiful?" Myra said.

Ellie went to her and embraced her, in silence, as though silence alone could say enough. Myra was an unwilling partner to an open conspiracy of suffering. Releasing her, Ellie sighed with courage enough for two, and, rearranging herself before the colonel, who, she thought, looked very smart in his riding clothes, she crowned her visit by remarking, like one bestowing an honor, "I am so awfully glad that Myra has you people. I know you do wonders for her. You do live right over there, don't you? With the jacaranda trees?"

Colonel Rumson nodded.

"Yes. And now I must fly," said Ellie. "Myra, phone me, day or night, any time, if there's the smallest thing I can do. Promise me?"

"Thank you, Ellie. And thank you for my white rose."

Ellie left, trying, for the colonel's benefit, to make her face and her movements express loyalty, common sense, grace of spirit, and intoxicating physical appeal. They watched her, returned the last little wave of her white glove, and then looked at each other and burst out laughing.

"A floral offering, what's more!" said Myra. "I could kill her. How does she do it? I see her coming and I lock my jaws and swear I will not tell her one thing. And the next thing I know, she is on her way, with my brains picked clean. Even now, after she's gone, she makes me speak. I can't let you wonder what it's all about." And she told him briefly.

"Well, Myra," he said, with his head cocked to one side.

"Thank you."

"Yes," he said, "and that was what you told Barbara, then, this morning."

She nodded.

He smiled. "My faith is restored, then," he said. "It's all clear. Poor child." He sighed. "How desperately the young ones repeat the primitive acts of long ago! Poor Barbara, and her colt. She made a sacrifice of him, didn't she, a victim, an innocent, to the blind powers that suddenly fell on her. Out of anonymous ages and ages. The blood was an accident, but not the sacrifice. Did you see her face, while she was watching me work? She's grown up a big jump today."

"Yes. I wish it might have been without so much hurt."

"Oh, there are two ways. That's one. Don't forget the other way. She'll know that in her time. Just as your friend Ellie isn't the whole world. She's only half of it."

[66]

Myra looked at him and saw in him the other half, and was thankful. She saw him make up something to say.

"Amy said to ask you if you wanted to come and have a bite of supper with us tonight."

"I'd love it," replied Myra.

"Good, then."

They nodded, and he went down the lane.

How I love him, Myra said to herself, and she meant Tom, who was gone, and doubly gone, now that everybody knew.

Then, with a start, she came to her future self, and found a clay dish in which to set the rose tree box, and went into the house looking for other trifles to do, and gratefully found them.

Black Snowflakes

"Richard, Richard," they said to me often in my childhood, "when will you begin to see things as they are?"

But I always learned from one thing what another was, and it was that way when we all went from Dorchester to New York to see my Grandfather off for Europe, the year before the First World War broke out.

He was German—my mother's father—and it was his habit, all during the long time he lived in Dorchester, New York, to return to Germany for a visit every year or two. I was fearful of him, for he was large, splendidly formal in his dress and majestic in his manner, and yet I loved him for he made me know that he believed me someone worthwhile. I was nine years old, and I could imagine being like him myself some day, with glossy white hair swept back from a broad, pale brow, and white eyebrows above China-blue eyes, and rosy cheeks, a fine sweeping mustache and a well-trimmed white beard that came to a point. He sometimes wore eyeglasses with thin gold rims, and I used to put them on and take them off in secret. I suppose I had no real idea of what he was like.

There was something in the air about going to New York to see him off that troubled me. I did not want to go.

"Why not, my darling?" asked my mother the night before we were to leave. Before going down to dinner, she busily came in to see me, to kiss me good night, to turn down the night-light, to glance about my room with her air of giving charm to all that she saw, and to whisper a prayer with me, looking toward my small blue and gold statue of Our Lady, that God would keep us.

"I don't want to leave Anna."

"What a silly boy. Anna will be here when we return, doing the laundry in the basement or making *Apfelkuchen* just as she always does. And while we are gone, she will have a little vacation. Won't that be nice for her? You must not be selfish."

"I don't want to leave Mr Schmitt and Ted."

My mother made a little breath of comic exasperation, looking upward for a second.

"You really are killing," she said in the racy slang of the time, "why should you mind leaving the iceman and his old horse Ted for a few days? They only come down our street twice a week. What is so precious about Mr Schmitt and Ted?"

"They are friends of mine."

"Ah. Then I understand. We all hate to leave our friends. Well, they too will be here when we return. Don't you want to see Grosspa take the great ship, you can even go on board the liner to say goodbye, you have no idea how huge those ships are, and how fine? This one"—she let a comic effect come into her voice as she often did when pronouncing German words—"is called the *Doppelschrauben Schnelldampfer Kronprinzessin Cecilie.*"

"Why can't I go the next time he sails for Germany?"

At this my mother's eyes began to shine with a sudden new light, and I thought she might be about to cry, but that did not seem possible, for she was also smiling. She leaned down to hug me and said,

"This is one time we must all go, Richard. If we love him, we must go. Now you must not keep me. People are coming for dinner. Your father is waiting for me downstairs. You know how he looks up the stairs to see me come down. Now sleep. You will love the train as you always do. And yes: in New York you may buy a little present for each one of your friends and bring them back to them."

It was a lustrous thought to leave with me as she went, making a silky rustle with her long dinner dress that dragged on the floor after her. I lay awake thinking of my friends and planning my gifts.

Anna came to us four days a week from the Lithuanian quarter of town and I spent much time in her kitchen or basement laundry listening to her rambling stories of life on the "East Side." I remember wondering if everybody on the "East Side" had deep pockmarks like those in her coarse face, and one day, with inoffensive candor, I asked her about them, and she replied with the dread word, "Smallpox."

"They thought I was going to die. They thought I was dead."

"But you weren't?"

"Oh, no," quite as serious as I, "I fooled them all. But look at me. There was a time when I thought I would have been better off dead."

"Why, Anna?"

"Who wants a girl looking like this?"

"Did they care?"

"Oh, my man came along, and I forgot about it."

"What is it like to be dead, Anna?"

"Oh, dear saints, who can tell that who is alive?"

It was all I could find out, but the question was often with me. Sometimes in late still afternoons, when I was supposed to be taking my nap, I would think about it, and I would hear Anna singing, way below in the laundry, and her voice was like something hooting far away up the chimney. It always seemed the same song that she sang, and I think now that she simply made up a tune long ago, and was satisfied with it, and so hooted it over and over, with words I never understood. Drowsily I wondered if the song were about dying. What should I buy for Anna in New York?

And for Mr Schmitt, the iceman. He was a heavy-waisted German-American with a face wider at the bottom than at the top, and when he walked he had to lumber his huge belly from side to side to make room for his great jellying thighs as he stepped. He had a big, hard voice, and we could hear him coming blocks away, as he called out the word "Ice!" in a long cry. Other icemen used a bell, but not Mr Schmitt. I waited for him when he came, and we always exchanged words, while he stabbed at the high cakes of ice in his hooded wagon, chopping off the pieces we always took—two chunks of fifty pounds each. His skill with his tongs was magnificent, and he would swing his cake up on his shoulder, over which he wore a sort of rubber chasuble, and wag his way in heavy grace, hanging his free hand out in the air to balance his burdened progress up the walk along the side of our house to the kitchen porch. He made two trips, one for each cake of ice, and he blew his breath with extra effort to interest me.

"Do you want to ride today?" he would ask, meaning that I was welcome to ride to the end of the block on the seat towering above Ted's rump, where the shiny, rubbed reins lay in a loose knot, because Ted needed no guidance, but could be trusted to stop at all the right houses and start up again when he felt Mr Schmitt's heavy vaulting rise to the seat. I often rode to the end of the block, and Ted, in his moments of pause, would look around at me, first from one side, and then the other, and stamp a leg, and shudder his rattling harness against flies, and in general treat me as one of the ice company, for which I was grateful.

What to buy for Ted? Perhaps in New York they had horse

stores. My father would give me what money I would need, when I told him what I wanted to buy, and for whom. I resolved to ask him, provided I could stay awake until the dinner party was over, and everybody had gone, when my father would come in on his way to bed to see if all was well in the nursery. At such times I might hear him and awaken and answer him still dreaming. He called me "Doc" because he believed that I would one day study medicine and carry a narrow black bag full of delicious colored pills like coarse sand in little phials, like the ones in the toy doctor's kit which I owned. How much love there was all about me, and how greedy I was for even more of it.

Having no voice in the decision, I was with everyone else the next day when we assembled at the station to take the Empire State Express. It was a heavy, gray, cold day, and everybody wore fur but me and my great-aunt Barbara—Tante Bep, as she was called. She was returning to Germany with my grandfather, her brother.

This was an amazing thing in itself, for first of all, he always went everywhere alone, and second, Tante Bep was so different from her magnificent brother that she was generally kept out of sight. She lived across town on the East Side in a convent of German nuns who received money for her board and room from Grosspa. I always thought she resembled an ornamental cork which my grandfather often used to stopper a wine bottle opened but not yet emptied. Carved out of crisp soft wood and painted in bright colors, the cap of the cork represented a Bavarian peasant woman with a blue shawl over her flat-painted gray hair. The eyes were tiny dots of bright blue lost in deep wooden wrinkles, and the nose was a heavy wooden lump hanging over a toothless mouth sunk deep in an old woman's poor smile. Despite the smile the carved face showed anxiety. The same was true of Tante Bep. Left alone in Germany many years ago, she might have starved, if her splendid brother, who had become prosperous in America, had not saved her. He sent for her and gave her what American life she knew with the German nuns who reassuringly kept the ways of the old country. Her gratitude was anguish to behold. Now, wearing her jet-spangled black bonnet with chin-ribbons, and her black shawl and heavy skirts which smelled rather like dog hair, she was returning to Germany with her brother, and I did not know why.

But her going was part of the strangeness which I felt in all the circumstances of our journey. In the Empire State Express my grandfather retired at once to a drawing room at the end of our car. My mother went with him. Tante Bep and I occupied swiveled armchairs in the open part of the parlor car, and my father came and went between us and the private room up ahead.

"*Ach Gott!*" exclaimed Tante Bep many times that day, looking out the window at the passing snowy landscape, and then at me, moving her tongue inside her sunken mouth, as she smiled to console me and blinked both eyes to encourage me—for what? Tante Bep prayed her rosary, trying to hide her beads in the voluminous folds of her skirt. But I could see the rosewood beads and the worn, heavy crucifix now and then as she progressed by Hail Marys, using her work-toughened old thumbs to advance the stages of her chain of mercy.

In the afternoon I fell asleep after the splendors of lunch in the dining car. Grosspa's lunch went into his room on a tray, and my mother shared it with him. I hardly saw her all day, but when we drew into New York, she came to awaken me, saying,

"Now, Richard, all the lovely exciting things begin! Tonight the hotel, tomorrow the ship! Come, let me wash your face and comb your hair."

"And the shopping?" I said.

"Shopping?"

"For my presents."

[73]

"What presents?"

"Mother, Mother, you have forgotten."

"I'm afraid I have, but we can speak of it later."

It was true that people did forget at times, and I knew how they tried then to render unimportant what they should have remembered. Would this happen to my plans for Anna, and Mr Schmitt, and Ted? My concern was great—but just as my mother had told, there were excitements waiting, and even I forgot, for the while, what it had seemed treacherous of her to forget.

We drove from the station in two limousine taxis, like high glass cages on wheels. I worked all the straps and handles in our cab. My father rode with me and Tante Bep. He pointed out famous sights as we went. It was snowing lightly, and the street lamps were rubbed out of shape by the snow, as if I had painted them with my watercolors at home. We went to the Waldorf-Astoria Hotel on Fifth Avenue. Soon after I had been put into my room, which I was to share with Tante Bep, my father came with an announcement.

"Well, Doc," he said, lifting me up under my arms until my face was level with his and his beautifully brushed hair which shone under the chandelier, and letting his voice sound the way his smile looked, "we are going to have a dinner party downstairs in the main dining room."

I did not know what a main dining room was, but it sounded superb, and I looked pathetic at the news, for I knew enough of dinner parties at home to know that they always occurred after my nightly banishment.

"It won't be like at home, will it," I said, "it will be too far away for me to listen."

"Listen? You are coming with us. What did you think?"

"Well, I thought—"

"No. And do you know why you are coming with us?"

[74]

"Why?"

"Grosspa specially wants you there."

"Ach Gott," murmured Tante Bep in the shadows, and my father gave her a frowning look to warn her not to show so much feeling.

A few minutes later we went downstairs. I was in a daze of happiness at the grand room of the hotel, the thick textures, the velvety lights, the distances of golden air, and most of all at the sound of music coming and coming from somewhere. In a corner of the famous main dining room there was a round table sparkling with light on silver, ice, glass, china and flowers, and in a high armchair sat my grandfather—rosy face, blue eyes and white beard. He inclined himself forward to greet us and seated us about him. My mother was at his right, in one of her prettiest gowns, with jewels. I was on his left.

"Hup-hup!" said my grandfather, clapping his hands to summon waiters now that we were assembled. "Tonight nothing but a happy family party, and Richard shall drink wine with me, for I want him to remember that his first glass of wine was poured for him by his *alter Münchner Freund, der Grossvater."*

At this a wet sound began with Tante Bep, but a look from my father quelled it, and my mother, blinking both eyes rapidly, which made them look prettier than ever when she stopped, put her hand on her father's and leaned and kissed his cheek above the crystal edge of his beard.

"Listen to the music!" commanded Grosspa, "and be quiet, if every word I say is to be a signal for emotion!"

It was a command in the style of his household terror, and everybody straightened up and looked consciously pleasant, except me. For me it was no effort. The music came from within a bower of gold lattice screens and potted palms—two violins, a 'cello, and a harp. I could see the players clearly, for they were in the corner just across from us. The leading violinist stood, the others sat. He was alive with his music, bending to it, marking the beat with his glossy head on which his sparse hair was combed flat. The restaurant was full of people whose talk made a thick hum, and to rise over this, and to stimulate it further, the orchestra had to work with extra effort.

The rosy lamp shades on the tables, the silver vases full of flowers, the slowly sparkling movements of the ladies and gentlemen, and the swallow-like dartings of the waiters transported me. I felt a lump of excitement where I swallowed. My eyes kept returning to the orchestra leader, who conducted with side-jerks of his nearly bald head, for what he played and what he did seemed to me to command the meaning of the astonishing fact that I was at a dinner party in public with my family.

"What music are they playing?" I asked.

"It is called *Il Bacio*," answered Grosspa.

"What does that mean?"

"It means *The Kiss*."

What an odd name for a piece of music, I thought, as I watched the musicians who went at their work with a kind of sloping ardor. All through dinner—which did not last as long as it might have—I inquired about pieces played by the quartet, and in addition to the Arditi waltz, I remember one called *Simple Aveu* and the Boccherini *Minuet*. The violins had a sweetish mosquito-like sound, and the harp sounded breathless, and the 'cello mooed like a distant cow, and it was all entrancing. Watching the orchestra, I ate absently, with my head turned away from my fork until my father, time and again, had to turn me to face my plate. And then a waiter came with a silver tub on legs which he put at my grandfather's left, and showed him the wine bottle which he took from its nest of sparkling ice. The label was approved, a sip was poured for my grandfather to taste, he held it to the light and twirled his glass slowly, he sniffed it, and then he tasted it.

"Yes," he declared, "it will do."

My mother watched him in this ritual, and over her lovely heart-shaped face, with its silky crown of rolled tresses, I saw memories pass like shadows, as she thought of all the times she had attended the business of ordering and serving wine with her father. Blinking both eyes rapidly, she opened a little jeweled lorgnon she wore on a fine chain and bent forward to read the menu which stood in a little silver frame beside her plate. But I could see that she was not reading, and again I wondered what was the matter with everybody.

"For my grandson," said Grosspa, taking a wineglass and filling it half full with water, and then pouring it full with wine. The yellow pour turned pale in my glass. There was too much ceremony about it for me not to be impressed. I took the glass he handed me, and when he raised his, I raised mine, and while all the others watched, we drank together. And then he recited a proverb in German which meant something like,

> *When comrades drink red wine or white*
> *They stand as one for what is right,*

and an effect of intimate applause went around the table at this stage of my growing up.

I was suddenly embarrassed, for the music stopped, and I thought all the other diners were looking at me; and, in fact, many were, and I had a picture-like impression of how all smiled at a boy of nine, ruddy with excitement and confusion, drinking a solemn pledge of some sort with a pink and white old gentleman.

Mercifully the music began again and we were released from our poses, as it were, and my grandfather drew out of one vest pocket his great gold watch with its hunting case, and unhooked from a vest button the fob which held the heavy gold chain in place across his splendid middle. Repeating an old game we had played when I was still a baby, he held the watch toward my lips, and I knew what was expected of me. I blew upon it, and—though long ago I had penetrated the secret of the magic—the gold lid of the watch flew open. My grandfather laughed softly in a deep wheezing breath, and then shut the watch with a lovely cushioned click, saying,

"Do children ever know that what we do to please them pleases us more that it does them?"

"*Ach Gott,*" whispered Tante Bep, and nobody reproved her, and then he said,

"Richard, I give you this watch and chain to keep all your life, and by it you will remember me."

"Oh, no!" exclaimed my mother in an uncontrollable waft of feeling.

He looked gravely at her and said,

"Yes, now, rather than later," and put the heavy wonderful golden objects into my hand.

I regarded them in silence. Mine! I could hear the wiry ticking of the watch, and I knew that now and forever I myself could press my thumb on the winding stem and myself make the gold lid fly open. The chain slid like a small weighty serpent across my fingers.

"Well," urged my father gently, "Richard, what do you say?"

"Yes, thank you, Grosspa, thank you."

I leaned up out of my chair and put my arm around his great head and kissed his cheek. Up close, I could see tiny blue and scarlet veins like something woven under his skin.

"That will do, my boy," he said. Then he took the watch from me and handed it to my father. "I hand it to your father to keep for you until you are twenty-one. But remember that it is yours and you must ask to see it any time you wish."

Disappointment spread heavily through my entrails, but I knew how sensible it was for the treasure to be held for me instead of given into my care.

"Any time you wish. You wish. Any time," repeated my grandfather, but in a changed voice, a hollow, windy sound that was terrible to hear. He was gripping the arm of his chair and now he shut his eyes behind his gold-framed lenses, and sweat broke out on his forehead which was suddenly dead white. "Any time," he tried to say again through his suffering, to preserve a social air. But stricken with pain too merciless to hide, he lost his pretenses and staggered to his feet. My mother quickly supported him, and my father left my side and hurried to him. Together they helped him from the table, while other diners watched, staring with neither curiosity nor pity. I thought the musicians played harder all of a sudden to distract the people from the sight of an old man in trouble being led out of the main dining room of the Waldorf-Astoria.

"What is the matter?" I asked Tante Bep, who had been ordered with a glance to remain behind with me.

"Ach, Grosspa is not feeling well."

"Should we go with him?"

"But your ice cream."

"Yes, the ice cream."

Though we waited, my family did not return from upstairs. Finally, hot with wine and excitement, I was in my turn led to the elevator and to my room where Tante Bep saw me to bed. Nobody else came to see me, or if anyone did, long later, I did not know it.

During the night more snow fell. When I woke up and ran to my hotel window the world was covered and the air was thick with snow still falling. Word was sent to me to dress quickly, for we were to go to the ship almost at once. I was now eager to see the great ship that would cross the ocean.

Again we went in two taxicabs, I with my father. The others had gone ahead of us. My father pulled me to him to look out the cab window at the spiraling snowfall. We went through narrow dark streets to the west side of Manhattan, where we boarded the ferry-boat that would take us across the North River to Hoboken. The cab rumbled its way to the deck and into the cold damp interior of the ferry.

"Let's get out and stand out on the deck," said my father.

We went forward into the clear space at the bow just as the boat moved into the blowing curtains of snow. All I could see was the dark green water where we sailed, a little sideways, across to the Jersey shore. The city disappeared. We might have been at sea, as Grosspa would soon be. I felt something like loneliness, to be closed away by the storm from sight of what I knew. Yet I noticed how the ferryboat seemed like a great duck, and the trundling action of her power underwater seemed like the engine-work of huge webbed feet. At a moment I could not exactly fix, the other shore began to show through the snow, and we docked with wet, grudging blows against the old timbers of the slip.

When we returned to the cab to disembark, my father said,

"We are going to the piers of the North German Lloyd."

"What is that?"

"The steamship company where Grosspa's ship is docked. The *Kronprinzessin Cecilie.*"

"Can I go inside her?"

"Certainly. Grosspa wants to see you in his cabin."

"Is he there?"

"Yes, by now. The doctor wanted him to go right to bed."

"Is he sick?"

"Yes."

"Did he eat something?—" a family explanation often used to account for my various illnesses at their onset.

"Not exactly. It is something else."

"Will he get well soon?"

"We hope so."

He looked away as he said this. I thought, He does not sound like my father.

The cab was running along the Hoboken docks now. Above the snowy sheds rose in silent grandeur the funnels and masts of ocean ships, and now I could see how huge they were. They made me ache with a bowel-changing longing. The streets were furious with noise—horses, cars, porters calling and running, and suddenly a white tower of steam that rose from the front of one of the funnels, to be followed in a second by a deep roaring hoot.

"There she is," said my father. "That's her first signal for sailing."

It was our ship. I stared up at her three masts with pennons pulled about by the blowing snow, and her four tall ocher funnels, spaced separately in pairs.

As we went from the taxi into the freezing air of the long pier, all I could see of the *Kronprinzessin Cecilie* were glimpses through the pier shed of white cabins, rows of portholes, regiments of rivet heads on the black hull, and an occasional door of polished mahogany. A hollow roar of confused sound filled the long shed. We went up a canvas-covered gangway and then we were on board, and I felt immediately the invisible but real lift and slide and settle of a ship tied to a dock. There was an elegant creaking from the shining woodwork. I felt that a ship was built for boys, because the ceilings were so low, and made me feel so tall.

Holding my hand to keep me by him in the thronged decks, my father led me up a stairway whose curve was like the gesture of a sweeping arm. At the top we came to an open lobby with a skylight whose panes were colored—pale yellow, pale blue, pale green, orange—in a fancy design. From there we entered a narrow corridor that seemed to reach toward infinity. Its walls were of dark shining wood, glowing under weak yellow lights overhead. Its floor sloped down and then up again far away, telling of the ship's construction.

[81]

Cabin doors opened on each side. There was a curious odor in the air—something like soda crackers dipped in milk, and distantly, or was it right here, in every inch of the ship around us, a soft throbbing sound kept up. It seemed impossible that anything so immense as this ship would presently detach itself from the land and go away.

"Here we are," said my father at a cabin door half-open.

We entered my grandfather's room, which was not like a room in a house, for none of its lines squared with the others, but met only to reflect the curvature of the ship's form.

At the wall across the stateroom, under two portholes whose silk curtains were closed, lay my grandfather in a narrow brass bed. He lay at a slight slope, with his arms outside the covers, and evidently he wore a voluminous white nightgown. I had never before seen him in anything but his formal day or evening clothes. He looked white—there was hardly a change in color between his beard and his cheeks and his brow. Seeing us, he did not turn his head, only his eyes. He seemed all of a sudden dreadfully small, and he gave the effect of being cautious in the world where before he had magnificently gone his way ignoring whatever might threaten him with inconvenience, rudeness, or disadvantage. My mother stood by his side and Tante Bep was at the foot of the bed in her black crocheted shawl and full peasant skirts.

"Yes, come, Richard," said Grosspa in a faint wheezy voice, searching for me with his eyes anxiously turned.

I went to his side and he put his hand an inch or two toward me—not enough to risk effort which would revive such a pain as had thrown him down the night before, but enough to call for my response. I set my hand in his and he lightly tightened his fingers over mine.

"Will you come to see me?" he asked in gallant playfulness.

"Where?" I asked in a loud clear tone which made my parents

look at each other, as if to inquire how in the world the chasms which divided age from youth, and pain from health, and sorrow from innocence, could ever be bridged.

"In Germany," he whispered. He shut his eyes and held my hand and I had a vision of Germany which may have been sweetly near to his own; for what I saw in mind were the pieces of cardboard scenery, lithographed in dusty color, which belonged to the toy theater he had brought to me from Germany on one of his returns from his journeys abroad—the Rhine in printed blue haziness with a castle high on a wooded crag; a deep green forest with an open glade in the far distance where gold lithographed light played through the leaves; a medieval street with half-timbered houses; a throne room with a deep perspective of white and good pillars, a golden throne on a dais under a dark red canopy.

"Yes," I replied, "Grosspa, in Germany."

"Yes," he whispered, opening his eyes and making the sign of the Cross on my hand with his thumb. Then he looked at my mother. She understood him at once.

"You go now with Daddy," she said, "and wait for me on deck. We must leave the ship soon. Yes, Richard, *schnell,* now, skip!"

My father took me along the corridor and down the grand stairway. The ship's orchestra was playing somewhere—it sounded like the Waldorf. We went out to the deck just as the ship's siren let go again, and now it shook us gloriously and terribly. I covered my ears but still I was in the power of that immense deep voice. When it stopped, the ordinary sounds around us did not come close again for a moment. I leaned over the top of the railing and looked down at the narrow gap of water between us and the dock, where the spill and filth, the snake-like glide of small eddies, so far down below, gave me a chill of desire and fear. Snow was still falling— heavy, slow, thick flakes, each like several flakes stuck together, the way they used to stick in my eyelashes when I went out to play in winter.

A cabin boy came along beating a brass cymbal, calling out for all visitors to leave the ship.

I began to wonder if my mother would be taken away to sea while my father and I were forced to go ashore. Looking carefully, I saw her at last. She came toward us with a rapid, light step, and saying nothing, she turned us to the gangway and we went down. She held my father's arm when we reached the pier. She was wearing a spotted veil, and with one hand she now lifted this up just under her eyes and put her handkerchief to her mouth. She was weeping. I was abashed by her grief.

We hurried to the dock street, and there we lingered to watch the sailing of the *Kronprinzessin Cecilie*.

We did not talk. It was bitter cold. Wind came strongly from the North, and then, after a third shaking blast from her voice, the ship slowly began to change—she moved like water itself, leaving the dock, guided by three tugboats which made heavy black smoke in the thick air. Everything went by in a trance-like slowness, but at last I could see the ship, all of her, at one time.

I was amazed how tall and narrow she was as she stood out to the river at a long angle, stern first. Her four funnels seemed to rise like a city against the blowy sky. I could squint at her and know just how I would make a model of her when I got home. In midstream she slowly turned to face the lower bay. Her masts were like lines I drew with my pencils. Her smoke began to blow forward. She looked gaunt and proud and top-heavy. At a moment which no one could fix she ceased backing and turning and began to steam clear and straight down the river and away.

"Oh, Dan!" cried my mother in a caught sob, and put her face against my father's shoulder. He folded his arm around her. Their faces were stretched with sorrow.

Just then a break in the sky across the river let light open on the snowy day and I stared in wonder at the change. I was the only one who saw it, for my father, watching after the departed liner in his thoughts, said to my mother,

"Like some old wounded lion crawling home to die."

"Oh, Dan," she sobbed, "don't, don't!"

I could not imagine what they were talking about. In my own interest and wonder, I tugged at my mother's arm and said with excitement, pointing to the thick flakes everywhere about us, and against the light beyond,

"Look, look, the snowflakes are all black!"

My mother suddenly could bear no more. My witless excitement released all her feelings. She leaned down and shook me and said in a voice now strong with anger,

"Richard, why do you say black! What nonsense. Stop it. Snowflakes are white, Richard. White! White! When will you ever see things as they are! Oh!"

Her grief gave birth to her rage.

"Come, everybody," said my father. "I have the car waiting."

"But they *are* black!" I cried.

"Quiet!" commanded my father.

We rode to the hotel in silence.

We were to return to Dorchester on the night train. All day I was too proud to mention what I alone seemed to remember, but after my nap, during which on principle I refused to sleep, my mother came to me, and said,

"You think I have forgotten. Well, I remember. We will go and arrange your presents."

My world was full of joy again. The first two presents were easy

[85]

to find—there was a little shop full of novelties a block from the hotel, and there I bought for Anna a folding package of views of New York, and for Mr Schmitt a cast-iron model of the Statue of Liberty. It was more difficult to think of something Ted would like. My mother let me consider by myself many possibilities among the variety available in the novelty shop, but the one thing I thought of for Ted I did not see. Finally, with an inquiring look at my mother to gain courage, I asked the shopkeeper,

"Do you have any straw hats for horses?"

"*What?*"

"Straw hats for horses, with holes for their ears to come through. They wear them in summer."

"Oh. I know what you mean. No, we don't."

My mother took charge.

"Then, Richard, I don't think this gentleman has what we need for Ted. Let us go back to the hotel. I think we may find it there."

"What will it be?"

"You'll see."

When tea was served in her room, she poured a cup for each of us, and asked,

"What do horses love?"

"Hay. Oats."

"Yes. What else."

Her eyes sparkled playfully across the tea table. I followed her glance.

"I know! Sugar!"

"Exactly"—and she made a little packet of sugar cubes in an envelope of Waldorf stationery from the desk in the corner, and my main concern in the trip to New York was satisfied. My father returned with all the tickets and arrangements to go home.

At home, in the next few days, I could not wait to present my gifts. Would they like them? In two cases I never really knew. Anna accepted her folder of views and opened it up to let the pleated pages fall in one sweep, and remarked,

"When we came to New York from the old country, I was a baby, and I do not remember one thing about it."

Mr Schmitt took his Statue of Liberty in hand, turned it over carefully, and said,

"Well—"

But Ted—Ted clearly loved my gift, for he nibbled the sugar cubes off my outstretched palm until there was not one left, and then bumped me with his hard itchy head making me laugh and hurt at the same time.

"He likes sugar," I said to Mr Schmitt.

"*Ja.* Do you want to ride?"

Life, then, was much as before until the day a few weeks later when we received a cablegram telling that my grandfather was dead in Munich. My father came home from the office to comfort my mother. They told me the news with solemnity in our long living room where the curtains were now closed against the light of the world. I listened, and I had a lump of pity in my throat for the look on my mother's face, but I did not feel anything else.

"He dearly loved you," they said.

"May I go now?" I asked.

They were shocked. What an unfeeling child. Did he have no heart? How could the loss of so great and dear a figure in the family not move him?

But I had never seen death, I had no idea of what death was like. Grosspa had gone away before now and I had soon ceased to miss him, what if they did say now that I could never see him again? I could show nothing. They shook their heads and let me go.

Anna was more offhand than my parents about the whole matter. "You know," she said, letting me watch her at her deep zinc laundry tubs in the dark, steamy, confidential basement, "that your Grosspa went home to Germany to die, you know that, don't you?"

"Is that why he went?"

"That's why."

"Did he know it?"

"Oh, yes, sure he knew it."

"Why couldn't he die right here?"

"Well, when our time comes, maybe we all want to go back where we came from."

Her voice, speaking of death, contained a doleful pleasure. The greatest mystery in the world was still closed to me. When I left her she raised her old tune under the furnace pipes and I wished I were as happy and full of knowledge as she.

My time soon came.

On the following Saturday I was watching for Mr Schmitt and Ted when I heard heavy footsteps running up the front porch and someone shaking the doorknob forgetting to ring the bell. I went to see. It was Mr Schmitt. He was panting and he looked wild. When I opened the door he ran past me into the front hall calling out,

"Telephone! Let me have the telephone!"

I pointed to it in the bend of the hall where it stood on a gilded wicker taboret. He picked up the receiver and began frantically to click the receiver hook. I was amazed to see tears roll from his eyes and down on his cheeks which looked ready to burst with redness and fullness.

"What's the matter, Mr Schmitt?" I asked.

I heard my mother coming along the hallway upstairs from her sitting room.

Mr Schmitt suddenly put down the phone and pulled off his hat and shook his head.

"What's the use," he said. "I know it is too late already. I was calling the ice plant to send someone to help."

"Good morning, Mr Schmitt," said my mother coming downstairs. "What on earth is the matter?"

"My poor old Ted," he said, waving his hat toward the street. "He fell down and just died in front of the Weiners' house."

"Oh—" and my mother spoke words of sympathy.

I ran out of the house and up the sidewalk to the Weiners' house, and sure enough, there was the ice wagon, and in the shafts, lying heavy and gone on his fat side, was Ted. There lay death on the asphalt paving. I confronted the mystery at last.

Ted's one eye that I could see was open. A fly walked across it and there was no blink. His teeth gaped apart letting his long tongue lie out on the street. His body seemed twice as big and heavy as before. Without even trying to lift it I knew how mortally heavy it was. His front legs were crossed, and the great horn cup of the upper hoof was slightly tipped, the way he used to rest it at ease, bent over the pavement. From under his belly flooded a pool of pale yellow fluid—his urine—and from beneath his tail flowed the last of his excrement, in which I could see oats. In his fall he had twisted the shafts which he had pulled for so many years. His harness was awry. Melting ice dripped at the back of the hooded wagon. Its wheels looked as if they had never turned. What would ever turn them?

"Never," I said, half aloud. I knew the meaning of this word now.

In another moment my mother came and took me back to our house, and Mr Schmitt settled down on the curbstone to wait for people and services to arrive and take away the leavings of his changed world.

I went and told Anna what I knew. She listened with her head on the side, her eyes half-closed, and she nodded at my news and sighed.

"Poor old Ted," she said, "he couldn't even crawl home to die."

This made my mouth fall open, for it reminded me of something I had heard before, somewhere, and all day I was subdued and private, quite unlike myself, as I heard later, and late that night, I awoke in a storm of grief so noisy in its gusts that my parents came to me asking what was the trouble.

I could not speak at first, for their tender, warm, bed-sweet presences doubled my emotion, and I sobbed against them as together they held me. But at last when they said again,

"What's this all about, Richard, Richard?" I was able to say,

"It's all about Ted."

This was true, if not all the truth, for I was thinking also of Grosspa now, crawling home to die, and I knew what that meant, and what death was like. I imagined Grosspa's heavy death, with his open eye, and his loss of his fluids, and his sameness and his difference all mingled, and I wept for him at last, and for myself if I should die, and for my ardent mother, and my sovereign father, and for the iceman's old horse, and for everyone.

"Hush, dear, hush, Richard," they said, and it was all they could say, for who could soften or change the fact of death?

A pain in my head began to throb remotely as my outburst diminished, and another thought entered with rueful persistence, and I said in bitterness,

"But they were black! Really they were!"

They looked at each other and then at me, but I was too spent to continue, and I fell to my pillow, and even if they might insist that snowflakes were white, I knew that when seen against the light, falling out of the sky into the sliding water all about the *Kronprinzessin Cecilie,* they were black. To children—as to artists—all life is metaphor. Black snowflakes against the sky. Why could they not see that? Black.

PART
TWO

A Start in Life

It was near dusk when the train stopped at Mead and the woman passenger came across the platform toward the little dock where the launch was waiting. She hurried in the twilight and seemed to gather herself against the chill that was coming with the autumn evening. Halfway down the dock, a young man met her and took her bags. He handed her into the launch that tipped toward the dock as they stepped aboard, and when she was settled on the red canvas cushions in the little cabin, the young man went to the wheel in the stern and started the engine which sat in a tin basin in the open cockpit. There was a canopy of maple slats and canvas, with scalloped edges, over the cockpit.

As the launch pulled away from Mead, the train whistled and began to wind into the darkened country of the shore.

The woman turned and looked at her skipper, and then looked out again over the water to the opposite shore where the black pines stood against a stormy silver line of the evening sky. The launch rocked on the blackening water. A stubborn wind blew off the lake, driving white caps up the inlet where the white launch moved. From a distance she looked like a beautiful little boat. Within her, she was a homely and battered launch that yet managed to cross the inlet between Mead and Port Raeburn whenever she must.

The two people in the boat were pulsing with the same rhythm, that of the engine in its oily pan. It gave them an odd and secret intimacy, subject to a force beyond themselves, now trivial, but prophetic of much to come.

The woman in the cabin came nearer the cockpit on the side bench.

"I suppose everybody is gone, by now?" she asked.

"Just about," the young man answered. "We had a big crowd all summer. But they're gone now. Place seems mighty deserted."

"That's just what I want," she said, smiling almost sorrowfully. "I have to rest."

He grinned at her and kept quiet.

"My name is Mrs Morgan."

"Yes, ma'am. I'm John Guelph. You wrote to my mother."

"Oh yes, Mrs Guelph was recommended to me by some friends who stayed here three summers ago. They enjoyed it, the food, and the lovely scenery, and the good beds. They remembered you and spoke of you. I suppose you were much younger, then."

She smiled, and after a moment, added,

"How far is it to Port Raeburn?"

"We're nearly there. We cross the channel and then you can see. But it's getting pretty dark. Maybe you can just make out the long pier, way down there, to your right?"

"Oh yes. I can just see it."

"Then this way along the shore, that red light? That's our dock."

"Oh, it's not far, then."

"No, I cross ten times a day in season, sometimes. This old boat knows it by heart."

"It's a rather sweet old tub, isn't she: what do you call her?"

"The Comet," he answered, a little resentfully, for he had never considered her a tub.

The engine tappets clicked along. In a little pause, they sounded like part of the conversation. Mrs. Morgan and John looked at each other and then laughed companionably.

"—How dark it turned, suddenly."

"Yes, it always does."

"You can just see the pines. What marvelous air! I'm going to take long walks on the beach. I saw from the train all the way coming up how far the beaches run in this country. And the forests right near the edge!"

The Comet was rocking and rising on the waves which were higher. It was dark overhead. The last silver glances of day were closing. Mrs Morgan turned a little fearful. She said nothing but looked anxiously at John. He felt this, and leaning down, he touched an electric switch under the seat, and in the ceiling of the cabin, a small light turned on, steady yellow. It added a sort of pathetic luxury to the cabin, with its red cushions and faded red curtains at the four little windows on each side.

"That was nice of you. I felt nervous."

"We might as well travel in style."

"Why is it so rough?"

"It's the channel. The lake seems to push right up here inland. When we have storms, this inlet is worse than the open water. I've seen waves twice's high's this boat."

"Do you have many storms?"

"Long about now, we get a few. Sometimes the big steamers have to lay up at Mead for a few days."

"The freight boats?"

"Yes. They used to dock on our side of the inlet, at Port Raeburn; my father was captain of one. That's what the long pier was for I showed you a few minutes ago. But the railroad and the lumber mill developed at Mead, and the big boats come up the channel now instead, and dock across the way.—But we still get the tourists," he added with a trace of irony. "Look: you see how much calmer it is? We're pulling in."

The water was dark and quiet. The shore was suddenly waiting for them right at hand. Through the pines windows shone with light. The Comet hissed and coughed; then her engine died, and she coasted on a long curve in toward the short dock above which loomed a weather-wracked boathouse.

"We're here," he said.

Mrs Morgan sighed. Why could not any voyage last forever? She stood up, and in a moment, climbed on the dock and followed him up the slope where the path was covered with pine needles that she could smell, and feel in her step, but could not see. The air was blowing with strong fresh strains of scent from the lake, the fishy shore, the pines which cut the winds into strange minor chords overhead. As she walked she was aware of small houses, unpainted pine shelters that were empty and dark. A summer resort, closed for the winter. She remembered a post card from her friends here three years ago, "Port Raeburn, Ontario," which showed a one-sided street with souvenir shops and candy stores facing the water.

The next morning she confirmed her impressions of the land and its map. It was a sunny day, with a brisk wind. The opposite shore of the inlet lay glistening and jeweled with light—the lumber yard, the sawmill, the station, the dock. On this side, once past the abandoned site of the summer resort the beach was clear and the forest was innocent. A path ran along its edge toward the point where the white sand piled up against tumbled rocks. Here began the long pier, going from the rocks out into the inlet for a hundred yards. Its wood was black and gray. The waves heaved in under its planking, and its piles, some of which were loose, winced audibly with a rotten softness.

Mrs Morgan walked out to the far end of the pier and saw Lake Ontario, moving in boundless light like a great sea.

She saw in the piles the evidences of many summers. There were carven initials and monograms; hearts grained with the pocket knife into this old fiber, which was staunch, a testimonial to a still older fiber in men and women. Thinking of the picnics and the pledges of such summers, she became saddened. Something knocked in her breast.

She was almost forty years old, and of medium height. Her face was young and thin, with enormous dark eyes which had stains of trouble under them. Her hair was brown. She wore her cheeks white, but her mouth was fresh peony red with lipstick. Her facial bones were true and clear under her skin, and her narrow hands often felt of them. She smoked constantly, even while taking a walk like this morning's. She told herself that she was right to go away and think things through, and in her tired dreaming and planning, it seemed to her the most desirable thing in the world, to leave Buffalo for a while, and get off somewhere where there was no chance of fooling herself any longer, and come to decisions that had to be made to suit Howard Morgan, her husband.

He had reminded her of what fun the Lancasters had had in Port Raeburn three summers ago. He agreed it was wise of her to go off alone. He told her if there was no one to talk to she might get some rest, and for once in her life not magnify her troubles by talk, talk, talk. She had heard this criticism of herself many times and sometimes she earnestly tried to find out if she really considered herself indiscreet. But she would conclude helplessly that some people were born with too much feeling, all they asked of life was permission to give; and when the giving was so easy, it very often was not wanted, which had wounded Mrs Morgan many times in her married life and before.

"It does no good to be lonely," she thought, gazing out across the lake. She was looking at a long freighter out there, moving so slowly down the wind that its smoke hanging forward like a mermaid's hair seemed to impede its going. The water danced in the sunlight as far as she could see. She lighted a cigarette and its taste was rueful in her mouth; the pleasures of life were pitiful now that life was hurting her. She began to weep.

Mrs Guelph, who ran the best boarding house in Port Raeburn, was glad to have a post-season guest. But she was a speculative woman, and she asked her son John many questions.

"What does she *do,* all day, going out alone?"

"I see her taking walks. I took her to Mead yesterday morning to get some things at the store."

"She seems troubled."

Mrs Guelph caught her breath and bit her loose lips in a rush of sympathy. She was a tall and bell-shaped woman, her head small with white hair, her eyes blue and sharpened by glasses, her cheeks sagging past her toothless mouth. She grew wider and wider from the shoulders down, until her skirts went awide to the floor. In her sixties, she could work like a man. Her hands looked like a man's with heavy veins coursing along their backs.

"Yes, she's troubled, but then so am I, and how can I afford to waste my sympathy *there.* —I don't know. —It's the same old thing. Since Cap'n died: that is: Johnny, I never can get a penny ahead, now here we had a big summer, and packed to the roof, and reservations turned down: and I was counting up today, there's barely enough money to get us through the winter! I tried and I try, I can't seem to save a shilling!"

Since Cap'n died: thought John. Every thing was new since then, the death of his father turned them into a new world because it was a world without him, though they did not change to accommodate it.

"Where do people get their money, Mother?"

"You poor child, if I had *my* way—"

"I know."

He teased her with his very being sometimes.

She would mourn over his good looks, the cheeky face of his nineteen years, his gray eyes and curly brown hair, as if in fostering them, she had lost everything to the world. He was a young man of imperious flesh and he would go off before long. He was ambitious. Longing to help him to go, she feared losing him. His life, as much as anyone else's, was secret from her. She remembered him even as she gazed at his white grin, the sly muscular charm he had moving. People in the summer always spoke of him as a typical Canadian, pink-faced and polite. He was rather reserved, and sometimes merry, and with not the strength of initiative, but rather the strength which waits to be used, and then becomes powerful as directed.

"Well, this Mrs Morgan didn't say how long she'd be here; but God help us, I hope she stays all month!"

"I'll try and be nice to her, Mother."

She was stricken by a thought about this and was ready with a warning plea; but she gazed into his face, refused him his growth, and turned away, troubled by the thoughts of his secret future. He felt something of this, and after it embarrassed him, it made him smile, for the suggestions it made and his taste for them.

"What's the matter with her, then?"

"What do you mean," said John. He was in the souvenir and grocery store, which stayed open all winter. The storekeeper was talking.

"She goes out walking, all alone, don't she?"

"Well, yes."

"I saw her, and Bea saw her, next day, and she was crying."

"I don't know."

"Looks mighty funny."

"Well, *I* never saw her!"

"Maybe not. No need to get wild about it!"

"I know. —She's just up here for a rest."

"I see. Does she get much mail?"

"I never noticed, specially."

"Oh, all right. Here's your bacon."

John left the store.

"Are you going to Mead this morning?"

He looked at her as if he hadn't heard the question but were listening to a question in his own mind instead.

"I'd like to go along, and get some things, if you are," she added.

"Yes."

She saw him start as if to awake and smile.

Presently they were down on the dock, getting into the Comet. The inlet was calm and deep blue. Over the opposite shore among the trees there stayed a veil of light blue vapor, autumn pausing in the woods before overcoming the whole land. The launch headed out over the water. Mead was sparkling with yellow sunlight.

"Indian summer!"

"Sometimes it lasts weeks up here. Sometimes it goes all of a sudden, and we get snow. Or storms."

"I'm sleeping much more since I came ten days ago."

"That must be what you do all day. I never see you around much."

"I didn't feel like fit company for man or beast," she said, with the first lightness she had felt for weeks.

"There aren't many men *or* beasts up around here this time of year. I get lonesome in the winter. There's not much to do."

"What *do* you do? What do you *want* to do?" she asked. Her brow worked, promising all her sympathy.

"Oh, I go to school, that is, I graduated from high school in town, and I read whatever I can find. I help mother. There's some repairing to do every year, and I work for the carpenter, Mr Cunningham."

He spoke hesitantly. He was thinking of something else.

"Yes, but what are you going to *do!*"

"I don't suppose you'd take it very seriously, but I want to study singing."

She felt the blush take her cheeks, until they felt hot in the cool air, because he was a little defiant as if sympathy would never come his way. She leaned toward him feeling her eyes sting with sentiment.

"That's very fine! Will you sing for me, John? I can play the piano. In fact, I play very well. I'd love to help you! It means so much to a younger person to have someone else take an interest in them—"

"I'll sing for you. I need to learn new songs. —So mostly when I have nothing else to do, I go out on the long pier, or down the beach toward Point St Albans and practice singing."

"You are ambitious!"

"Yes. —I want to be a concert singer."

She saw that he took these desires so seriously that they must lead to something for a life. She felt a rushing warmth in her heart, and was afraid he might see how needful she was of a chance to give: to make use of her spirit in that way, which was the very way that now bored her husband and gave him what he considered license for freedom. She was afraid that a man impersonally would resent the betrayals of her interest unless he was in love with her, which her husband was no longer, and John would never be. She thought if her marriage had not turned into this bitter mockery of each

other's most integral ways, Howard would love her for her sentimental enthusiasms, instead of sneer at them, and she would admire
his cold, critical mind instead of beat on its dispassion with her
passion.

So she simply turned and did not talk any more until they reached
Mead in the launch.

In the afternoon a fog rolled across the inlet about three o'clock,
tasting like cold smoke, and darkening the house into the very
woods where it sat. Mrs Morgan came downstairs from her bedroom looking for company. She found Mrs Guelph in the kitchen.

"It's chilly! But rather pleasant, for a change, isn't it!"

"Oh, you vacationists!" declared Mrs Guelph with a laugh. "Anything happens in the country is all fine with you!"

"Well, anyway, I came downstairs to find something to do. —May
I play the piano? Where's John: will he sing for me?"

"So he's told you *that*."

"Why: yes: I think it's splendid."

"Yes, and how will he make a living at it? And how will he get
money to go to Toronto to study singing?"

The room was darkened with the gray cloud on the window-
panes. The fog itself seemed to fill the room.

"If he's good enough, and has enough ambition, he'll—"

"Psst! —He's coming up the back porch. I never can talk about it
if he—"

Mrs Morgan turned and went to the sitting room at the front of
the house. Here it was even darker, for great pines stood by the
windows and turned the shadows inside black even on a bright day.
The room was lined with stained pine boards, dark green, and the
furniture was made of heavy, varnished oak. The upright piano
stood in a corner. It had a carved grille backed with red velvet. Over
its top lay a green velvet lambrequin. On this was a row of family

photographs. The keys were creamy with age, not wear. Mrs Morgan sat down and began to play. The tone was dank, much as if this very fog had lived in the strings till they had caught cold.

"You'd better have some light."

She stopped playing and turned around.

"Oh, John! Now will you sing?"

"If I can find my music. —I haven't sung for a long time, I mean with the piano. —I don't know if I—"

"You're nervous! But not *ever,* with *me!* I am very understanding, my dear boy!"

It was the very sort of remark that always enraged her husband. It excited John still further. But together they looked for his songs in the music cabinet in the other corner of the room. Bending together, they were oddly intimate. Her hair wired along his cheek, and made him taste the flavor of faint electricity in his tongue. He wished, without conscious plan, that they were alone in some other house. He suddenly felt like singing. They found some music. He lighted the gas mantle in the center of the room. A citrous light fell on them. When Mrs Morgan heard his fine natural voice she shivered and her shoulders shrank together, for she heard youth, and bright truculence, and the secrets of beauty in a man's heart which he knows so few ways to tell.

They played and sang until late afternoon.

From time to time Mrs Guelph appeared in the living room doorway timid before the mystery of this trial, and resentful of it for its threat to all the ways in life she knew about. She conceived a dislike for Mrs Morgan. Mrs Morgan looked prettier, she was flushed, her eyes shone, her mouth was sweetened by something Mrs Guelph didn't like, and she seemed less thin and resigned. Mrs Morgan would stop and turn to John and admonish him about phrasing. He listened and nodded, thinking that he liked her.

[103]

At a moment, she stopped, and asked him softly if he had ever been in love.

"I don't—I guess so. Why?"

She closed her eyes and clasped her white fingers together over her mouth and seemed to "pray" to them for a pause.

"What?" he said.

"I thought so, something in your voice, do you want to tell me about it?"

"What do you mean?"

"Who *was* she? Did you *adore* her?" she said, softly, to revive his tenderness. "And were you *lovers:* would she know *how much* you had to love to be *that* to each other?"—with no rebuke implied, but rather a teasing suggestion that life with its gifts, all of them, must be taken.

John began to blush, but he steadied his gaze on her eyes, and she shook her head a little, as if to say "You darling," and he said,

"It was a girl I knew in high school."

She saw that he intended to tell her no more about it. But his reddened face had done it for her. She patted his hand.

"I'm sorry. I didn't mean to—" she said.

"Oh, no, that's all right."

He laughed in troubled excitement, wondering what she was thinking, and training his own thoughts.

Mrs Guelph appeared again in the doorway, wondering about the long pause in the music. She said wryly,

"Johnny, the fog is lifting a bit. Maybe you'd better run over to Mead for the mail. —And see if there's a show tonight that I might want to see."

She would not withdraw until their musical resolution was broken.

Outside, later, the inlet was revealed below the rising fog, which had drifts of vapor smoking up from the dark water. John crossed and came back before it was dark.

"Any mail?"

"There wasn't any."

"That woman upstairs will be disappointed. She's been looking for a letter for a week. Time she went back home, perhaps."

"Why Mom!"

"—Well, how about the movie?"

"Yes, but's one of those mystery murders, you hate them."

"I hate them, you'd think they'd get a good show once in a while."

At supper Mrs Morgan said,

"Do you want to take me to the movies, John?"

"If the fog stays up, I promised to go and take Caroline Cunningham, I saw her yesterday morning."

"Oh."

"—I'm sorry, Mrs Morgan."

"So am I, it gets very lonely."

"How do you think *I* like it," said Mrs Guelph, "day after day and year after year! Since Cap'n died—"

"Yes, well, excuse me: I think I'll go upstairs and write some letters."

Mrs Morgan left the dining room and once in her own room, she felt that she had been foolish, betraying irritation at John's refusal, and then she was washed by a wave of relief. Hadn't she come up to Ontario to think out a way to spend the rest of her life? Wasn't she supposed to be sick and tired of emotional strife and entanglement? What was the truth, after all: her husband Howard Morgan was ready for a divorce, and though he was trying to be civilized about it, his temper broke out at her time after time, for he felt injured by the sixteen years they had been married, the best years of his life, he called them, taken and wasted by her, and what had she given him

[105]

in return? She had cited their home: she had helped him in his engineering business by entertaining his business friends. She had loved him singly and desperately. He had invited her to take a lover, and leave him free to do as he liked. She had become accustomed to drinking to please him, but when he saw her drunk and high-voiced she disgusted him. When she asked him what she could do to keep his love, she would do anything if he would only tell her what, he told her that the trouble with her was, she tried too *hard* to be wife to him, which hurt her so bitterly that she could only gasp, and wait for miserable days for the relief of one of her sick headaches and tears.

Now she had written Howard that they were, after all, two civilized people. Why should they destroy the fabric of their lives together completely? If something was gone, it was gone, but there was so much left to go on with. "I have been too possessive, I see it now," she had written. "I clung for years to my girlhood ideals of marriage and the response that I thought had to come from both partners. You have sinned against me by your cruelty and abuse and philandering and worst of all, your cold withdrawal from any contact but that of sex. I have sinned against you by my refusal to try to understand you as you are, instead of what I wanted you to be. Isn't this a reasonable and honorable view of the situation? If we only recognize what the wrongs are, darling, we can clear them away and leave nothing but the rights! Isn't that true? So don't you see how barbaric it would be for us to be divorced, when you still need me to carry on at home, and I still need you, because there is no one else, and nothing else, that I could rely on if I were cut adrift? It will be only fair to ask you to make the terms on which I come back to you, and also to ask you to accept a few conditions on my part. I will write these next time, if you answer this right away, showing me that you can be and are sympathetic again, and ready to know that my love is one that goes beyond the petty squabbles of day to day and sees something larger for both of us than we ever had before. Your devoted, Ruth."

—But he had not written. A week had passed and no afternoon trip of the launch Comet brought back one of his square engraved envelopes, Morgan, Deeman, Inc., Construction Engineers, with his writing that seemed to grow on the paper in the image of grass, determined and leaning backward, with heavy downstrokes and blade-edged light strokes.

—But if she meant her letter, and she knew she did, how foolish and false it would be of her to fall in love with John! She was glad he had had to go to the show with a girl at Mead. Having seen so clearly what was threatening, she felt strong and able for the rest of what she now thought of as her lonely but gallant fight.

In the morning, she felt that there was a new lap finished, and she was gay with Mrs Guelph, following her around the kitchen, and even into the old woman's bedroom at the back of the house on the ground floor, where the woods came down the slope of the low hill that rose away from the inletside. Mrs Guelph sat down on her immense bed that had a depression in the middle of its expanse, which her body and that of the dead Captain had molded there.

"How much longer, perhaps, will you be going to stay, Mrs Morgan?"

"—I don't quite know. I should surely know by the end of the week. My husband will either come and get me, or write me his plans."

"Oh? Your husband is living?"

"Why of course! Why, whatever made you—"

"Nothing. No, I just didn't know. I just wondered."

The old woman got up and pushed her small glasses up on her forehead and wiped her right eye with her thumb that was pink and shiny like leather from much wear. She suddenly seemed more happy.

Mrs Morgan said,

"Well, I'm going to go down to the village and get some post cards. I'll be back for lunch. —Where is John?"

"He got up early and took the launch and went down to Point St Albans for the day, he's helping Mr Cunningham get some timber. That's the old carpenter over to Mead. They arranged it last night. Johnny says the picture was outlandish."

Mrs Morgan went out. At the souvenir and grocery store she bought cards. They all had robin's-egg blue skies, olive green forests; clouds like erasures; views of the long pier strung with bunting; picnics on the beach, corn roasts by moonlight, canoes and rowboats manned languorously by figures that looked no longer romantic, for the old fashion of their holiday clothes of twenty years before, when the cards were made. She could have bought raffia baskets, miniature birchbark canoes, sweet grass doilies, and the like. But it was autumn, and cool, and lonely: none of this sentimental refuse meant anything even to the storekeeper, out of season. He was a stringy native, with a hush in his voice. An old man, with life almost gone, he felt that things were escaping him.

"Enjoying up here?" he asked.

"Oh, very much."

"Nice folks, the Guelphs. Knowed all of them."

"Mm."

"—That's a comer, that John, I tell you."

She saw his old eyes water with intensity as he searched her face. So! she thought. They are watching me with John! She felt coolly angry.

"He's gone to Point St Albans, by the way," she said. "I wonder if you will be kind enough to bring our mail back with you. He may not get back in time to get over to Mead before the post office closes."

"I will. I always go. You wouldn't care to go along, now, then?"

"No thank you."

A little past five the storekeeper's launch came back across the inlet, and in the acid yellow light of dusk on the sky-white water it was transfigured. Even the put-put of the engine was caught in an echo and doubled and blurred, so that it seemed like a noise from the sky. Mrs Morgan was waiting on the dock, at peace except for the ache of the scene's beauty in her heart. Far down the inlet toward the lake she kept watching for the Comet, coming back from Point St Albans. It didn't come.

The storekeeper shut off his engine.

He glided his boat in to the dock. Standing as it went by like a low bird with a wing in the still water leaving a wavy trail, he handed a small packet of mail up to her, and then sat down, put his tiller over, and was off to his own dock.

"Thanks, very much," she called.

He waved back by his ear, a grudging acknowledgment.

She went up to the house. The top letter was addressed in the grass-like writing of her husband. Here it was. She put Mrs Guelph's mail down on the table in the dark hall and ran up to her room. The corridor was dark, the boarders' rooms all empty but hers, which was the large one at the front of the second story. Yet for the reading of her letter she had an impulse without much sense, to go up to the attic, to be remote and alone. But that was where John slept, and if he should come in, he would be embarrassed. She went to her bedroom, closed the door, and moved to the window for the last light.

"Dear Ruth," she read. "I've been a long time getting around to answering your letter because it was just the opposite of what I

[109]

expected to receive from you. But I might have known that you'd never get cured of wringing the daylights of any situation, and as for trying to patch up and go on at this stage, I think you must be crazy. I don't mean I'm being funny or saying that the way one does to imply incredulity. I mean I think your emotional unbalance has gone further than either of us has ever wanted to admit. You asked me to write to you. I said I would. It isn't easy. But evidently one of us has to be realistic about the situation, and evidently it's got to be me.

"When I sent you up to Port Raeburn it was to give you a chance to pull yourself together and think the thing through, and see that the only thing to do is for us to go ahead and get the divorce. God knows I've given it a fair trial and more than a fair trial. There's no use repeating what we've been over and over until I'm sick and tired of the whole damned thing. And now you sit down and write to me that you'll come back to me on my terms, *and* make a few conditions yourself. I gather that it has just occurred to you that after the divorce you'll have no one to rely on, as you say. It popped out unconsciously, evidently. You want to stay tied to me so I'll support you and that's all. There's no use kidding each other, not that we could do it. Marriage at least has taught us to know each other. So that's another proof that we might as well own up and get it over with.

"It's not a question of petty squabbles that go on from day to day. I could stand that. No, it's the drag, drag, drag of our never wanting the same thing at the same time, and of mutual suspiciousness, and resentment for all the things we thought we would have and haven't had, and each blaming the other. Can't you tell when a thing is done and finished with and dead? Lord knows you've threatened often enough to clear out and leave me. I don't feel I am being unfair now in saying, all right, go ahead, I'll take you up on that.

"I'm glad to hear you're feeling better and getting some sleep. I've been busier than hell at the office lately, and ought not to even think of it, but as soon as I get a break in the schedule, I am coming up there to have a talk with you, and I want you to be ready for it, and sensible. I'll meet you halfway on any reasonable conditions, you'll never starve, you know that, Ruth. That can be taken care of. And don't begin *imagining* the way you do. There is no other woman anywhere near me, I'm not ready to fall into anybody else's arms at the drop of a hat. I'm getting too old for that sort of thing. Naturally, you'll get the house here in Buffalo. I had Seedenham come over and arrange to take care of the garden and the shrubs through the winter again. Maybe you could rent the house and take a little apartment somewhere. Deeman and I may have to go to Washington any day now on a Government project that we may get a look-in on. I'll let you know when I think I can get up there and settle things up. I think it would be an advantage to do it up there, away from all the familiar surroundings that could mean too much to us one way or the other and influence our feelings in the case.

"Keep well, and get a lot of sleep. Love, Howard."

The stillness of the house seemed a living quality, for the wind was whying through the pines outside, and the soft inhaling sound of the little waves on the beach became part of the silence without seeming to interrupt it. The house would now and then speak in its weathering boards. It was cold and clear that night. A boat starting out from the dock at Mead could be heard all the way across, growing not much louder as it neared Port Raeburn. It could be seen, too, as a shadow on the starry water as it came this way. It was the Comet, coming back late.

She had listened for it.

Mrs Guelph too, in her room downstairs, had listened. Now hearing it, the two women were changed in their hearts. Mrs Guelph was relieved and immediately drowsy, but waiting till John should come to tell her good night. Mrs Morgan was no longer frightened for the sound of his boat coming home. Hearing it, she was resolved, and her heart knocked fast with little velvety strokes. Perhaps it was almost midnight. She had not slept. She had not eaten. The letter rang in her mind like an anvil and its cruelty may have been all in her imagination but since there it was, she suffered a stricken feebleness of will and hope. So, she thought over and over, everything she tried to do that might help her to a fine and dignified life was turned back and scorned! The meaningless but familiar words, "How could he!" kept running through her mind, no, through her heart, for it was there that she was most alive.

Then she had thought of John.

He was in the house now. She could hear him moving carelessly around below, not thinking anyone perhaps asleep. Then she heard Mrs Guelph call him, in her voice like a rusty bugle, hoarse and manly like many old women's voices. He answered her and went back to the downstairs bedroom.

It seemed long before he came up the stairs.

When she heard him Mrs Morgan went to her door in the dark and opened it. There was a drift of wind in the hall. He was coming toward her to the attic door. He didn't see her until she moved.

He felt the draft and shivered.

His instinct warned him to be silent. He asked himself in a racing leap of his thoughts if what he imagined was what she meant too. He stopped and waited but she was motionless again in the dark. His body was tired from a day's work in the woods up the lake, and he was close to a dream-like acuteness of vision and feeling. It was only a moment of doubt. He could see better in the dark with every second. He put his hand out and touched the loose warm nightgown over her. She took his hand.

[112]

"Quiet, quiet, quiet," she whispered, drawing him after her into her room and trembling and closing the door.

In the following days, they hardly thought of each other though they were together constantly; but each searched the inner judgments of himself to find out how this infatuation had come about, and what could be done about it, and whither it might lead.

For Mrs Morgan, the thing was like passage between two states of life. She had seized John in her bitterness and rage, her betrayal; and by her sudden acts of love with him, she had done violence to the loyalties and hopes of the life she had made and which was now shattered.

John was drunkened, though he was careful to betray nothing to his mother. He had never known an older woman with any intimacy. Now his countryside romances faded from his memory, the nourishment of the past forgotten, with its clumsy sweetness and its pathetic enlightenment. He went every day on picnics with Mrs Morgan. They would meet beyond the long pier as if by accident; or setting out for Mead in the Comet, they would head for Point St Albans instead and there in the smoky sunlight of autumn spend the day among the big shadowed rocks and watch the gulls and hear one another out while they talked of the ambitious lives they desired; and in the feverish reality of insatiable desire they saw their wants as attainable—John as the future concert star, if only he could find the money to start his study; Ruth Morgan as the attractive middle-aged matron whose wisdom would always draw young men to her long after she could expect her body to. They were as aimless, self-centered and voracious as two children, when they were together.

In moments of aloneness, two other outlines of their worlds would show through their clouded content; and Mrs Morgan would know that any pleasure undertaken for the moment could last no longer, and that a life while it was made up of moments had yet to relate them in some harmonious design or character for the sufferance of it. She would heat with shame every time she had a long view of her infatuation for John; and as the days went on she discovered that the only cure for that feeling was to see him at once, to be alone with him for a tempest of assuagement of her wretched loneliness and her shame—shame not for taking a lover but for losing a husband.

And alone John would regard himself in the glass, and wonder if what he was doing were wicked or good. He looked just the same. His eyes were the same gray with shadows half over them from his level brows. His vanity remembered the compliments Ruth had made, exclaiming over every discovered and shared secret of his ripe young body with lustful rapture. Things she said sounded often in his mind, and made him stir again with discovery. "You are coming to life!" she cried once. "And you'll have to pay for it! You won't be unhappy for a long time, perhaps, but eventually it'll hit you, and then all you'll have to remember and live on will be the lovely things you've grabbed and stolen and tasted!" The more her emotion grew, the more symbolic and dramatic her language became. John noticed it, and thought it curious to talk so elaborately in times when he was completely inarticulate from an overburden of feeling. Nothing seemed to interrupt the rhetoric of her sentiments—calling him "My dear," and "Dear one," and murmuring, "That such a thing should come to us!" and "Everything in life is beautiful if you see it reverently!" and "Was it for refusing this so long that I have broken my heart!"

Her last remark disturbed him.

"Yes, but I keep thinking," he said.

"But what—"

"You *are* married, and sometimes I feel like a—"

"Listen to me! I have given unstintingly of my best years to that

man. I owe him nothing: it is not *his* judgment of me that matters
to me and that I want to meet with a pure feeling in my heart, it is
my judgment of me that matters to me and that I want to meet
with a pure feeling in my heart!"

"Well, just the same—"

"Will you trust me, dear heart? Your Ruth?"

"I suppose so."

"Why do you never call me by name? For days I worked on you
to stop saying 'Mrs Morgan.' "

"Ruth!" he said with a little scowling grin of irritation.

She could be whimsical and tender and understanding.

"Never mind. Only call me something dear when you think of
me," and saying a thing like that she could make him feel that she
was tender and wise, and that her loving him was the most amazing
and fortunate thing that could ever have happened to him, so much
so that subterfuge seemed almost an honorable undertaking to keep
the thing from his mother.

Ruth's imagination, her desperate need for a shape to her life,
began to build a future out of John. Between the times of their
passion, she thought to enrapture him with appeals to his vanity,
and so bind him to her. She said she could "see" the whole thing.
They would go somewhere and take a little apartment. He would
study, practice for hours every day, learning the great song literature
and the baritone roles in the operas. She would coach him and play
his accompaniments. He would be the first good actor in American
opera—for of course he would end up in New York. His debut
would be tremendous. She knew so much. He could have all of it.
Had they not proved exquisite sympathy and fulfillment with each
other? It must have been for this that her parents had sent her
abroad to study piano years ago. She had thought of a career, but
(she smiled with engaging self-appraisal) she was not first-rate by
herself. What she had was great musical knowledge and style, and

oh, my dear, feeling for life itself, that would make someone else a first-rate artist.

His eyes sparkled at the future she painted, even while it frightened him with its intensity and its possessiveness. He did not demand to know practical details as to how all this was to be achieved; what her situation in life was; but only drank up her plans as he did her gasping kisses. The plans really seemed a substitute for the propriety which the love-making wanted.

Mrs Guelph went suspiciously around the house when they were out together, searching their rooms half-ashamedly for anything that might tell her a secret. She had noticed for several days the sudden high spirits showing between her son and their boarder, and following their previous state of fumblement and politeness, it troubled her, and made her bugle soft little sighs of deep woe in her throat. Then she would shake her head with vigor and her eyes would flush with tears and loyally she would say aloud to herself alone, "No sir! My Johnny's a good boy!" and the tears would gather at losing him, as she was certain she had; whether to a career or an evil woman she could not say; but she had lost the Captain and nothing would ever again be the same.

The days fell more sharply with more cold.

Fogs came oftener; fires were built and burned all day in the house. Walking on the beach meant a lonely gray time, bundled in a coat, and harried by the melancholy gulls that drifted on the winds off the lake.

John brought the mail one noontime in the Comet and a telegram from the station at Mead. It was for Mrs Morgan. He took it to her bedroom. She called him to come in and in her face he saw the instant light of his presence. He tipped the door softly to and shook his finger before his mouth, warningly, in humor. She nodded to show she understood; they both knew Mrs Guelph might discover them any day. They were cautious. She kissed and fondled him urgently but silently. She took the telegram he handed her and read it.

His heart was knocking against his gullet, for he had been believing that the telegram would take her away, a summons, a deprivation, the wan aftertide of excitement. She handed it to him with a gesture of fatalism.

He read it.

"Arrive on evening train Saturday stop reserve accommodations stop stay till Monday morning stop sure you will agree with carefully made plans Howard."

"Who is it?"

"My husband."

"Saturday evening!"

"Till Monday morning. And then?"

She shrugged and snatched the telegram from him and tore it into little bits.

"What's the matter, Ruth?"

She looked at him haggard and real. He was shocked. He felt some strange reducing of her spirit. Misgivings came alive in him. She put her arms out to hold him and her whole quality begged for comforting; but that was not what he sought to give her now. He backed away and said,

"Good Lord, your husband is coming here, and you have never told me a thing about him! —What'll I do, what do I say to him?"

"I'll say whatever has to be said."

"—You surely won't tell him—"

"Are you scared? Or ashamed?"

He shook his head.

She saw that he was appalled at the realistic consequence of his actions; she saw how he perceived for the first time the ironical interlocking of people. She was a little contemptuous.

"Never mind, leave him to me," she said.

He nodded, and then suddenly blushed, for he saw his cowardice in her face. This must not survive. He went to her and kissed her. She was stony motionless, suffering him, as a drowsy dog might, to caress her. His lips felt cold to himself on her face. He left her.

All he saw was from a distance. He had taken Ruth over to Mead Saturday night to meet her husband, had brought them back to Port Raeburn, and then had seen them walking out on Sunday for a picnic at the long pier. He had listened all the night, it seemed, as they had talked in her room below him. The voices were monotonous and there were sometimes silences in which sleep seemed to have won over their droning; but then a voice would begin and be answered at great length, and the strife of communication would be resumed.

To tell the truth, John had to recognize that he was almost scared to death. He thought that Mr Morgan, Howard F. Morgan, looked like a formidable man. He was not very bulky, but he was somehow strong-looking. His head was a little too large for his body. His brow was white and bland. His eyes were wide and startlingly black-and-white, and he wore over them huge rimless spectacles with slim gold fittings that looked very expensive. The gleaming glass gave his eyes a jeweled look, polished black stones. He wore a tufty black mustache under his straight blunt nose. John thought he resembled a doctor in an advertisement. He was darkly dressed, with elegance. He looked efficient and sure of himself. John noticed that on arriving at Mead, Mr Morgan had taken charge of everything, giving him orders about the launch and taking them back over the inlet to Port Raeburn, and talking to his wife almost officially.

"You look fine, Ruth. You must be getting fat. The food is good? And the beds. —That's fine. You're having a good rest, the best thing in the world for you."

Ruth was silent.

As they came and went on their walking expeditions of the weekend, John would try to be where he could see them, and meet them casually, and judge how things stood between Ruth and her husband, and whether she had told him of the past week, and whether Howard Morgan would get him into trouble for it.

But there was no hint of anything that might concern him. He could not guess what they had to talk about at such length. When they left to go for a picnic on the long pier they were in sober discussion; and when they came back in the late Sunday afternoon, Mr Morgan was still earnestly haranguing his wife in a low tone. John saw them come in. He thought Ruth looked drawn and dispirited. That night the talking went on, seeming to enter the fabric of the house and vibrate there, the burry drone of the husband's voice, and endless, level replies from Ruth.

In the morning Ruth was not in evidence.

Mr Morgan asked John to take him across to Mead to catch the train. The fog was hanging and the inlet was choppy. John had been dreading a time alone with Mr Morgan. The Comet bumped and sprayed, rocking and chilling them with broken waves. Now and then her exhaust would be submerged and gurgle and chuckle drowningly.

Mr Morgan turned up his coat collar.

"You must have heavy winters up here," he remarked.

"Yes. We do."

"Feels in the air today."

"It certainly does."

"—Lake looks sort of rough, out there."

"We may get a storm."

"That's what I was thinking."

The Comet was crossing the channel now. It was rougher.

"Well, my wife was telling me about you."

Mr Morgan was looking at him with his huge lenses in which the polished black eyes were enlarged against white.

"Oh."

Mr Morgan whistled a little in a whisper. He seemed to be waiting for John to speak.

"Well, I—"

"It would be a great thing, all right," said Mr Morgan.

"What?"

"She told me all about your plans and ambitions, to study singing, and so on. I have a young cousin in Philadelphia who has been studying for six years. They say he'll get there some day."

"Oh. —Yes. —Mrs Morgan and I've been practicing some songs together, too. She has helped me a lot."

"Well, you've been very nice to her, and probably helped her not to feel so lonely. She's crazy about music. I can see how she might be, without sharing the enthusiasm myself. I go wild about bridges and so on. —By the way, that pier—"

He paused and turned around, leaning over the gunwale of the Comet, and pointed up the gray inlet toward the lake against which the old long pier showed like a thing drawn in charcoal.

"What about that? Why isn't it kept in repair?"

"Oh, the steamers go to Mead now, instead of tying up at Port Raeburn the way they used to. —The summer people use the pier for picnics, and have a lot of fun. That's all it's good for."

"It's pretty rickety. A *lot* of good timber wasted because somebody won't use a *little* good timber to repair it. I hate waste. Besides, it may be dangerous."

Mr Morgan brought his intense black regard around and gazed at John for a long time, and John was thinking, "Is that all he knows? Maybe I'd better tell him. Maybe it would make me feel right again. Maybe Ruth would hate it. I don't know."

Mr Morgan shrugged.

"If I had a summer cabin up here I'd have a lot of fun working out improvements on the pier, with concessions, and so forth. —You could make it very attractive."

His enthusiasm was cold and without inner tone.

The launch was nearing Mead.

They heard the train whistle far away up the shore.

John helped Mr Morgan to bring his bags out of the boat and up to the train platform. Mr Morgan thanked him and pulled out a dollar to give him.

"Oh, no, thanks. Thanks anyway," said John.

"Why not? You do me a service, and I wish to acknowledge it?"

"That's all right."

John felt like a boy again. He was unable to interpret the shrewd look, the long and dark and expressionless gaze of Mr Morgan. He felt miserable. He felt in panic the need of virtue. His whole action of the past week was clear; he saw what he had done. He could not undo but he could reform. The train shrieked again, the extra shrill cry of the Canadian engine, and Mr Morgan held out his hand.

"You needn't wait, Guelph. Thanks very much. Goodbye."

"Goodbye, Mr Morgan."

Nodding once or twice as if to tie a thought into a bundle and put it away, Mr Morgan went down the platform toward the incoming train. Nothing about him seemed mysterious or unusual. He left with John nevertheless a feeling of insecurity and doubt, and when John went back to the Comet to head her across the inlet, he was almost filled with hatred for Ruth Morgan.

When he got home, his mother told him to stay quiet all day, that Mrs Morgan had a sick headache and was not to be disturbed. He thought that he must see her and find out how much had happened between husband and wife that might concern him. But in late

[121]

morning the weather howled down worse and he had to go and take the Comet into the boathouse, and tie her with just the proper play in her ropes, two at bow and two at stern, so that when the huge rollers came up the inlet, she might rise and fall safely in her covered slip. Working muscularly, and tending to his boat, John was restored to a certain respect, for himself, for life, for the tasks a man had, and he felt for the first time since summer a waft of his old affection for the launch. When he had her tied, he decided to clean her up; and he spent the rest of the day washing the cabin out, beating the cushions, cleaning the engine, scrubbing the tiny decks, and sewing up some rips in the canvas canopy over the stern cockpit. The water in which she rode in the boathouse was madder as the day advanced. By nightfall, when he was working by lanterns, the Comet was bobbing and wincing at her ropes. The wind was in fury. He went outside and saw the blown fragments of last daylight flagging into darkness over the woods beyond Mead. The inlet looked like earthquaking mountains of stone, dark gray water rising and sliding into sharp peaks and breaking down into black valleys. He could imagine hearing the scrolled combers riding up the beach beyond Point St Albans, and falling on the sand with a sound like far-off cannonading; and fans of spume pushing toward the edge of the woods, rattling driftwood and hissing the beach-grass out of its rooted hold, and tumbling the million pebbles and shells into further barriers of land against the ferny darkness of the forest.

After dark came rain and one or two splits of lightning. But it turned too cold for a long electric storm. The drive was on before winter, and the air was damp and put an ache in the bone. Fog stayed after the rain in a short calm spell in the sky in which the aftermath of wind kept the waves rolling. Boats knocked on the docks, and the rollers trundled and simmered on the beaches. Old wood groaned with the waves. Before morning the wind set up again and more rain; and the day came in a driven sort of light,

[122]

yellow gray in the shredding sky, and steel blue over the water, which rode so wildly that no boats could put out into it.

Inside the house they had to talk loudly to be heard, over the noise outside, until they sounded like people on a train. It was comforting to talk; the house was shivering under the weather; built for summer mostly, it was always miserable in the winters; the stained pine boards sang and quivered at the cracks when there was a wind. The fires inside flowed up the chimneys in an answering song of security and defense.

Mrs Morgan was unable to rise for breakfast. Mrs Guelph was rather worried about her. She looked ill, and said the storm had terrified her. There was a great branch of pine outside her window that the wind brushed over the panes every few minutes. It startled her each time. She wanted to know how long the storm would last. Mrs Guelph said she didn't know but would ask John.

"I'll ask him," said Mrs Morgan. "Can he come up for a second?"

"I'll see."

The old woman went out and rocked herself side to side down the stairs, like a traveling bell. In the kitchen she found John, slicing strips of bacon for breakfast.

"She wants to see you, ask you about the storm, upstairs."

"I'm—I'm busy."

The mother put her hands on her waist-long breasts and pressed them there, silently saying some vague thanks for relief and the safety of her son. She said,

"Well, you better go up later."

After breakfast she told him again to go up. With ill temper that was unlike him, he rose from the table and went upstairs.

Knocking at her door was harder than the rest of it would be, he thought. He finally did so.

"Come in. Is that you, John?"

He went in.

They were both shivering from a draft the door released; and from something else blowing in their hearts.

"I waited all day yesterday for you to come, John!"

"You were ill. I thought you were resting."

"You'd be ill too! If you knew what I've been through those two days with Howard Morgan!"

"—I'm sorry."

"What's the matter, dear heart?"

"—Nothing. Be careful! Don't call me that here!"

"The wind. Nobody can hear."

"I'm sorry you feel low."

She began to weep.

"You're not really sorry. —What's the matter? You are different. What have I done?"

"Nothing. No, I'm not. —I don't think we ought to talk here. The wind. We couldn't hear anybody *coming.*"

"Oh, the wind! It's driving me crazy! I didn't sleep all night! —When will it stop?"

"Yes. I thought I'd go out right now and see how it looked. If I went down to the lake I could see how the sky looked there. It's the worst one I've seen in years. —Can I get you anything? Mother is setting you a tray."

"Come back, if you don't I'll die, I am cold, and alone, and exhausted. —You will come back?"

He nodded. He felt guilty that her misery should make him impatient to be gone. Her misery was like part of his own guilt. It was the same feeling he had from standing in the path of Mr Morgan's gaze. He nodded again, seeing her last wretched drawn effort of mouth and eye at prettiness in a smile, and closed the door. He ran downstairs in a fury of escape, and on his way down the front hall took his heavy mackinaw and hurried through the front door. He ran down to the path toward the boathouse and the dock, scrambling into his coat. The wind hollowed his mouth out and took his breath. The waves were higher than last night's, and he was afraid for the Comet. He went into the boathouse and saw that she strove at her ropes and rose and fell like a fever patient assuaging pain with ceaseless movement. Her hull was scratched in spite of the woven hemp snubbers he had hung over the gunwale. Two of the dock boards inside the boathouse were torn loose. The cockpit was awash from spray thrown up by the slap of heavy rollers as they passed under. He nailed the loose boards down at once. He tested the slack of his tie-ropes. Then he went walking up toward the long pier.

He had to earn every step, leaning into the wind. His hair blew and stung as the wind pulled at it. Several times he had to trip sidewise to miss the rush of a wave up the beach towards the high water mark of drift. When he reached the long pier he saw her topside wet. The great waves rolled in past Point St Albans and the first thing they hit coming up the inlet was the pier. They would charge in a long rise and then hit the end of the pier that angled out from the shore, and as they hit, there would start the cold explosion of the wave into a traveling ruffle of white spray going down the whole length of the pier which turned black under the wet and creaked with velvety sounds and made rotten splinters sometimes down under the piles. From the pier end he would be able to see out past Point St Albans, and he started to walk down the soggy length of slippery wood. But the farther out he got the harder it was to walk against the wind and the slimy footing, and the sharp drift of spray on the blowing air. He put his head down and strove on, but when he'd look up, the flying spume beat his face down again, and he knew that even if he got out to the far end of the pier, which looked miles off, he could not stand to see. So he went back. The old timbers shook under him. The piles gave with the waves. It made walking feel dizzy. He could see no sign of the weather's break. The sky was low, and clouds blew over in running shreds. He had got wet. He went home. His thoughts were like the day, confused and vaguely terrified.

Toward dawn of the third day the sky subsided and so did the waters, and the daylight came with the sun wanly showing behind thin clouds. John crossed to Mead in the Comet after the mail and some groceries. It was an adventurous voyage, for he found in the channel that every now and then by the caprice of diminishing storm, a tremendous wave would form out of several big gentle rollers and rise and tremble and break fussing with white down its own advancing breast. Encountering one of these, the Comet heeled over and shipped water; she gasped at the exhaust and he brought her about to face the wave, and she rode over it. His heart trundled with excitement and challenge; he shook his head, and thought, "I'd've hated to see that wave hit anything much solider and bigger than the Comet, only a little boat could've gone over so sweetly."

In his imagination the Comet was proud of the event, and once on her course again went with charm and gallantry to the dock at Mead. He felt deep love for the boat. He loved the luxury of her faded cushions and her mahogany stained woodwork. The Comet seemed to know his hand on the wheel. The sound of her engine working steadily in a chord of hiss, click, rumble and patter, always made him feel like singing. He sang almost every time he went out in the launch. Sometimes the tenderness of his voice would make him feel tearful, and at that he would laugh. He had a beautiful voice and he knew it.

When he returned from Mead, Mrs Morgan was downstairs dressed in a sweater coat and a rough skirt. Her face was made-up. Her mouth was thick with rouge and the white strain of lines on each side of it made her look consumptive. She was in a new mood

[126]

of gaiety with tones of charm in her voice, and she held out her hand trembling a little for her mail.

"There's no mail for you, Mrs Morgan."

"But of course not! I haven't written anyone for weeks. Why should there be?"

"These cards are for Mother. Where is she?"

"She's upstairs doing the room. —Listen: come here!"

She became intense and eager and he scowled.

"Take me on one of our picnics today, the weather is better, and I haven't seen you in days, what has happened? Oh, I have so much to tell you!"

"How can we manage it? Where?"

"Let's go up to the pier, meet me there. Maybe the Comet could take us around Point St Albans and we'd be absolutely alone, and if it was stormy out, we could sit in the cabin and be so snug and private and just have ourselves. —*Wouldn't* you? For *Ruth?*"

He was close enough to put his arms around her and he half wanted to, but he simply stood, looking at her anxious, thin face which had so few hints in it of the almost mighty passion she was capable of, and the engulfing tenderness she felt happiest in giving out to anyone who would take it.

But he saw her with another eye than that of the lust-enlivened youth of last week.

He looked at her now and he saw her with the eye of Mr Morgan, perhaps; the memory of that eye was disturbing, for it seemed to see too detachedly for any mercy. He saw her working her eyebrows and imploring him with her tragic eyes and smiling. Whenever she wanted pity, he felt angry. It decided him now.

"We have a lot to say to each other. I'll meet you a little after one. You wait for me at the land end of the pier."

"Will you bring the Comet?"

"No. I'll walk."

"But we'd be so cozy . . ."

"No, I don't want to take her out. The water is still very rough."

"But you had her out this morning . . ."

"No! I don't—"

He stopped talking. She saw him red and shining with anger. He couldn't tell her that he would not take the Comet for what he knew must end as an unpleasant scene. Inarticulately, he loved his boat better than that. He managed to smile and reassure her with a touch on the shoulder. He left her, scowling. She thought he looked so much less like a handsome, healthy boy; he was making men's gestures and treating her as if he were the older one. She went upstairs to help Mrs Guelph with her room, and she vaguely asked herself how anyone could find it in his heart to be unkind to her, who had so much to give and such desire to give it!

John was hardly hearing her. There was a long freight boat halfway to the horizon, and he was watching it rise and fall with the lake, and its smoke yaw with the wind. The long pier trembled with the sliding waters that pressed below.

The steamer looked at moments like something made wholly of smoke. At others she looked solid, like something built on the horizon and never moving.

There fell a silence.

But the quarrel continued into it, and they knew how their bitterness was choking them. He was indifferent and unwilling to go into long excuses and withdrawals; Ruth Morgan kept telling herself that just now of all times she could not undergo two betrayals. Yet so emotionally inventive was she that even now she asked herself how might she have failed, that two men so dear to her should give her up with every sign of self-need and restoration.

"Should I have told you long *before* that I was married, and that my husband might appear at any time? Is that it?"

He shrugged.

"Why don't you talk to me?" she insisted.

"What good does it do."

"—I have meant nothing, then?"

"Oh, good Lord, yes. Only, it's time to call it off."

"You've said that. You're sorry? What are you ashamed of?"

"Not ashamed. It's just good sense."

"Good sense, he says! —You aren't willing to trust my understanding? —I know: it is that Cunningham girl, the carpenter's daughter you took to the movies that night. Do you know something? This will amuse you," she said bitterly, and he was afraid she might be going to cry. He turned to see her. The midafternoon light was clear on her face, and her ruefulness made him feel guilty without making him feel affectionate.

"What is it?" he asked.

"The night you did go and take that girl to the picture show, I went up to my room, and I *felt relieved* that you weren't taking me. I said to myself, what's the use of getting involved with anyone ever again as long as you live. I rejoiced that you were indifferent to me. I said to myself that it would be easy to fall in love with you, and you know just's well as I do that when we first played and sang together, it could have come about much sooner and very easily. But I was full of good intentions and it wasn't until I had that cruel letter from Howard that I saw myself with time going by and life all around me and none of it for me. Then you came home late that night from Point St Albans and I remembered how you looked, and how your eyes were when you looked at me, and I said to myself, why not, maybe I am wrong, but if I am not, how much I could do for him, he has such talent, and I called you as you went upstairs in the dark. —And now I, now you—"

"I'm sorry, Ruth."

He rejected the wan rekindling she sought from repeating the tale of their first loving, and by references in it, to light his own fire again.

"After all," he said, "I wasn't realizing what all this might have to do with other people. When your husband arrived, and spent that time, and then when I took him back, he said you had told him all about me, I thought he meant he knew about *us*. He looked at me so strangely. I felt like a thief. It wasn't worth it. I thought it wasn't fair."

She laughed hysterically, like the wind itself.

"Wasn't fair! Wasn't worth it!" She began to cry bitterly. "And after all I thought I meant to you! Oh, my God."

"Don't cry, Ruth. I can't stand it. After all, Mr Morgan does come into this."

"Howard Morgan! He doesn't care what I do. He'd be tickled to death, I didn't tell him just because he could use it for a divorce if he wanted to, he could bring it up when he wanted to punish *me* or humiliate *me*. He wouldn't hold a thing against you."

"Well, all right. But I know I'm right."

"And all our plans, all that means nothing, either?"

"You know it was all just a part of *that*. I never stopped to think, and work anything out."

"Don't you love me at all, any more, then?"

She tried to stop crying, to make herself pretty. She leaned toward him. In her mind her thoughts raced. She saw the truth. But if only he wouldn't admit it, if only it were not spoken aloud between them, she could, she knew she could make it come true somehow that he would finally see her as she saw herself, and love her forever.

"Don't you?"

"It isn't that. I mean, *love,* after all—"

"You're a boy still, what do you know about it?"

"Well, it ought to be comfortable, for one thing."

It was like a blow to her heart.

She stood up and threw her wind-eaten cigarette down into the water that rose so highly near the floating pier.

She gave him a long look, and then turned and began trudging against the stiff breeze out toward the far end of the long pier. The wood was slippery. She nearly fell to her knees once. She had on a long rough cloth coat that made her body seem bulky though it was so frail. John waited a moment, and then he thought he heard her sob or speak and he went after her.

"Ruth, wait a minute!"

She bent down and hurried more. There was something foreboding in her walk, and he was impatient and afraid.

"Ruth, wait a minute, I tell you!"

He caught up with her and took her arm. She wouldn't look at him but shook his hand away.

"Ruth, come back, it's very wet out there, the waves still break over the pier occasionally. You'll get soaked. The channel is still rough. It's getting late. It's getting dark!"

"I don't care!" she said in a low voice, staring out toward the lake. He followed her gaze and in so short a time, his freighter was nowhere to be seen. Not even the smoke showed against the whitening fall of afternoon.

"No, come on back, Ruth. After all, we can't talk here, it's wet and cold."

"And we can't talk at home, your mother is always there, watching us!"

This irritated him.

"After all, it's her house!"

"Oh, certainly! She can snoop all she wants!"

He held his tongue. It was not easy.

There was a drummed booming underwater as the waves coincided against the lakeward piles.

[131]

Without any preparation but pulling her hand from her pocket, Mrs Morgan sharply slapped John on the face. Then she clapped her fingers to her mouth and gasped.

"There!" she said. "I've tried not to do that for the last twenty minutes. It's the only way I can hurt you. I want to hurt you only one tenth as much as you are hurting me!"

"You're not hurting me, you're just being silly," he said. "I'm going home. Are you coming?"

Now she did begin to weep and turned from him and ran blindly along the pier. She stumbled and seemed to be foolishly running toward the edge. He ran after her again and caught her and shook her.

"Be careful! You nearly fell in the water!"

"Who would care—you—nobody!"

"Don't be foolish, Ruth. Come on, are you coming? I'm cold and damp. The weather doesn't look very good again. It's getting darker."

"I don't care!"

"Well, come on. Here, give me your hand."

He spoke like a bored teacher. She snatched her hand away, and said,

"Well, go on, I'm not keeping you. You can go."

"You'd better come, too."

She smiled with a feverish hope of the hint in his voice that he was worried. Yes, maybe he thought she would do something desperate. Maybe it would be good for him to think so. She hugged her shoulders and shuddered and nodded to him.

"Go on. You needn't wait. It'll be a long time—"

"What do you mean! Now, Ruth—"

She turned and went again. He thought she was a fool and he felt like one himself. He said,

"We are being childish!"

[132]

She waved back at him, a taunting sort of goodbye, with a pretense of gaiety in it.

"Well, goodbye, then!—I don't care!" he cried. He turned the other way, toward shore. He wanted to look back and see if she had noticed his going; but he would not. The waves rose and trembled against the piles. The old wood waved, supple in the wet, and shifted underfoot.

He stopped and listened.

He didn't know if it was his thought that stopped him first, or something he heard, or whether she had called him in various ways.

"It might be dangerous!" he said aloud, and turned around and ran far after her. She was still moving out to the pier end, and the pier looked so familiar and sturdy that he sounded his voice on a grunt of relief. "But yes, it might," he thought, and he went now, calling to her, and when the waves from the channel began to show him their reflected strength against the pier, about at its middle section, he was really concerned.

"Ruth! Come back!"

She stopped and waved.

She couldn't have heard his words, just his cry. This far out on the pier the wind was strong, coming off the lake, and the water was rougher. He saw the whitecaps assembling and rolling in around Point St Albans. It was getting worse, he thought.

"Yo-o!" he called, and waved her to come back.

His voice lifted like a gull on the wind.

A wave hit and traveled with spray down the pier. The pier didn't tremble, it leaned, slowly.

"It's going to fall!" he thought and looked aft of him. It seemed a long way to shore. The leaning section of the pier didn't right itself again, as the waves reflected.

"Ruth!" he cried, and started toward her, waving his coat over his head. She saw. She saw him and the dark shadow of the pier flooring where it leaned away from the light. It looked already like a gap, though it was merely a sag. He saw her clutch her coat about her and start to run toward him.

"That's right! Come on, Ruth!" he cried, running.

The waves began to mumble again, and then as had happened that morning on the way to Mead, several combers steamed together and fell into a kind of team and came galloping like horses with flying white manes and with a breasted thunder charged upon the leaning pier and trampled it down in a muffled sound of her scream as she was thrown free, and the velvety crack of waterlogged timber, and the broiling of the waves as they went on through the fury of debris and carried much of it with them, tumbling shadows in the fading afternoon.

This he had seen, and at the gap's edge he saw what he must do. The wet knocking crash had broken down the rotten piles. They lay making black currents in the waves that rolled through the gap in the pier. The far end of the pier was still standing, and so was the most of the shoreward approach. About thirty feet of the middle section was gone. He threw down his his heavy mackinaw and pulled off his shoes.

"Mrs Morgan!" he shrieked in thoughtless formality, staring into the water. "Can you hear me!"

Feeling hollow from fear, he climbed down the nearest exposed pile and let himself into the water and began to swim, looking for her under the pier where she might be holding to a timber; and swimming as near as he dared to the tumbled wreckage that lay up-inlet. But he saw nothing. He kept calling. His heart kept tightening. He could hardly swim. The water was heavy and cold. It sounded in his ears, running and sighing. When it was so dark that if he were to find a way back up the pier he must do it now, he left the search, and hauled himself from pile to pile shoreward, feeling for the rise of the beach as it must slope, and at last he touched bottom and trudged to the dry sand.

Later in the same evening, men came back to the pier with lanterns and boats. They looked at everything. Yes, the pier was gone, all right. The boy's story must be so. They found his mackinaw blown against a pile that jutted above the pier flooring, near the break. The motorboats moved carefully in and around the pier and the wreckage. The men grappled in the currents. Late in the night one of them walking on the beach found what they were looking for, and the searching party returned to their homes in Mead and Port Raeburn, and one of them properly telegraphed to Howard F. Morgan for instructions.

The station agent at Mead brought Mr Morgan across the inlet on the morning after next in his outboard motorboat. Mrs Guelph and her son were waiting at their house. They had done what they could. John had gone on all the necessary errands, and the Comet had made several trips to Mead and back. In all these hours he had not looked at Ruth Morgan. She lay in the downstairs living room, where the piano stood, with its keys closed away and the shades drawn.

Everyone had told him repeatedly that he must not blame himself for the terrible accident. He wanted to tell them they had been quarreling. But the slightest explanation of her death would have had too much to do with his life.

He kept silent. He seemed to be grieving. His mother was worried about him. When the news came that Mr Morgan was arriving to take the body back to Buffalo for burial, he went to his mother and said that since there was nothing more he could do to help with the sad affair, he thought he would take the Comet and go off for the day and get his mind off this thing.

[135]

The old woman groaned like a distant horn, and her mind pieced together an image of sinning and guilt and it stirred her like truth, but she must never admit it, and instead she grasped her son by the ear as if he were ten years old and pulled him to her.

"You'll be staying right here, and I never heard of such manners! The poor man! Nobody to be kind to him here but us!"

Her eyes watered behind her diffusing lenses. She had the almost evil relation to truth of some old people, incapable of indulgence, and shrewd for its moments in others.

It was a sunny day.

The inlet was innocent, running long mild swells off the lake which would hardly have troubled a canoe. Mr Morgan came across in the outboard rowboat in perfect comfort. He was met at the Guelph dock by Mrs Guelph herself, standing memorially there as if she had been wheeled down the little hill for the occasion. When she grasped his hand, she began to weep and speak at once.

"It's just so terrible, Mr Morgan, may God have mercy on us all! I said to John, 'John, what can we say to Mr Morgan?' "

Mr Morgan faced her with his arms crossed at the wrists against his neat overcoat. He had his hat off and the sunny breeze could not disturb his shining dark hair. He listened to Mrs Guelph with an intelligent composure, and when she had finished he said,

"No, Mrs Guelph, pray don't blame yourself. —Where is the boy? He will be able to tell me all about it. A very shocking thing."

"Yes, come up to the house. He's there. He's waiting. He feels so terrible, he was with her, you know."

They went up the pine-needled slope to the house. Mrs Guelph rocked side to side climbing. Mr Morgan helped her with his gray gloved hand at her elbow.

"The train connections are so bad," he said. "I took a special from Toronto, just an engine and a car. I have to be back in the office tomorrow, and I'm leaving for Washington the day after."

"I see."

The old woman was enraged at his calm.

They came to the house. In the hall, John was waiting. His face was white. In certain lights, his eyes glowed red, coals in a furnace burning within.

"Hello, John," said Mr Morgan, holding out his gray hand. They shook.

"Hello, Mr Morgan. I can't"—

"Yes, yes, well, what arrangements remain to be made?" said Mr Morgan.

"The—she has to be taken to Mead to the train. That's all. We've done what we could, way up here, away from—from everything."

"Yes. Indeed, of course. Perhaps I'd better see the body?"

"This way. The front room."

They started to it. At the door, Mr Morgan turned.

"John? You're not coming?"

"No, I—please."

His mother intoned, loosing her anger at the formal indifference Mr Morgan had brought with him:

"John Guelph. You come here. Everybody has to learn to pay respect to the dead."

John followed. They went into the living room.

The coffin lay supported by two kitchen chairs at each end. The box was of pine covered with black cloth. The upper half of the lid was off. They could see her.

It was the shell of her impostures without the little furies of her desires inside it. It was as if they had found her out now, without her defenses of argument and impulse, her small cunning ways of love or generosity. She looked thin and her mouth was almost bony-looking, like a ridge of suffering exposed. Once John looked, he could not look away. He was not ready to cry. His soreness was toward himself. Mrs Guelph began to weep with a deep and distant windy noise. Mr Morgan looked up at her.

"No, come, come, Mrs Guelph. Thank you, that will be sufficient, I should say. Have the coffin covered. We shall start back in a few minutes."

They left the living room. John called in the two men from the back porch who had handled the coffin. They put down the lid.

Mr Morgan said,

"Now I think it would be somehow satisfying, though rather unpleasant, to go up and see just where and how it happened. I'll walk along with you, John, if you'll show me. You say it was day before yesterday afternoon? What time? Wasn't it chilly to be out all day on the old pier? Or were you in the boat? The telegram was, of course, insufficient. Naturally, I would like to know."

They went down the beach to the pier.

John told him the story.

Maybe the last thing he could do for Ruth was keep her secret. She had said she didn't care. But that was while she lived. He wanted to clothe that poor frail corpse with whatever dignity he could now. At the same time, he must meanly disclaim her love. He told a simple tale, unable to keep some emotion out of it.

"Mrs Morgan and I sometimes went and had a picnic lunch on the old pier, and she was rather ill after the weekend, we had a very hard storm. When it was clearing, she wanted to be out. So we went about noon, I guess a little after. We had our lunch. It must have been really half past one. Then we just sat and talked and—"

"What about," asked Mr Morgan, almost without interest.

"We—about my future, the career I want to work on."

"Oh, yes, you want to be a singer, I remember now. Go ahead."

"Well, there were still a lot of high waves now and then."

"Ah-hum. There you are. Do you remember my telling you that

that pier would crack one of these days? I believe I remarked that it was dangerous, didn't I? Or did I?"

"Yes, well, then, you know the whole story. She wanted to walk out to the far end, and I said better not. But she insisted, and I didn't feel I could argue, and I think, well, I got irritated, she wouldn't listen to me, but just went on—"

"That's very like Ruth," said Mr Morgan, with a remote smile of intelligent association.

"And I began strolling in the other direction."

"You remembered, of course, that it was likely to be dangerous after the heavy buffeting?"

"Yes, when it did occur to me, I turned around and called her, and I ran after her and she heard me, so she turned around. It was wet, you could hardly run. Then I heard that cracking as it began to go. But before she could—"

"Before she could make it," interrupted Mr Morgan in a level voice which he seemed to intend as a rebuke for John's cloudy and quivering tones, "the break came."

"Yes."

"Now we can look at it. Here is the pier."

They walked out on the old boards that were drying pale gray under the autumnal sunlight.

"It is just where the current would bring the greatest stress, yes I see," mused Mr Morgan. "And was it here that you jumped in and tried to rescue her?"

John nodded and gulped.

"That was very courageous."

They stood in silence.

It seemed like a pause in which John must suddenly, almost with violence, tell Mr Morgan the whole story of his week with Ruth. John saw that sturdy body of the man, his pale fleshy face, the cool clearness of his black eyes behind their crystal glasses. The man was

[139]

looking over the whole detail of the scene, making a faint little tune exhaling breath through his nose into his black clipped mustache.

John put his hands behind him and gripped them together. He cleared his throat and began to talk rapidly.

"Mr Morgan, I guess there is probably a lot more that you ought to—"

The man snapped his face around toward John and his black eyes fired. He poked his gloved right hand on John's front and stopped him.

"Never mind! There's no use going over and over the gruesome details of the thing. It's happened, and done and over with, and all we can do is take it in the best grace possible. Come on, we'd better be going back. I don't want to hear another word about it. —Don't you suppose it's difficult enough as it is?" he demanded, staring over his arm at John, as they walked.

It solved nothing but it saved them much.

By the time they were back at the house the large supply launch from Mead was loaded with the coffin.

"I'll go back with you in the Comet," said Mr Morgan.

He said goodbye to Mrs Guelph and pressed her hand reassuringly. Mrs Guelph felt that their proper parts were reversed. She coldly accepted his folded bills for his wife's last room rent and meals.

They talked very little until the Comet was nearing Mead. Then Mr Morgan turned to John and said,

"There are several ways of looking at things, one is full of emotion and a lot of style, and the other is from the standpoint of use and value. I am going to do something for you. I try to make my judgments most of the time from a useful and abstract outlook, if possible. I want to help you to get a start in life, the life you want. You were kind to my wife— No, be quiet! Let me finish. You were kind to her and sometimes it was hard to be that to her. She evidently had much faith in what you might accomplish in the field of music. Here is five hundred dollars. I brought along a lot of cash because of the incidental expenses of this kind of journey. I want you to take it and go down to Toronto or Rochester or Philadelphia, and begin your study. If you're good enough, you'll find ways to hang on and finish by yourself."

John could say nothing.

"Go on, here's the money, take it," said Mr Morgan. "Almost everything anybody accomplishes in this world is at the expense of somebody else. Don't let a sad affair confuse your attitude toward your future. I believe Ruth would applaud my giving you this, and would want you to take it. She'd think me cynical, because she always thought so. But some other accident of friendship or tragedy might be the very thing to give you your start. After all, you might have become involved with the Morgan family in any one of a thousand other ways, which might have ended differently, without opportunity for you."

The money was in John's hand now.

"But talking has nothing to do with it," finished Mr Morgan, standing up as the Comet veered in to the dock at Mead. "Maybe I could never convince you that it is right for you to take the money. But you will take it, because what you *have* to do is perhaps stronger than what you *ought* to do. Good luck to you. If you are ever famous, I will feel your career to be in some small measure a creation of mine. Don't think too hard about the way Ruth died and all the rest of it. If there's anything worse than a hypocrite it's somebody full of idle regrets. Nobody can conceal much of anything, anyway. Goodbye. —I believe they are ready for me at the train."

He jumped out of the cockpit, holding on to his hat on his head, for there was a brisk sunny breeze. He put his hand out and John scrambled up to the dock and shook hands with him. Mr Morgan

[141]

regarded him somberly through his large elliptical lenses with his dark eyes in their grayish-white fields. There seemed to be nothing more to say. Neither of them noticed that John had not said "Thank you." When this long look was full for both of them, Mr Morgan nodded, dropped John's hand, turned, and walked rapidly up the dock to the land, climbed the wooden steps to the station level, and hurried into the little funeral train, which was ready to go.

In Summer's Name

Because as a doctor I was abroad in the streets at such frequent and irregular times of the day and night, I think I saw more of the town's temper than anybody else. I mean the weather on the vast Texas plain where the town sat, and what the weather in its season did to the gracious hood of cottonwood trees that stood up and down all the streets. Coming to town from far down the plain, I would see the little mound of light-crowned green haze, the trees locating the town for me. In summer, especially, I loved those towering cushions of glittering leaves. In daytime, when the heat tried to press everybody to the earth, the trees breathed forth some fragrant essence that was refreshing; and at night, with chance bloom from the few remote street lamps of the little town, the leaves looked cool and delicious.

In the summer evenings all life was lived out of doors.

I came to know it as a seasonal symptom when the summer afternoon was spent at dusty hot sunset on the yellow plains, and the evening came, and cars moved out along the streets, and in one way or another the whole town was moved by the spirit and yielded to it whatever contribution its people could make.

The revival meetings began in May and continued until late August.

I used to see them as I drove on my rounds. Sometimes I stopped in the dark, and turned off my car lights, and watched and listened to those working souls who tried the summer night with their calls and cries, their rude apprehensions of beauty and their clamorous denunciations of fear.

I came to realize that the town went as two classes to the meetings: one was the class of the earnest, poor, plain people to whom this kind of thing was theater; it was opera, and ballet, and poetry. It took the lame knowledge that so hindered their lives and, by the infusion of several dozen human spirits with the same belief, lifted that knowledge up into a dizzy and golden certainty that raced the blood, and made the heart powerful, for a little while. People who lived violent lives, in the sense of unease and grapple with the very forces of the earth, needed to alleviate their trials as violently.

The other class I supposed I belonged to: the ones who went to observe; but in observing I always felt too a responsibility somehow, some share in this ecstatic devotion to those powers in life which rise and fall as mysteriously as the droughts on the plains where we lived. Mostly, the others, like LaVerne Dicely, the banker's son, and his crowd, simply came to make soft catcalls, daring to see how soon they'd be caught or chased off by outraged Christians.

At one time during the summer several revivals would be going on at once.

On an empty corner near the business blocks they had erected poles and a skeleton roof, over which they laid pine and cottonwood boughs, making a great arbor. When the light was burning in the gasoline lamps under the leafy roof, and the men and women and children were working in their chairs, it made some sight, I can tell you.

There was another which I always thought of as the Tree and

[144]

Lantern. In an empty lot by the railroad tracks there stood a single venerable cottonwood, and from its lowest branch an electric light of great power had been strung; and beneath the tree, in the open field, under the ice-bright stars of the West, humbles came and called and bent, so that an unconscious poetry seemed to rise from their worship of whatever it was before the great tree.

On the outskirts of town a wooden tabernacle had been built. Here in the summer nights the air was boxed and stifling. People sweated and steamed, lost themselves and sang.

Late every summer a professional revival troupe came and set up an enormous tent with cherry-colored rope lacings, and a trombone quartet, and a jingle harness worn by a pretty plump blond girl whom the revivalist drove through the tent shouting a pious sentiment about "Trotting Home in Glory." They all looked like vaudeville actors; they preached God and sang Jesus and made cajoling sounds, winning their audiences with familiar sentiments, but delivered by clever boys and pretty girls and distinguished middle-aged men who looked anything but Godly: which made the hearts of the hearers sink and then rise; first, because these visitors looked so smart and seemed so rich; and, second, because, with all those worldly qualities, they should still shout and praise the Lord God of the plains. . . .

One of the most extraordinary things, I always thought, was the way boys and girls from the high school used to get caught up in the emotional tug that fetched the town.

Many of them came to me in panic-stricken privacy for the usual reassurances or, if those were not possible, then the proper care. I knew that young people anywhere were open and eager before any emotion whatever. Yet I was always a little chagrined for my faith in the old blind gods of the body when boys and girls I knew would skulk on the edge of the revivals and now and then enter into the arena with shouts in a hymn, and then retreat in pairs or threes or

[145]

fours to the shadowy outskirts of the spirit's circle and there taste the fruits of conversion, so easily plucked when the daily presence was dropped and the exalted promise of glory raced in the blood, and filled every head. . . .

Some youngsters even in a fairly large town become personages at early ages.

Some achieve this by some physical brilliance which they properly cultivate; like the boy, whose name I never knew, who because of his hair like the whitest corn silk, which grew off his forehead like a plume, was recognizable everywhere.

And some were individuals by sanction of circumstance, like La-Verne Dicely, the son of the banker.

And some, like Trillie Dee Spelzer, received the public homage which is given beauty everywhere. She was a junior in high school and, like most of our high-school children, rather old for her class. She was dark-haired. She was brilliant with the loveliest colors of earth in their loveliest and likeliest places—eyes like the little precious pools of blue water on the plains, full of sky; skin like the skin of fruit protected by shade. Her body was wieldy and she could afford to pretend she was awkward, which she frequently did. I suppose mostly what she had was vitality, properly expressed in physical ways; but it was quite enough.

Her father was very poor, a carpenter and cabinetmaker. Her mother was dead. She used to work after school as a house servant. I knew the people who employed her from time to time. One of them was the high-school principal, a patient of mine. He used to shake his head over her, and screw up his eyes which felt hot and smarting at the precious dangers he detected everywhere.

"I'll be glad when she graduates and gets out," he said. "She's hard on the boys."

This was clear to anyone who ever saw her.

I talked with her several times, casually, and she was instinctively gifted as a flirt. She had but one vehicle for her relation to life. It often happens so. Great loveliness, great poetry, fine music, a good painting sometimes result from it. But the custodians of the power of love most often end worse off for it. Perhaps Trillie Dee was an exception here, as in so much else.

She was not stupid; she made average grades in school; she was clever and careful at her housework; but she was a half-wit in appetite and love, an emotional fool.

It was a thing you never could remember when you looked at her.

And during the summer I am speaking of, all these things were demonstrated.

It was a contest between religion and boys, for Trillie Dee.

The drugstore was a sort of forum or club for the younger leaders of the town. There I would see them, gathered about the soda fountain, where Martha Rooks, the druggist's girl, presided like a charming hostess with all the authoritative graces which the position required anywhere. Martha had the quizzical prettiness of any young creature, without any suggestion of what she would turn into as a woman. She blushed easily; her father watched her in sullen suspicion, down the length of his glass showcases or as he came from the back room bringing me my prescription. He was conscious of his family's place in the town; the Rookses were nearly as "leading" as the Dicelys. It was typical of his fatherly conscience that when Martha went out with LaVerne Dicely all he had ever heard about the boy disappeared from his memory.

Martha and Trillie Dee each had the power of symbolism; for the one, propriety and charm; for the other, adventure and furious beauty.

And now it is time to describe the stuff on which these symbols worked. LaVerne Dicely was a tall boy, with a rather small head on which there sat tight yellow curls always highly lustered. He must have used brilliantine. His clothes came from Fort Worth, and in consequence were masterpieces of inventiveness and novelty. He always looked too long for them, in arm and leg, and the buttons were strained across his bony chest. But he had three suits to other boys' one, and was highly complacent over it. He kept talking about going away to college.

He was the acknowledged leader of the high-school set. Nobody liked him very much, really; but he boasted a certain power which was effective, the power of riches and skepticism among people who were mostly poor and credulous.

Martha Rooks worked at the drugstore all that summer. The boys and girls dropped in and out. The town was tired and empty-looking all the hot days. Trillie Dee worked for some people I knew all day long until after the early supper which was customary in summer. Then as the dusty light of the day failed under the clarifying stars, life began to move. The movie-theater sign came alive, and red light chased white light around and around the frame of the sign. Rooks's drugstore took on the life of a smart café where friends met and the day was redone. And in wafts of silence during the evening, a vagrant breeze would bring the thump and whinny, the scrape and bellow, of the herded worshippers making noise unto their aspirations. The revival meetings sounded over the plains.

Trillie Dee Spelzer went one night with LaVerne Dicely to sit in his car and watch, and kid, and carry on, and wisecrack, and use what others did as clumsy and joking references for their own usage of each other. LaVerne smoked and roved her with his hand and she kept pushing him away, saying it was too hot. The music from the Tree and Lantern, where they were parked, had an animal beat to it. The next thing you knew, Trillie Dee was out of the parked Ford and scampering into the area of light from the blazing electric bulb in the lower branches, her arms raised and her fingers quivering, her mouth slack and happy, her eyes almost milky with inner sight, her voice wailing in the bleat of the pitiful, her lovely breasts rigid with intention and excitement—until she fell forward on the plain plank mourners' bench directly before the great trunk of the cottonwood, crying to be saved, to be taken up, to know Jesus, oh, yes!

LaVerne was dumfounded.

He was suddenly aware of his delicate position, and thought how humiliating it might be to be invited in with his girl friend to know God.

He started his car and backed away from the trodden lot, and went downtown, smoking gloomily.

He could hear the cry and bump of the congregation singing and stamping.

He turned around the block and left his car in an alley under the shadow of a lumber shed and sneaked down the tracks until he came within sight and sound of the Tree and Lantern again.

There she was.

She was white and startling in the fascinating light, the blazing globe that hypnotized and revealed. She was in a tight dress. She stood on the bench whimpering loudly and straining her arms upward. He could see people's faces shining from sweat in the heat of the night and the soul's labor. She was crying words. The benched people moved with her; they confirmed her with glad yet suffering cries, "Oh yes . . . isn't it so! . . . Know me, God! . . . Hear the tongues!" and she was saying, "Anna-ballie-shillalioh! Bally-annie-shall-ibanny-oh! Oh, sha-mallay-ash-a-malley-she-nannie-oh!" over and over again, with the same limited variations. It was received as revelation.

She was alive in another world; and, lying in the dusty and coal-smoky grass between the tracks and the live area of light, LaVerne

Dicely was quivered alive by the animal possession of all the listeners.

He watched and waited until the spell was broken, and Trillie Dee had sat down among the washed. When the meeting ended, he watched for her and he believed in an excitement of certainty that he would take her in his car to his will.

But she went away with another young man, who had played the guitar during the meeting. They looked sober and earnest, going up the street toward Main, with the great shadow of the guitar box between them.

LaVerne was disgusted.

For several days he let Trillie Dee alone.

He would go and sit for hours at Martha Rooks's soda fountain and stare at himself in the big mirror behind it, where the soft-drink menu was written in rose-colored washable paint. He could turn his head without losing sight of himself in the glass. Martha served him sundaes and Cokes until he was drowsy. They hardly ever conversed; sometimes he offered his attention by becoming a jazz orchestra, all by himself, making poop and beep noises with his mouth, and tapping with his feet on the fake marble floor of the fixture, and scraping one hand on his corduroy leg, and jazzing the other hand with loose change on the counter top. It was an authentic representation of his feelings, and at such times Martha really felt intimate with him. She would make up her mouth and kiss the air in the accepted idiom of her time.

They were silent and comfortable together.

Sometimes they kissed, in the back room, while Martha blushed. She began to have a mental picture of him that was wholly different from what he really was. The heartless chemistry of love was effecting its delusive changes in her very view.

Then LaVerne heard that Trillie Dee was making a great success as a convert, at all the other revival meetings. She went the rounds, pounding her heart and confessing her wickedness as often as they would let her. It was always a ravishing performance; and she achieved a tiny little fame, and brought tears to old eyes and hot breath to young mouths among her listeners.

The Fords were parked under the cottonwoods every night.

Trillie Dee worked all day and took her wages to her father, who was silent, and looked wry, and had a legend, as any "eccentric" is likely to have in a small town. Somehow, long ago, the word had gone around that he was a German baron. The town absently believed it. He gave himself no airs, unless that of being remote in a small and teeming town were one.

In the evenings LaVerne and his crowd ranged the streets, the revivals, the countryside roads where cars stopped in the dark. It was the old repetition of the roving blood, LaVerne and his gang like the rascals of the Renaissance in Paris, exacting pleasure from the historic sense of privilege. They had privy knowledges. They got drunk together and stretched the boundaries of their permitted license. They dumped produce trucks that were parked near the trackside warehouses. They toured the revivals and mocked and cheered.

And they all knew that Trillie Dee was having a summer in which her stars compelled her strangely.

In her triumphs as a convert she found for the exhausting floodwaters of her emotions a way to burst. Her fantastic loveliness went very well with the role of the pleading sinner.

She came to look upon herself as the theater of a war between Christ and Satan.

She told about it in her strange tongue and with dancings of her beautiful body.

When LaVerne heard from one of his gang that Trillie Dee was going off after the meetin's with a new man every night, he felt a private strike of rage and renewal in his breast; but he pretended that he'd known it all along, and whistled an experienced tune.

But the next night he was alone and watching, outside the North Hill tabernacle, whose plain pine walls clapped and rang with the high doings within. It was so hot that he had to wipe his face now and then. He could see Trillie Dee inside, working and at love with her spirit; her face gleaming with silvery lights in the heat and the hard light of gasoline lamps; dancing the people with her into the state that would spell freedom from torment, whether about body, or soul, or love, or death.

A fat girl sat down at a piano without any front to it, and began banging a rapid rhythm out in primitive chords.

The listeners began to sing.

Trillie Dee swayed before them and shouted, with her eyes closed:

> "There'll be pastures bright with clover
>   When He comes;
> There'll be pastures bright with clover
>   When He comes;
> There'll be pastures bright with clover
> When the long hard day is over
> And Lord Jesus is my lover
>   When He comes."

The piano tongued along, *bung*-bung-bung-bung, and the voices sounded like those of herded spirits in tired joy at the end of the hot hard work of life. The song dealt in terms of their earthly wants with the bright destinies of their desires. Another song said:

> "My heart is like a red, red rose,
> My heart is like a living rose,
>   Just like anyone's heart is
>   That the good Lord knows!

[152]

"My soul is like a big white bird,
My soul is like a flying bird,
Just like anyone's soul is
That has heard the Word."

Now and then a hollow trumpeted fume of glee arose from some man's throat, confirming above the sound what they all believed.

LaVerne, in the shadows outside, smoking nervously, felt a lump in his throat at the possession within.

He was prickling with the impatience of lust.

He, like all the rest, was a creature of the hot, hot summer, and the eternally youthful trial toward God and life which knew so many different terms.

The high-school principal and I had agreed several times that Trillie Dee was a complete fool in one direction. Now we had to add LaVerne Dicely to the category. He had recaptured her; and they were locked by all the pressures that overwhelmed them that summer, and for which they were essentially ready. Weeks went by and he never went to see Martha Rooks. Trillie Dee lost her job with my friends because if she came to work at all it was with such sleepy resentful eyes, such sluttish ways of laziness and pretension that she was insufferable. LaVerne revealed a cruel streak; took to bullying littler boys on the corner of Main and Arroyo streets; became glossy in some new snake-like way, his yellow tight curls oiled under the sunlight. Days long he and Trillie Dee would cruise slowly around town in his Ford "job" with the top down, stopping for a Coke, under the immense old tree at the eastern edge of town where the summer sang in the leaves and the wings of bugs droned; or again, pulling up in front of the movie theater on Main and merely sitting to watch the people go by at their hot duties of commerce and meager prosperity. The movie theater was two doors down from Rooks's Pharmacy.

Everybody saw what went on. LaVerne's own gang sneered at him. So he couldn't take it when someone else went out with his girl, eh? So he had to monopolize her and snub everybody else?

They were envious and hated his easy powers.

They thought bitterly, "Let his old man's bank go phooey, and see what happens to him then! Nobody'll look at him!"

But Martha would still.

Her face became actually grayish, from ill health in her thoughts; she served her young public at the soda fountain and matched their wits with the proper wisecracks. But she had no rich sway over her own heart. Several boys dutifully flirted with her and took the conventional liberties with her when they were alone. Her agony made her honestly angry at them for it. They told her LaVerne wasn't worth all that. She admitted to herself for the first time in her life, but not the last, that this was perfectly true; and that it made no difference.

At the proper time in August the professional revival troupe arrived, set up their tent on the same corner, out north of the business blocks, a large empty lot with a towering hedge of salt cedar and many trees; rather a picnic ground, it looked. Just beyond it to the east, the open country began, though the town continued north and west for several blocks.

Trillie Dee and LaVerne went the first night. A huge crowd came.

The show was glorious. I sat there myself for a while. The star was a white-haired man with a kind face and merry blue eyes and a snappy suit. He laughed between every two or three words he uttered. His assistants were several young women made up prettily, and several young men, with slicked hair, confident baritone voices, and all the physical unity of cheerleaders in college. That's what they were, in effect. They played harmonicas, trombones, accordions, and one did a novelty number with a jazzy tin whistle, a child's toy, while one of the girls sang, in a baby voice, a semi-sacred verse about "Baby's First Prayer." It wasn't until the second hour of clever speeches and smooth harmony numbers that the devotional quality received release; but then the actors skillfully drew the audience into the performance; and in less than half an hour the whole tent was an orgy. Everybody making some odd sound of remorse, resolve, or desire; women wailing and fluttering their hands; men sitting with closed eyes, slumped bodies, and making lowing sounds like the hungry kine; while down in the mourners' space, the scented, slick boys tugged and yearned at the poor bleating sinners who sought something beyond their powers of recognition. The slick young men embraced and murmured, and winked, and stroked. The pretty girls of the troupe made noises of rejoicing. The kindly boss evangelist went from one to another, laughing hollowly and alight in his eye at the powerful miracle he was performing—the turn of a population from its daily sense into this scene of abandon and collapse. His power was sincere. At the moment when the ice in people's hearts began to melt, he always felt some surge of restatement, his life bloomed anew, he fed on its results. His eyes flared and glittered. His hollow laugh continued. I had seen possessions like it in hospitals. I didn't like it. I got up to leave.

Just then Trillie Dee stood up and began to go down the aisle between the circus chairs yelling and waving. I saw LaVerne reach out to hold her back, blushing in a rage. But he was too late. She was down there, and the handsomest and glossiest of the young men received her into Glory.

There was no denying the superb liveliness of the child, the lavish scatter of sparkling vitality she made; most of all at these, her idiot moments.

I felt very gloomy, almost like LaVerne, I suppose, at the odd combination that dwelled in her.

I drove off on some routine calls of the early night; and later, coming back, I saw the tent emptied and only one light burning.

A faint warm night wind was going through it. The salt-cedar hedge was whispering warmly. The tent sides were not yet rolled down for the night. The hedge had received much of what had been generated inside the tent, I knew. There was a precise tapping of people's wells, in all the work by the troupe. Young men and women found the shadows discreetly enough, going out of the tent which was open all around. The hedge was a long whispering shadow far enough away, and not too far. Beyond that was the country of the open plains. Beyond that was our oldest mystery.

When you are a medical man, you are apt to think of everything that happens each day in terms of the consequences it might have.

After a while the consequences spring to mind, and carry no opinion, no sense of shock or judgment, simply recognition.

When fall came, and school opened, and the nights were a little cooler, and the summer's possession relaxed, and life turned more willingly to work, all these factors were reflected in the lives I have been talking about. It was as if a normal rhythm returned to the pulse, after a period of febrile agitation. You might say the town was well again.

Trillie Dee returned to school, and so did Martha, and LaVerne, and the gang.

The proper hours, the lessons, the pleasure in organization which young people feel, the worried love of the principal, a keen new show that everybody looked forward to at the movie theater, most of all the inexorable demands of contingency as against those of memory brought everybody back to normal ways.

Trillie Dee got her job back.

She worked soberly and worried about losing the heavy tan the summer had left on her, and which made her blazingly beautiful.

But now formal society was in force, with the school going, and LaVerne could not go with a girl who worked as a servant and who went to his same school; so he pleaded his need for her to Martha Rooks, in his own odd way, and she paid attention. He gave a little show for her in assembly one day, with his purple felt hat, with the half-inch brim. He made it into funny shapes, and put it on for her, each time with a new face. She finally had to smile at him. He pulled out his pocket comb and combed his hard yellow hair in triumph. Later he skidded his Ford to a stop by the sidewalk as she went down to the store to finish out the afternoon. She got in, and once at the soda fountain she had a chance to see him again as she *knew* he really was: his eyes not hazed with pink veins, but clear and loving; his face not buckled at the mouth in an insecure sneer, but cleverly smiling; his body not long and animal-frank, but graceful and modest.

They fell in with the autumnal mood, and had together a superior air of virtue and security.

Trillie Dee smoldered at them from the distance they preserved.

She said to anybody who would listen that she was dying to get to Dallas.

There was somebody in Dallas who would make them all sit up and take notice around here. He was just waiting for her. Let them look out!

But these fiery sentiments went oddly or not at all with her actions. Trillie Dee was claimed by normality again, and the early autumn went along through its cooling tempers; the plains were clear and exhalant of some sweet breath; the little town, or city as it called itself, prospered spiritually under the well-being of the weather; I had the sense of people happy, as we do receive that sense in the intervals of trouble and pain.

This is where it would be comfortable to end my story.

But one day in late September, Trillie Dee came to see me at my office. She had the tragic tact of a human being forced to utter the most painful realities. Her dignity was astonishing. She was bitter, underneath; but rather than show it to me at first, she assumed a face of social charm, smiling and posing as if to reassure *me,* when the roles were actually reversed. She confessed her suspicions, and only too readily was I able to confirm them.

We sat staring in silence at each other, and I feel sure the pulse of the spent summer was revived in her memory as it was in mine.

Then she began to talk, and told me in flat, curious eloquence, of the things I have already set down; and my mind filled out the details when she talked.

She declared that her father would kill her if he ever found out about this.

She said he had one passion in life and that was his independence. If his daughter fell into disgrace, then the whole town would "have something on" him. She said quite soberly that she had nowhere to go. Then she snapped her fingers and licked her lips, looking infantile and exquisite, and declared that if she could only get to Dallas: the evangelist young man had left her his address; and she got to know him pretty well here, and she felt pretty sure that he . . .

Her cheeks began to redden at another thought; and she spoke of LaVerne Dicely, with the utmost hatred now. She also mentioned Martha Rooks, and, so to speak, spat upon her virtue.

"I think I'll know what to do now," she said, and stood up to go. Her eyes had a yellowish cat gleam and she was breathing deeply, consciously looking superb and making me want to laugh at this

[158]

clumsy imitation of a movie star, which yet had its flashing style and physical loveliness.

I told her to be a sensible girl, and make her decisions slowly and carefully.

She asked if she might come back for advice when she had made up her mind. I said of course. She held out two dollar bills to me—a week's wages, I imagine. She had that sort of propriety—the only thing of her father in her character, I imagine; the pride of a poor person who insists upon paying for indispensable services. I handed the money back to her and said,

"I'll send you a bill when the case is finished."

She squinted suspiciously, then snickered.

The next thing she did was that evening.

At half past six, when all families in town had got up from the supper table, Trillie Dee, in her finest clothes, strolled up to the house of the Dicely family, rang the bell beside the screen door, and demanded to see the banker himself.

The man's wife received her and fetched her husband. Mr Dicely was more like an undertaker than a banker. He wore starched collars that stood away from his yellow neck, and his face was gray where he shaved, and his eyes were hollow with some permanent misery in shadows about them. His mouth was like a fold of skin over a skull, without the life. When he spoke it was oddly soft, and he cleared his throat often. I often thought he had a tubercular larynx.

He took Trillie Dee into his den.

He stared out the window at the front yard, where no grass grew, only wind-raked throws of gravel.

He never opened a conversation: part of his cheap and sinister strategy as a man of affairs.

Trillie Dee told him, first, that she was pregnant; second, that his son was responsible; third, that she wouldn't marry him if he had good sense; fourth, that she only wanted one thing.

Mr Dicely looked at her and shivered. I could imagine the rattling dusty blow of the dried leaves of life which might go through him at any reference to passion.

In a very few minutes Trillie Dee left the room on her way out in triumph. In the hall Mrs Dicely was waiting. She was a tall woman resembling her son—yellow hair, long spare bones, a cheek that burned quickly with hysterical flush. She detained the girl now with her pale hand and demanded to know what was up.

Mr Dicely told her in a few ashen words, burdened with contempt that mocked the very pattern of a family.

Mrs Dicely turned and clutched at Trillie Dee with her sharp fingers and nails.

They were fixed in a tableau of impotent furies when a noise on the stair landing made them turn.

It was LaVerne, trying to back upstairs without being seen or heard. He had been listening all the time. He couldn't get away without knocking into a mahogany pedestal that stood there with nothing on it.

His mother called upon him to come down and deny this horrible story.

This is just what he did.

But his father's dark and rubescent eyes pierced him like a bird's, a creature which with all its selfish pursuit of function still and without a sense of virtue recognizes a threatening circumstance.

The boy gangled and blushed and tried to wisecrack his way to safety.

But his mother perceived the hollowness of his efforts.

She turned and slapped Trillie Dee and began to cry and ran up the dustily carpeted stairs. It was one of the few two-story houses in town—white wood with stone corners, an unroofed porch, a shingled cupola, a short driveway bordered with stone cairns between which black chains were stretched; the whole sitting on a wide corner lot where there was no grass, and looming over that end of town on the very edge of the dwelling section. Behind the house, the grand, fair plains stretched away.

Trillie Dee came to see me late that night, and told me all this.

She exhibited money which Mr Dicely had given her to go to Dallas on.

"And I'm going."

"Have you told your father?"

"No, I'll write him."

"Do you want me to tell him after you leave?"

"I guess so. . . . Say, that'd be keen!"

"All right, I will."

The train went shortly after midnight.

She was on it.

I heard it.

It gave me some catch of feeling. There was a certain bravery about it, though perhaps I'd be hard pushed to say exactly how. Perhaps to take the burdens of your very quality as simply as she did was the point. Anyway, the train whistled a long faint windy chord through the dark and I thought of the lighted windows and the silent spacious land; and Trillie Dee Spelzer setting out for Dallas, where she would seek and find and undertake further folly, without a doubt; and I thought again of how pretty she was.

But hardly that obvious quality of hers was remembered in the next few days, when the town was thoroughly sure of her flight.

She was damned and scolded everywhere.

People drove slowly by the gray board shack-like building on East Arroyo Street where Spelzer had his shop, and where Trillie Dee

[161]

had lived with him. They looked to see if anything of this extraordinary performance were somehow *visible* about the premises, or in his face, chanced he to show for a moment.

I wondered where the truth leaked out, and was dumfounded to discover that Mrs Dicely had gone clacking to her friends with it, not mentioning her own son, of course, simply saying that Trillie Dee had been caught *doing* with a high-school boy, and run out of town for it. She had a withering wryness about her, an instrument of strength, some decadent current alive in her, a desperate and miserable woman.

I went to see her and told her that I knew the truth, and that it was not fair to go around with a half-truth to the damage of only one of the parties implicated.

"The surest way to save my family's name," she said,, "is to be the first to tell the facts, without telling the circumstances."

"But if you must know, Mrs Dicely, the whole town knows it is LaVerne."

"Yes, but they aren't admitting it."

There was some truth in this.

The older people were simply not agreeing with the truth: that a son of Banker Dicely (to whom they all owed so much, in both cash and power for their small concerns) had created a scandal.

"There isn't anything anybody can tell me about my relatives, doctor," said Mrs Dicely, with hot spots on her cheekbones. There were tears in her eyes. She seemed to pour at me all the unsatiety of her womanly dreams and their crude half-fulfillments.

She was wry and starved and difficult.

I went off and left her.

I didn't know then that she had cancer.

I contrasted the way she behaved with Spelzer's behavior the morning after his daughter left for Dallas on the night train.

He heard what I had to tell him with a critical smile on his face, his teeth gently chewing a pencil, his head nodding.

If he really were a German baron in unexplained exile, he could not have more clearly disdained showing his sentiments to a stranger with unpleasant news.

But a night or two later his shop began to burn.

The town was stirred and summoned by the light in the sky and the noise of the fire truck.

Spelzer wasn't around. The gray boards of the shop, the decades of shavings inside, the very dryness of the life it reflected seemed to blow upward in the strenuous relief of flames. In the crack of the wood and the calling of the firemen and the glass-like break of the hose-water in the blackening walls, everybody kept looking for Spelzer. But he was gone. The next day it was understood that the fire was his *congé*.

The acts proceeded to their ends.

A year or so later LaVerne and Martha Rooks married. It was jubilantly understood in the town that the boy had decided to give up his college career and not wait any longer for the girl he had been in love with since they both learned to toddle. A sentimental seizure followed. The happy proprieties were indulged to an almost hysterical degree. There were showers for the bride, and vestigially obscene festivals for the groom; and on their return from the honeymoon (which they'd spent in Galveston, seeing for the first time the mystery of the sea and the communion of two human spirits, and understanding neither, like many a better man or woman), the "younger married set" set upon their brick bungalow at ten at night with flashlights, tin pans to beat, rattlers to whirl, and ticktocks to fasten on window frames: a shivaree, in which all the crude impulses of savage and naïve society are formalized, given sanction by numbers, and license to make sport of the generative act, without

[163]

violating any local laws. The newly married couple had their lights out; but somebody cried in the street:

"They're there; I saw them drive in and go to bed; don't give up!"

It was a very important occasion in their communal life.

The crowd went on making noise and peering.

Inside, LaVerne and Martha whispered in humorous terror. He was all for pretending they were not home; hiding his head, as he always did in danger. But she, who felt secretly outraged by the vulgar nuisance and its instinctive meaning, yet saw how it was meant in friendship, and that to refuse the shivareers' entry would be hostile and even ungracious. So, blushing and hanging her plump head, which was so pretty and still maidenly, she got out of bed and shivered, put up her hair and threw an overcoat of LaVerne's on, and went out to the little cement stoop, reached up, and turned on the amber coach lantern that was their "porch light," and called:

"Come in! —I'll make coffee for us all!"

They surged in, dropping their bushmen's implements on the bald little lawn.

It was a tribal union.

Everybody spoke of how sweet Martha was, and once you got LaVerne over his odd and fumbling bravado, how nice he was.

He retired with some of the men and produced a gallon of bootleg corn. The girls and Martha had coffee until the drunkest husband came back to the front room with its tinted wrought-iron and sponged-color walls, and they all decided to "make whoopee." Martha drank too, and it made her weep. But somehow it seemed like a night of nights, and the scheme included so much that was reassuring and proper because it was always done to honeymooners; so she tried not to think of the noisy and unattractive part of it, but only of the confirmatory part of it; and she thought of Trillie Dee, knowing a great deal more than anyone thought she knew; and the

[164]

evening seemed to become a triumph of goodness, in Martha's eyes, for this was the thing, the way of life, that poor Trillie Dee could never know.

The first winter passed, and everyone spoke of how gay the town was that year.

When spring came, it got around that LaVerne Dicely's wife was going to have her first baby, and that he himself was drinking heavily. I knew (as I knew so many unutterable pieces of news) that he was consorting with the prostitutes on South Ranger Street. He would go off to Fort Worth and Dallas, too, on "business," and come back looking ill and resentful. He worked at managing his father's cotton gin west of town.

In summer the season of the Holy Ghost broke over the town as it always did.

Memories were revived now and then by the tokens of emotion which had had such visible results the previous summer.

In the march of the seasons this coming of holy men and the lofting of their obsessions and voices resembled some perfectly natural phenomenon, the heat which brought forth desert creatures, the song of the locust, the cry of the prophet in the plains.

Martha had her baby, a boy.

I took care of them, and both were brave and everything was quite usual.

The generations stretched away in the future, and the grandparents on both sides tried to possess what they could of it through the favor of the baby.

But he was like his mother, sober, yet simple; questing with his eyes, and uncomplaining at finding so little.

The years came along.

There was another baby at the younger Dicelys.

The winters were windy and full of loneliness for those who

stopped to listen to those great travels of hurrying air across the plains.

The summers were hot and needful and dry.

One day at the movie theater the town was amazed and stirred by a face on the screen.

The heroine of a serial film was perfectly and unmistakably Trillie Dee Spelzer.

I hurried to see it as soon as the news reached me.

There she was, under the name of Laura Marsh, performing those breathless antics with all her old zest and child-like intensity, all her liveliness magnified and yet somehow made stony by the odd light of the photograph. She rode horses and avoided cliffs and was swept down canyons, and she wrecked railroad trains and saved lives and shot a man and stabbed a mad dog and performed countless other fascinating stunts through the duration of the serial. When she looked out into the theater of her home town during one of her silent soliloquies (this was before talkies) and stared right at us, many people were heard to say it gave them quite a turn!

There was a tremendous amount of speculation about the actress.

What do you suppose she makes?

How did *she* get into pictures?

"Where does she *get* that?" wondered many a mother with a daughter of her own.

So, revisiting us, Trillie Dee had perhaps one further set of consequences for our lives.

LaVerne now showed much of his mother's spirit. It was the winter she died, and it took her months of wretched agony to do it.

LaVerne drank more and more heavily, and had gradually been eased into the role of the town bum by the very people in whose "social set" he moved.

Mrs Dicely had insisted on going to see one installment of Trillie Dee's serial.

This was the supreme tribute, we all felt.

It dramatized the dying woman's will, and was the peg upon which many appeals were hung and presented to her son: to stop drinking and doing all the other things that distressed his sweet little wife so, his lovely children, his aging father. They *knew* he didn't *have* to work for a living, like everyone else. But if he went on he'd kill himself. . . .

He was so uncertain of his wants and his desires that he would agree readily with the last person he talked with, and then go on his way.

He was fattening at the belly, though his arms and legs were still gaunt, and his face and yellow curls foolishly young.

Mrs Dicely died in April.

One of her last utterances had some fierce grandeur in it, I felt, and I've never forgotten it; for even to a doctor, there is sometimes a prophetic and terrible weight about words that come from the last burning in the human intelligence. She said,

"*You'd* never've admitted a thing, *either.*"

She looked at me straight, after this, and her face was pathetic and dreadful, the effort to communicate.

There was no use telling LaVerne the defensive words which confessed so much. He came to the funeral weeping and drunk.

Martha had her third baby a little later.

Warm weather, and the hot heaven of summer.

The tents and the lanterns, the cry and the bellow, the prayer and the kiss, all the summer possession returned.

So did Trillie Dee, or rather, Laura Marsh, in another movie. I said to myself, seeing it, that in the film she was just like the old Trillie Dee of the revivals: the same emotional sprees, done with the same artful and commonplace genius for projecting her body, bearing the very same results; only, as her movie popularity grew, the results affected a million men and women, perhaps, where in my town and in my time it affected some one only.

For LaVerne went that summer drunkenly down to Jesus at the mourners' bench.

It might have been in memory of Trillie Dee.

He was a violent convert.

He moaned and sang and smashed all the liquor bottles he could find, anywhere.

He was now a terror in his house, instead of a familiar, disgusting responsibility.

So the bitter seed of Trillie Dee's planting so long ago meant something strong, now that it had grown in them; even though it meant something different to each.

To LaVerne, was it all the beauty he had once touched, not in recognition but in lust, and had now lost?

Was this a reminder, this convergent return of her likeness, and the shoutin' of the preachers?

Was Trillie Dee right, all this time?

Whose virtue?

Martha Rooks loved her children and cared for them and hoped for them until she felt sometimes her breast would open under the weight of her image of a proper life for them. She *knew* that everything she had was a synonym for the proper life. She would tell them over so often—a lovely home; three dear little children, so clever and so pretty, so promising; a devoted circle of friends; a husband who was everything everybody said he was, but still a man whom she knew in humility and perhaps that was really the core of love. . . .

But a haggard sense of guilty judgment always came alive behind these proper beliefs.

Martha had a lot of character, at last, if not much of the grander

[168]

and more spectacular style in people. I remember thinking when she was a high-school girl that I couldn't have imagined what she'd turn into. That now seems unintelligent of me. For life had written down its facts upon her and her spirit had illuminated each one as it came. I suppose she was the one person in town who might have understood poor Mrs Dicely's valedictory sentiments, but I never told her what that bitterly faithful sentence was. Martha was a proof of the real goodness there is in people. It is best undisturbed by the mysterious intelligence of bitterness, such as her late mother-in-law's.

And if everybody felt, even Martha, that Trillie Dee had cheated them, had broken all the rules, and had received no penalties, this was still another way in which her destiny wielded its influence.

What they felt was that Trillie Dee had seized life, and condemned them to existence.

It is so easy to console people, if they really know what troubles them.

But as for me, though it wouldn't have made sense to tell anyone so, I remembered the vanity of blame and the words of Socrates, who, when informed that his fellow citizens had condemned him to death, replied,

"And Nature, them."

So Little Freedom

One morning, after he had been in Taos about a week, young Roger Warrington went into the Plaza Drug Store for a chocolate soda at about half past ten. Just being in Taos, New Mexico, was almost enough, he had thought; but his astonishment and delight were almost like being a little sick when he saw, reflected in the soda fountain mirror, the two rather large women come in, followed by the small, spring-footed man with the fiery red beard. Roger could hardly believe his eyes. The three people sat down noisily at one of the drugstore tables, ordered soft drinks, and sat regarding each other. There was quite a crowd in the Plaza Drug; nobody paid them any mind but Roger; but his heart was beating fast, and he felt almost weak, because it was unmistakably his favorite novelist, Edward St David, especially now that he had pulled off his ten-gallon hat, and the thick hair fell fox-red over his incandescent white brow. The soda jerker took them their drinks, and one of the women said in a comfortable voice, unconsciously loud so everyone could hear, but in a German accent,

"*Ja!* the chocolate szoda is yours, St David; it will give you cr-r-amps again."

This must be his Austrian wife, Roger had read about their romance, and he gazed at her and felt somehow comfortable about her. St David screwed up his eyes and merely stared at her, and took the straw into his mouth like a greedy child.

The other woman was impassive; she seemed almost like a governess for the two of them. Roger suddenly knew who she was; it was that rich woman from Boston who had built a medieval castle of adobe out near the pueblo, with a high wall where at night the lanterns shone deep in the roadway leading to the door; and now everybody came to Taos to visit her, from anywhere, famous writers and painters and publishers and symphony conductors; her name was Mrs Gerald Boree. Most everybody in Taos was always saying her name, "Mrs Boree, M'ss B'ree," a sort of refrain of curious respect, except that the young painters who idled in the Plaza spoke of her with comic intention and effect simply as "Bertha." She had left her husband, Gerald Borce the artist, in Rapallo, and had come here alone "to find herself," as she had so often tried to do.

St David sucked air at the bottom of his soda glass, and began to speak to Mrs Boree, who appeared to be enacting the conception of placidity.

"A new kind of manorial bad manners," he sneered. "My ancestors used to have to put up with getting beaten and robbed and starved and bastardized by the manor folk, who carried on like this in full view of the county, elevated above common decency and poor trouble, as if just and right. This is a new dimension of the same thing. Moving in and taking over a whole town, a damned whole contented and centuries-old secure people, and putting them on like a new rag to wear around your shoulders, to show to the rich and famous and talented and frightful people you drag here from all over the world to see your show, your personal mountains, your

[171]

private desert, the spiritual reservoir which you did not fill, but only saw others filling and taking from."

In embarrassment Roger lowered his eyes from the big soda fountain mirror where he had seen all. The drugstore was full of the midmorning glisten and drift of casual life. Everybody could hear. Roger was blushing; his ears were like red lampshades, he knew, with light coming through them. When he dared look again, he was astonished to see the group at the round iron table sitting in simple composure. Mrs Boree was gazing at the great man without resentment, almost with love? do you think? and her face was like a daytime moon under her black hair with its Pueblo bangs. Mrs St David looked almost bored, a bored lioness, sleepily licking the sweet edge of her chocolate glass. St David himself was hunched bonily down, sucking on the straw, scowling. And even then, he looked up, and smiled sort of washily, his resentment free, his blue eyes striking out with a look of misery and power which gave Roger a pang in the breast. But the shrill, bitten voice was not yet able to be quiet.

"And do not sit there understanding me with possessive tolerance," he said. "I won't have it. Whatever I owed you I have paid you. I came, did I not? You have exhibited me, have you not? We have had our thrust and parry; I like your damned insolent landscape, and I shall flee it the moment I can afford to, and you shall have suitable credit for discovering my inner appropriateness with it."

"St David!" said his wife, richly chiding in her Viennese accent, "I beleef it is your manners which are too bad. You are too *bad,* to sit here in vront of all these beople, and show your temper like a stomach-ache."

"Ha!" he cried, turning on her, "if there is one thing worse than to be mooned over, it is to be shut off, like a doll! I know you! Mocking me with your big female calm, waiting . . ."

[172]

"Come, Bertha," said Gerda St David rising. "He is going to be dreadful all day."

Roger saw the three of them leave the drugstore, St David in the rear of the two large women, his new blue jeans sticking stiffly out behind where his bony hams failed to fill them, his head dwarfed like a rabbit's by the tall, ear-like rise of his ten-gallon hat, his rough woolen lumberjack shirt, bright red plaid, bagging pitifully around his thin shoulders and arms with a sort of childish pretension and failure. St David coughed as he disappeared into the blazing sunshine of the sidewalk crowd. His cough shook him throughout his whole skeleton. Roger Warrington swallowed in sympathy. Then even genius was not free? Could look ridiculous? Was tortured and had to cry out, over even the silliest things?

No matter. Roger's youthful loyalty was truer than that. He had actually set eyes on Edward St David, and if he accomplished no other thing, his trip to Taos that summer was already worthwhile.

But his hungers, too, were truer, harder to satisfy than by such a glimpse. He went out to the country where Mrs Boree's house was, and sure enough something happened. Mrs St David came walking out alone, toward the dirt highway, and before he knew it, they were talking together, and he never felt so easy with anybody in his life. She had him saying in two minutes that her husband was his idol, and it didn't make her laugh, or be modest, or anything; she simply said he must come back with her to the house and meet him. Her warmth, her allowance of him, right off, made Roger a little blurred with joy; after all, look who she was, a former countess, and the wife of the greatest living writer, and she said she thought she had seen Roger before, at the drugstore? drinking a szo-da? *Ja?*

He was too scared to go with her to meet St David. But he wrung her hand, and she smiled broadly, said she had two sons of her own, and hoped he was a happy boy, "— — are you content, here, in Ta-os?" She didn't wait for him to reply, but went on to say that he must not break his heart if he didn't have any tal-ent, but go home, and be happy with the good, and dear, kind things at home; sometimes they were hard to find, but *ja!* they existed, everywhere. She blinked both her light blue eyes at him, and went back up the long road to the house of which so many mysteries were reported in the village, and left him staring after her, startled and moved.

No talent? . . . It had never occurred to him.

That would mean they were right, the others, who were ashamed of him, back home in Whitewater, Texas, and of the love he had in him and could not conceal, but had to reveal as art. Yet how kindly, how immediately, Mrs St David seemed to know him.

He didn't know which one he loved more, St David or his wife. Roger had the disturbing and exciting belief that anything could happen in Taos. Drifting up and down the dried mud streets, he conceived of himself as living the most adventurous life possible. It took so little freedom in the realm of the possible to make him happy. He was blond-headed, as they say in Texas, pink-cheeked, and slow moving. He longed to think and feel and believe as independently as his grandfather had pioneered and killed and colonized.

But when he got back to his room by the alfalfa field, he found a letter from his mother, Texas-Anne. It was an edict. Big Roger said if he did not take the next bus out of Taos, they would never send him any more money, and they were going to settle once and for all about this thing. And Grandfather had deeded his stock in the Bank to Little Roger, and if he came right home, and went to work in the Bank, and learned the business, they'd put him on the Board of Directors on his twenty-first birthday. So wouldn't he do this, hon? just for her? She missed her little baby boy, and was sure he couldn't bear to refuse Texas-Anne the only thing she ever asked of him?

His exultation vanished. He bitterly thought of how both Mrs St David and his mother had in effect asked him to do the same thing.

[174]

How could they both be right about him? He dawdled for several days, not even answering the letter. He still had enough money for a while, even if they never gave him another cent. He said to himself that he was too upset to paint. He found himself hanging around in front of Mrs Boree's gateway; or out in the fields beyond her house; or down in an arroyo from which everything was out of sight but the tip of the blue mountain. Approaching the place, one afternoon, he heard St David talking, and he could not go away. In a moment he saw St David, and that he was talking to a large sandy-looking cow.

"Life uncritical; life absolute; life abstract," he was saying, almost in song. "You ruminate and gestate and let your generous bag to anyone who desires it. Oh purity of un-thought! Heavenly vacuity!"

But he knew whenever anyone was looking, and he turned swiftly on Roger, and slitted his blue-eyed glance suspiciously. Roger stammered something, and started away, but St David began to laugh, a high delighted laugh.

"The drugstore baby!" he cried. "Gerda told me you came to call the other day and then dwindled off in a storm of nerves. . . . I wouldn't bite you. . . . I have been having the sweetest of all arguments with my cow here, a one sided argument. Come here!"

St David took his hand.

"Why is your hand cold?"

Roger explained that—that he was excited, meeting this way after years of admiring him from afar.

"Rot."

St David sat down on a clump of salt grass and waved Roger before him. In a twinkling, Roger was pouring out his troubles, and St David was nodding, as if ahead of him in the tale. His eyes smoldered and began to fire. His spirit always burned at the news of cruelty, of anyone's hope being maimed; and he interrupted Roger by jumping up and walking away and coming back.

[175]

"Never, never, never, *never* give in!" he almost shrieked. It took all his strength, and he began to cough. He hugged his wracking ribs and bent over, and the coughs traveled up from the ground and shook him as if he were a fiery red cat in the grasp of a huge dog. Roger was alarmed, but St David managed to wave off his concern. In a little while the seizure was over, and in the sunlit silence they met each other with little smiles. In that recuperative quiet, another voice then sounded. It came from the rim of the arroyo above them. It said, coolly, musically,

"Well if you need proof there it is, Edward. If you will waste yourself on everything else but the one thing that matters, which is your work, which I could protect for you—"

It was Bertha Morgan Boree, looking down upon them impassively. But her eyes had lights of ire in them, and she looked from the boy to the man and back again. Roger thought she even looked jealous, but he at once said to himself *that* was a crazy idea.

St David seemed for a moment too outraged to speak. When at last he could speak he was so controlled that he was more terrifying than he was in his outbursts.

"You have been watching me in secret," he said. His voice was thin with contained rage. "When will I ever learn to believe my wife! Nobody could have seen me come here otherwise. It is all I needed to know. — — Come along, you, lad, we will finish talking in the fields, in broad view of a purer heaven."

He turned and scrambled up the opposite slope of the arroyo with costly energy. The dirt flew down under his hands and feet. Roger clambered after him, astonished at the power within that delicate frame.

"Edward! Oh, *do* be sensible and careful," called Mrs Boree, raising her voice but still sounding most cultivated. "How you misunderstand me! I only feel a duty — —"

On the opposite edge of the red arroyo he turned and made an obscene gesture at her across the gap, and then fled to the fields, walking loosely and with incredible speed. Words trailed back over his working shoulders to Roger, angry words, foul, execratory. At last, a long way across the field, they stopped, and turned, and looked. The bulky figure of the woman was still at the arroyo. Her hands were to the sky. She was posed like a priestess. Roger was impressed. Feeling that, St David said to him,

"She knew we would turn to look."

They walked on in silence for a quarter of an hour, and the calm of the day, the desert scent, wry and pungent, the peace of the looming mountain, the gold of the wheat in the fields before the pueblo, which was darker gold in the sunshine, came back into them, and St David finally said to the boy,

"Well, *I* never, never, never, never gave in, and I never shall! *I would rather be killed by what I am than by what somebody else wants me to be.*"

His eyes in the white face, under the dark red bang, raked and swept Roger with a sort of rough compassionate tenderness. He seized the boy's hand and crushed it in his, and then he nodded, saying "Goodbye, goodbye, we know each other now, those things keep. Goodbye!" He turned and walked away in a solitude which defied further intrusion.

That night Roger slept out on the roof of the adobe house where he was living. It was a sort of ritual, under the stars of Taos, farewell, made of joy and grief both. One thing he was sure of. It took a "genius" to say that about *never, never, never, never*: and he vaguely felt that he had been *through* something, but he wasn't quite clear about what it was. He lay awake a long time, thinking of everything he had seen and done in Taos, where he loved the busy, commercial, gregarious to-do about "art."

But he knew, too, after those brief but somehow total glimpses of the St Davids, yes, and of Mrs Boree, that there were trials he had never suspected about art in the souls where it lived, and required delivery. He fell asleep at peace, knowing that he carried no fires within him such as were consuming Edward St David; and the next day he went back to Whitewater, Texas, and the Bank.

The Huntsmen

East of town about a dozen miles ran the river. To a place near its edge before dawn on Saturday came Mr Pollock and his younger son, Madison, accompanied by their dog, Punch. It was a cold morning in autumn. The boy was hardly awake yet. His father had to nudge him to get a move on and climb out of the car when they stopped in a clump of rust-brown salt cedar at the end of the sandy road Mr Pollock knew about. For years it had brought him from the paved highway and through the low dunes of sand and clay to his favorite spot for duck hunting.

Madison left the car, carrying his own new shotgun. Over his bony little shoulder was slung his canvas bag for shells. In the darkness the air tasted like snow. As they moved forward to walk beside the river to Mr Pollock's favorite blind, the father did not have to tell Madison to be as quiet as possible. He wasted no words, but merely gave by example a lesson in the caution and delicacy of how to move when there were surely ducks out on the river. Punch, an elderly rat-tailed spaniel, went heavily but silently on the sand, pausing at intervals to be sure the others were following. As they came between two huge clumps of salt cedar that rattled in the faint cold wind before daylight, Mr Pollock halted and held his freezing fist by his ear. Madison could just see him. The gesture said, "Listen!"

Madison turned his head and held his breath.

Then, yes, how could his father ever have heard it, it was so faint, but now he could hear it too—the reedy, murmurous sound of ducks disturbed and talking over there, out of sight under the high carved clay banks of the red Pecos River earth.

The boy's heart began to pound. He loved his father for this experience. They stood shivering in the graying dark until there was no more sleepy music from the hidden water. Then they walked carefully up the river, keeping away from the bank until Mr Pollock found the shallow dirt canyon which led to his favorite blind. They entered into it, a miniature wilderness choked with brittle weeds which grew from dry alkaline earth. Nearing the river, they began to walk in mud and marshy water. The bank rose before them a little, making a small peninsula screened at the edge by a spare rank of young willows. Here was the place. They knelt down on the cold sand and allowed the day to come.

It was now not far off.

Though nobody knew it, Mr Pollock came for this as much as for anything else. In the spectacle of the natural world he found his poetry, his music, his art gallery. This was his culture, and what it meant to him he had no way to tell, except through example, for the benefit of his sons. All his feelings were buried, anyhow. He was a short, heavy man who walked leaning backward, to carry his weight evenly. He was a director of the local bank and the manager of a building-and-loan association. During business hours he was a leading citizen of Main Street. Many people felt about him as they would about a doctor, for he knew and helped with serious problems in their families which had to do with the possession and safety of their homes. Under his low hat brim his large light eyes saw everything and betrayed nothing. His mouth was small in his big face, and habitually he said little, but when he spoke, he was believed.

Wherever the town showed its composite mind or strength, you'd see a Pollock. If Mr Pollock would sit on platforms as a silent endorsement of civic desires or ambitions, his wife was likely to be one of the speakers. She did not speak with skill, for her voice was loud and harsh, somehow inappropriate to her small size; but everyone was always impressed as she struggled to bend the public will to her personal belief. She governed her family in much the same way, overwhelming them with her anxious vitality, which was a happy joke among them all until in some issue she yielded to the tears that always seemed to lie in waiting behind her pinch-nose eyeglasses which trembled before her face. But she was as apt to weep for happiness and her good fortune in such a kind, sober husband and in two such wonderful boys, as she was out of vexation or "just nerves."

The parents embraced so completely their station in middle life that it was hard to imagine either of them as ever having been boy and girl. Especially was this impossible for their sons to do. It was as though Mr and Mrs Pollock had ceded to their young all graces of person and fiber, and were content to lose those beauties which had once served their mindless purpose in the founding of the family, whose sons now contained the future's desires.

Living life again through their sons, Mr and Mrs Pollock knew the elders' eternal wonderment about their children: *They may be bright, but are they good?*

Edwin was eighteen, his brother Madison twelve. Both were already taller than their parents, and far more communicative than the father. Give either of the boys something to take part in, and, according to their ages, they would fling themselves into it, and pretty soon end up in charge of it. Edwin was a great local athlete.

He was also an honor man in high-school studies. Boys and girls alike admired him as a terrible cynic, and the yearbook in his senior year said that if you ever wanted a shock, just ask Edwin Pollock for his honest opinion of anything. But it added that he always grinned when he gave it, which accounted for all the "broken hearts" he left scattered around him. So tribute was already paid in pathetic and heartfelt ways to Edwin's powers of comeliness, strength and warmth in life. He was a junior public figure in the small city, and was loved most of all because he never seemed to know it.

Now, before going to college, he was taking a year to learn the value of a dollar—his father's favorite words—by selling farm-implement machinery up and down the Pecos Valley, which lay fertile and prosperous in the wilderness of dry plains all around, graced by the far-distant lift, loom and day-long change of the southernmost Rocky Mountains.

Madison Pollock at twelve had the energy and the laughable daring of a half-grown cat. Of all the Pollocks, he was the funniest and the most high-spirited. He loved to show off, knowing exactly how to make people take delight in his antics. He, too, was a good student, and he had a few pygmy enemies because he seemed to have been born with all the schoolbooks in his head, for he never studied, or said he didn't. He probably didn't. He was as excitable as his mother, but, unlike her, he made more than evasions come of his excitements, whether in play, work or mischief. He was the only blond Pollock. His eyes were dark blue, his cheeks a furious dusky pink, and his whole self, no matter what he did, seemed always to look dry and clean.

The last member of the Pollock family was Punch, the spaniel, who was an actual character because they had all put their characters into him ever since his puppydom. Now, in his privileged later life, Punch was a leading citizen of the alleys of town, and with his mornings to himself, he made his daily tour of inspection and gluttony along the back yards of countless friends. They would hear him coming, with his collar chain and tags tinkling to his heavy trot, and would know that this day, like all the others, would pursue its reassuring course, under the great sky whose light, beating upon houses, and streets, and highways squared to the points of the compass, and plains, and the long river, could show everything except what the future would bring.

Waiting for daylight by the river, Mr Pollock and Madison shivered companionably. Behind them rose the escarpment of the river's eastern bluffs in cold shadow. But they could see the edge of the sky line now, outlined by a faint lift of pearly light.

Before them across the river reached the great plain still held in night. A few far lights showed sweetly and steadily where the town was, and every half minute the faraway beacon of the airport swept suddenly out of the darkness, showing now a white light, and next time a jeweled green. Madison knew exactly where it was, twelve miles away. He admired it and in half-thought wished it were his, for it was pretty, and perhaps it did belong to him, if he said so.

As still as the rest of the river world, they waited. But they waited in growing excitement, for over and about them proceeded the immense arrival of day. It seemed to start slowly, but vast events, as they watched, happened more quickly, and the light gained behind them, and turned to the color of embers, and in the dome of the sky came a smoky blue, and then the western sky showed a pale rose against which the curved shadow of the sleeping earth swept a dying image. Little clouds that were lost in the dark now came to show like wisps of flame in the east. What was that now, on the endless western horizon? The rosy light came down, dispelling the

[183]

blue earth shadow, and struck the tips of the mountains which so remotely faced the coming sun.

How was this? Before the sun was up, its light rested across the world on the rocky faces of the mountains and made them show great sweeps of stone, as though heat and light were within them. A green glow filtered into the sky and far-off irrigation canals picked up the reflection and made ribbons of silver and green in the hazy ground. It suddenly seemed colder. Madison hugged himself around his gun. The grand vision before them arose in their spirits, too, and their faces were open with the wonder and promise of this splendor. All this was what Mr Pollock meant and said nothing about. His greatest moment was still to come, and nothing must destroy it.

Down the distant mountains crept the growing light, until soon there was a blade of golden light cutting across the whole plain at the mountain base, and behind the escarpment to the east blazed visible rays of glory as the sun showed itself at last, tearing the long quiet horizon clouds into silken rags of fire.

Just then another sense than sight joined in the tremendous arrival, and the air was filled from everywhere with sound as startling as the vision which grew and grew and spilled over the world. Up from the black lazy water rose the birds in salute to the sunrise. Their wings beat and beat until they seemed to beat on the very ear itself. Their calls made a chorus that veered and varied like the wind. The hard stout birds seemed to hurl themselves at the day. They wheeled and shuttered, stirring like a strike of life itself, and went off to taste the sky.

Madison was half standing in the big commotion of all nature. His empty gun was raised. His father reached up and pulled him down again. They could now see everything. Mr Pollock's face betrayed nothing of the high achievement of feeling which the dawn flight had brought him.

[184]

"They'll come back and settle down again," he said in his mild, grainy voice, "if we keep still."

Madison subsided. He swallowed. As thoughtlessly as a duck, he himself had saluted the day, out of an excitement older than memory, and a recognition of glory as near as his impassive father.

The light was now drawing eastward across the plains, and the airport beacon seemed to dwindle. Farmhouses began to show, little cubicles poured with gold. Trees stood plain. Green fields of winter wheat looked out of the receding twilight. In a few moments there would be no mystery, no startling grandeur, but only daytime, and a forgotten sun climbing overhead showing, common, the red rocks of the cliffs, the endless sweep of the plains, the smoke-defined town, and the mountains with their faint hovering clouds.

The ducks returned. Madison saw them before he heard them, little twinkling specks of black that moved together against the dove-wing colors of the northern sky. Then came their sound again, from everywhere, as though a cloud could be heard.

Mr Pollock nodded and silently thrust two shells into his gun and then closed it.

Madison copied him, watching his father now, instead of the flight, which came staggering yet orderly on the beaten air. Punch quivered, his nose lifted to the sky.

Mr Pollock gave Madison a half look and raised his gun in a trial sight. Then he indicated that if the birds came over them and started to settle on the river beyond the willows, they would shoot.

The river was chocolate brown, shallow, snaking its way around mudbanks of the same color which gave off a rich smell.

Here they came, growing specks along the silver reflection of the gun barrels, with silver streaks in the sky beyond. The air drummed. All sound vanished and only sight was left, tense, as the guns made their arcs with the circle and swift descent of the ducks.

Then, by a common power of agreement, they both fired. The shots broke the whole adventure in stunning strike, and dawn, and boy, and father, and sky life, and river world, blazed into an instant of ringing silence.

The flight struck upward again from the waiting water, and were gone beyond speed. But two fell, and they saw them, and they knew where—heavy black bullets with ragged wings from which a few feathers drifted separately so long after.

Madison jumped to his feet. He was charged with love for the birds he had helped to kill. All huntsmen from before his own small lifetime stirred in him. His teeth chattered with mindless power and memory.

But his father showed him in silent example how to break his gun and lay it for safety's sake on the ground, and lovingly, because of its exciting oily smell, its sweet smooth wood, its power of compressed dominion over living things. With a hand on Punch, Mr Pollock led the way through the little willow brake to the shallow water and beyond, where their game lay on the long mudbank in midstream.

Madison's belly felt full to bursting with joy. He ached with longing for even more happiness. He wished his brother Edwin could see him now. He wanted to be like Edwin in every way—his body, his style, his mind and his famous cynicism. He felt like Edwin right now, having killed some ducks out of the sky, and as he walked he spread his legs somewhat as Edwin did, walking, and made a rather hard-boiled expression on his face, looking ahead. This was more like it. None of that childish excitement. Madison retrenched his spirit, and did his best to seem offhand; the master of his gun, and of his power to kill, and provide.

Later they moved downstream. They had chances to shoot three more times, and did their best, before Mr Pollock said that they'd better think about getting back, as he intended to be at his office by ten o'clock, where there was other quarry to size up and bring to terms. He had his canvas pouch pockets full of birds whose blood smelled like marsh weeds, and whose inert weight bumped against his stride with the majestic bother of all trophies.

Madison carried three ducks by hand. They were, it was agreed, his first three. There was still enough baby in him to want to hold them forever, just as they were, just as he had made them, with their tiny head and neck feathering of green and blue fire, their stripes of white, black and brown, their leathery bills, their dear death. Punch was allowed to carry one bird in his important jaws. He almost pranced in slow dignity as they all returned down the river to the hidden car. All three of them felt the same feelings.

Mr Pollock unlocked the car and opened the back door on the left side. The back seat was covered by heavy brown wrapping paper— Mrs Pollock's contribution to the good sense and economy of the expedition. There they put down their bleeding ducks.

This was about nine o'clock. There were no mysteries left in the day. True, it was turning a little colder, for low gray clouds were unfolding from the east. But everything stood clear and simple, so far just like another day.

"Mad, you take the guns and put them in the car," said Mr Pollock. "I counted one more duck that we knocked down last time. I'll take Punch and go back and find him. You wait here, so's I won't have to lock up the car all over again."

All of this seemed reasonable to Madison except the claim of another duck. He hadn't seen an extra one fall. He'd have seen it, he'd been watching, he said to himself.

But one thing that was never done was to question the father— aloud anyhow. He took Mr Pollock's gun, which was left open at the break, and empty of shells. He saw the man and the dog trudge off. He went around the car to the other side and opened the front door. There he hurriedly put the two shotguns on the seat, side by side, making the same angle with their open chambers and barrels, muzzles outward. He shut the door on them with a vague feeling of forgetting something, but it seemed more desirable at the moment to get around to the other side of the car in a hurry, in order to watch the progress of the retrievers. He could tell where they were. Mr Pollock and Punch rattled and cracked through the tall reeds up the river. There were a few pauses, way up there, while the father would halt and reconstruct the angles of flight, sight, fire and fall. Then the search would continue. Finally Punch gave out his wheezing bark, at the very instant Madison was saying to himself, *They'll never find it, because there isn't one.*

Presently the two others reappeared from the blurred brown ranks of weeds and walked patiently back toward the car. Punch carried in his proudly lifted jaws one more dead duck.

Well, sure enough.

But Mr Pollock was short about his triumph. He had a good eye, a faithful sense of numbers, and a lifelong principle of collecting what was due to him. He simply trusted these faculties. Impervious to compliments, he took the duck from Punch, and leaning somewhat backward, walked heavily around the car to the right side and opened the front door to see where the shotguns were.

So it was that everybody else came to find out where Madison had put the guns, and how. Madison's gun was released by the opening of the car door, and slid along the mohair covering of the seat toward the floor of the car. It struck with force. The breech closed as the butt thumped on the floor, and what Madison had half-forgotten then took effect. He had not removed the shells from his gun. The impact of the gun stock on the floor jarred the gun sharply. One barrel fired.

Madison was right there, for he had come around the car to watch, and finally to take his place on the front seat.

That flash of color and sound—what did it do—go off?

The duck fell from Mr Pollock's hand. It trailed a trifle of slimy blood on the dried mud earth. Mr Pollock bent forward and made a long agonized sound of groan on the word, "Oh-h-h," and fell down, bleeding, too, slowly, until he was humped leaning against the car with his arms around his middle, his head forced back and his eyes closing from the lower lids up, slowly, shutting out the light of the sky and the mind, both.

He was alone with his younger son and his weight of authority now passed to the boy. Madison, as if he were being watched by a host of people, pursed his lips and pinched them with his fingers, and said, nearly aloud, "Now let's see."

But his heart was banging with sick hurry in him, and choking him in the throat. He wanted to talk to his father, but his father was gone, for the time being—he could see that—and he was afraid to reach him, for he knew whose fault it was that Mr Pollock lay there like something else, after that ringing explosion and the sudden strike of dream.

He knelt down and put his stalky arms under Mr Pollock's shoulders, thinking to lift him into the car. He could not budge him.

Maybe it would kill him to move him, anyway—echoing the Red Cross lessons in first aid they had learned in school during the war.

Plans occurred to him. Perhaps if he waited a little while, Mr Pollock would wake up refreshed from a little nap, and they would get into the car and go back to town, and he and Edwin would clean the ducks in the back yard, and, yum-yum, Mom would cook them, with an apple and an onion inside each one. Or perhaps Dr Dave Sessions would come by here duck hunting, and operate at once, with the heroic assistance of young Madison Pollock, who also happened to be there.

Or perhaps he, too, would simply die. He closed his eyes to feel how this would be. When he opened them again, he was crying and fully aware of what he had done.

As reality returned to him, he came into himself and saw what he must do. He managed inch by inch to move his father down to earth from the side of the car. Mr Pollock was breathing wetly. He seemed to shake his head blindly at Madison as the boy moved him. Now the car was free.

Madison put Punch on guard. The dog looked hungrily after the boy, but stayed where he was meant to be, beside his still master. Madison got into the car, and remembered the few times he had stolen rides alone in it, against every law of the household: no boy of twelve should be allowed to drive, think what could happen—and all the rest of Mrs Pollock's timeless obedience to the whimpering gods of worry.

He pinched his lips and again said, "Now let's see," as he re-hearsed the technique of driving. He started the engine, put the gear into reverse and let the clutch go, but too suddenly. The car leaped backward and then stopped, for he stalled the engine with too much gas. He started over again, this time swinging in a wide arc to turn around and head for the highway over the sand dunes, whose profiles were now blurred by the play of a low hard wind which had come up. Just before he drove forward, Madison glanced back fearfully to see if perhaps his father would sharply call to him, asking, "Where do you think you're going with that car? You know you are not supposed to drive it."

But there was no such threat, and he whined along in second gear, swaying with the lift and boggle of the car over the uneven road. On the back seat, the inert necks and heads of the dead ducks rolled from side to side in little arcs. Mrs Pollock's brown paper was moist and stained in places.

When he reached the highway, he stopped the car just off the paving on the shoulder of the road. He sat there, numb, for a little while, as three or four cars went flashing by.

Now let's see. What would he have to say if he stopped someone? How could he ever say it? He hoped nobody would stop.

He looked both ways. The highway was now empty as far as he could see. His heart fell with pity and relief, even as he licked his dry mouth in a panic of disgust over his great betrayal.

But here came a car, way up at the crest of the cliff, where, in a deep cut, the highway took its course toward the sky, and found its level to cross the great wilderness which led to West Texas and beyond. The car came fast down the long slope toward the bridge.

Inviting his own doom, Madison got out and stepped into the near lane. Long before he could see the driver he began to wave his arms. He ended by leaping off the ground a few times. He never realized that he did this.

The driver began to slacken his speed, and when he saw that this was a boy, he slammed on the brakes, as he said afterward, and did not overshoot the mark very far. Something told him before he stopped that here was bad trouble, which spoke so powerfully through that young, jumping figure alone in that big spread of country. The boy did not come to him, so he left his own car and walked back to find young Madison Pollock, with his teeth chattering and his right arm pointing off up the river and trying to tell.

"What's it, son?" asked the driver. He was Tim Motherwell, of the Soil Conservation Service. It was lucky he came along. He was a young man in whom the outdoors had reposed its secrets and its ways during all his life. At ease with the natural world, Tim was one of those who could wring an essential note of goodness, or hope, or respect out of people at their worst. He squatted down before Madison and began to chew on a match, not looking at him, but musing in his presence as though they were two men with all the time in the world to decide or exchange something important. He had noticed blood on the boy's field jacket. What might have put it there he was already imagining, when Madison managed to tell him what lay up the sandy road by the river, and what was needed.

Tim nodded mildly, but he lost no time. He pulled his weathered green Government pickup truck well off the highway, where it was a familiar sight, and returned to Mr Pollock's car. He drove Madison back up the river. As they went, Madison tried to tell him how it had happened.

"I did it," he kept repeating.

"We'll see," Tim replied, and wondered, like so many people in the next few days, what could ever reclaim this boy from this morning.

Madison was awry in every possible way. His thick yellow hair was tangled and upright, resembling the straw-like weeds by the river. His face was white generally, but even so, square patches of dusky-peach red tried to show on his cheekbones. His eyes were wild. He kept trying to put his hands on his round young thighs in composure, but they would not stay there, but would spring up in the air as though moved by counterweights.

"About there?" asked Tim, pointing to the terminal clumps of salt cedar which at last they could see.

Madison nodded.

In a moment they came to a halt and got out of the car. Punch was there, trembling with fear and strangeness, and stood up to greet them with a high, stifled yawp. He cringed in an agony of humble love, but did not leave his post. They came forward and Tim bent down. Almost at once he saw that the father was dead.

They got to town as soon as they could manage, and in ten minutes the news was everywhere.

If people did not say it aloud, they spoke plainly with their eyes. "Oh, that poor boy! He will never get over this for the rest of his life!"

In everybody's face, Madison read, "That is the boy who killed his father," and somehow a buried mythic purpose stirred in those who looked at him or talked about him; and awe was mingled with their pity, and guilt with their forgiveness.

After the three days—the rest of Saturday, all day Sunday, until Monday afternoon, when the funeral was held—Madison Pollock was in danger. Edwin knew it. The boy's teeth would chatter suddenly and for no immediate reason. By turns he longed to be with his mother, and could not bear facing her. "My baby," she would sob, smothering him with crushing sympathy. And then again, she would have hours during which she would exile him in silent grief and widowhood. He was afraid most of all that Edwin would not like him any more for what he had done. He spent hours awake at night breaking his will on terrible schemes to make everything up to everybody. But an imp of maturity abided in him, and told him how useless were these waking dreams. He must shrink even from them.

Tuesday morning he did not want to go back to school, giving as his reason that someone had let the air out of his bicycle tires. Edwin went to see, and it was true. The brothers looked at each other, both knowing who had done it. They did not discuss it. Instead, Edwin drove Madison over to school in the car, but he could not make him get out of the car and fall in with the tumbling boys who played touch football on the pale Bermuda grass of the playfield.

"One of these days, you know, Mad," said Edwin, meaning that he'd have to start school again sooner or later.

Madison shook his head. "Never. I can't."

"You can't?"

"Nope."

"Why not?"

Madison shrugged. He didn't know.

"How about trying, say just the first period?" asked Edwin. "I'll promise to be here when the bell rings after the first period, and if you still want to then, I'll let you out of it."

Madison shook his head.

"Well, then, what do you want to do?"

"Nothing."

The brothers sat in silence, staring straight ahead through the windshield while Edwin played a little jazzy tune on his teeth with his thumbnail. A couple of boys spotted the car and ran over to get Madison, calling his name.

Madison crouched down and said hoarsely, "Come on, come on. Let's go, let's go."

Edwin drove off. The other boys watched after them, and then one of them went loose on his legs, pointed a forefinger at the crown of his own head, made his eyes cross, and hung out his tongue, enacting the goofiness of what had just happened. Then they went back to the game of touch football.

Without further discussion, Edwin simply let Maddy stay with him that day, in the front seat of the car, as he went on his business calls down the valley in the interest of selling farm implements and checking up on servicing those already sold. This made an idle and drowsy day for Madison, and when it was over, and they were home for supper, he was ready to go to bed early.

It was barely half past seven when someone drifted with heavily shod steps up on the wooden porch and, unable to find the bell button in the dark, knocked once or twice on the beveled plate-glass pane of the front door.

Mrs Pollock pressed her cheeks with both hands and silently gasped that she could not stand another trial of any sort. Edwin caressed her shoulder and went to see. He put on the porch light and could see through the white net curtain inside the glass that a familiar figure stood there, slowly spinning his fawn-colored felt hat on his forefinger. It was Tim Motherwell, offhand and mild.

He came in and shook hands, saying that he just happened to be driving up this street, and thought of looking in for a second, to see if there was anything he could do, and to tell Mrs. Pollock that he certainly felt for her. At this, she raised her head with a hazy social smile conforming to the best of manners, as though to say that people like her should not inflict their misfortunes upon others, but the imposture lasted only a moment before her little face with its passionately trembling eye lenses appeared to dissolve like molten glass changing to another set of shapes, and she lay back in her chair, subject to the grief that pounded upon her from without, and made her say in a choked treble like a child's, that she did not know how she could go on living.

Edwin asked Tim to sit down, which he declined to do. In a minute or two, Mrs Pollock recovered enough to ask Edwin to show Tim the messages of sympathy they had received, and the long list of those who had sent flowers. Tim examined these gravely, still standing, while the widow watched him hungrily for signs of dolorous pride in the tribute paid to the stricken family. With his mouth shaped for silent, musing whistling, Tim read what people thought and said about Mr Pollock, and gave the papers back to Edwin without a word, but with a black sparkling look in his eyes which was like thought itself made manifest. It satisfied Mrs Pollock. She covered her eyes and wept again. Edwin felt ashamed of her, and then, for feeling so, ashamed of himself.

[195]

Well, he had to be going, said Tim. Edwin went out to the pickup truck with him, and the real purpose of the call became clear. They talked for about fifteen minutes, Tim at the wheel, Edwin leaning his chin on his fists on the open windowsill of the car. Their conversation was muted and serious. Tim felt younger, Edwin felt older, and both felt like good men, assembled in honor of what needed to be done for someone—in this case, Madison Pollock.

Edwin said, yes, his brother was in a bad way, and said something had to be worked out. Tim said he suspected as much, and with modesty and diffidence told what he would do about it if it were his kid brother. Their conversation had many gaps of word, but not of thought.

When the essential matter was finished, there was a long terminal pause, after which Tim, where he sat, jumped comically, as though he felt an electric shock, and said, "I'd better get a move on or my little woman won't act so little, time I get there. See you, Ed."

"See you, Tim. Sure do thank you."

Tim switched on his car lights and drove off. Edwin watched him round the next corner. The red tail light on the SCS truck spoke for Tim as long as Edwin could see it, admire it and covet the goodly strength it stood for.

The next morning, Mrs Pollock, in the name of what Dad would have wanted, declared that this time Madison must go to school, and ordered Edwin to drive him there again.

Madison turned white. "No, I can't."

"Yes, you can. Oh, what have I done to deserve— You know how your father slaved to give you boys a good education, and now, here you sit, and won't—"

Her brokenhearted righteousness welled up in her, more powerful than grief itself, and she crushed the boys with the very same love which had given them being.

Madison left the table and went to the back yard. There he was violently sick at his stomach. Edwin found him there, shuddering on the back steps like a starving cat.

"Come on, Maddy," he said, and practically dragged the boy to the car. They drove off, heading south toward the school. Madison set his jaws and braced his feet against the floorboards the closer they came to the red-brick school building, but Edwin, without a glance, drove right on past the teeming block of the school and its winter-blanched playing field, and continued on south and out of town down the valley.

"I'd gain his confidence," Tim had said. "I wouldn't hurry."

So once again—this time defying the suffering authority at home —Edwin took his brother with him, and did the same all the rest of the week. The brothers were together all day long. They visited farms in the broad flat valley, and while Edwin talked business, Madison was let alone just to fool around. They spent one afternoon tinkering with an ailing tractor. One evening they lingered with a little crowd of itinerant cotton pickers who had a bonfire going under some cottonwoods by an irrigation ditch; and to guitar music, clapped hands and country song, the illimitable twilight came down like forgiveness—for a little while—over Madison and everyone in the world. Sometimes Edwin took him along to have a glass of beer, though Mad drank only soda. Another time they called on a girl Edwin knew in the little town of Dexter, and the conversation, full of evocative memories and half-suggested plans for the creation of more such, brought Madison a wondering sense of more trouble, sweeter than his awful kind.

And then on Saturday—one week after Madison's first time out hunting—Edwin, having made a few preparations in private, got up at four in the morning and went in his shivering nakedness to Maddy's sleeping porch and woke him up, turning on the light and picking up scattered garments off the floor.

"Come on, get up," he said.

[197]

Madison was stunned with sleep. "What for?"

"Never mind what for. Get up. Come on. I've got your clothes. We can dress in the living room, where it's warm. Be quiet. Don't wake Mom. Turn out the light."

The boy followed his brother. In the front room they got dressed stealthily. It was exciting.

"Where're we going?"

"Never you mind. Come on. We'll get some breakfast downtown."

Edwin was dressed first. Waiting for Maddy, he sat down at the dining-room table, which bore marks on its brown oak surface of a strenuous life, and wrote a note which Mrs Pollock told everybody later she would keep forever.

"Dear Mom," it said, "don't worry. Mad and I have gone off on a job. Back during the day. Taking Punch along for the buggy ride. Be a good girl and don't worry. Love and kisses. E."

He propped it up against the crystal fruit bowl in the center of the table, where she would easily find it, for the bowl held her darning materials and her glasses. He knew, too, that when she came to his fond, impudent advice to be a good girl, she, in whom there remained no degree of girl whatever, would weep over it with famished pride, to see that the power of the family had passed to him, the first-born, now escaped into his own life. It was not cruel to make her weep. It was almost a kindness, for she enjoyed it so, and in these days it gave her solace to feel anything but the main dream of her shocking loss.

The boys went gently out the front door, and around to the back yard to Punch's house, which they had built together so long ago. One of the family mysteries was that they had never caught Punch asleep out there. He knew them now as they approached, and mildly banged his ugly rat tail on the floor of his residence.

"Come on, Punch, old boy, old boy," said Edwin softly. The self-important old dog got up slowly and stretched himself, first fore and then aft. And then with a prankish lunge he assumed the gaiety of a puppy, but could not sustain it, and soberly followed his masters to their car, which was parked in the alley. Edwin unlocked it, they all got in, and Edwin drove off. The night was black and empty in the cold streets of town.

They had coffee, canned orange juice and ham and eggs in Charlie the Greek's, without conversation, though not without communication, for Edwin could feel Maddy throbbing beside him with doubtful wonder. Edwin once turned on his swiveled stool to face Madison and cuff him near the ear—an action which said that he was not to worry, or be afraid, or in doubt, for this was still the family, doing its best for him, no matter how things might look; indeed, if they became too much for anyone to bear, never mind; there was someone right here who would stop everything before that point was reached.

It was still pitch dark when they went out and drove off again. They crossed Main Street, whose neon signs and traffic lights were dead, and headed out toward the east, where the road forked to go either down the valley or out to the river over the bluffs to West Texas.

Madison looked sidewise to question his brother, who drove. Edwin, though he felt the look, did not acknowledge it, but merely drove on in general confidence and repose.

At the crossroads they were slowed down by a traffic light which blinked all night long. Madison looked to the right, along the highway which would take them on one of their familiar days of salesmanship at the valley farms. But Edwin, resuming high gear, drove straight ahead on the other highway, which led to the river. Maddy's teeth began to chatter.

The first pale strips of day now showed ahead of them in the east.

Suddenly, as though between looks, it was there. With it came a colder feeling. Edwin speeded up as though to race the dawn.

Maddy saw the highway unreel before and under him. Where were they going? He put his hand on the door handle beside him with an unformed motion that he might open the door and, speed or no speed, get out right now. Why not? Edwin caught this out of the corner of his eye in the half-light of the instrument panel. He began to whistle a little tune inside his teeth, leaned over and snapped the door handle up to a locked position. Again it was an action which said more than it appeared to.

By the time they saw the river, its slow sparse waters were reflecting the faint early light in the midst of heavy shade over the earth. The watery course in the black nearing distance lay like tarnished silver knives, curved and jagged. They were driving fast.

Maddy, in terror, both did and did not believe it when the family car slowed down at the far end of the Pecos River bridge and took the sandy turnoff of the road that ran over the dunes, in the same darkness, by the same willows, in the same cold, to the same screen of salt cedars as a week ago this morning.

Edwin stopped the car and got out. He opened the rear door for Punch, who scrambled forth with his head lifted amid the marshy smells on the faintly stirring air. At the luggage compartment, Edwin unlocked the handle and flung open the lid. He took out two shotguns, a canvas musette bag full of shells, and two pairs of rubber boots.

"Come on, Mad!" he called.

The front door opened and Madison stepped out, against his wish. Edwin threw Maddy's boots to him. "Put them on."

"What for?"

"Put them on."

Everything was greater than Maddy. He was overwhelmed. He was numb, inside and out. He put the boots on.

Edwin handed him his own gun.

"No."

"Take it. Go on. We're going to get some ducks."

Madison took it. He could hardly feel it in his grasp.

Edwin led the way up the river to the blind where, long ago, he, too, had first come with his father. The day was nearing. Again, sky, mountain, plain and earth's own curve evolved toward the moment of glory and revelation.

Once again not only all light but all sound and all space beat upon the senses when the sun rose. The ducks were there again. They fled the shadows and streaked noisily into the lofty light. Like his father, Edwin stayed their fire at the dawn flight. The birds would return. To be ready—

"Load," said Edwin.

Madison fumbled with his gun. He could not handle it. Edwin took it from him and loaded it, closed it, which cocked it, and handed it back.

"You take the first one, Mad."

They waited. The older brother set his jaws. He knew what he was doing, and the pain he was causing.

Presently the birds were coming over again. Edwin pointed. Madison saw only a dazzle of flying black specks in the yellowing day.

"Now," whispered Edwin.

Madison raised his gun and tried to sight, leading the flight, which seemed everywhere. He was shaking. He fired alone. Nothing fell. He brought down his gun. His head was ringing. He looked at Edwin.

"Tough," said Edwin.

Madison thrust his gun at Edwin for him to take. "Let me go," he said in pitiful modesty.

Edwin shook his head and pushed the gun back in his brother's grasp. "You'll do better next time."

"I will?"

"Sure."

Edwin, whistling silently, turned his gaze over the sky.

What? thought Madison. And then this was astounding: powerfully like a wind, free and lofting, the idea blew through him, and he thought, *Of course I will.*

He looked at Edwin to find an explanation of the excitement which spread so fast in his being. But Edwin was immovable, watching the lower reaches of the sky.

"I will get some next time," whispered Madison. "I got three last Saturday, and I'll get more today."

Edwin nodded briefly. His heart began to thump with relief. Maddy's excitement could not be hidden. He could never have said so, but Edwin knew they had come here to put death in its place, and were going to succeed.

The Treasure

to Victor Bubin

Now let's see. Since I am not ever going to write it all down, it would be well to put some sort of order into my thoughts. This will help me to be certain that what I am doing is right.

First, then, I must recognize what a violent break I want to make with all that is expected of me; and I must face the fact that certain people close to me would necessarily find it hard to believe what they may hear of me, Archer Wilmington, Jr., who, if any young fellow ever had, seemed to have a clear course set for him from childhood.

Second, I must follow, from long ago to today, how I came to be where I am.

And third, I must keep it clearly in mind who it is I am addressing in my mind. It is you, Father, and I think—I must think—that somewhere, you know this and you hear me. If I couldn't believe this, I doubt if I'd ever have the courage to go ahead. But just as I was meant to find the treasure, so are you meant to hear me now.

I am living on two levels, to use the expression which is rather sternly fashionable among my friends at the university. In your day there, they probably had other famous formulas by which to measure their attempts at giving pattern to life. Someone told me there at Kingston that along in the 1920s everybody was talking about the *élan vital*. Well, if you had the "vital impulse," we have "levels of meaning"—and the more we can find in any simple little thing, the more profound we feel.

So now, while one part of my mind is flowing out of my past as lucidly as a little stream before rain hits it, another part is active in the present, and I see what is around me, in the bus station, and I think I see it more vividly because of that stream which flows out from me to you, wherever you are, Father.

It is a big, new bus station, and it is lighted tonight, as every night, with long pallid tubes of glass set against the ceiling which put a shadowless glare over all. We all seem to be creatures without substance because we cast no shadows in our air-conditioned terminal, where as many paths end as start. We are crowded together. The hours before midnight seem fateful, and many buses are due to arrive, many to leave. The stages of life all about me make their claim upon me. I see aged men and women who move slowly—they even seem to wait slowly; and what they wait for seems an open secret, as it always has been to mankind which having been born must die. I see children inhabiting with various degrees of destructive animation the abstract universes which they all invent for themselves, and which they impose on people about them, with varying degrees of success—and by success we always mean the evocation of love from others. I see the middle-aged, still busy with various pretensions of excellence and purpose, nicely balanced between ignorance and futility, as between youth and age. And I see the young, the youths and girls, alive first of all to their own well-being and beauty, and second of all to the excitement of chance in human affairs, sweetened by the certainty in each sailor's head, and in each girl's willful self-possession, the certainty that here: tonight: one minute from now: the big thing is going to happen, to change

[204]

everything forever, that will simply cause life to continue, and by their power.

Meanwhile, coffee is taken out of paper containers, and newspapers are bought, read, and, dampened by hold, are left on the waiting room seats, and doors open and shut, on what, and for how long, anybody could guess, and the odors of disinfectant float from the rest rooms on the air-conditioner's invisible beam, and anxiety goes to the ticket counter, and returns to sit down and wonder, and a heart is heavy, another one light and rippling for what lies ahead, and walking on patented floor composition polished to shine the sound of many feet rises in a sandy whisper to mingle with the words in the air, which are spoken to be heard. You will understand me, Father, if I say that I pray they are heard, for I, if not aloud, am speaking too.

Another thing occurs to me, and it will make you smile as it does me, too, I imagine. This is what my mother always thought of bus stations and traveling by bus. It was all right for those who had to do it, but it certainly was not for people like us.

But of course, this sentiment of hers would belong more properly to those other days, the great time of Used-To-Be, when you were still with us, and we had what she calls Position, which came to us from your great place in the Kingston faculty, which though it never made us rich made us what Mother calls Comfortable, and brought us the house I grew up in, and still inhabit, in a way, but not in the way that Mother still lives in it, for I know it is gone for good, while she hardly admits that it has been bought and sold twice since we lost it. How often I have seen her gazing about her living room in her rented apartment in Elizabeth, New Jersey, and watched her shudders of comic gallantry. Surrounded by some of her Things which she saved from the breaking up of home, she would say,

"Your father never intended for me to come to This."

Such a remark always made me angry for a minute, because it

seemed to imply that if I would only do my duty, I would rescue her from what she had come to.

But she would see the look I could not withhold, and she would laugh, and her eyes would mist with the prettiness she could summon to waft away her habitual veil of regret, and she would say,

"Archer, darling, don't stand there and feel sorry for yourself. We're doing the best we can, and nobody can ask more of us than that. Sit down, and stop being deliberately well-mannered, like every other Kingston boy, manners should be entirely thoughtless, and tell me what you've done to the dean lately."

This was a joking little contrivance to bind together Used-To-Be, when as a faculty wife she knew what deans had to endure from fellows like me, and the time of Now, when already, as a student living away from home, I was in danger of getting lost. By this she meant—though she could never bring herself to say it—that she was in danger of losing me. If this was a danger that simply came with the acts of life, like the commonest danger of all, which is the act of death, she would, I think, rather have thought of dying than of losing me, after having lost you.

You can imagine, then, how hard it was for me to think of her in connection with what came to be my whole life this spring—if your whole life consists of what you suddenly know you have to do for the rest of your days.

What this was, for me, I don't have to tell you, for if you are hearing me as I try to give shape to my desire, you must know what that desire is. It need never be mentioned, and to tell you the truth, I feel safer, and stronger with it, somehow, if I hardly mention it to myself. I just feel best when I am thinking of how to meet its demands as truly as it deserves.

Anyway: the season of spring at Kingston is all bound up with it, for me. You remember Kingston in the spring.

When you wonder if you can ever leave that which you love, it

[206]

seems suddenly nearer and dearer to you than ever before. This is how I felt about the university when springtime and my hope came to me together. I always regarded the yearly classes who came and went as if I were an old-timer; which indeed I was, for my childhood was spent on the campus, or near it, when you would let me come to walk home with you after your work. The university, in my childhood eyes, was there to last forever, and so were you, and so was the scholarship that I was bound to win, which would take me straight to my degree in science. After that would come the great career in the course of which I would change the world with my discoveries about the nature of life.

I used to lie on my belly at the edge of the campus lake with my microscope and "prepare" slides of matter from the rich slime of the waterline. Looking through my lens, I saw movement and pale color and occasional blank dazzles of the whole sky caught in my optical tubes, and all this thrust a deep stroke of joy and authority in my belly, for I knew I was then in my boyhood dreams the master of abstract secrets.

Human beings could be seen in just the same way, I was sure. I could hardly wait to grow up to capture them as specimens.

And in fact, the whole university seemed to provide me with a laboratory of life, wonderfully abstract, always changing, yet always the same—the classes who came and went as I grew up. When I became a Kingston man myself, I could smile at my image of the race of students, and see how astute I had been in my youthful regard of them. Kingston men always seem to work at approximating the abstract, in their conventions of restraint in manners, their famous haircuts, tailoring, accent of voice and the code which embraced any expression of behavior provided it was inconspicuous. To a quite wonderful degree Kingston men have always—at least in my time—managed to feel like each other. Despite all my scientific detachment, I came to find my image in them, and most of my impulses in all those common to the group within our Gothic quadrangles.

On the nights of moonlight in early spring, I would walk—usually alone—around the campus, coming in and out of shadow along the walls and by the towers; and I would wonder just how it was that so tender and fugitive a thing as the impact of a human creature could leave its meaning, in some quite impossibly actual way, in our very stones and vines, the pattern of our lighted windows and the shape of Gothic pinnacles printed on clipped grass by the rising moon. Kingston was the sum of all who had ever come there since before the War of the Revolution to feel the body grow while working to harness the mind.

Sounds before midnight came clearer the later went the clock. From my open window in the tower over the sally-port of Duffield Hall I could always hear the last train from the junction come grinding into Kingston station. I could hear voices emerging from the old gritty red-painted cars and presently steps coming up the inclined walks and then words making excitement in the air as fellows finished talking of where they had been that evening. Then silence would fall in suddenness as sleep struck down with almost violent power the healthy fellows who needed it in their well-bred exuberance.

After midnight came little winds off the meadows of New Jersey, bringing the start of wild flowers and blossoms; and on certain nights, when the wind was stronger, and from the east, I could taste the sea in my tower.

When my light went out I often traveled the whole campus in my darkened eye, and I saw you, Father, in many a lecture hall, and along many a walk, and deep in many an aisle of the library stacks. I saw you in your portrait which hangs in Steuben Hall since the alumni, after World War II, had it painted and put there. Having been painted from photographs, it doesn't look much like you, but I know what you look like, so it doesn't much matter. When it is viewed eventually by people of the future who never saw you, it will look to them like a fine likeness of a distinguished university professor in his doctoral robes and hood, showing repose, serenity and a lighted mind behind a clear blue eye—for even at several removes, that look survives. The artist got your ruddy color, too, and the beginning of silvery hair above your ears. The mouth, no, for he never heard you speak. Fellows who never heard you, either, often asked me about how you spoke, for older men remember how, and tell about it still. It is amazing to me, and, I always feel, a trifle disrespectful, that I am taller than you now. Mother says I look like you. She knows it pleases me, though I can't see it, but of course at Kingston we are expected to question everything until we come to our own conclusions; and whether these do or do not coincide with those of our professors is not so important as the process of questioning.

I counted on this, when, just about in the middle of this past springtime, I knew what I must do.

I went to see the dean about it.

He listened to me in silence. When I stopped talking, he made a ritual out of selecting a pipe from the handful he kept in his top right-hand desk drawer. He scraped it out, he filled it, lighted it, examined his burning match critically, softly blew the match out, laid the burnt match exactly in the middle of his ash tray, and then said,

"Archer, I could have, of course, an objective, even an abstract, respect, for your purpose. Knowing you ever since you were a small boy, I could hardly feel otherwise. But I wonder if—"

And he began to develop one of those monologues for which he is famous. His intention, in fact his duty, was to "bring me to my senses." He never used any expression so vulgar or unsympathetic. But in his arguments he spared me nothing. How—he gleamed and twinkled at me over his pipe, and his voice was grainy with droll wit, and his syntax was both original and faultless, and his tone was confidential as between two grown men of obvious intelligence and superior style talking in their club—how could I think of throwing away my scholarship? Did I not realize that it carried not only privileges but also obligations? Might it possibly be that I was rather comically subject to the gentlest form of dementia praecox which as dean for many years he had, with an amused smile, seen come and go with springtime in many an otherwise steady and knowing chap? Was there anything in my intention which my father might perhaps have held other views about? Did Grace, my mother—that gallant, bewitching and pretty woman—did she have any inkling of my thought? Moreover, how about that other, that larger, that seemingly impersonal but actually keenly watchful mother, Kingston University herself: would what I had in mind really be quite the sort of thing Kingston would ever have expected—with a smile he almost said suspected—of me? What, in any case, was so urgent about it that for it I would in the springtime of my junior year withdraw from college, abandoning every advantage which at some sacrifice by certain persons had been placed at my disposal? The young, he must, with every accent of respect mixed with whimsy, remind me, often had these little storms of revolt against conformity; but he would add, not without a sigh of pride for his small part in the continuing tradition of Kingston, it all depended upon what you were asked to conform to. In his view—and that of thousands long gone before us—what Kingston asked me to conform to was, when all was said and done, pretty well the best tradition of civilized life a chap could ask for.

It was odd that I had hoped to hear anything else.

I could have written his remarks out before seeing him—though I could not have delivered them with such an affectionate and drolly dry-voiced air of amused satisfaction. He even seemed rather grateful that I had brought him an occasion for the exercise of his professional powers.

I sat silent, trying to invent a way of departing without rudeness.

"Still urgent?" he asked.

"Yes."

He sighed and played a little tune with the tip of his tongue against the bit of his pipe. Then,

"I'll take no action," he said, "until you talk to Grace about it. You may trot over to Elizabeth to see her during the week if you like. I'll let you have the necessary cuts. You and your mother have always seemed very close, Archer. I'd trust her to advise you in the best way."

Here, Father, I must confess to an unworthy emotion. I had a leap of hope, for I felt that I had a certain persuasive power with Mother, and I intended to make it work now. I said,

"Sir, if my mother approves of what I want to do, will you agree with her?"

"Oh-ho: a trap. My position, my dear Wilmington, will have to arise out of—but this is academic," he said with an ironic smile at his use of the word. "She will agree with me, not you. And in any case you do not need my *agreement* to do anything at all. You may walk right out that door and go merrily to the devil without any *permission* from me. It is entirely up to you, in any case. But if you want my *advice,* which is wholly another matter, you already have it."

He stood up to terminate the interview. He had an uncrackable, tinny strength behind his cultivated signs of jolly tolerance. He was the enemy. He was the world. I left him. In my head was an angry question. Why did I have to bother to get approval from anybody to do what I must? But I did have to, for two reasons, I guessed. One was my youth: I was not sure enough of myself. The other was fear, mixed with my great resolve—fear that I might not after all be right in reaching out for what so dearly called me.

It was too bad that the dean was right about anything at all, but right he was about my going to see my mother.

I went over to Elizabeth, New Jersey, later the same day, taking the bus. I thought the world looked bright and fair. The cars streaking by in both directions made a ribbon of constantly changing and shining color. People in them looked like the cast-iron "men" in my childhood toys who sat smiling, stiff and bolt upright in an endless propriety that was touching to think of. How good people were. What order there was in the world. And the roadside restaurants, with their Old English oriel windows, and their ranch fences, and their air-conditioners camouflaged as Georgian stable cupolas with gold weathercocks, gleamed and invited and proclaimed "good" taste in perfect innocence and content. From them I had a reminder of Mother's apartment, for her place has just such innocent and false references to style. When she complains of "This," to which she is reduced, I cannot help agreeing with her, even as I feel cross that anyone's surroundings should have that much power over them. Why can't she accept the Edgemere Manor Estates as simply as the other tenants do? They all seemed content to come and go with the Edgemere Manor Estates as their focus of life, happiness and the future.

But of course my heart would sink with hers, as I in my turn would once again see the long succession of L-shaped red brick buildings with Tudor references at every third window and identical half-timbering on the street end of each block of apartments. One day she said to me,

"Archie, do you know what Edgemere means? —The word, I mean?"

"No, Mother."

"Well, *mere* means pond, or lake. Edge-of-the-pond. Tell me. Do you know of any lake or pond anywhere near this place?"

"Well, no, I don't."

"You see? I looked it up in your father's dictionary. That's what I mean about it. It's all so desperately—" She paused and gave me a chance to speak the word which seemed a little too vulgar for her as a professor's wife.

"Phony?"

"Phony!" she cried with comic relish, now that it had been said for her.

But what really saddens her, I think, is the uniformity of the units in the Edgemere Manor Estates. Whenever I come to see her I always remark on how charming she had made her small sitting room, with flowers, books, family photographs and your collection of little Italian landscape drawings in their gold-lined mats and gesso'd frames. She has two bedrooms, of which the spare is used as a storeroom for boxes and boxes of "Things" kept from the old house which she cannot part with, even to put them in storage, which of course would be expensive. Now and then she will think of a "Thing" which she has not seen for a long time, and she will begin systematically to hunt for it, going through carton after carton of her possessions in the spare room. These journeys past family landmarks give her deep pain and pleasure. As the years went by since you left us on that day to go into the army, the time of Used-To-Be grew always more vivid, for her, rather than less so.

She was startled to see me in the middle of the week.

"Archer! What is wrong!"

"Nothing is wrong, Mother. I have the dean's permission to come."

"The dean! Then something *is* wrong. Wiley Braxton would never let you cut classes if—"

She dwindled away out of my embrace and sat down in her bay

window armchair, and the dropping sun printed her with diamond shapes cast by the leaded panes. I came and sat down on the footstool facing her. She couldn't bring her fingers away from shielding her eyes, just yet. She murmured into her gesture,

"—More than I can stand. First, Daddy, and I think every day, day after day, that this will be the day when I will hear from him, or at least something about him, but then it never comes. And then staying here, hardly daring to go out to shop, for fear of missing the message. And now you, today, something is fearfully out of order, or you wouldn't be here." She looked at me. She was suddenly haggard. "Then tell me. I can bear it, I suppose."

I must laugh, or submit to the contagion of her love, which would weaken me.

"Laugh," she said. "It is all you have ever done for me."

I took her hand and said,

"Mother, Mother, please. Please, Mother. Just listen to me, and don't *think,* or *feel,* until I am done. Then we can talk. I have something wonderful and important to talk about with you. You can make me terribly happy if you will see what I see."

And then in a rush, hardly breathing between words, I told her what I must do. In my grasp her hand seemed to go dry and to diminish, until it felt impersonal, like a bird's claw, or even dead. Her eyes grew hot and dry and bright with horror. Her lips whitened. They grew taut across her teeth. She let me finish only because she had not the physical resource at the moment to interrupt me. I saw from the beginning, then, that my case was lost with her. Why did I always come back? come back? back? and always think that this time, at last, we would meet on common ground? But no. I was nothing of a man in her eyes, only the child who had come to life through her joy and pain, and whatever he did the child must bring her only further pain as he tried to go his way.

When I was done, she gave a gasp, threw herself upon me and

[214]

kissed my brow with a tempestuous hot sigh and then breaking into sobs which wracked her small body so properly groomed and dressed for the afternoon and evening, however empty these must be, she flew to her bedroom and shut the door and turned the bolt.

I was left to silence in the empty sitting room, where all the Things accused me by their fabric of reference to Used-To-Be, when we were all together, and I did as I was told, and had such promise, and nothing would ever end.

Why did I think I might, this time, persuade her with my healthy excellence, and with my love? I could hear her in my mind.

"Your obligations to your father's memory. Is this what he would have wanted of you? To throw away everything he saved for, and planned for, and worked for, to give you the life you always said you wanted, and that now you want to dismiss? Yes, and who ever heard of any of our family going in for anything like what you have on your mind, no Wilmington ever did, and I am sure no one on my side ever did. It may be all right for some people, but that you should think it would do for us—! Yes, and then, the university, my God, if Wiley Braxton knows of this, it will be all over the place, I don't know how I will ever face it, to think you would throw away the scholarship, and not stay to take your degree, and go on to honors in graduate school, and use the budget which we have kept sacred for this purpose, my God, yes, how I have slaved and pinched, giving up the house, and living here and coming to This, the Edgemere Manor Estates, just so you would be able to finish your education, if it is the last thing we manage to do, we must keep this sacred, it is all-sacred, my God, how can you do this to your father, Archer, how can you do it to me, to me, to me. . . ."

An hour later when her door opened she found me sitting in the dusk looking out of her Tudor window, while I watched lights flowing by a quarter of a mile off on the turnpike. Every pair of

[215]

lights beamed bright and sure as signals of somebody else's will which took them fast to where they intended to go.

When mind is thrown aside as an instrument of communicating, and feeling takes its place, the power that governs is as catching as disease.

Her wild grief and fury were displaced now by even more authoritative tenderness and wan pity. Finding a thread of voice, she asked,

"When would you intend to carry out this—this absurd plan of yours?"

"I see no point in waiting, Mother. Immediately."

"Now? Before the semester is even over?"

I nodded.

"And your obligations to your father's memory?" she asked, and I heard then the recital of all the arguments I had listened to in my mind in this hour. Virtue gave her animation. It was rooted in a familiar concern which in all honesty she saw as the dearest duty. She was busy with what she wanted me to be—not what I wanted to be.

So we had our intimate little epidemic of the same illness; and as I listened to her, I knew I must manage, for now, some desperate compromise. Looking attentive and regretful, as she talked, I sought wildly for some formula to save at least a promise of my hope.

"So once again," she said, "it seems that I am always the one to give in"—for she really thought this gave the history of her life. "Supposing I must accept this shocking plan of yours in the end, at least, Archer"—for she had come to her own compromise which would gain time and who knew what could be managed with more time?—"at least you must agree to complete your college work first, and take your bachelor's degree. Then we will see."

She had by now so weakened me with the powers of her feeling that my resolve was shaken. How did I know she might not be

[216]

right, Father, in her view of what I owe to you? Would it truly betray your sacrifices for me, and your hope, if I went my own way now, without further regard to what the family had always expected of me? I was being put to work, all over again, at the job of finding myself. I could not make a promise to her which I might after all have to break; nor could I break the promise I must make to myself. Therefore, my own compromise ran like this:

"I'll tell you what, Mother," I said, pressing her hand reassuringly. "I'll hold on for a while. I'll go back to Kingston and think over very carefully what you have said to me. I'll do my best to be true to what seems to me the truest thing. But Mother, if it should come around again to what brought me here, it will have to be faced. I wish you could give me your blessing and let me go."

"Go:" she said, "to what: to the first headstrong notion that comes into a young man's head in the middle of spring!"

She smiled delightfully, with all the air of wisdom and charm which she could summon. It was the best I could get.

"Well, Mother, as you say, 'we'll see.' "

"At least," she said, "this delay won't make the loss of the house seem quite so useless, will it. It gave us the trust fund for your education, didn't it."

There were two things in this—first, she was binding me to her world by alluding to sacrifice made on my behalf; and second, she was as usual reaching for peace by going back, through the memory of our house, to the time of Used-To-Be.

And as usual she took me with her, until I too, could see the house where I was born and where I lived my first life—the life of a boy. It was a life which ended on that day when you left to accept your commission in World War II. Beyond a boy's power to say I was proud of being the son of Major Archer Wilmington, Army of the United States. When I would tramp through the university, I would see your fellow faculty members, and I would say to myself,

"See, *you* are not on leave of absence from Kingston, to serve the country as an expert in your field. My father is a major. He wears two gold leaves like this one on my lapel which he gave me. You are not going overseas in an Army bomber, but he is, and when he gets there, he will win the war."

All we were told by the War Department—all they have told us to this day—is that your flight from Washington to North Africa by way of Belem and Dakar vanished over the Brazilian jungles and was never heard of again. "Presumed lost," they said, and yet they have never felt able to announce the death of all on board.

The colonel from the office of the Secretary of War who came to see Mother about it thought he was being encouraging when he said that men had been caught in those jungles for years and in the end had come out again, to be restored to civilization. I have often wished he had never given her that consolation. As much as anything else, it is this which has held her bound to Used-To-Be. I would want you here again as much as she does, Father, but after all these years, how can I think it could be? I do not feel disloyal to you in looking ahead.

But meanwhile, with Mother, on that midweek evening, I had to look back.

She not only found peace as she went about the sitting room to touch Things—she gave the effect of changing the subject, which was what she always did when disagreeable and threatening matters loomed. If she could get me interested in anything else, for the moment, however trivial, perhaps I would forget all about the disturbing affairs which had brought me here to upset her.

"There are so many," she said, "so many things I don't seem able to find. I've been going through my boxes lately—for example, do you remember the perfect little model of a brass naval cannon of the period of 1812 which your father kept on his desk? You used to love it so, you used to pretend to make it shoot, I remember, you always

[218]

used to imitate first the sound of the fuse—'s's's's—and then the 'boom'! That was when you loved Stephen Decatur so. I made you a little blue naval frock coat just like Decatur's, with white facings, and the tails buttoned back with brass buttons. Well. I cannot find the little cannon anywhere, and I know I could never have lost it, or given it away, even though I was in such a state when we had to move. Do you remember it?"

"Yes, it was my best toy that I could not have for my own."

"No, it was too valuable, it was a perfect antique scale model. Daddy thought then he might give it to the Smithsonian. If I don't have it for him when he comes home, he will miss it, and look for it. Oh, Archie."

Looking through me at the day and the hour when you would come home, she was brave and frail and secretly hopeless.

"We'll find it," I said, just as falsely as I would have said, "And he will come home again."

"Yes, well, I did find these," she said, taking up an envelope from her desk. "Some old snapshots I thought you'd like to have, taken of all of us, on the last day at home before Daddy left. Do you want to look at them with me?"

"No, oh, thanks, Mother, I'll take them with me, and look at them in my room in Duffield. I have to get back now, if"—I blinked and smiled at her and put up her chin with my knuckles—"if I am to continue the high degree of excellence so far displayed by me as a junior in Kingston University."

"You will go back, then, and stay on?" she insisted, in a sort of legal maneuver, to make a firm contract.

"I told you I would change my plans to the extent of not going away at once. I will keep that promise, until I know beyond doubt about my idea. But try to remember, Mother, that this is not a whim, or a little change of scene. This is what I hope to do with my whole life."

She let me go with a brave little shift of tactics. She kissed me lightly and gave me a pat on the shoulder, and winked back cheerfully the light of frightened tears in her eyes, and said,

"I'm not afraid. I know my boy better than that. You will think it over. You will do the right thing. You always have. I think all of us always have tried to, at any rate."

It was like pulling against actual tethers that bound me to leave her so.

But in quite another way than it did with her, the time of Used-To-Be put its power over me a few days later.

I returned to Kingston and put away the envelope of pictures. I did not want to see them. I was too raw in my feelings of defeat by the established authority of my two mothers to risk any further emotions for a while. I threw myself into my work, trying to close my mind against all that had moved me in that springtime, and though I knew my private day of reckoning could not be put off forever, I was tired and glad to have it postponed. Even so, I was glad to think of the few dollars I had managed to save in case I should ever need to go my way.

But one night a week later when I had come in from a walk around the lake, I took down my physics textbook to take one last look for a test to be faced in the morning. I was feeling fairly good—that is to say, so sleepy and tired that only the concerns of my foreground were important for the moment. My roommates were already asleep. I had had a good letter that day from a friend of mine at Radcliffe. It was pleasant to half-think about what she thought of me. The hungry lump of frustration that had hung in my belly since the week before was now only aching instead of paining me. I thought I would look at the snapshots.

Well, Father, there we all were, and there was the house, with its four white columns in front, against the warm gray of the fieldstone walls, and there were the little evergreens along the driveway, and the big windows downstairs and the small ones upstairs, with the window of my room at the corner, where, in honor of the war, at that age, I had hung outside a string of little silk flags of the allied nations. You were photographed with us not only because you were going away, but because you were in uniform, and we all wanted a record of that. There was one snapshot of me wearing your new cap. It was too big. It engulfed my ears, but I brought my hand to its visor in a salute anyway. It was a faintly embarrassing glimpse into the sentiments and ardors of a small boy in the fond sanctions of his family, and I turned hurriedly to the next picture, and saw the garden out in back of the house, and the gate which led through the picket fence at the end of the garden to the hillside beyond, and the little woods that rose all upon it, and the course of the brook that went winding along at the base of the hill. That brook, though it did not belong to us on our property, was the most precious thing of all to me. It carried water all year round, muddy in spring when it rained, cool and somewhat depleted in summer, iced and mysterious between its stones and little snowy shelves in winter. I remember how you said that you bought the property because of the brook. You said you had me in mind, for imagine what a fine place it would be for a boy growing up to play in.

The woods were my great forest. The hill was my mountain. The brook was my river. In my imagination there was plenty of scale to enlarge all these things. I peopled them for myself and I lived intensely the hours of dreamy invention which I spent along the brook with toy boats, and miniature forts, and, in the woods, tiny Indian stockades built of twigs and whittled branches. Best of all I loved the great rock that rose like a castle at the bend of the brook just opposite to our back gate, and a hundred yards from it. I loved it most in the autumn, when the leaves of the oaks on the hill were falling like warriors' shields of bronze. The leaves drifted down the slope and made a deep and mellow furniture about the base of the rock where I could lie and read and think. Near enough to my house and my people to be safe, I could yet be secret and at large in my own concerns out there by the rock castle. I gave it a name. It was the Castle of Torquilstone, in honor of scenes from Ivanhoe, which I had read many times.

On some days in spring, when winter was breaking from frozen waters to mists that rose into the woods from the brook, you could see actual shafts of golden sunlight coming down through the hillside trees. Some of these shafts always touched the rocky crown of Torquilstone. When this happened, I would stare and stare at the beauty and the wonder of it, until the mists dissolved, and there was nothing left to serve as the medium of the sun's own light divided by the airy shadows of oak tree boughs.

The snapshots told me all this again. They tried to tell me more. I would not have it. I put them away and went to bed.

But Used-To-Be was not done with me.

Late that night I awoke from a strong dream which made some reference to our house, and the rock, and the brook; and I struggled awake to remember what I tried to remember. It came. I wonder if you remember it, Father.

After we took the pictures that day, you returned to your study overlooking the garden, saying you had some last things to attend to. In a little while I followed you there, and I said,

"Come and play with me."

"What do you want to play?"

I said the first thing that came into my head.

"Treasure."

"How do you play treasure?"

"You take and bury some things and then try to forget where you put them, so if you come and dig them up again, it is a surprise."

You looked long at me, and then said,

"Have you any treasure?"

"Lots."

"Am I to bury some too?"

"Oh, yes. In the same chest."

"What shall we do for a chest?"

"I have a chest."

"What kind?"

"It is a nice tin chest, painted with colors and designs, that Mother gave me. It came with lots of different cookies in it. It is *called* a treasure chest. It *says* so in gold print on the front."

You looked over the objects on your desk—that collection containing so many items which I longed to possess.

"How big is it?"

"About like this—" and I measured off in the air about eight inches of treasure chest, four inches deep.

"I think we can manage quite a respectable hoard," you said. "Very well, this will take a little time to prepare, suppose you put your things in first, and then bring me the chest, and I'll add mine. Then we'll bury it."

It was a fine excitement that held me aloft in my breast. I put my things into the chest, and I brought the chest to you, and waited; but you dismissed me, saying,

"No, Archie, trot along. I'll put my things in by myself. Thank you?" you said, in the rising thanks by which you often had me leave you. I was suddenly sobered with new delight at the seriousness with which you took my game.

It was easily half an hour before you came with the treasure chest to find me. My impatience was so great that I was almost discouraged and ready to give up the game. But presently you found me in the garden.

"By the brook, of course," you said, carrying the chest.

I jumped and capered alongside you with happiness at your having the same thought as I, without any previous discussion of it.

"Now where shall it be, precisely?" you asked.

"Oh, there, there, by Torquilstone!"

"That great rock?"

"Yes, yes, the castle. If robbers come to dig for it the knights in the castle will fight them off and protect the treasure."

"Good enough."

You gazed about, considering the land.

"If this brook should rise in flood," you said, "its waters would sweep around the brookside face of the rock, and carry away the earth in front of it, and anything else that might be there. We should find our place on the uphill side of the rock."

It was glorious—to have the matter taken so gravely. I was so moved and excited that I almost had to run back to use the bathroom. But I stayed, and we got to work. With garden tools which you had brought, we dug a deep hole for the chest. When it was time to lower the chest into its neat grave with nice flat walls of fresh-smelling earth, I saw that you had sealed the chest with great discs of the red sealing wax which you always kept on your desk. It was a detail which gave the contents—whatever they might be—new, and incalculable, value.

We settled the chest and poured displaced earth back upon it and around it. We tamped the earth home. We left a good three inches of earth on top of the chest. We put twigs and old humus over the fresh scar in the ground, and we covered all with leaves of the oaks above us, and then we gathered up the loose earth left over from the operation and carried it to the brook where we dumped it in.

"The water will carry the surplus earth away," you said, "and nobody will ever see any trace of the buried treasure. Only you and I will know it is there."

I thought, Oh, why can't my father be here to play with me like this every day, and now he is going away to the war. No boy would ever know so well as he how to make things so real; for the

[224]

essence of wonderful play was to create by it as much reality as possible.

I could not help asking you,

"Daddy, what did you put in the chest?"

"That would be telling," you answered. "It may be that some day you will be looking for treasure—I'll have another word about that for you in a minute. But then you will dig this up, and you will find out what is there."

How fine. Such fine, settled plans for things in the world. Things were really arranged wonderfully, I thought—a small boy's feeling of satisfaction and safety. Then you said in a voice I now remember again,

"Archer, look at me."

I did.

"Listen to me," you said.

I did.

"Don't ever dig this up and open it," you said, holding my chin with your hand, "till you really believe you need it. Till nothing else will seem to be of any help to you. When you think that way, come here and look for our chest. Perhaps you will find what you need. That's part of what treasure is for. Hear me?"

"Yes, sir."

Subdued and robbed of magic, I followed you back to the house, toward the rest of that, our last day together.

These events are what my dream took me into awake. It was late and dark and quiet all over Kingston. I put my head out the big window of our tower, and I marveled at my rediscovery of what I had so long forgotten. For after you went away, and after you did not return, and when we had to sell the house and move, I was so confused by all the changes in my small life that the treasure by the brook never again entered my thought, not even on our last day at home, when mother and I made a point of saying goodbye to everything there.

But now: now I knew that, if only to touch again the last touch of your life, I should go back to our old house, and find the brook, and the treasure, and see what it was you put into my tin box so long ago—nearly ten years, actually—and through an act of childhood once meant so seriously, to feel again the strength of your mind and the steady humor of your heart.

Except for my test in the morning, I would have cut classes; but I held on, and after lunch, when I had no class to make, I borrowed a bicycle from one of my roommates, and rode out past Library Road, turned into Mountain Avenue, and followed that road which goes parallel to the Trenton highway and about three miles west of it. To my right the ridge of hills rose and fell, and in the spring afternoon, the hills were vaporous with blue shadows amidst the hillside groves of young green. I did not know who now owned our house. I rode fast, rehearsing just how I could come to a halt a few hundred yards before our driveway; and how I could hide the bicycle in a clump of rhododendron and climb over the roadside fence and disappear into the woods I knew so well. So I could come to the Castle of Torquilstone from the far side, and avoid seeing anyone and being seen by anyone of the house.

How thoroughly well I knew every step.

Yet when I came down our own hillside, and searched for Torquilstone I was a long moment in finding it. There it was, of course, but something was all wrong about it, and about the brook, and about the house, which I could see through the beeches we had planted in the garden and which were now tall and thick with their polished dark red leaves. My rock castle was only a small boulder, now, which reached hardly above my waist. My house, which had always seemed immense, a palace, to me, was only a moderate-sized suburban house, like a thousand others. The brook was hardly two footsteps wide, though it was there, there, that I had sailed fleets, and had fought under Decatur before the forts of Tripoli, and there I had launched voyages which, flowing through my boyhood mind, had come finally to the sea. How could it be that these places which once I had made great I had now quite literally outgrown?

But if, as I have been told, I am taller than you in my body, I was still reaching to come up to you in my mind; and I set to to find the treasure.

I scraped away the deep carpet of oak leaves blown against the hillside face of my rock by the wind and packed there by the rain and snow of ten years. As I came down to the spring damp of the earth itself, I released with my clawing fingers and the hunting knife I had brought along a dark, sweet, rich scent which took me powerfully back to the day when together you and I dug our treasure deep into safety. I smelled burial and resurrection, by which I mean the place of roots underground, and the break into air of early flowers—crocus, narcissus, hyacinth, the campanula, lilies of the valley—all the sweet-starred flowers that first light the dark of winter and that yet in their beguiling odors carry something of the moldy climate of the grave.

If life rested eternally in the earth, so did death, and both told me to hurry, hurry!

Over my shoulder a vagrant near cloudling drew away from the afternoon sun; and, as in the old days of my imposed magic, shafts of golden radiance poured out of the sky into the trees of the upmost woods, and down through their branches, and struck the crest of Torquilstone rock where in tiny veins of granite a myriad points of diamond light winked and shone with intimate dazzle. It was a powerful effect, for just then I struck the tin lid of the treasure chest. My heart took a tumbling bump, and my breath went short.

"This is silly," I said to myself, "to get so worked up over something a child and his father made a game out of years ago."

I was glad to be alone. It would not have done for anyone to observe a grown man, a junior at Kingston University, scratching away at the floor of the woods behind a rock by a little brook, and turning flushed and breathless in the act.

In another moment I had the chest in my hands.

It was rusty, but intact. The red wax seals were whitened by some deposit of salts in the earth, but otherwise they were secure. I was about to crack them open with my knife when I saw I was not alone.

Across the brook, standing in an attitude of grave regard, was a boy about ten years younger than myself. He wore a paper hat with skull and crossbones painted on it in nursery watercolors. He carried a wooden sword. He looked at the tin chest in my hands, and then raised his large brown gaze to look at my face.

"Have you been digging up treasure?" he asked with hungry interest.

"Why, yes, I suppose I have," I said.

"I wished I'd'a known it was there all this time," he said. "I'd'a dug it up myself. I buried lots of it around, but I never thought of that place."

"It was a good place."

"Did you know it was there?"

"Yes."

"What is in it?"

"I don't know exactly."

"Well, let's look."

It was what I wanted to do even more than he. But I must be alone when I opened the treasure chest.

"Well, no, thanks, I'll have to go along now, with this. Goodbye."

"Goodbye," he said. His voice in the woods by the reflecting brook had a note of unblaming sorrow in it, like that of a dove. All the disappointments of childhood sounded in it, and vanished without meaning. I turned and, feeling oddly guilty of having betrayed both manhood and childhood in being caught at my task by a boy, I scrambled hastily up and along the hillside, holding my tin box against my ribs. I found my bicycle and rode back to Duffield Hall. If I got there soon enough, I would have the tower room to myself, for my roommates were both out for the swimming team, and would be in the crowded natatorium until after five. I could lock the door and be alone to open the chest.

I found, when I opened the chest, that all my ancient contributions to the hoard were scattered amidst yours. I found again what I had regarded as treasures when I was young and owned magic: from the drawer of an antique table a broken glass knob which once looked to me like a large diamond; some chocolate money wrapped in gold foil; two knights in armor made of lead and painted; a gold tassel with cord from a dance program brought home one time by Mother; a small key meant to open what I could not say; one large and one small brass button; five detonated shells caliber .22 long; and a folded print cut from a newspaper of battleships burning at Pearl Harbor.

I felt like an archaeologist, excavating for the evidences of his own past, and turning up objects which in his special knowledge he can interpret to make a likeness of a lost stage of civilization. With an indulgent smile I put aside my own history and took up your contributions.

They consisted of three long manila envelopes whose contents varied in weight and thickness. Each bore an inscription. This is how they read, and I arranged them in the suggested order:

"To my son if he is still eleven years old."
"To my son if he is about sixteen years old."
"To my son if he is over twenty years old."

I took up the first. It was the thickest and heaviest, and feeling it with both hands, I had a notion of what was inside. I was right, for when I tore open the cover, there revealed was the miniature brass cannon of 1812 which I had coveted so longingly, and which had come to me instead of to the Smithsonian Institution. My throat thickened with memory and pleasure; and I gulped away the surge of boyhood that threatened me.

The second envelope was perfectly flat. Was there anything at all inside? I opened it and found two ordinary uncanceled three-cent stamps. Treasure, yes—with actual value, even though this of extreme modesty. But why stamps? "—If he is about sixteen years old," you wrote on the envelope. After some thought, I concluded that you meant to symbolize by these postage stamps a boy's joining of the world: taking up the common acts of communicating: not so far from becoming a citizen and a taxpayer whose most thoughtless relation to his government, perhaps, is the buying of postage stamps. Or perhaps, I thought, it was simply a desperate and comic solution for a small problem, when on the day when you were to leave for the war, you had greater worries than to find treasure for your young son in a romantic game.

But in this thought I was wrong; for your third envelope told me how truly I lived in your mind, and why it took you some little while to come out of your study with the treasure all prepared. I opened the third envelope and found your letter. It covered all four sides of two pages. How well I remembered your handwriting. I can speak or think all of the letter. I will never forget any of it.

Archer, my dear son,

this is addressed to you for the time when you will have crossed the threshold of manhood. God alone knows whether you will ever read it, or if you do, under what circumstances. If you find it too soon, please try to keep it against the day when it might be useful.

Today, as I prepare to go away to meet a duty that may be full of hazard, I find myself delivered from the constraints of conventional thought and even logical behavior. I've never gone to a war before, and at my age I'd never have gone to this one, if the government had not reached out to pluck me from my comfortable and obscure academic treadmill. I'll certainly never go to war again, and, smile as I will about being made a major, and being asked to put on clothes which I shall never be able to wear with any plausibility, I am impressed by all the unspoken pressures of tradition and occasion which come at us from long out of the past at a time like this. I, the head of a small tribe, am become a warrior; and before I vanish into the conflict bearing my shield and spear, I am moved to leave with my son and heir such words of counsel as seem necessary. If these seem to lie somewhere between duty and irony, you will recognize the manner as that which prevails in academic groves; and hear the matter with an open mind, like a good student. This letter may be only an elaborate way of controlling and spending the emotion I feel just now; but whatever, I address you seriously and with love; and I may hope you will listen to me in the same way.

When you asked me for treasure a few minutes ago, I wished that you were more nearly grown up so I could speak to you what is in my mind instead of write it to you.

But if I here address the future blindly, I must also address it with confidence.

Now: if you are like your father, a situation may arise for you when you will have an agony of indecision about a matter of vast importance to you. Should you, as sons sometimes do, happen to repeat the experience of your father, you may find yourself taking up a position against all the sensible people—the people in charge— the powers of your world.

This happened to me when I was in my twentieth year.

There was something I desired to undertake with all my heart and soul. It did not seem suitable to those who were then responsible for my welfare and my development. I used every means of my youth and inexperience to persuade them to my view, but without success.

If I had succeeded in my desire, I might have found all they promised for me in it—obscurity, failure, waste of my natural endowments, perhaps disgrace, and the rest. I have no way of knowing whether they were right, in terms of all the visible and worldly aspects of the values which ruled, and which I was trained to inherit and preserve.

On the other hand, who—even among those others, the powers— who could prove that I, in following my inmost want, might not have attained to greater success even in the very terms they sought to insure for me? This should be noted, quite apart from my own certainty that my inner life would have been a wholly different, a vastly finer, a more truly grateful one for the bounty of God, than it has ever been.

For I gave in to the demands made upon me—demands imposed with every mark of love and worry and respect for "the right thing."

Archie, listen to me. It doesn't matter so much, now, *what* I wanted to do and believed in heart and soul; but *that I did not do it* matters enormously. More enormously than I can ever confess to anyone.

So today when you proposed that we play together a game of burying treasure, there came into my mind a desire to leave here for you the greatest treasure I could bestow upon you if events should bring it into my power to bestow.

In other words, in this little cookie box I give you freedom, if you should ever come to find it here.

And even if you should not, it has given *me* some sense of

freedom, as I leave you for a long while, to commit you to freedom as I never was.

I will take the risk to believe that if you should ever want to do for your life something that lies in opposition to what others, even those close to you and dear, want you to do, it will be a good thing which you want to do.

Assuming this, then, I solemnly charge you to do it.

Let no one dissuade you.

Ask the blessing of God on your hope, and go to find its fulfillment.

If when the war is done and we are all together again I should ever come to be one of those who would oppose your best desire, I hope you will confront me with this document. I will honor it, even if I have forgotten the feeling of today— today, when I see clearly what my life has been and what in all hope yours may be.

Goodbye for now, my son. With my blessing, I am

Your loving,

Father

So it is that late at night I am waiting with all those other people in the bus station. You have told me what to do and I am doing it. You gave me strength to do the big thing. I do not have enough strength to do the little ones—arranging matters in an orderly way before departing, saying goodbye to classmates, having a cordial handshake with Dean Braxton, above all, telling Mother. I will write to them all. The one last thing I did do was to send, by registered mail, the little brass cannon to the Smithsonian Institution in Washington in your name.

It has been hardest of all to wait here in the bus station and not go to the bright aluminum telephone booth and there place a call to Elizabeth, New Jersey, and tell my news. I know how it will give pain to my mother that I have not shared my intention with her.

[233]

But her power, in all its pliant softness, is great; and offering it another chance to wield its pity and its pathos is too dangerous.

The shadowless light of the white ceiling tubes shows us all to each other in the waiting room. We are tired and exposed. All sorts of little truths and pitiful beauties show on the faces which are now too tired to bother about *being* anything. The old people, the middle-aged people, the young people, the children and babies, all live for me in a new way since I read your letter today. I'll never cease wondering, Father, what it was you wanted to do when you were my age. Wondering about you makes me look at those people around me now, and ask what lies behind their daily faces. And I know that because I am able to ask myself this, and to feel that in my work, some day, I must help them to answer it for themselves, I am waiting for the right bus.

The loudspeaker has just called it.

It is a westbound limited.

Others are taking it with me. We are given new spirit by the beaded voice that fills the glaring room. We rise and take up our possessions. Our energies return and give us again our public natures. We file considerately to the gate, we show our tickets, we go down the concrete ramp with its hooded golden floodlights, and we enter the open-folded doors and take our seats. Our engines are idling in a rich soft rumble. People of experience in travel are settling themselves with little amenities. The children have hardly awakened long enough to move from waiting room to vehicle. Old men and women are bright awake. The night is no stranger to them. Younger ones can feel their own hearts. When the bus starts to move, certain passengers lean forward and look ahead through the front windows, as though to take us faster and more certainly where we want to go.

When a young man knows where he wants to go, he must take his way, whatever it may be, against the obstacles not only within himself, but also against those outside, however these may be shown to him, in mockery, misunderstanding or love. Acting for myself, Father, and even for you in your desire abandoned so long ago, I like to think I may be acting for all youth as I go away toward my hope on the westbound bus tonight.

National Honeymoon

to Vitya Vronsky

Somewhere an electric organ began to play the trumpet notes of the Mendelssohn wedding march. The audience began to applaud, for at the same moment a sunburned, heavy man in a flowing gray flannel suit came out of the darkness beyond the stage into a spotlight. He came to the microphone with his head bent, his hands crossed before him in mock solemnity. Footlights caught a sparkle in his eye which flashed over the full studio with suggestive hilarity. He stood for a long moment, creating suspense for the whole throng, mostly women. Behind him on the stage was an orchestra. A sign in scarlet electric letters overhead read ON THE AIR.

Out of sight backstage, standing in the darkness, a young man and a young woman faced each other, trembling.

"I don't know why you had to go and do it," the young man said.

"Please, darling, I didn't dare to tell you before."

"I don't know why not. We've always talked about everything."

"It means so much to us," she said urgently, "and you wouldn't have agreed if I had told you before."

It was his habit to try to be fair, and he thought this over. She studied his face, guessing at his thoughts. In the light that faded

[236]

over him from the stage she saw that he was honestly troubled now, lost in a little struggle between authority and love. Finally he acknowledged with a grudging smile how well she knew him.

"No," he said, "I don't suppose I would have agreed."

She shook her head at him, and tears threatened to come to her eyes. "It was my surprise for you," she said.

He knew this was not an entirely sincere claim, and he whispered, "Here I get you to Hollywood for our honeymoon, and the first thing I know you drag me to a radio show and the next thing I know we have to be in it. How did you get it all fixed up, anyway?"

"Get what fixed up? What, darling?"

"Now listen. They met us at the plane. They brought us here. They took our picture, and you kept telling me to be quiet and smile."

"Well, you hate to be conspicuous, you know that. It would all have been much more conspicuous if we'd refused and made a scene."

"You didn't answer me. How did you arrange it all?"

"Oh. Why—the radio station at home did everything. So when our plane landed here this afternoon they were ready for us."

"I wish I'd known it before this morning."

"You mean before we were married? Do you mean to stand there and suggest that if you'd known, you'd have— Don't you love me that much? And us married just a few hours ago?"

He made a helpless gesture, conceding all that she wanted to know. She put her hand on his arm.

"Darling. Listen, oh, please be nice."

She motioned toward the brightly lighted stage, where the man at the microphone was changing his personality.

"Dearly beloved, we are gathered together," he said reverently, and then brightened, "for *another* excursion of *romance* and happi-*ness* on National Honeymoon, and this is your favorite father-in-

[237]

law, Gail Burke Himself, broadcasting to you from *Hollywood, California,* the honeymooners' *dream* city, over USA, the United Stations Association, with another *brand-new bride and groom* to present to *all* America, a fine young *man* and a beautiful young *girl,* who are going to tell us *their story,* and share their happiness with *every*one, and when *they* are *through,* we have some *surprises* for them that will take their *breath* away, and *yours too!"*

Backstage, the bride smiled brightly at her husband to make him accept such promises of good fortune. "See, darling?" she whispered; and then she clung to him for safety, for their time was about to come, and excitement, stage fright and strangeness overwhelmed them.

The orchestra began to build up to their entrance with brassy chords and flying runs on violins. At the microphone, Gail Burke Himself enriched his voice, and cried,

". . . ladies and gentlemen of America's favorite wedding party, *our honeymoon couple!"*

He pointed to the wings. Someone came up behind the bride and groom, gave them a pressing caress at their waists and sent them walking out into the glare.

Burke advanced to meet them, leading the applause. Low cries of pleasure arose amid the clapping when everyone saw how beautiful today's honeymooners were. The young man's hair shone like polished white gold when he turned his head under the stage lights. He stood with physical pride, in the new suit whose lines showed how comely he was and strong. He held his wife's arm, which was trembling. She wore a small flowery hat way back on her silky brown hair. There was an orchid on the shoulder of her smoky-blue suit. Her eyes were blue. Her hands gloved in white held her huge, black leather purse with her initials—the new ones—in silver. She

[238]

kept close to him, looking up at him for safety and forgiveness. Her face, lifted so, was an imploring mask of sweetness.

Burke observed this. He sliced the audience noise into silence with a sharp cut of his hand, and said as though confidentially to the packed rows of seats, "She can't take her eyes off him for a minute!"

The audience roared.

"She hasn't had him long enough," added Burke, and they roared again. "Aren't they sweeties?" he asked, pressing home the aching spectacle.

"Now let's see who they are, shall we, people?"

The crowd cried, "Yes!"

Burke turned.

"First, our groom. My, what a fine-looking young fellow, about six feet two, a hundred and eighty pounds—am I right?" The young man nodded. "Blond hair, good-looking suit. All right, what's your name?"

"G. A. Earickson."

"Aha! What does the G stand for, Mr Earickson?"

"Gustavus."

"Gustavus!" cried Burke at the audience. "Get that? And what's the A stand for?"

"Adolphus."

"No! Gustavus Adolphus, Gadolphus Astovus," chanted Burke in delight. *"People, do you love it?"* he cried to the audience, and his listeners responded with applause. When he could, he resumed. "What do people call you?"

"Gus."

"Adda-boy, Gus; mind if I call you Gus? I never would get around that Gavvovvus Gusdolphus routine. Say, you must be a Swede. Are you a Swede?"

"No. My grandfather was."

"He was? *Vas a Svaydish jantle-mann* from *Svayden?"*

[239]

"Yes."

"And what're you, Gus?"

"I'm an American."

"People, get that? He's an *American!*"

The people cheered back at him.

"Oall right, Gus what do you do for a living?"

"I travel in wholesale produce."

"Wholesale produce, you mean groceries?"

"That's right."

"How do you travel?"

"By car. I use a company truck."

"Where do you go?"

"I make all the valley towns."

"Aha! That's fine, simply fine," murmured Burke. "I suppose you have to be away overnight sometimes?"

"Sure."

Burke whirled on Roberta May and called over her head at the crowd, "She'll have to watch that, won't she, people? Hubby off by himself, who knows what he might get into, hey?"

This brought a kind of innocently cynical laughter.

Turning back to Gus, Burke said, "Wonderful, wonderful? Now tell us, Gus, how long you been married."

"Today."

"*Today?*" said Burke with sudden quietness. "You mean you have been married only a matter of hours?"

"That's right."

"And how have you spent the time between getting married and now, Gus—would you tell us that?"

Gus, seeing the import of the question, began to blush.

"Say, people, he's *blushing,*" cried Burke, making a magician's pass over Gus's head. "What could he have to blush about? Shall I ask him?"

Roar.

"Oall right, *oall* right. Gus, what are you blushing for—is there anything you can't tell us?"

"No. I'm not blushing."

"Oh, he's not blushing, eh? Very well. Oho, *that's fine.* Then just tell us, Mr Earickson, how you have spent the day."

"In an airplane."

"Getting here?"

"Getting here."

"I see. And what did you do?"

"Nothing."

"*Nuth*-thing?"

"That's right."

There was a dry edge to Gus's voice. Burke got it. He decided it was time to switch.

"Thank you very much, Mr G. A. Earickson; we'll ask you some more questions later. But now, to this lovely, lovely girl standing before me, holding on so tightly to her new husband's arm—let us ask you your name; will you tell us that?"

"Mrs Gustavus Adolphus Earickson," she said with great clarity and pride, to reject any mockery that might linger about Gus's name.

Laughing, bested, Burke struggled to recover in the face of his audience.

"Well, I didn't think you were Mrs Joe Palooka," he said. "I mean your own given name. I can't go on all day calling you Mrs Garruphus Astovvus Earickson. What do they call you, honey?"

"Roberta May."

"Roberta May!" Burke pointed straight at the audience. *"Isn't that wonderful?* Let's give her a hand on that!" And they did, to her dismay. But they made her a heroine, and she felt her heart pound more easily, and she looked up at Gus as if to tell him, "You see?

[241]

This isn't so bad—it's sort of fun, and happens to not many boys and girls in the United States!"

"Now Roberta May," continued Burke, "where did you two meet? Tell us that."

"At home. We grew up together."

"You did! Did Gus carry your schoolbooks back and forth for you?"

"No."

"Did he put your pigtails in the ink bottle of his desk in the schoolroom?"

"No. We didn't go to the same school, at first."

"Where *did* you see him, then?"

"Down the street. His house and my house were only a couple of blocks apart."

"I see. And did he ride by on his bike and take you for a spin?"

"No. He just rode by."

"Didn't stop?"

"No, he didn't."

Burke faced the crowd with dismay.

"Say, how're we ever going to get these two together?" he asked, and then turned back to his work. The audience was touched by the simple pride and dignity of the bride and groom, who just stood up there and said what they knew.

"Did he have other girl friends?"

"I guess so."

"Did you, Gus?"

There was a little pause, and then Gus decided to answer, and said, "Yes, when I got to high school."

"Now we're getting somewhere," said Burke. "And did Roberta May go to high school at the same time?"

"Yes, a class behind me."

"Did you fall in love with her then?"

Gus looked at him and kept silent. Burke shifted to her.

"Did you fall in love with him then? In high school, Roberta May? Want to tell us that?"

"Why, yes, I'll tell you. No, I didn't fall in love with him in high school."

"But you saw each other every day?"

"Oh, yes."

Burke turned in comic silence to the audience. They laughed in sudden friendliness; there was a sense that a silent wing of life itself was brushing through the big red-and-gold plaster room, and they stirred unconsciously in response to it.

"Well, when—did—you—fall—in love with him?" chanted Burke. "Can you remember that?"

"Yes, I can remember," said Roberta May. "It was when I heard he was reported missing in action, overseas."

The beat of the wing grew heavier. There was a second of absolute stillness. Presently Burke asked in quiet masterly calm and false respect, "Would you consent to tell us a little more about that, Mrs Earickson?"

She looked at Gus, who lifted his chin a trifle, as though to say, "Go ahead and tell him." Her heart thumped at his loyal wish that she do well, now that she was there.

"All right," she said. "Why, I was home from the office that day; it was a Saturday—"

"Pardon me, Roberta May," interrupted Burke, whose duty it was to bring out all possible facts in his interview, "did you have a job?"

"Oh, yes."

"What was it?"

"I worked as a secretary at the Building and Loan."

"And do you still?"

"Oh, no. I wanted to keep on, but Mr Earickson wouldn't let me."

"Wouldn't let you!"

"That's right," said Gus levelly.

"Why, Gus? Would you tell us why?"

"I can support both of us."

At Burke's gesture, applause exploded.

"Thank you. Now go ahead, Roberta May."

"Well, we didn't stay open on Saturday afternoon, and so I was home that afternoon, and the phone rang, and I thought Mother would answer it, and it rang and rang, but she didn't answer, so I went and it was Mrs Earickson."

"Gus's mother?"

"Yes. Well, she wanted to talk to Mother, and I said she wasn't home, and she didn't say anything for a while, and I said, Is there anything wrong, Mrs Earickson? And then she said, Oh, Roberta May, and then I heard her voice sort of close up. So I said I would be right over. Well, I hung up, and I went right over, and she was waiting for me on the front porch, sort of hiding behind one of the fern baskets out front there and crying. She had this telegram in her hand and she just shoved it at me, and that was how I found out."

"What did you find out?"

"It said he was missing in action over Germany, and it said they would send more news as it was available."

"Then what did you do?"

"I kissed Mrs Earickson and took her inside and we sat down and we talked and we talked—she needed to have somebody to talk to. There was a picture of Gus in uniform on the piano, and she pointed at it and said she couldn't bear to look at it. I asked her if she wanted me to turn it around and she said, No, let it alone. But I looked at it, and thought about things, and I knew I was in love with him. I thought it was too late. But I just couldn't get used to the idea of there not being any Gus, anywhere, any more. It left a hole."

She paused. Burke kept quiet, and the audience leaned forward, rapt. She resumed.

"So then I decided Mrs Earickson needed a daughter—she didn't have anybody else. I was there day and night, and we never gave up believing he was safe and would get back to us. But the funny thing—Mrs Earickson was worried about *me, too."*

"Why, Roberta May?"

"Why, you see, she found out I was in love with him, and she tried to make me think what would happen if he got back and wasn't in love with me. We just knew each other as kids before, you see, and his mother didn't want me to be let down. So she worried and she worried. But I didn't worry."

"You didn't?"

"No. I didn't."

"Why not?"

"Why, I said to myself, If he comes back, and he doesn't—*you know*—why, I'll just be sensible and look around elsewhere."

It was a relief to crash with laughter and applause at the innocent realism and strength of this statement, which now struck Roberta May as faithless so that she rode above the applause saying loudly, "But the real reason I didn't worry is because I just knew he would feel the way I did when he got back."

"How did you know that?"

"I don't know. I just did."

"And did he?"

"Even before he got back."

"He did? Tell us!"

"Why, when he escaped back through France and got back to his outfit, he wrote to Mrs Earickson, and at the end of the letter, he

[245]

said, Give my love to everybody, and especially Roberta May when you see her. So I knew then."

"So what did you do?"

"So I began writing to him regularly, and he began answering, and that was all there was to it."

"Isn't—that—wonderful! *Come on, everybody!*" The audience obliged with deafening applause. Burke added, "And when he got home, what did he do?"

She was puzzled a little, and smiled with diffidence. Burke coaxed her.

"Come on, Bridey, what did he do when he saw you?"

"Oh," she said. "Why, he shook hands."

A short laugh.

"Didn't he kiss you?"

"Not right away."

"He *didn't*? When *did* he?"

"It took him two weeks, about."

"Two weeks to make up your mind to kiss a honey chile like this one! What are we coming to?"

"Oh, no," said Roberta May with reproof, "he was serious. He wanted to be sure."

"Serious—wanted to be sure. *People, do you love it?*" demanded Burke, and they did. "Wonderful, wonderful," he continued. "And then did he pop the question?"

"Oh, no, not then. We went together, but we got engaged just last year."

"You waited all that time? Why'd you wait?"

She looked down as though in utmost modesty over something which she could confess, if at all, in the most refined way.

"Why," she finally said, "we couldn't afford to get married at first."

Oddly, there was an instant of fixed silence, and everyone seemed to feel ashamed. Burke was equal to this failure, and said reassuringly, "But you finally made it, didn't you, and got engaged? Will you tell us how you announced it?"

She brightened at once, happy and proud of what she could remember and tell.

"Oh, why, yes—we had a party at my house for all my girl friends. It was cute."

"Cute, so're you," said Burke, imitating a cartoon convention of a bashful boy who scrapes his bare toe in the dirt and twists from side to side. "What'd you do?"

"Why, Mother helped me fix it up, and we had all the drapes drawn, and candles, and refreshments, and—this was the cutest part —we had the mantelpiece in the living room fixed up with a wide white satin ribbon painted with gold paint, and it said, Gus and Roberta May, June twenty-second. And on the mantelpiece there was a toy white kitten just like it was just getting out of a bag—we had a brown paper bag tipped over, and that was our idea to tell the news."

Burke clutched his brow. "You mean *the cat was out of the bag?* Is that what it meant?"

"Yes."

Burke whirled on the audience.

"D'you get it, people?" They did. "Isn't it wonderful? Thank you, Roberta May, thank you. And now—" He turned to Gus. "Now, Gus, can you tell us a little something about how you courted this lovely, lovely bride of yours? Could you tell us a little about that, h'm?"

"We just had dates, I guess."

"Aha, dates. And what did you do on your dates?"

"Oh, ride out in the country, mostly."

"Use a little moonlight, and play the radio, is that right? Park under some trees and thissa and thatta, like all the boys and girls, h'm?"

Gus murmured something. Nobody could hear it.

"What was that? A little louder, please—right here, right into the microphone, please."

"I said, yes, I suppose so."

"Thank you. And what else did you do on your dates? Go to the movies?"

"Yes."

"Fine. Fine. Tell me, Gus, did you ever have a fight over anything? You know, little lovers' quarrels, disagreements?"

How hungry the listeners were to taste the experience of that pair of lives.

"Well, sure, I guess so, yes."

"Oh, you did, eh? What about?"

"Oh, little things—they didn't mean anything."

"Like what, though, son? Tell us."

"I told you they didn't mean anything," said Gus.

"Oh, so you won't talk, eh?" snarled Burke in a burlesque of severity, because what he and his national instrument feared most was a moment's silence.

He was saved by a flushed inspiration from another quarter. Roberta May, swept along by the contagion of the moment, broke in, saying, "We had quite a row over that job question. I was really worried, there, for a while."

"Sweet-heart!" cried Burke. "Tell us!"

She felt lightheaded, but even so, she knew now that she was betraying her husband in public. Trembling for what she did, she could not, under the lights, the power, the applause, the national hookup, help doing it.

"Why, he sprang it on me without warning," she said, "that when we got married I would have to quit my job. So I said I didn't want to, he'd be gone all day, what would I do all day, and I said I could help with payments on the house, and our things, and besides, I liked my job, it brings you in touch with lots of people and everything. So I said no"

"What did he do?"

"Nothing. He just didn't come around, or call up or anything."

"Why, Gus, you old *meanie*," said Burke, trying to make him laugh. Sick for her betrayal, Gus decided to share in it for her sake. He laughed.

"Go on, go on, I can hardly stand it," Burke said to her. "Did you ever marry the guy?"

Smiling, she went on, enjoying the occasion now to the fullest.

"So I went and I asked Mrs Earickson what to do. She said to wait a few days, and if he didn't really mean it, he would get over it by then. But if he did mean it, then he wouldn't get over it, and I would have to make up my mind which meant more to me —keeping my job, or getting married to him."

The outcome was already known, and Burke turned out front with his familiar, *"People, do you love it?"* and when they answered him as he wanted, he took it as love for himself, and made a cozy face and hugged himself.

But Roberta May could not quit. She said, bright and charming, as though talking on the telephone to an intimate friend, instead of over a microphone to the nation, "So I finally said, all right if that's the way you feel about it, I'll give up my job, but I hope we have a lot of babies right away, I said, just to give me something to do, I said."

There was a shock of silence, and then the crowd took a meaning that she had not meant. They shrilled hysterically.

Burke began to sweat. The thing could get out of hand. They could get put off the air. He yelled above the storm.

"Wonderful, wonderful! A *wonderful* little girl, here, all right, and a fine boy. We wish them *all* happiness and success, and in a minute we will prove just how much we mean it, but in the meantime an important message from our sponsor."

No chains held the Earicksons there. No guards restrained them. There was free passage off the stage, and out to the alley, across the parking lot, to a bus line. But they stood there under the light waiting to be told what to do next.

After the sponsor, the orchestra played again, then faded down, while Gail Burke Himself returned to the microphone. The stage lights slowly darkened, and white spotlights came up on the bride and groom and Burke. The auditorium was hushed to a panting stillness, for everyone knew what was coming.

Dimly off the other side of the stage Gus and Roberta May could see movement. More people were gathering out there in the shadows beyond the silver velvet curtains.

From the audience came an almost visible wave of emotion. More than a thousand eyes glittered with material desires.

"And now," cried Gail Burke Himself, "we want to do our part to make *today's* National Honeymoon the *greatest* one *ever yet,* and I feel humbly grateful that it falls to me to speak for all America's families and families-to-be, in presenting today's wedding presents to our guests of honor, Mr and Mrs Gustavus Adolphus Earickson— *got it that time, eh, boy?* So let's move on to the wedding presents and see what we've got for you!"

The orchestra played a smashing chord.

"*First,* placed at the free disposal of the bride and groom during their entire stay in Hollywood, a super-de-luxe convertible sports coupe with all expenses maintained by the proprietors, the Wil-Bev Motoria!"

A young man with hair like gold leaf over scrolled carving, dressed in a page's scarlet uniform, stepped out from the far wings holding a large colored picture of such a convertible coupe. A spotlight hit him like lightning. There was applause; he stepped back and disappeared.

Each item, heralded by a blast from the stage band, was exhibited in fact or effigy by the uniformed pages.

"Next, for the groom," chanted Burke, "two complete changes of sports clothes, presented by The Male, Incorporated, of Hollywood!" The garments made their appearance while the audience avidly imagined Gus as he would look in his new clothes.

"And now for our lovely bride. Wait till we put her eyes out with this, a lovely, lovely half-carat solitaire diamond ring from Lydia Lennox, Limited, Fine Jewels, of New York, Miami and Hollywood!" And as the gray velvet box was thrust into Roberta May's hands, sighs rose like a prayer.

They rose higher and higher, sometimes with applause, as the catalogue continued: fresh corsages, for day and evening, every day, for the bride; a honeymoon patio suite for two weeks at the Beverly-Westwood Hotel; a conducted tour of the motion-picture studios, with autographs guaranteed and lunch with favorite stars; a chest of flat silver specially monogrammed; one dozen silk sheets with lace trimming and embroidered initials; and more; and more.

"And now, Roberta May, you must have something in your heart you want more than anything else. What is it? Tell us on National Honeymoon, and if we can possibly give it to you, we will! Can you tell us?"

She licked her lips. She looked at Gus where he stood beside her with his head bent, his legs spread, as though to be strong under assault. They were beaten and stunned with munificence. He shook his head to tell her that he was out of this.

"Why, yes," she said. "Some day, when we can afford it, I want a special kind of room in my house—we have the *room,* I mean, but there's a certain way I want it done. There's this extra room, and I

[251]

want two sides of it paneled in knotty pine, and the other two sides of it papered in something bright, and the ceiling the same way. I want a fireplace in it, and a solid-color carpet all over, and drapes just like the wallpaper so the wall where the windows are would all look alike?"

"What, no furniture?" asked Burke.

"Why, yes, we would get some red-leather furniture, because my husband would like that."

"What would you do in this room, Roberta May, tell us that?"

"Oh, why, *everything*, I—"

The audience laughed. She flushed.

"Oh, I don't mean *everything*, I—"

They laughed again, harder than ever.

She tried to rise with her voice over the crowd.

"I mean play cards, and have buffet suppers, and read, and just talk."

"Oh, I see, just talk, eh? You and Gus have a lot to talk about?"

"We just love to just sit and talk."

She confessed so much in this, so quietly, that for a moment the snickering in the big hall was hushed. When the thought and its meaning came home to everyone, a wave of applause began with some sensible woman's hard, virtuous, single handclap, and spread in a roar through the house. Burke, after a glance at the clock, let it ride for a few seconds, and then he stopped it with his hands.

"Well, Roberta May, I'll tell you what National Honeymoon is going to do for you. We are going to see that that room is decorated and furnished just the way you have described, and just the way you want it done! *Would you like that?*"

She brought her hands together and seemed to pray. Her eyes misted. Her voice quivered.

"Oh, yes, Mr Burke—"

"Fine, fine," Burke said, with a look at the clock, whose hand was falling toward the end of time. "And now to wind up, we have a lovely, lovely gift for our guests of honor on National Honeymoon today, Mr and Mrs Gustavus Earickson of New Mexico—two sets of special trousseau garments exquisitely handmade. Here they are—*think how they'll look in these!*"

He pointed dramatically and the pages came to center stage, one bearing a long transparent black silk nightgown with much lace and embroidery, and a flesh-colored silk negligee; the other bearing a pair of red silk pajamas and a blue silk robe.

The garments swam in mid-air, fantastically animated by the pages as they walked; an illusion of life filled the nuptial vestments and erotic images began to glow in the heads of Burke's public, while all eyes were fixed on Gus and Roberta May. The young couple bowed their heads in confusion. Applause rolled over them in unnecessary sanction. Until the end of the program, the pages stood in sight, holding the symbolic garments.

"And now, Gus and Roberta May, and ladies and gentlemen of National Honeymoon, here in the Hollywood studios of the United Stations Association, and all across America, I see that our time on today's Honeymoon is just about over. But before we play our Grand Recessional, we have one more little remembrance for our happy couple here today, and here it is—"

Burke pointed to the last page, who, to the sound of tiny, tinkling musical bells playing a nursery tune, wheeled a baby carriage out on the stage and over to the group in the center, while in climax, a storm of cries and laughs and beating of palms arose.

"—a brand-new Storkmaster Baby Coach, *big enough for twins,* if our happy couple *should* have occasion to use it, God bless them! *How about it, people, do you love it?* Goodbye, goodbye, and until tomorrow's National Honeymoon, this is Gail Burke Himself saying—Goodbye-Now."

The music rolled up with organ and orchestra, and the crowd

[253]

whistled and called and clapped in exhaustion and fulfillment, and at thirty seconds before four o'clock National Honeymoon went off the air.

Late, late that night, Gus and Roberta May lay sleeping in a patch of light from the waning moon which shone through the window of the hotel suite whose daily rate was equal to a week's pay at home.

The moonlight moved slowly and came to rest on their faces. In his sleep, Gus passed his hand across his eyes against the quiet brightness, and the act awakened him. He found that he was gazing at Roberta May, who was sleeping with her cheek on her hand, with tears going slowly down her face in the moonlight.

He wanted to touch her tears with his fingers, softly so as not to awaken her. But he was clumsier than he knew, and his touch awoke her. She threw her arm upon him and fell to his shoulder sobbing like a child.

He asked her what was the matter.

She pressed her face against his breast and shook her head. He knew that in a few minutes she would try to tell him; and she did.

She said she was sorry with all her heart for what they had given away that day.

It was theirs alone, and smilingly they had let it be given to everybody else—their very own love story.

"I want it to belong just to ourselves," she sobbed. "And it's too late now."

"Hush. Hush."

"It was all my fault. I started it all. And I told out loud all the things that meant so much to us, just us. Talk, talk, talk. I just kept on talking. And some of the things I said!" She choked with grief and pity for what was gone. "The way everyone laughed at them!"

"Ro, honey."

"Why did you let me?"

He would have thought that this would make him angry; but not at all; a wave of choking tenderness went through him.

"Never mind," he said softly, "never mind, never mind, never mind, never mind."

"If we could only get it back!" she sobbed.

He thought for a moment.

"Do you want me to?" he asked against her cheek.

"You can't."

"Yes I can. Most of it. The important part of it."

She stopped crying and rose to look at him in the moonlight. "You're crazy," she said.

"Will you leave it all to me? No matter what?"

She leaned down to him again and rested her head on his heart in aching humility.

"Forever and ever, in everything," she said.

She fell asleep again before he did. He now knew that things could happen to two people together which nobody else would understand, and that yesterday's experience was one of them; for if to marry each other did not mean to marry the very world, in its terms as well as theirs, what did it mean? Now everything took its proper place in the good knowledge that among the great things that had come to them were the power and the desire to forgive each other and be forgiven, for all of their lives.

At four o'clock the next afternoon Gus and Roberta May were waiting at the stage door. Presently the musicians, the attendants and the star of National Honeymoon came through the stage door after their day's work, talking it over.

"How *was* I?" asked Burke.

"But wonderful, Gail," one of the attendants assured him wearily.

"I don't know—yesterday was *tougher,* but it was somehow better. Say, look who's here!"

Gus came forward.

"Mr Burke," he said, while Roberta May, proud of what he had made her understand, nodded yes, yes, yes, "we've come to return all the things. Here." Gus put the jeweler's velvet box into Burke's hand.

"Return—the boy is *but mad!*" cried Burke, consulting his fellow showmen with a comic look. They stared back at him impassively. Something in them began to rejoice.

"Yes," said Gus, "we left all the other presents at the hotel when we checked out, and the car is back at the garage, and you needn't send the things to us at home. If you do we'll send them back."

"You can't do this to me!" snapped Burke. "In all my *years* on National Honeymoon a thing like this has *never* happened to me. Think if it ever got *around.* You people here—" he swept the other members of the show with a fierce look "—you people just keep this quiet, hear?"

But someone laughed, "Ha!" and one or two in the little throng whistled approval at Gus.

"And the room," insisted Burke, "and the furniture. You said you *wanted* all that!" He was almost pleading.

"Well, if we do," said Gus, "I'll buy what we need, and if we can't afford it yet, we'll wait till we can."

Burke stared at everyone, his heavy, tanned face sagging tragically.

Roberta May felt a pang for him. "Never mind, Mr Burke," she said with sweetness. At that final punishment, everyone else laughed out loud.

"All right, Ro," said Gus. "Come on." He took her away.

They kept in touch with everybody back home by post card every few days, and had a glorious time on their own for the rest of their honeymoon.

PART
THREE

The Surgeon and the Nun

Here you are. I haven't thought of this for thirty years. I don't know what called it to mind. I'll tell you anyway.

When I was a young doctor just out of internship, I left Chicago to come West, oh, for several reasons. I'd worked hard and they were afraid my lungs might be a little weakened, and then besides, I've always been independent and wanted to get out on my own, and I'd seen enough of the society doctors back there. Anyway, I came on, and heard of a new section of country in New Mexico, opening up, down toward Texas, and thinks I, I'll just go and see about it. The hottest day I ever spent, yes, and the next night, and the next day too, as you'll see.

The railroad spur had been pushing down south through the Pecos Valley, a few miles a week; and it was in July that I got on the train and bought a ticket for Eddy, the town I was thinking about trying.

The track was completed all the way, by then; but they had a lot of repairing to do all the time, and no train schedule was maintained, because we'd move, and crawl, and then stop, baking, with nothing but dust to breathe, white dust like filtered sunlight; outside the car window was naked land—with freckles. I remember thinking: spotty bushes and gravel. Above, a blue sky like hot metal. The heat swam on the ground.

You couldn't sleep or read or think.

There was nobody to talk to in the car.

Two seats across the aisle from me was a Sister of Mercy, sitting there in her black robes, skirts and sleeves, and heavy starch, and I wondered at the time, How on earth can she stand it? The car was an oven. She sat there looking out the window, calm and strengthened by her philosophy. It seemed to me she had expressive hands; I recalled the sisters in the hospital in Chicago, and how they had learned to say so much and do so much with their skilled hands. When my traveling nun picked up a newspaper and fanned herself slowly, it was more as if she did it in grace than to get cool.

She was in her early thirties, I thought, plump, placid and full of a wise delicacy and, yes, independence, with something of the unearthly knowingness in her steady gaze that I used to see in the Art Institute—those portraits of ladies of the fifteenth century, who look at you sideways, with their eyebrows up.

She wore glasses, very bright, with gold bars to them.

Well, the train stopped again.

I thought I couldn't stand it. When we moved, there was at least a stir of air, hot and dusty; but at that, we felt as if we were getting some place, even though slowly. We stopped, and the cars creaked in the heat, and I felt thick in the head. I put my face out the window and saw that we had been delayed by a work gang up ahead. They were laborers from Mexico. Aside from them, and their brown crawlings up and down the little roadbed embankment, there was nothing, no movement, no life, no comfort, for miles. A few railroad sheds painted dusty red stood by the trackside.

I sat for ten minutes; nothing happened. I couldn't even hear the sounds of work, ringing pickaxes or what not; I felt indignant. This was no way to maintain a public conveyance!

It was around one o'clock in the afternoon.

Mind you, this was 1905; it isn't a wilderness any more out here. Oh, it was then. Every time I looked out at the white horizon my heart sank, I can tell you. Why had I ever left Chicago?

Then I wondered where the Sister was traveling to.

It was strange how comforting she was, all of a sudden. I had a flicker of literary amusement out of the Chaucerian flavor of her presence—a nun, traveling, alone, bringing her world with her no matter where she might be or in what circumstance; sober, secure, indifferent to anything but the green branches of her soul; benign about the blistering heat and the maddening delay; and withal, an object of some archaic beauty, in her medieval habit, her sidelong eyes, her plump and frondy little hands. I almost spoke to her several times, in that long wait of the train; but she was so classic in her respose that I finally decided not to. I got up instead and went down to the platform of the car, which was floury with dust all over its iron floor and coupling chains, and jumped down to the ground.

How immense the sky was, and the sandy plains that shuddered with the heat for miles and miles! And how small and oddly desirable the train looked!

It was all silent until I began to hear the noises that framed that midsummer midday silence—bugs droning, the engine breathing up ahead, a whining hum in the telegraph wires strung along by the track, and then from the laborers a kind of subdued chorus.

I went to see what they were all huddled about each other for.

There wasn't a tree for fifty miles in any direction.

In the heat-reflecting shade of one of the grape-red sheds the men were standing around and looking at one of their number who was lying on the ground with his back up on the lowest boards.

The men were mostly little, brown as horses, sweating and

[261]

smelling like leather, and in charge of them was a big Texan I saw squatting down by the recumbent Mexican.

"Come on, come on," he was saying, when I came up.

"What's the matter?" I asked.

The foreman looked up at me. He had his straw hat off, and his forehead and brows were shad-belly white where the sunburn hadn't reached. The rest of his face was apple-colored, and shiny. He had little eyes, squinted, and the skin around them was white too. His lips were chapped and burnt powdery white.

"Says he's sick."

The Mexicans nodded and murmured.

"Well, I'm a doctor, maybe I can tell."

The foreman snorted.

"They all do it. Nothin' matter with him. He's just play-actin'. Come on, Pancho, you get, by God, t' hell up, now!"

He shoved his huge dusty shoe against the little Mexican's side. The Mexican drooled a weak cry. The other laborers made operatic noises in chorus. They were clearly afraid of the foreman.

"Now hold on," I said to him. "Let me look him over, anyway."

I got down on the prickly ground.

It took a minute or less to find out. The little cramped-up Mexican had an acute attack of appendicitis, and he was hot and sick and, when I touched his side, he wept like a dog and clattered on his tongue without words.

"This man is just about ready to pop off," I told the foreman. "He's got acute appendicitis. He'll die unless he can be operated on."

The heat, the shimmering land, something to do—all changed me into feeling cool and serious, quite suddenly.

"I can perform an emergency operation, somehow, though it may be too late. Anyway, it can't do more'n kill him; and he'll die if I don't operate, that's sure!"

[262]

"Oh, no. Oh-ho, no, you don't," said the foreman, standing up and drawling. He was obviously a hind, full of some secret foremanship, some plainsman's charm against the evil eye, or whatever he regarded civilization as. "I ain't go no authority for anythin' like that on my section gang! And, ennyhow, they all take on like that when they're tarred of workin'!"

Oh, it was the same old thing.

All my life I've got my back up over something no more my business than the man in the moon; but seems to me when it's a matter of right or wrong, or good and bad, or the like, thinks I, there's no choice but to go to work and fight.

That blasted foreman infuriated me. And I can swear when I have to. Well, I set to and gave him such a dressing-down as you never heard.

I called him everything I ever heard, and then I made up some more pretty ones for good measure.

I told him I'd have him up before the nearest district territorial judge for criminal negligence. I told him I was a personal friend of John J. Summerdown, the president of the new railroad, and I'd, by God, have his job so fast he wouldn't know what hit him. I told him that anybody who'd stand by and let a man die instead of taking every chance there was to save him—I said was lower'n— anyway, you can't go through medical school without picking up a few fancy words.

He cocked his elbows and fists at me a couple of times. But when I'm right, I know I'm right, and that's all you need to handle a peasant like that.

He got scared, and we both wiped the sweat off our brows at the same minute, the same gesture, and glared at each other, and I wondered if I looked as hot and messy and ignorant as he did, and I laughed.

The Mexicans were curious and asking questions and clawing at him. I turned around, like a nervous old maid, or a scared child, to see if the train was still there.

It had become a symbol of safety to me, the only way out of that yellow, yellow plain streaming with sunlight. Yes, it was still there, dusty black, and dusty white where the light rested.

The foreman talked to the men . . . there must have been about three dozen of them.

He may have been a fool but he was a crafty one.

He was talking in Mexican and telling them what I wanted to do to Pancho, their brother and friend. He pantomimed surgery—knife in fist and slash and finger-scissors and then grab at belly, and then tongue out, and eyes rolled out of sight, and slump, and dead man; all this very intently, like a child doing a child's powerful ritual of play.

"Oh, yo, yo, yo," went all the Mexicans, and shook their fists at me, and showed their white teeth in rage. No sir, there'd be no cutting on Pancho!

"You see?" said the foreman. "I told 'em what you aim to do, and they won't have it."

I am no actor, and certainly no orator, but I turned to those poor peons and tried to show them as best I could how the only way to save Pancho, lying there like a baked peanut, was to operate right now.

The foreman kept up a kind of antiphony to my arguments.

You know? It was something like the old lyric struggle between good and evil—enlightenment and superstition.

There we were, miles from everything, on that plain where the heat went up from the fried ground in sheets; nothing but a rickety line of tracks to keep us in the world, so to speak; and a struggle going on over the theory of life or death, as exemplified in the person of a perfectly anonymous wretch who'd eaten too many beans once too often!

I'd be damned if I'd quit.

I went back to the train and had more on my mind now than chivalry and Chaucer and Clouet.

She was still sitting there in her heavy starch and her yards and yards of black serge.

Her face was pink with the heat and her glasses were a little moist. But she was like a calm and shady lake in that blistering wilderness, and her hands rested like ferns on the itchy plush of the seat which gave off a miniature dust storm of stifling scent whenever anything moved on it.

I could hear the argument and mutual reinforcement in cries and threats going on and gathering force out there in the little mob. It was like the manifest sound of some part of the day, the heat, the desert life, which being disturbed now filled the quavering air with protest.

When I stopped in the aisle beside her, she looked up sideways. Of course, she didn't mean it to, but it looked sly and humorous, and her glasses flashed.

"Excuse me, Sister," I said. "Have you ever had any hospital experience?"

"Is someone ill?"

Her voice was nearly doleful, but not because she was; no, it had the faintest trace of a German tone, and her words an echo of German accent, that soft, trolling, ach-Gott-im-Himmel charm that used to be the language of the old Germany, a comfortable sweetness that is gone now.

"There's a Mexican laborer out there who's doubled up with appendicitis. I am a surgeon, by the way."

"Yes, for a long time I was dietitian at Mount Mercy Hospital, that's in Clefeland?"

"Well, you see what I think I ought to do."

"So, you should operate?"

"It's the only thing't'd save him, and maybe that'll be too late."

"Should we take him in the train and take care of him so? And operate when we reach town?"

Yes, you must see how placid she was, how instantly dedicated to the needs of the present, at the same time. She at once talked of what "we" had to do. She owned responsibility for everything that came into her life. I was young then, and I'm an old man now, but I still get the same kind of pride in doctors and those in holy orders when they're faced with something that has to be done for somebody else. The human value, mind you.

"I don't think they'll let us touch him. They're all Mexicans, and scared to death of surgery. You should've heard them out there a minute ago."

"Yess, I hear them now."

"What I think we'd better do is get to work right here. The poor wretch wouldn't last the ride to Eddy, God knows how long the train'd take."

"But where, doctor!"

"Well, maybe one of those sheds."

"So, and the train would wait?"

"Oh! I don't know. I can find out."

I went and asked the conductor up in the next car. He said no, the train wouldn't wait, provided they ever got a chance to go.

"We'd have to take a chance on the train," I told Sister. "Also, those men out there are not very nice about it. Maybe if you came out?"

At that she did hesitate a little; just a moment; probably the fraction it takes a celibate lady to adjust her apprehensions over the things she has heard about men, all of them, the very authors of sin, ancestors of misery, and custodians of the forbidden fruit of knowledge.

"It would have been more convenient," I said, "if I'd never got off

[266]

the train. That groaning little animal would die, and when the train went, we'd be on it; but we cannot play innocent now. The Mexican means nothing to me. Life is not that personal to a doctor. But if there's a chance to save it, you have to do it, I suppose."

Her response to this was splendid. She flushed and gave me a terrific look, full of rebuke and annoyance at my flippancy. She gathered her great serge folds up in handfuls and went down the car walking angrily. I followed her and together we went over to the shed. The sunlight made her weep a little and blink.

The men were by now sweating with righteous fury. Their fascinating language clattered and threatened. Pancho was an unpleasant sight, sick and uncontrolled. The heat was unnerving. They saw me first and made a chorus. They them saw Sister and shut up in awe, and pulled their greasy hats off.

She knelt down by Pancho and examined him superficially and the flow of her figure, the fine robes kneeling in the dust full of ants, was like some vision to the Mexicans, in all the familiar terms of their Church. To me, it gave one of my infrequent glimpses into the nature of religious feeling.

She got up.

She turned to the foreman, and crossed her palms together. She was majestic and ageless, like any true authority.

"Doctor sayss there must be an operation on this man. He is very sick. I am ready to help."

"W', lady," said the foreman, "you just try an' cut on that Messican and see what happens!"

He ducked his head toward the laborers to explain this.

She turned to the men. Calmly, she fumbled for her long rosary at her discipline and help up the large crucifix that hung on its end. The men murmured and crossed themselves.

"Tell them what you have to do," she said to me coldly. She was still angry at the way I'd spoken in the train.

[267]

"All right, foreman, translate for me. Sister is going to assist me at an appendectomy. We'll move the man into the larger shed over there. I'd be afraid to take him to town, there isn't time. No: listen, this is better. What I will do; we could move him into the train, and operate while the train was standing still, and then let the train go ahead after the operation is over. That way, we'd get him to town for proper care!"

The foreman translated and pantomimed.

A threatening cry went up.

"They say you can't take Pancho off and cut on 'im on the train. They want him here."

Everybody looked at Pancho. He was like a little monkey with eyes screwed shut and leaking tears.

The little corpus of man never loses its mystery, even to a doctor, I suppose. What it is, we are; what we are, must serve it; in anyone. My professor of surgery used to say, "Hold back your pity till after the operation. You'll work better, and then the patient will be flattered to have it, and it might show up in the bill."

"Very well, we'll operate here. Sister, are you willing to help me? It'll mean staying here till tomorrow's train."

"*Ja,* doctor, of course."

I turned to the foreman.

"Tell them."

He shrugged and began to address them again.

They answered him, and he slapped his knee and h'yucked a kind of hound-dog laugh in his throat and said to us:

"W', if you go ahaid, these Messicans here say they'll sure 'nough kill you if you kill Pancho!"

Yes, it was worse than I could have suspected.

This was like being turned loose among savages.

You might have thought the searing heat of that light steel sky had got everybody into fanciful ways.

"Why, that's ridiculous!" I said to him. "He's nearly dead now! Halsted himself might not save him! Nobody can ever guarantee an operation, but I can certainly guarantee that that man will die unless I take this one chance!"

"W', I dunno. See? That's what they said." . . .

He waved at the Mexicans.

They were tough and growling.

Sister was waiting. Her face was still as wax.

"Can't you explain?" I said.

"Man, you never can 'splain nothin' to this crew! You better take the church lady there, and just get back on that train; that's what you better do!"

Well, there it was.

"You go to hell!" I said.

I looked at Sister. She nodded indignantly at me, and then smiled, sideways, that same sly look between her cheek and her lens, which she never meant that way; but from years of convent discretion she had come to perceive things obliquely and tell of them in whispers with many sibilants.

"Come on, we'll move him. Get some help there."

The Mexicans wouldn't budge. They stood in the way.

"Give me your pistol!"

The foreman handed it over. We soon got Pancho moved.

Sister helped me to carry him.

She was strong. I think she must have been a farm girl from one of the German communities of the Middle West somewhere. She knew how to work, the way to lift, where her hands would do the most good. Her heavy thick robes dragged in the dust. We went into the tool shed and it was like strolling into a furnace.

I hurried back to the train and got my bags and then went back again for hers. I never figured out how she could travel with so little and be so clean and comfortable. She had a box of food. It was conventional, in its odors, bananas, waxed paper, oranges, something spicy. Aside from that, she had a little canvas bag with web straps binding it. I wondered what, with so little allowed her, she had chosen out of all the desirable objects of the world to have with her and to own.

My instrument case had everything we needed, even to two bottles of chloroform.

I got back into the dusty red shed by flashing the foreman's pistol at the mob. Inside I gave it back to him through the window with an order to keep control over the peasants.

What they promised to do to me if Pancho died began to mean something, when I saw those faces, like clever dogs, like smooth-skinned apes, long-whiskered mice. I thought of having the conductor telegraph to some town and get help, soldiers or something; but that was nervously romantic.

It was dark in the shed, for there was only one window. The heat was almost smoky there, it was so dim. There was a dirt floor. We turned down two big tool cases on their sides and laid them together. They were not quite waist high. It was our operating table.

When we actually got started, then I saw how foolish it was to try it, without any hospital facilities. But I remembered again that it was this chance or death for the little Mexican. Beyond that, it was something of an ethical challenge. Yes, we went ahead.

I remember details, but now, so long after, maybe not in the right order.

I remember a particular odor, an oily smell of greasy sand, very powerful in the shed; the heat made the very dirt floor sweat these odors up, and they made me ill at ease in the stomach.

It was early afternoon. The sky was so still and changeless that it seemed to suspend life in a bowl of heat. The tin roof of the shed lowered a very garment of heat over us.

[270]

Faces clouded up at the window, to see, to threaten, to enjoy. We shook them away with the pistol. The foreman was standing in the doorway. Beyond him we had glimpses of the slow dancing silvery heat on the scratchy earth, and the diamond melt of light along the rails of the track.

The camp cook boiled a kettle of water.

Sister turned her back and produced some white rags from her petticoats.

She turned her heavy sleeves back and pinned her veils aside.

The invalid now decided to notice what was going on, and he tried to sit up and began to scream.

Sister flicked me a glance and at once began to govern him with the touch of her hands, and a flow of comforting melody in Deutsch noises. I got a syringe ready with morphine. And the mob appeared at the door, yelling and kicking up the stifling dust which drifted in and tasted bitter in the nose.

I shot the morphine and turned around.

I began to swear.

That's all I recall, not what I said. But I said plenty. Pancho yelled back at his friends who would rescue him. It was like a cat concert for a minute or so.

Then the morphine heavied the little man down again, and he fell silent.

Then I shut up, and got busy with the chloroform. Sister said she could handle that. It was suddenly very quiet.

My instruments were ready and we had his filthy rags off Pancho. Sister had an instinctive adroitness, though she had never had surgical experience. Yet her hospital service had given her a long awareness of the sometimes trying terms of healing. In fascinated silence we did what had to be done before the operation actually started.

There was a locust, or a cicada, some singing bug outside somewhere, just to make the day sound hotter.

The silence cracked.

"He is dead!" they cried outside.

A face looked in at the window.

Now the threats began again.

I said to the foreman:

"Damn you, get hold of that crowd and make them shut up! You tell them he isn't dead! You tell them—"

I began to talk his language again, very fancy and fast. It worked on him. I never cussed so hard in my life.

Then I turned back and I took up my knife.

There's a lot of dramatic nonsense in real life; for example: my hand was trembling like a wet dog, with that knife; but I came down near the incisionary area, and just before I made the first cut—steady? that hand got as steady as a stone!

I looked at Sister in that slice of a second, and she was biting her lips and staring hard at the knife. The sweat stood on her face and her face was bright red. Her light eyebrows were puckered. But she was ready.

In another second things were going fast.

I once told this story to someone, and later heard it repeated to someone else. I hardly recognized the events as my friend described them, because he made it all sound so dramatic and somehow like a scene in the opera, grand and full of high notes. No, it seems to me that the facts are more wonderful than all the things time and playgoing can do to a person's imagination. The whole situation couldn't have been meaner; more dangerous from forces like dirt and stupidity, instead of forces like fate or fascinating Mexican bandits. There was the hazard, too, of my own youth, my inexperience as a surgeon. There was my responsibility for Sister, in case any trouble might start. There was the heat and a patient with temperature and no way to cool off boiled water in a hurry, and the dust rising through the cracks of the door and window and walls of the shed as the outraged men kicked and shuffled outside. We could see the sheets of dusty light standing in the room's dusk, sliced from the gloom by a crack of that sunlight and its abstract splendor.

Oh, my surgery professor and my colleagues would've been shocked to see some of the things I did, and didn't do, that day!

I tried to hum a little tune instead of talk.

But now and then the noise outside would get worse.

Or the foreman would creak the door open and stick his varlet face in to peer.

Or the patient would almost swallow his tongue, making a noise like a hot sleeping baby.

So I'd swear.

Sister said nothing all the time.

She obeyed my instructions. Her face was pale, from so many things that she wasn't used to—the odors, the wound, manipulation of life with such means as knives and skill, the strain of seeing Pancho weaken gradually—she was glassy with perspiration. Her starched linen was melted. There was some intuitive machinery working between us. Aside from having to point occasionally at what I needed, things she didn't know the name of, I've never had a more able assistant at an operation in all my long life of practice.

I think it was because both she and I, in our professions, somehow belonged to a system of life which knew men and women at their most vulnerable, at times when they came face to face with the mysteries of the body and the soul, and could look no further, and needed help then.

Anyway, she showed no surprise. She showed none even at my skill, and I will admit that I looked at her now and then to see what she thought of my performance. For if I do say it myself, it was good.

[273]

She looked up only once, with a curious expression, and I thought it was like that of one of the early saints, in the paintings, her eyes filmed with some light of awareness and yet readiness, the hour before martyrdom; and this was when we heard the train start to go.

She looked regretful and forlorn, yet firm.

The engine let go with steam and then hooted with the exhaust, and the wheels ground along the hot tracks.

If I had a moment of despair, it was then; the same wavy feeling I'd had when the train had stopped here what seemed hours before.

The train receded in sound.

It died away in the plainy distance.

Shortly after, there was a rush of voices and cries and steps toward the shack.

It was the laborers again, many of whom had been put back to work on the track ahead of the engine, in order to let the train proceed. Now they were done. Now they were crazy with menace.

It was about four o'clock, I suppose.

Fortunately I was just finishing up. The door screeched on its shaken hinges and latch. I heard the foreman shouting at the men.

Then there was a shot.

"Most Sacred Heart!" said Sister, on her breath, softly. It was a prayer, of course.

Then the door opened, and the foreman came in and closed it and leaned back on it.

He said they sent him in to see if Pancho were still living. I told him he was. He said he had to see. I said he was a blankety-blank meddling and low-down blank to come bothering me now; but that I was just done, and if he had to smell around he could come.

I showed him the pulse in the little old Mexican's neck, beating fast, and made him listen to the running rapid breath, like a dog's.

Then he looked around.

He was sickened, first, I suppose; then he got mad. The place was dreadful. There were unpleasant evidences of surgery around, and the heat was absolutely weakening, and the air was stifling with a clash of odors. Sister had gone to sit on a box in the corner, watching. She, too, must have looked like a challenge, an alien force, to him.

He grew infuriated again at the mysterious evidences of civilization.

He began to wave his gun and shout that next time, by God, he'd fire on us, and not on them Messicans out yander. He declared that he, too, was agin cuttin' on anybody. He was bewildered and sick to his stomach and suffering most of all from a fool's bafflement.

He bent down and tried to grab back the meager sheeting and the dressing on Pancho's abdomen. He was filthy beyond words. I butted him with my shoulder (to keep my hands away and reasonably clean) and he backed up and stood glaring and his mouth, which was heavy and thick, sagged and contracted in turn, like loose rubber.

Sister came forward and, without comment, knelt down by the wretched operating table which might yet be, for all I knew, a bier, and began to pray, in a rich whisper, full of hisses and soft impacts of r's upon her palate, and this act of hers brought some extraordinary power into the room; it was her own faith, of course, her own dedication to a simple alignment of life along two channels, one leading to good, the other to evil.

I was beginning to feel very tired.

I had the weakness after strain and the almost querulous relief at triumph over hazard.

I'd been thinking of her all along as a woman, in spite of her ascetic garb, for that was natural to me then. Now for the first time, listening to her pray, I was much touched, and saw that she was like a doctor who thinks enough of his own medicine to take some when he needs a lift.

The foreman felt it all, too, and what it did to him was to make him shamble sullenly out of the shed to join the enemy.

We watched all night.

It got hardly any cooler.

Late at night Sister opened her lunch box with little delicate movements and intentions of sociability, and we made a little meal.

I felt intimate with her.

I had a sense of what, together, we had accomplished, and over and over I tried to feel her response to this. But none came. We talked rather freely of what we still had to do, and whether we thought the Mexicans meant it, and whether the train crew knew what was going on, and if they'd report it when they reached Eddy.

We had an oil lamp that the foreman gave us.

When I'd get drowsy, my lids would drop and it seemed to me that the flame of the wick was going swiftly down and out; then I'd jerk awake and the flame would be going on steadily, adding yet another rich and melancholy odor to our little surgery.

I made Sister go to sleep, on her corner box, sitting with her back against the wall.

She slept in state, her hands folded, her body inarticulated under the volume of her robes, which in the dim lamplight looked like wonderful masses carved from some dark German wood by trolls of the Bavarian forests . . . so fancifully ran my mind through that vigil.

I saw morning come, like a cobweb, on the little window, then steal the whole sky that I could see; and then, just as a flavor of cool sweetness had begun to lift into the air off the plains, the sun appeared (rapidly, I thought; but then it was I, not the sun, whose fever hurried life along that day).

Early that day Pancho become conscious.

We talked to him and he answered.

He was inclosed in the mystery of pain and the relief of weakness.

When he identified Sister by her habit, he tried to cross himself, and she smiled and crowed at him and made the sign of the Cross over him herself.

I examined him carefully, and he was all right. He had stood the shock amazingly well. It was too early for infection to show to any degree; but I began to have a certain optimism, a settling of the heart. It had come off. I began to think the day was cooler. You know: the sweetness over everything that seems to follow a feeling of honest satisfaction.

The the crowd got busy again.

They saw Pancho through the window, his eyes open, his lips moving, smiling faintly and staring at Sister with a child's wonder toward some manifest loveliness hitherto known only in dream and legend.

In a second they were around at the door, and pushing in, babbling like children, crying his name aloud, and eager to get at him and kiss him and gabble and marvel and felicitate.

They were filthy and enthusiastic, flowing like life itself toward that which feeds it. They were, then, infection personified.

I shouted at them and made them stay back. I let them see Pancho, but from a distance of three feet.

He spoke to them, thinly; and they cried "Aiee!" with astonishment, and nodded their heads in homage. They couldn't have been more friendly now. They went yes-yes, and my-my, and how wonderful to have such a man! and he is my friend, and so forth.

But their very presence was dangerous, for they kicked up the dirt floor, and they hawked and spat on their words, and I finally put them out.

The foreman's mood was opposite to theirs.

He was now surly and disgruntled that we had pulled it off successfully.

He knew, as I had known, that the Mexicans really would kill if Pancho died.

We had the unpleasant impression that he felt cheated of a diverting spectacle.

We watched Pancho carefully all morning; he grew uncomfortable as the heat arose. But, then, so did we. It rose and rose, and the bugs sang; and the tin roof seemed to hum too, but that must have been dramatic imagination. I had all our plans made. When the noon train came along, we would flag it, and carefully move Pancho on board, and take him down the valley to Eddy, where he could spend two weeks in the company hospital.

Midmorning I stepped outside and called the men together and the foreman, and made them a speech. Now they had their hats off listening to me. Their little eyes couldn't have looked more kindly and earnest. *Sure,* I could take Pancho off on the train. *Sure,* they wanted him to get well. *By all means* the *señor médico* must do what he thought best. So, with a great show of love for them, I shook hands with myself at the little mob, feeling like a gifted politician.

The train finally arrived; and as it first showed, standing down the tracks in the wavering heat, it looked like a machine of rescue.

There was only one more thing there.

When we went to take Pancho on the train, the foreman refused to help.

"I won't he'p you," he declared. "I ain't got no authority t' move none of my men, and I won't he'p you."

I picked out two of the less earthy natives, and they helped me to bring the patient on board the train. We carried him on a camp cot. It belonged to the foreman. When he saw that, he got so mad he threw down his hat and jumped on it. The dust flew. His fish-white brow broke into sweat. Then he came running to stop us. We barely got Pancho on the train in time, and the door closed and latched. It was a state of siege until the train went again. It must have been ten minutes. Fortunately I'd brought my bags on board the first thing, and Sister's.

We finally pulled out.

We looked out the rear window, and saw our desert hospital recede into the slow pulsing glassy air.

We could see the little figures, most of them waving.

Just at the last, one of them held forth his arm; and we saw a puff of smoke, and heard an explosion in our imaginations, and then heard the actual ring and sing-off of a bullet as it struck the rear of the car.

It was the foreman's farewell, the last, and futile, opinion of the ignorant.

The afternoon passed slowly in the train.

The heat and the dust were hard on everyone, and especially Pancho. I kept wetting down the cracks of the windows, and the doors, to keep the dust out if I could.

But soon the water was gone, and we had to sit there and hope.

We reached Eddy in the evening, and it was like a garden, after the endless plains and their sear life. We found green trees and artesian wells and cool fields of alfalfa.

There is little more to tell, and what there is, is not about Pancho, except that he made a recovery in the proper time.

It is about my saying goodbye to Sister.

It seemed to me we had been through a good deal together.

Now we were going to separate, for she was taking a stagecoach from Eddy on down into Texas somewhere, and I was going to stay a few days and see my patient out of the woods.

So we said goodbye in the lobby of the wooden hotel there, where she was going to spend the night.

Nobody knew what a good job I had done except Sister; and after we shook hands and I thanked her for her wonderful help, I waited a moment—just a little moment.

She knew I was nervous and tired; and it was vanity, of course, but I needed the little lift she could give me.

But she didn't say anything, while I waited; and then as I started to turn off and go, she did speak.

"I will pray for you, doctor."

"What?"

"That you may overcome your habit of profanity."

She bowed and smiled in genuine kindliness, and made her way to the stairs and disappeared.

Duty is an ideal and it has several interpretations, and these are likely to be closely involved with the character that makes them.

You might say that Sister and I represented life eternal and life temporal.

I never saw her again, of course; but if she's still alive, I have no doubt that she's one of the happiest people in the world.

The Other Side of the Street

Mrs Schluzer sat reading *The Agony of an Empress* in the warm afternoon. A glass of goldfish-colored orangeade stood next a fifty-cent box of chocolates on the wicker tabouret at her elbow. The sun ventured steadily in through the blinds that screened the side porch where she sat. Fudge, the fox terrier, panted fatly at the foot of his mistress's lounge, while from the lawn came the consoling whirr and spatter of the hose-spray.

It was a quarter to three, because Bertha was setting her ferns out in the sun next door. Mrs Schluzer turned another royal page and anointed her lips with the velvety, gradual kiss of a chocolate banana cream. Across the street Mrs Klobstock came out on her front porch a moment and then, after a swift look whose rays shafted both up and down the street, retired within again. In a moment the lace curtain just behind the "Room and Board Available for Gentlefolk" sign was twitched and settled, as it always was in mid-afternoon after Mrs Klobstock had had her "breath of air." Remote in the sunny afternoon, the other side of the street was somehow active and interesting.

Mrs Schluzer lazily stirred in discontent. If only the Empress

Euphemia would appear now, and sit down to chat with her! The same old life repeating one of its afternoons! Harry Schluzer would, at five-forty, return, and—

Harry had strolled across her consciousness for the first time one sunny Sabbath morning in Reward, where she had gone to visit her cousins the Zimmendahls. In the dusty areas of the square before the church, he had sauntered by, his derby hat on his oiled curls, and his buggy whip rakishly switching in one hand. He had halted, stared, and gone on; and that evening, by a Divine Coincidence, Emma Gressing had brought him to call, and the harmonium in the parlor had tried its bellows to the point of rupture, so great was the good will of the little party, and so uncontrollable was Hortense's infatuation.

The wedding: in the best taste. The honeymoon: two days in Chicago, a lake ride to Duluth, and back home by way of Monamossee, where they inspected the famous caves with reverence and hidden alarm. The removal: Harry's fine job in the freight office in Advantage—and that was all: all: except that she grew pinker and plumper, and he grew softer and lazier, though his rise had been steady, for he was now district freight inspector for the Midland and Central Railway, and had had two personal letters from the president, Mr Pennybannock, on business.

Oh! life was comfortable, and happy; but who, she thought, wanted anything but magnificent misery, or superb despair, or persecution that lighted the days with an inner glow richer than the mere sun's that daily revealed the city of Advantage?—

With a shrill denunciatory shriek, Fudge leaped to the screen door, scolding a young man who stood on the cement steps of the porch. He held his cap and a black leather professional case in one hand, while in the other a wicker suitcase proclaimed the transient.

Mrs Schluzer edged her round legs off the plump mattress of the swing lounge, pretending for herself and the young man that her legs had never been up. This pretense made it difficult to find her stance easily when she arose to play the hostess. She laid away her novel, and chewed very rapidly to dismiss the banana cream.

"Fudge!" she commanded, with a smile of apology to the visitor that her animal should have been so uncordial. "Fudge! stop touting the gentleman." "He's very careful about strangers," she explained, pulling a corner of her waist down over her rear hip, and ignoring the action.

"Psoui, psoui," said the young man, kissing the air at Fudge and snapping all his fingers at him. The little white dog finally accepted peace and tried his small hams in a comfortable sitting position. Then, Mrs. Schluzer, having found in her examination of the young man that he looked like her cousin Emil—the same pink compactness about the cheeks and neck, the unsurprised blue eyes, and the meaningless but agreeable smile, the same observable thickness of flesh under his checkered suit whose lapels pointed quite bravely upward—leaned towards him, and asked, "You were wanting—?"

He looked at her, and set his suitcase down, and rolled his cap up and put it into his coat pocket. Then, with a frank relapse into a confidential air, he said: "I've just moved here to Advantage. My home is in Calliope, and my sister used to live here; so she told me of a good place to live, where you can get your food, and all; she said Mrs Elsie Klobstock had a good house along here, somewhere, I couldn't find it. Are you Mrs Klobstock?"

Mrs Schluzer widened her elbows in a slightly magnificent gesture. Harry Schluzer could keep his wife, thank you, and no work for her. (One of the worst episodes of the unfortunate Empress's later days was the humiliating mistreatment of her by her former courtiers. It is on record that she was once taunted with her alleged likeness to a certain Frau Gebbert, a fishwife!) The young man, however, was very simple in his question. She therefore said with equal simplicity, smoothing the white embroidered ruffles of her waist, "*Hum*-uh. I'm Merz Harry Schluzer. Merz Klobstock lives—"

Suddenly it came to Hortense that if this young man left her doorstep, and went across the street with his cases, she would see his slenderly bulging back, and the opening of the lace-curtained door, and Mrs Klobstock's rapid intense inspection of him, and then the closing of the door, and—the end. It would be another victory for the other side of the street, which always had everything, all the fascinations of life: the house where the Italian bootlegger lived with his un-wife, the doctor's office where dramas of life and death (she knew from short stories and films and "ads") were acted hourly, the busy church on the corner where weddings often happened, Mrs Klobstock's house where really refined people boarded.

"Come in: I'll tell you all about local living facilities," she said, and the young man, lifting his suitcase and the black box, followed her into the ferny places of the porch. Fudge begrudged him the honor; but only sniffed, wetly.

"Sit down," said Hortense, and the young man did so, with a certain elaboration of the act, so that she noticed the elegance of his movement, and the bland acceptance of the chair that his body made.

There fell a silence. (My gracious! she thought, how shall I?—) He relieved matters. Looking at the house next door, where the ferns turned in the sunlight, he said, "There's a pretty picture, composition, we call it."

She looked at the shadows made by Bertha's bay window. Composition? "Are you an—?"

He nodded. "Sort of. I take pictures. That's my camera, there. I've studied color work, too, and free-hand. But I like photos best."

She became, suddenly, pitapalpitant, and handed him the chocolates, trusting to her God to quiet the tumult in her shirtwaist.

What was it? She had seen plenty of photographers—

He took a candy, and knowing, as a male, that she had made an undeniable overture, he relaxed further, until he was appraising her patronizingly with a warm eye.

But if Hortense had seen plenty of photographers, she had never had one in her house before, who perhaps would take her picture in the favorite pose. It was a dream, in its suddenness, and in the excitements it suggested to her.

"Why, how perfly fine," she said, urging the candy on him again (until he said to himself, Hell! she's easy, she'll fall over). "I've always been interested in photos. I haven't had one made for some time now—"

He studied her. " 'D make a good one," he said, with a friendly suggestiveness.

They sat looking at each other for a long moment, and then they both blushed and stirred. "I have some plates—"

She rose and adjusted the waist over the hip. "Lovely—I'll go get ready—I want a royal photograph, so come in, come in."

He followed her, his legs confused with the ambulating body of Fudge, into the front room. There she showed him the heavy plush portières, the mahogany pedestal on which a long-white-gloved elbow could rest with dignity, the fern that could be put into the background with the gilt chairs.

"Look," she said, bringing him *The Agony of an Empress,* and pointing to the frontispiece, which revealed the unhappy Euphemia in the ninth year of her reign. She was *en grande tenue,* and the tiara, the orders, the ribbon, the ermine over the chair, the crown on the table, the cushion for the scepter and the lesser orb, the brailed curtains at the back with heavy gold cords and tassels, the earring that must have been an emerald. . . .

"I see," said the young man. "You get ready, and I'll fix the background." She breathed eagerly, like a little girl. "Run along," he

[285]

added, patting her stout shoulder blade, which she couldn't resent because he was entering into the spirit of her happy desire.

He pulled the furniture about (thinking, She's some'm like Alice, over at Fort Scranley. I guess it don't pay to trifle with these married dames, in the afternoon, she may have a husband in town, she's nice and juicy—).

Hortense paused on the landing, and took a deep breath. Her half hour had wrought splendors upon her, and like every other woman of her class and period, she could assume a true histrionic effectiveness when some external agency released her from the embarrassed democratic canons of her daily life. Now, in her best evening gown (sequins and moiré) with all the false gems she possessed, with her fur coat worn as a cloak, and her mother's long white gloves on, she managed a rich feeling that was definitely conveyed in her bearing and expression. This was the enchantment of being something, which her wide laziness daily held away from her. Her friends were active, they went places and accomplished things; and happiness followed. But Hortense had never been able to say, "I had a good choir rehearsal"; or, "The preserved peaches is doing 'st fine"; or, "My! I enjoyed making those curtains," when her husband joined her for their dull little evenings.

She raised one shoulder slightly, and lowered the corresponding eyebrow; and descended upon the photographer, whose background was a masterpiece of the baroque. He leaned on the piano with a real admiration for her sudden beauty and splendor. (Jeest, he thought, husband or no husband—)

His reddish hair covered a skull whose extensive back spaces connected with a sturdy neck, that would, in time, be leathered by the sun and wind. He had pale blue eyes that seemed to be lashless, for the tiny foliage around them was almost white. Hortense, sensing his immediate respect for her now that she was panoplied, took advantage of his arrogant stares to move into the area of the palatial scene that he had built out of her gilt chairs, the ferns, the pedestal from Cousin Harriet, and the brailed, braided plush.

"I feel so silly" she said, coloring, because he was forgetful of his profession. "But I do want to try it—"

"Hep-hep," said Bruce, hopping into action. "Let's get busy. You sort of took the wind out of me sails."

He went to the window and began to arrange the shades for light, and became at once marvelously efficient so that Mrs Schluzer was in her turn suddenly respectful. It seemed to her with a quick insistence as if the young man had commanded her as a man to observe him, and then intrigued her instantly with the undeniable evidences of skill that he was now showing her: the maneuverings of the tripedal camera (in whose black accordion there lived a strange bird) she remembered from her childhood portraits (whose eyes would suddenly observe her, and register, in some labyrinth of that magic box, the lineaments of her features). (I don't mean it, she confessed to herself, but they always used t' say, "See the birdie." My God, if Harry was to see me with this rouge on!—)

The afternoon was advancing steadily towards the moment when the sun would be arrested by the turreted shingles of Mrs Klobstock's house; the evening papers were already turning warmly damp on the front lawns, and in the front parlor of Harry Schluzer's house—

"Now," said Bruce, "let me have a look!" He got inside his black tent and saw her, glassily granulate, and upside down, looking pursed and splendid, she thought.

(I think I might try to squeeze her a second, Bruce considered, but these wives—I dunno—)

They went through with it, and she decided that the Empress was not particularly inspiring today.

They planned another, and he twinkled his plates so that she found his dexterity in feeding and emptying the camera something fabulous.

"My robe—" she said a moment later, when he had moved her so that the light caught her earrings and made them burn gravely in its beams. He came forward, and knelt to arrange those spurious fur folds.

She regarded him from above, looking down, and her attitude was almost tender, simply because any attitude leaning over is apt to be suggestive of madonna-like gentleness. For his part, the handling of her furs was suddenly a symbolic thing—Alice, over at Fort Scranley, sure was like her (I remember how we used to do with Alice: these ankles are the same). A thick blush arose out of his covered body and surrounded his neck and head. Hortense thought it was only the strain of kneeling that turned him so cherry-ripe. But Bruce knew that if he sought this plumply winning girl with his ardors, she would be likely to resist with a panting smile for a moment, and then, like Alice, whom she so much resembled, let her lips tremble and then fall to his kiss, her eyes meanwhile strangely filling with tears—probably of self-pity, he decided with an amorist's shrewdness, for there were sulky shadows about her, and in her house, that he had long ago learned as the dark banners of a dull love.

The fur was trailed upon the Brussels. The eyes of Hortense found him strange and new momentarily. (Harry is so *same,* she said to herself.) Bruce seemed to be a fresh person every moment, for he was now the intent artist, a moment ago he had been the kneeling suppliant for the favors of an empress, and when he arrived in the afternoon sun, he was simply a young man with the same farm-lad looks of her cousin Emil, who had fascinated her years ago in the light of an August evening when the hay lay in windrows.

"Now: good," he said, while his left hand suspended her pose in the air, and his right described a slow, pneumatic circle at whose

[288]

final arc the bulb was released and the impression was filtered upon the plate within the black, boxy aviary.

She relaxed, her heart pounding a little; for he had compelled her eyes in the pose, and the jewels and the furs were suddenly a false part of her. She felt that this was trumpery. Empress? Dear God, she was only Mrs Schluzer, of Elmer Avenue, her robes were dyed rabbit, her emeralds were verdine glass, her long white gloves belonged to her mother. But Bruce made her ashamed of her momentary shame. He was there, looking at her, and it came to Hortense in an intense happiness that no woman need be more than a woman when love intruded rudely and successfully. The remoteness of Bruce from her life made him swiftly desirable; and instead of the idyll of the royal woman, she now underwent a narrow *frisson* that took her into those lazy days when Harry was a new dimension of her existence, and when the dust that arose from the lines as they walked tasted in her mouth like the divine particles of cloud that shrouded God in His Heaven.

The curtains at the window turned grayer, for the sun just now had suffered indecent eclipse by the black turrets of Mrs Klobstock's, and Bruce stepped towards her, confusion of purpose within him (for if she don't like it, he thought, I stand to get t'hell in trouble, but look at her!).

He wasted no more time. Like a dream figure, so astonishingly unknown was he to her, he embraced her shoulders, while she struggled backwards weakly, making the demanded resistances.

"Why, what do you mean, why I never in my life, you're so *next*—oh—"

He had found her lips, and had kissed them.

The street went its golden length in the dying sunlight, gentlemen were wending homewards; Harry Schluzer mounted his front steps with *The Reporter* under his arm, his cigar smoked short to meet his stubble mustache.

He let himself in with his house key, and took off his straw hat, leaving it on the newel post where his wife always found it with a little cry of regret.

He whistled—

—as he did every evening to tell her that he had arrived; and if there was nothing beautifully musical about it, it was at least suggestive of a contented robin announcing, as best he could, his safe return to the nest.

"My husband," said Hortense against the stifling embrace of Bruce, "no, don't."

He understood at once; and despite the rapid vision of shotguns, headlines, horsewhips, or, worse, the Klan, he could not desert her warm person as immediately as his reason urged him to. But it was, even so, in time enough. At the entry of Harry into the disarranged parlor, they were again in the positions of client and artist.

Harry never tried to understand anything that surprised him. Now, he merely thought how handsome his wife looked, and what a sunburned young man was taking her picture—though when the thing was over, and the young man came to shake hands with "my husband, Mr Schluzer," Harry noticed that far from being sunburned, the photographer was actually sallow.

"Well—Harry, you've spoiled my surprise," said Hortense, flicking at him with a tail of fur that her nervous fingers had found with gratitude in those piteously terrible moments when Harry had followed his elk tooth emblem into the room.

"Elch, elch, elch," laughed Harry, with a cigarry effusion. "Trying to fool the Old Man for his birthday, and the Old Man spoiled it, eh?"

(Thank God he thought of his birthday, she thought.)

Harry winked at Bruce, who had packed his equipment with preposterous speed. Bruce managed to wink back before saying, "I'll have proofs in a couple days. Thank you. I'm sure they'll be very tony."

Hortense smiled and came forward, so that Harry saw her rouge, and wondered angrily a moment; but he decided sensibly that pictures aren't like real life—"you have to bring it out."

"Now how do I get to Mrs Klobstock's?" asked Bruce, and Harry told him, took him to the door, escorted by Fudge, who emerged from a cubbyhole in the hallway to preside with silent skepticism at the parting.

In the parlor, Mrs Schluzer sank into a green plush chair, covering her face with her hands, her body lacerated by pains of the most unbearable frequency and temper. He had gone. But what was worse, he had not gone into a cloudy region of myth and memory, but across the street to the hated Mrs Klobstock, who always had the amusing things.

If Harry hadn't been there, she could have sent Bruce far off, and he could have come now and then like a Grail Sir Knight to see her—now she would see him every day, he lived across the street, there was nothing romantical in that. (Oh, my God!)

She was weeping when Harry returned, and every dull bitterness she had in her heart against him arose now clamoring for release upon the kind stupid front of him. But he leaned over her, and the thick smell of his cigar wrapped her, closely, familiarly, so that she relaxed into the known torpescence that was her life, confessing to him that her head ached from the photographing, and suffering his bristly kiss without a single sensation, and feeling within her that her idyll forever was melted away, for neither queen nor mistress was she, although Fudge panted at her feet with devotional rapidity. Harry had gone back to his paper, and had left her to herself.

Mrs Klobstock gingerly accepted Bruce. He went into her red and brown hallway, gave a look about him, and accepted her, in turn, with the jaunty deposit of his hat on the left antler of the mirrored coat-and-hat rack. The landlady, massaging a mole on her cheek, watched his retreat up the stairs with that strange sense of wonder that overcame her every time she took another boarder—lives crossed one another and patterns resulted—would this one be symmetrical, with the little decencies of community life casually observed? Or would she hear, with birds of alarm whirring in her breast some late night, the horribly tentative ascent of the stairs, the tragic mumble of the drunk, the assault upon the bedroom door, and the final, obliterating "ganunnk!" that would tell her he had slipped in the bathroom?

Perhaps he wouldn't; and there was always the chance that in the evenings he'd begin to talk to her in the green, or back, parlor. Her lonely bosom trembled at that sweet prospect, for no husband, or lover, required she; only someone to ask her now and then how her cat was, and if she'd care to look at his copy of *The Country Gentleman*.

Bruce, in a few weeks, liked Advantage. He liked Mrs Klobstock, because she nervously pampered him, and he liked Elmer Avenue.

Every evening, returning from his job with McLarney's Studio, where he retouched pictures, he walked on the side of the street opposite Mrs Klobstock's. (It must be, he thought, because of the Queen.)

That moment when he had held Hortense to his silk-shirted breast had left marvelous reverberations. It was the highest romance of his amorist's career, because never before had he failed to reduce to his furious, promising will the object of his attentions. Hortense —how she had refused him, how she had then wept in taking his kiss! How Harry had come in, and how narrowly the explosive aftermath had been missed! Bruce for the first time in his life took time to think about one of his affairs; and Mrs Schluzer, and her house, her side of the street, everything about her, became for him unutterably romantic, and touched with those divine rays of fancy like the sun's that would, in a few weeks, bring a perishing, dear beauty to the tall trees that patterned the Avenue.

Every evening at half past five, he walked by her house, and he always turned his head away from it; because, the first evening, she had sat on the porch and turned her head away after seeing him. (She's a real lady, he told himself, denying that glorious state to the countless girls he'd taken by surprise.)

And because she had not looked back at him, and because the pictures were all failures (not even a decent proof to show her), he mused, he had never gone back. She regarded him respectfully both as man and artist, he felt. It was another link in the chain of incidents that made Elmer Avenue (her side) especially romantic.

Mrs Schluzer, resuming her designed ways, was now and then bitter that Harry didn't know, that he'd never know, how near he had been to grass-widowerhood. In the weeks that unrolled before her like any other weeks, she was even surprised to find that she wasn't very unhappy—just tired and a little disagreeably dulled by the flow of existence.

But one morning, perhaps three weeks after the photographs had been taken, she awoke with a start to realize that Bruce had never brought her proofs. It was the last straw. She lay in her bed, which in daytime was covered with fancily colored satin pillows and cushions, and laughed at the ceiling. If anything were needed to free her of her last fondness for his unknown, near presence that day, then the fact of his incompetence was enough. Today Harry had gone down to the office, had kissed her through a familiar (not unpleasant?) mist of nicotine. She didn't have to wash the breakfast dishes until after lunch—and then she remembered that there was no lunch, for it was Harry's day at the Lions, and she could eat downtown.

She sat up. "I'll get a book to read," she said, happily, and a half-memory of the intimate joys that she'd had from between the inscrutable boards of countless past books shook her into joyous action. "I can get something romantical," she said, and when she dressed, she considered herself in the roles of all the heroines she'd ever met.

She got home at a little after three, tired, hot, but pleased at her day. A few minutes here, fingering stockings and gloves; there, a session with some quilted house robes; a bout with a stubborn hat that was too small for her, but whose comet-like spray of pheasant feathers entranced her; lunch in the tea-room of Dickinson-Smithers department store; and then, with a bated sense of approaching apocalypse, ten minutes in the rental library.

She settled now, in a cool dress and with a glass of lime freeze, on the porch swing. Fudge cocked an ear at her, remembering the million afternoons his mistress had gone to bed with a book on the couch, instead of playing with him at Shake-the-Furnace-Glove, a delirious game involving the white and blue cotton gauntlet used to bring up the coal.

Bertha must be out, she thought, absently, opening her book. (She always sets her ferns out this time of day.) The ferns were nowhere to be seen. Mrs Klobstock could be heard beating carpets in her back yard, and the strident song of a streetcar rounding a corner made a faint trajectory over the roofs to Hortense's warm, sweet reteat, where she lay reading *An Angel of Mercy*.

The battlefields were oppressed by sheets of dazzling heat, and men lay putrefying in rags, men lay dead, dying, wounded. On a distant, hazy knoll, the staff officers confused their brains with stained maps. The dogs of war belched behind bush clumps, and miles away, those febrile breaths scorched and exhausted a whole village. But in the midst of this furious misery, a cool balm, a presence like chipped ice sweetened with baby kisses went down the rows of agonized men, and laid a silvery hand upon each dying brow. It was the Angel of Mercy, it was Angelica Vann-Cecill, and Mrs Schluzer joined her so eagerly in the pages of that novel that five o'clock, and five-thirty came towards her unnoticed. Men walked home from work, such men as photographers and railroad men, in the falling evening, and Harry was obliged to disturb his wife so that they could have some supper.

She went into the kitchen and pinned on her whitest apron, and then went to the pantry, where she leaned over the potato bin, and selected the vegetables with a hand touched by the heavenly current of mercy and healing.

Tribute

The Apache Tavern in Hermosa, New Mexico, was run by a man called Captain and his wife Billie Jeane. Every time a customer came in for a meal, they were busied anew with the duties they enjoyed; and by taking a sentimental interest in their work and themselves, they cast over their little café a curious atmosphere of comfort and pity. They were very fond of each other, a fondness based on admiration as well as desire. When their coffee urn was hissing, and the swinging door between the cooking range and the eating counter was whapping in the winds of service, and Billie Jeane was cat-walking up and down with orders, smiling, her high heels making hard jolts on the floor that shook her frank breasts with each step, then she and her husband were happy because they were busy and because people needed their work for their own good.

They were frank with each other and with the world.

And they were successful. Hermosa was a small town, but right opposite the tavern was the county Court House, a sandy gaunt building with a wooden cupola on whose windy four faces a clock had been painted four times in 1897. The painted hour was thirty-five minutes after two. Time arrested in that town was a memorial to the death of Toby Gardenhire who had died by gunfire at the hands of cattle thieves at that hour on a Saturday afternoon in 1897, when Hermosa consisted of hardly one street.

But Highway 380 went by this way now.

There were four paved blocks in the center of town. The machines of city life were here too. A movie house, everybody's radio, cars with radios in them, and the transport planes crossing the same streak of sky this side of the mountains at the same hour every evening, when the evening settled over the immense veils of color that made the land there—roads taking the eye far down the terraces of plains; the blue hover above the river behind town with its dying willows and the white salt hollows; the level horizon blurred with light except the place where the mountains began, rising rock on sky and taking light into their depths all day in change. Slow things lived temperately there still, cows roving, old Mexicans paced by their burros, the fat sheriff who limped majestically and was beloved by his townsmen. But the lives of most people were rolled rapidly like spools leaving thinner threads as they rolled, along the roads in their cars. The roads called them. And the roads were good in all kinds of weather.

The Captain and Billie Jeane were proud of that, they said. It kept business moving, the coffee bubbling and sighing in their urn.

On a day like this, in early November, the café was somnolent in midafternoon; but when the door opened, it didn't surprise Billie Jeane unduly, though she glanced at the clock above the pie cabinet, and said to herself, " 't's quarter t'four," and went forward to wait on the man who sat down at the far end of the counter, near the street, where you could look out and see the second story-and-up of the Court House and the baring treetops in the yard before it. The sights below that were blurred by Billie Jeane's muslin curtains that veiled the lower half of her big front window.

[297]

The Captain came to his swinging door and looked across it at the new customer. The Captain wore a white flat cap on his head. He was tall and fat at the waist, with black hair and pale brown eyes behind black-rimmed glasses. His face wore an almost permanent kind of eagerness, as if he were inhaling a smell that nourished him, a sauce, or hotcakes browning, or gasoline running into the tank of his car. He watched Billie Jeane do her offices at the counter, the glass of water, the butter pat, the tableware, the napkin and the menu. She smiled and looked out the window and snaked her fingers in her hair, fixing her bob. About her plump cheeks rose a starched collar that made her look in silhouette, as the Captain now saw her, like an old court lady in the picture last week. Then she turned and got the order and came down the aisle, saying in a loud voice as if the room were full of clamorous diners:

"Bowl of chili, dry toast, one egg easy," and the Captain retired from his swinging half door to stir the chili pot on the range. He went at it with zeal.

Up front the customer pushed his hat back off his nose, and said:

"Say, got the papers today, there, sister?"

Pursing her mouth in humorous efficiency, Billie Jeane got him the papers off the top of the pie cabinet and then stood leaning by the counter, alert but not obtrusive, watchful and modest. He glanced at her once, rattling his paper, seeming to look for something. She coughed, accepting his notice, and fingered her hair again confidently.

She was a woman in the colors of electric light and fire engines and blue plush. Her hair was wiry yellow and every hair was part of a curl. Her face was flour-white, except at the cheeks where deep rosy stains bruised the cheekbones and faded down the jaw, and at the eyelids, where blue plush shadows winked and glittered. Her mouth was hose-cart red, and scrolled smaller than her lips; and it

[298]

was odd to see her talk and smile, with that miniature mouth. She thought of herself as beautiful, and so did the Captain, a face worthy of the hours she spent on it. She had never really understood why men had tried to pick her up in larger towns. She was virtuous by character, though she looked the opposite.

"Bowl of chili, dry toast, one egg easy," called the Captain from the range.

She lunged free of the counter with her hip, and went down the aisle to get the food which Cap had slid through the framed hatch between the counter and the kitchen table beyond the wall.

Billie Jeane carried the food down to the customer, and he laid down his paper and relished the sight of the dishes.

"Coffee?"

"Yes, no cream."

She got it.

Cap was leaning on his half door again, watching. His bare forearms were black with hair.

"Is this all the papers you got?" asked the man.

"Yes, there's the Denver *Post,* the El Paso *Herald,* the Albuquerque *Tribune.* I *did* have a Fort Worth—I wouldn't just know *what* become—Cap, did you see the Fort Worth *Star?*"

He closed his eyes and shook no.

"Never mind," the customer said.

"I read them all every day," said Billie Jeane. Her voice was like a wooden whistle that was wet. With her enlarged doll's face, the piping husky voice finished the picture. Her face got dreamy now, and she leaned on the counter toward the stranger. He glanced at her from his eating. "I think if I ever got my picture in the paper, I'd just *die,*" she said, and turned to Cap, shrugging and delighted with even the hopeless image of success.

"Shuh!" he exclaimed fondly, at such foolishness; but it was a cubbish scorn, full of agreement. He looked past her down the narrow room out the window. A car was just drawing up to the curb, vaguely visible through the muslin curtains. They all looked around as the door opened.

Two more customers, a man and a girl.

They went to one of the tables, the one nearest the door, and sat down. Billie Jeane was with them at once, holding her menus in their hinged leatherette bindings. She gave them water and butter while they discussed their food.

"Is the regular lunch still on?" asked the girl, glancing at the clock. It was four o'clock. The hour began to strike, whanging on the springs.

"The veal pie is still on, that's all," said Billie Jeane.

The man looked up. His look somehow shocked Billie Jeane; and she noticed him for the first time, taking him into her mind as an impression, which she rarely did with people. He seemed serious; his pale eyes were shuttered by puffed lids, though his face was lean and young with pale brown skin. He looked like a boy grown newly big, but no older, as if he were her young brother, in a dream, or a movie hero. She smiled at him and licked her rouge. In her breast her heart was a little faster, and she couldn't imagine why. The man said,

"Two veal pie, two coffee, hashed brown on two, and snap it up."

"I'd rather have—" began the girl.

"Cut it," he said. "All right," he added to Billie Jeane. A shining frond of his oiled brown hair had fallen across his temple, and he pushed it back on his skull with his raked hand and looked around the room. Billie Jeane turned and went, mad at herself for the fuss the man had put her into. She was critical of the girl, too, who was pouting thinly and clawing through her shabby bag for a cigarette.

"Two veal pie, plate lunch," called Billie Jeane at the kitchen door.

She came back to get the coffee.

Cap rattled his dishes and sliced bread and pushed it through.

The café was full of professional effort. Billie Jeane trod snappily on their clean linoleum, and every time she neared the table to begin serving the meal, while Cap was singeing the crust of the veal pie to warm it up, she couldn't understand what there was about the new customers to make her think so much; but she decided they were just married, and mad at each other. She winked at Cap when she turned around the next time, and saw him leaning on his half door, staring at the newcomers; and she thought Cap's face was rather white, and his mouth open made him look as if he had a cold. Now she was warm with cleverness, and she felt a breasty giggle of tolerance in her heart when she reconsidered what marriage did to a man and a girl, and what simply unreasonable terrors it gave the woman when the man was sulky; and how if the man got mad and took a swing at her, and knocked her face off, it was easier to bear than sulks. The girl sitting at the table smoked rapidly, constantly wetting her lips, and feeling her throat.

"They'll neither of them say a word till the other one does:" reflected Billie Jeane. She wanted to go up to them and join their hands, and smile at them with a flickering radiance while light beamed through her electric gold hair, and life opened into a sweeter reality, made of movie close-ups.

The man at the counter slapped down a coin on top of his lunch check; and while Billie Jeane was heading back to the kitchen, he left. They heard the door close, and turned to see, but he was gone.

"Ready?" she asked Cap sweetly, her eyes still full of a brooding thought for the man and the girl at the table.

Cap nodded, and turned half sideways, and began to talk out of the side of his mouth. He jerked his head at the table up front.

"Billie Jeane, who's that look like?"

She turned and looked and looked back again.

"Why, Captain, I hardly like t'say." . . .

"Billie Jeane, you look again!"

She looked at her husband, instead.

He was white. He was quivering, almost trembling. His brown eyes behind their refined glasses were hot and dry. She suddenly turned into a scare; and when Cap saw her begin to tremble herself, he flushed and felt a thunder of rage in his breast. He was furious at her for being scared.

"Two veal," he sang out. His voice faltered a little. But he followed it with a witless smile. Then he leaned and whispered, while she clanked the dishes putting them on a tray,

"Pay no mind; you just come back here and wait by *me* till they want you again. —Bring me the papers; his picture was in one of 'em. I'd want t'make *sure* before I—"

"Before you what?" she demanded.

She knew who it was now. The face of the young man at the table was always in the papers. She felt besieged. She faltered a look at Cap, and picked up the tray. She was feeling very weak. Her ankles felt shivery. But the white, gold, and crimson and blue design of her face concealed whatever feelings she owned.

And now, at the table, as she served the veal pies and the hashed browns, her customers sat there without mystery for her. She served them as fast as she could. It was warm and still in the café. The clock sounded clearly. There was nobody outside on the street. They couldn't telephone. —What could they do?

"Will you wish coffee?" she asked in her own propriety.

"I said, 'Two coffee,'" replied the man. But he didn't sound angry, and he looked up to smile at Billie Jeane. He looked more boyish than ever. His eyes gleamed in their narrow sacs, and his mouth turned up at the corners showing sharp eyeteeth. "Two coffee, sister," he repeated, and cleared his throat, and hunched around in his chair.

[302]

My *land!* thought Billie Jeane, going for the coffee.

The girl at the table murmured something that sounded like a sneer; and when Billie Jeane came back, she looked her over and snapped her eyes coldly back to the man's face, as if to say, "That bleached floosie, save your breath."

Billie Jeane felt much more calm now. The smile she'd got, the intimate and live relation between herself and the famous man soothed her fears. She was remembering so much about him. Everybody knew of him.

Cap winked her into the kitchen beyond the swinging half door, humming noticeably to cover their actions.

"The papers?" he whispered when they were private.

"They're gone. The man must've taken them by mistake, the fella at the counter. —Land alive, Cap, that's who it is, though--"

They were making incidental kitchen noises to cover their whispering.

"How you reckon he come *here?*"

The last they'd heard, or the last the papers had, was about Honeyboy Benton heading for Texas, probably alone, or at most with one or two pals, after their latest killing, four people during a bank raid in western Kansas. They'd heard of him going through Oklahoma three days ago. The picture was used everywhere, and reports were sent out every hour to track him down. The picture was a good one too. It looked more like him that he did himself, sitting up there at the table by the front window.

Billie Jeane and Cap peered out for a second. The two of them up there were still eating.

Honeyboy was like a man in a story to them, a story in the movies. They knew all about him. They knew from every way that news traveled. They understood his life because he was from the same part of West Texas they came from. All his experiences except those of killing and stealing were their own. They had even known flight, one time, in a desperate Model T Ford, getting out of town before a gang of Baptist raiders who heard that Cap and Billie Jeane served beer in their eating house . . . that was several years ago.

They could think of themselves wearing the fame of Honeyboy.

But he looked so young, and so good-looking, how could he have done so much in his short years? It made him a kind of prodigy, something to be marveled at and, marveling, to admire.

They'd seen Honeyboy in the movies; a newsreel shot of him being taken up the steps of the jail at Monamossee, Oklahoma. The day was still and hot in summer, with a dust haze hanging on the horizon, and the two trees by the jailhouse standing unshaken by any breath, their leaves limp (and bitter with wry odor). The steps were crowded; but the cars drove right up to them, and Honeyboy stepped out, wearing handcuffs. He had no hat, and the sun made him screw his face up, grinning, and he waved his coupled hands at the camera. He swallowed. The camera moved up. The sounds of people around him blundered gently on the microphone. He swallowed again, and they saw his throat where his collar was open. The genial peace officer standing by him remarked, "Well, Honeyboy, I guess this's just 'bout where you sign off," to which Honeyboy replied, "Just a little *rest* cure, folks," and turned to enter the jail, from which he escaped the same night, smiling on the guards he killed, and leaving a note saying, "Not tired any more."

The whole country had roared at that one.

In truth, they found him winsome. There was a cat-like sweetness about him, sweet like a boxer who has style and what it takes besides. He was called Honeyboy because he was so terrible in crime and so plaintively good-looking and child-like.

When he killed anyone or escaped from any jail or robbed a bank, why, who knew it? Why, the whole country knew it.

The radio talked about him. The radio said he was last seen heading southwest out of Monamossee, Oklahoma, and was believed to be heading for Texas, where he had many hideouts, long known to him from his boyhood days up and down the valley of a great red river that some months flowed like chocolate spilling nourishment over the plains; and other months barely trickled in a white cracked river bed half a mile wide, whose banks were deep cut back into baking hot shadow, little canyons left by the river at its time of rich flood, places where men could hide out.

It'd take a maghty smart posse to find Honeyboy, they all said. Ain't never *been* caught and *stayed* caught *yet,* they said.

The general opinion got around that Honeyboy's adroitness was a thing to be liked for itself.

Like a man in a story, then; a story composed in the very country where outlaws were heroes more than half the time.

The smiling, severe, babyish face staring out of newspapers all over the country was the face of a Southwesterner. Thousands of boys might have been his substitute—if they'd had the obsession and the courage it generated wastefully. It'd be a woman to get him, in the end, they said. They would shake their heads and spit, and know what they were talking about as news-educated citizens, and say a boy like that was always a fool over women; you could tell't t'look at him. Like most public truths, it was instinctive.

Gol dang him, it was such a human failing, that about the women.

For several months they'd been singing a ballad all over the West, about Honeyboy Benton. It was a recital of his exploits, and it sang out on radios and music stores that had loudspeakers on Main Street; and everybody heard it now and then, to the yang of guitars, the bee hum of jews'-harps, the yodel at each last stress of the chorus.

Right down the street from the Apache Tavern was a music store which played the record, a hillbilly performance for Honeyboy Benton's ballad. Cap and Billie Jeane had heard it time and again.

And there he sat, at their front window.

"Cap, I don't know how come I didn't know him raght *off:*" said Billie Jeane, humorously troubled. "I thought was somethin' strange; di'n' know what."

"Look t'me first glance like who it is," he replied.

They were both standing in the kitchen doorway, leaning on the half door and staring. Their minds and memories had been filled with reels of pictures unwinding; and now they came frankly to stare and admire, to fear deliciously with reverence, the same fear religion brought when glory ran high and the Lamb Lived Again, in tents by the railroad tracks on summer nights, full of heat, smoky light, and skidding hearts.

Cap was thinking, "If I ducked out back door, got round to Court House, I'd find Sheriff 'ere; they's a *re*ward"—the fuddled thought of a citizen who craves part of the celebrity of sin, the riches of virtue, and the good of the state.

Billie Jeane thought, "—a dried up skinny old girl like that. I'll bet she sure henpecks him; I'll bet he'd look at me twice if she'd'a let him."

Honeyboy and his girl were eating without words. But an atmosphere of better humor came up between them. After all, they were probably hungry. Four o'clock is late to eat lunch.

He kept glancing out the window, to look at his car, as if to be sure it was still there waiting for him.

They saw by now that it was a Chevrolet business sedan, with closed sides, and the name of a tobacco company on it. Billie Jeane was working her cheek in thought.

"That sure is a clever way to travel," said Cap, nodding to the car.

" 'm going to get a better look," she half thought and half said.

Cap dragged at her waist; but she eluded him; and adjusting her hair and smiling downward with a proud modesty, she strolled up back of the counter and leaned opposite their table, and yawned exquisitely, holding her fingers before her minutely opened mouth. The girl at the table looked up, and at once looked away again. She was disgusted. But she was also alarmed. She toed Honeyboy under the table, and flicked her eyes toward Billie Jeane. Grinning with his mouth full and showing food, Honeyboy looked up at Billie Jeane, and saw the elaborate languor of her pose, the female attention of her presence, masked by midafternoon idleness and peace. But his whole quality told him of danger and chance and the necessity of killing, as he needed to know these things. He knew now that he'd been recognized.

He looked back at his companion.

He began to lean over his plate and cluck the food into his mouth in great gusts. She pushed her plate back, lighted a cigarette and looked long and carefully around the room. She saw Cap still in his doorway. He smiled at her. In the colorless shadows of the late afternoon, he looked black-and-white, and his smile was toy-like, unfamiliar. This read as menace to the girl. She stood up.

Honeyboy looked up, and frowned.

"In a hurry?" he said, and drank half a cup of coffee.

"Come on, come on," said the girl in a drawl.

Billie Jeane came out from behind the counter.

"Would you wish dessert?" she asked. "There is pies and cake, and baked apple, walnut sundae, or preserved figs."

She smiled openly at Honeyboy, sharing the dread secret of his identity with him. He could tell by everything—the moist quiver of her voice, the bead and spark of her eye—that desirous fear so full of his legend that women gave back to him everywhere.

Cap was now coming down the aisle. His face, too, was an open secret. Honeyboy read there the fat shape of indecision.

"No, no more."

He rose and reached in his pocket for some money. He pulled out a handful of rumpled bills rolled up like wastepaper, and picked out a five-dollar note which he threw on the table. Then he looked rapidly around to be sure there was egress; and nodding to his girl, he went out to the street. How quickly he seemed to move! they thought, peering after him through the glass door.

Good God, he was gone, sure took out in a hurry.

The tobacco car whined and fluted as Honeyboy backed out from the curb. Then it curved forward and flew down Main Street, dusting the air where a little wind was beginning to blow. The sun was dropping toward the mountains. How soon would he be gone forever? He was heading South, toward the highway.

"Well, I *do* say," they thought.

Cap went to the table and picked up the five dollars, and rubbed it guiltily with his thumb.

Billie Jeane came beside him and started to pick up the dishes.

They could not look at each other, or speak. Their feelings began to clear, bitterly. Had she married a coward? Slow, and getting fat, and content to stay just where he was: she knew all that long ago. But there he'd'a stayed, and Honeyboy sitting there all that time, just waiting to be taken. Cap rubbed the wrinkled sweet-smelling five-dollar bill and suffered for the depths of his suspicions. —What had she done? walked down to get a look at Honeyboy, and stood there, grinning like a bitch bobcat, trying t'make him look at her. Billie Jeane! His own *wife,* by God!

The café was growing darker.

Light receded and left them far from each other.

Her panic broke before she could help it.

"You better *do* somethin'!" she cried, slamming down her tray on the counter and turning to face Cap.

"Why, you— Yes, and all that time," he said, "what *you* do? Stand and make eyes at him—that helps a lot, don't it?"

" 't could *I* do," she demanded, her reedy voice sounding like a bleat. "You could'a run out the kitchen door, got the Sher'f, collect'd reward, set us on easy street. Just stand 'ere and watch!"

"Leave you alone here, with 'im?" he demanded furiously, moving his little brown eyes side to side as he searched for new thoughts in defense.

"Oh, *my,* yes," she jeered, and began to sob on her breath. "Pertect *me.* —Honeyboy Benton don't go 'round shooting women!" she stormed, as if Cap did that very thing himself.

Her tears began to wreck her face. She could feel it happening. Her woe was abject.

"Say, time to do something raght now," said Cap with a sudden embarrassed energy. Her weeping always saddened him, melancholy as he was by nature. She nodded at this, with her face buried in her hands. He noticed her hands, thin from labor and dishwashing. The tendons stood there like the cords in her throat.

"You wait raght here," he said, and rushed out of the café.

Evening had fallen before he came back, and the lights were on, and supper started. He came back soberly and said,

"They'll get 'im, all raght. Sher'f sent out two cars raght away, heading down the highway. Said he didn't see what else I *could* do but what I *did* do.". . .

Billie Jeane looked around from the range, accepting the truce.

"Sure 'nough?" she sighed.

"Un-*hunh?*" he answered, meaning yes.

They both got busy cooking.

They spoke very little; but working side by side, and knowing how sobs will echo before they die down altogether, they felt something grow back between them, and recognized without words that, after all, a wild occurrence had transpired in their café, the Apache Tavern, that very afternoon, a passage unbelievable and unsettling, for the sudden intrusion of the movie-radio-newspaper world of power and fame into their lives.

[309]

Presently the front door was shaken open and they looked down the café to see. People entered.

"Where'd he sit?"

"Hunh?"

More people came in.

"Raght there, that chair by the window."

"Sure 'nough!"

"Uh-*hunh*." . . .

"Did he look like—"

"—like the pictures? Sure did." . . .

"What'd he do?"

"Well, I was serving a customer, and then this girl, she come in, and he follows."

They all nodded, hanging on her words. Their faces were child-like, their mouths piteous with wonder, and their eyes watching visions. The café was crowding up. The news had spread. The sheriff's cars had gone blatting out of town to the highway. The news got around very fast.

"Did he tote a gun?"

"Didn't *see* any."

"Did he *talk,* and *kid,* and carry *on* at all?"

"*Uh*-uh . . . never said a word."

They turned their heads and looked at the chair again, the window, the table. Cap showed them the five-dollar bill. A couple of boys in the crowd whistled, and someone said, "*Oh*-oh," and everybody laughed. Presently Cap looked Billie Jeane in the eye, and took her love for granted, and had to give back to someone something he felt he owed somebody, and he waved his hairy arm and took in the crowd, saying,

"Ev'body have a cup of coffee on the house?"

"Jabetcha," someone replied, and they all laughed again, crowding up the counter.

[310]

A boy fifteen scrambled over to Honeyboy's chair and sat down in it and made a face, a mock grin at himself and the world for what he had to do—sit in the great bandit's chair, and live life ahead, however briefly. The boy made pistols out of his hands and covered the room; and that compulsion over, he left the chair with his head full of dreams.

Nothing in the café was changed; yet it was all new—the gleaming counter rubbed with soap every day until it looked like beeswax; the art finish on the mottled walls, wavy plaster sponged with blue, red, and gold on a tan base; the dark green ceiling; the pie cabinet and the clock; the swinging half door; the merry coffee vat; the front window and door through whose muslin the night street showed, cars moving slowly and reverently by to let people look into the tavern where it had taken place, and across the street, the pale front of the Court House among its spindly trees, through which night light blazed from the windows of the sheriff's office.

In the sky beyond all that a faint drift of afterlight showed between the lowering curtain of the dark and the dark country where the chase was in progress.

"What kind of a car did he have?"

"He had a Chevvie . . ."

"Coop?"

"*Uh*-uh; it was a salesman's truck, *you* know, like a sedan, only closed up all solid behind the front seat?"

"I know."

"He drove it up and he drove it off."

"I *swear.*"

"Maghty clever."

"Where'd he get it?"

They didn't know until a man came in at half past seven with his wife and four children, to show them the place, the chair, the magic. Then he explained all about the tobacco truck.

He said that at three-twenty in the afternoon a man he knew, Sam Losey, by name, a tobacco salesman, driving his Chevrolet business sedan, was stopped just there on the highway where No. 380 joins the main road, about eleven miles outside of Hermosa; and he said they stopped him by blocking the road, they had their Lincoln touring car set right across the road, so he had to stop.

"So he stopped, and he got out, and quick's he sees who it is, he starts to turn around and run and get back t's car; but Honeyboy himself called after him, and he figgered he better stop. So he stop running, and come back. Well, they set him up in the back seat of the Lincoln, and the last he knew they was tying his hands and laigs; and Honeyboy and the lady and another bandit got in Sam's car, and they drove off toward town."

Billie Jeane tucked at her hair and said with almost a yawn,

"Yes, it was raght after that he came in here."

The man went on with his story.

"Then they drove the Lincoln off the road, down by the river, raght there—you *know?* where the willows begin? and you cain't see it from the road? That's where they waited."

"I declare."

"They had that big car waitin' there all that time!"

"Well I'll declare."

"Where's he *now?*"

"Who, Sam Losey?"

"The salesman."

"He's over to the *ho*tel."

"Honeyboy let 'im go?"

The man with the family smacked his lips, and ran his fat cracked fingers over his mouth in a humorous, waggling suspense, and chuckled in his throat, confidentially.

"Sho'," he said, privately, relishing what he knew about and would presently tell them.

[312]

"What's he *say* . . ."

"Who, Sam Losey?"

"Un-*hunh*."

"Says his head aches!" declared the man, and burst into a scream-ing wheeze of laughter that seemed like a wind whining gustily through telegraph wires. He bent slowly over and whacked his thick little knees, and his children danced up to him and laughed with Papa, while his wife looked modestly around at the wondering faces of the throng, deprecatingly and promisingly.

"Head aches?"

"Honeyboy—" he had to pause a moment to conquer another laugh, but presently went on. "Honeyboy come back in Sam's truck, and the Lincoln come back to the road; and they put Sam back in his driver's seat, and Honeyboy says to him it sure is too bad, after the loan of his car, to have to do this; but he says he has to do this, so he hauls off and cracks Sam on the *head* and Sam passes out! . . . Spaw-w-w-w!" was the noise he made as asthmatic laughter overtook him again.

The crowd began to laugh too.

They looked around at one another; Sam was alive and well, only with a headache, and Honeyboy was hissing far away along the road in his big Lincoln; when someone got cold-cokked it was a thing to die laughing at.

The laughter died gradually, and the man wiped his eyes with his hard, glistening little thumbs, and said further that Honeyboy gave Sam a souvenir.

"I saw it. He left it in the car by Sam, and Sam found it when he come to."

He paused and spaced his fingers out in front of him, and measured the space with his eye, and refined his calculations and nodded.

"'Bout that big, the prettiest little .38 you ever saw; reckoned he figgered Sam ought to tote a gun, be safe next time bandits holt him up."

There was a murmur.

"Sure 'nough, did he leave him a present?"

Billie Jeane nodded emphatically. She could see him do it. She understood by intuition that the grandeur that fetched her would also make Honeyboy himself its victim.

"Didja see the *otha* man?" asked the prominent father.

"Who?"

He waved at Billie Jeane and Cap and closed his eyes eloquently for a second.

"There was anotha man. He came in with them in the truck. Sam Losey says he goes along with Honeyboy ev' time they go town, and looks around first."

"Billie Jeane, you reckon that was the man?"

"Why, Cap, I *declare,* I think so . . ."

"He came in here before Honeyboy and the lady did," explained Cap. "He sat raght there at the counter, in that chair, and he ordered bowl of chili, and he asked for the newspapers. —By gravy, Billie Jeane, he took all papers, di'n' he?"

"Sure did, Cap."

Cap straightened up and palmed his hands out and upward.

"There y'are. See? —That man is the *ad*vance man. He comes in here; and if he don't come out in a hurry, then Honeyboy and the lady waitin' outside knows all is well, and in they come. Then the *man* goes out to keep guard, and he takes the papers to pri*vint* idintification by any picture that happenstance to be in the papers. —Then they pick him up on the way outa town."

A sigh went around, and the crowd moved in self-dismissal. Billie Jeane looked at Cap with a tender amazement and pride at his reasoning.

"Reckon, will they get him?" said someone.

"Who, Honeyboy? Man, you ain't *never* goin' see *any*body git that rascal!"

This was said admiringly, in tribute. It was a publication of everyone's belief, rooted in hope rather than sense. They all nodded, brightly eyed. Billie Jeane and Cap watched them all go, newly drawn together themselves by the fame of the Apache Tavern and their own authority from the occasion. As the crowd lessened, one of the young boys cocked his thumbs like hammers and crouched over and began to run slyly down the street. "Pow! Pow-pow!" he said, shooting.

The Small Rain

I was on duty late that night, reading. Then the night bell. Someone ringing. I went down from my room on the third floor. Nobody
else was in the house but a window was open somewhere letting in
cold air that followed me down the narrow carpeted stairway.
Finally, the frosted glass vestibule doors, and a man's shadow on
the outer one. I was a long time getting there, and he was moving
away just as I reached the knob, which was brightly polished as
always by old Maggie, poor soul.

"Yes?"

He turned back from the few steps that go up to the street. He
faced into the door light. Darkness behind him and the passing of
cars both ways on 79th Street.

"Oh. I was just—I thought nobody."

"Yes, I'm sorry. I had to come downstairs from the back of the
house. Come in?"

"Thank you."

I walked ahead to the downstairs parlor, turning on our weak
frugal lights. He followed. His steps sounded unwilling.

"In here."

"Thank you."

Overhead light, which seems always to exist only in itself. The brown walls stay dark. Pool of light over the flat desk and the chair behind it and the armchair facing it.

"Will you sit down?"

But he stood waiting. He didn't want his face to show. He said,

"Do you happen to know me?" On his breath drifted the damp smoky smell of Scotch whiskey. He was sober.

"Yes. We have met once or twice and then I think I have seen you on Sundays."

"Yes. —It was locked next door or I would have gone in and rung the emergency bell over there."

"Yes. In this neighborhood we have to lock the doors after nine. It's too bad. We would like to leave it open all night. But you know."

"Yes."

Even as we faced each other, he worked to remain unknown. I have often seen how hard that is. It was so hard that he finally did what only can be done. He fell to his knees and put his fists on the corner of the desk and his face to his fists and said in his private darkness,

"Father, will you hear my confession?"

"Of course."

And then waiting.

And I must be silent for him.

How much makes silence. Here, the beat of his thoughts. Far off, maybe on York Avenue, an ambulance or police siren. I once said the sound was like the scream of the city in pain. Then near, down the hallway, Monsignor's old standing clock, ticking slowly and it now seemed loudly. I leaned toward the caller, turning my face away. He was about my own age. I wished I could lift him up, offer him a blessing and tell him it was all over. Who was I—

[317]

youngish, and a short haircut like his—to loom over him. Did he feel my eternal sense of inadequacy? No matter. He rolled his face in his hands and made a small rusty sound in his throat, like a child's husky venture toward speech, yet could not begin.

"Yes?" I said. "I believe you said emergency?"

Whisper, "Yes."

"Yes. Well. Let's see. How long since your last confession?" Something to answer, then possibly, something to let go.

"Seven months."

"So. And then?"

"How can I. You wouldn't know unless I told all of it."

"Then do."

"Yes. Oh, great God. I don't feel I know who I am, even."

"Something brought you here."

"I have just come from the hospital." He had to swallow. "It's my wife."

"Ah? Ah."

"What have I done to her?"

He ground his head down into the dust of whatever it was.

"You sinned against her?"

"Oh, I, yes, I did, I did. And now she."

"Yes. Then perhaps it might help if you could tell how it began."

He left his darkness; looked up and away. He was haggard and yet comely. His face had a healthy color which nothing could drain away. His eyes were crackling black in startling whites. He opened and shut his lips—they were sharply defined, generously formed, and they echoed appetite—and in a crumb of a voice that yet rumbled deep in his chest he said,

"Last week I had to go to San Francisco on business. I am a broker. I wanted to take her with me, and our children, my little boy five and my daughter seven. They have never seen San Francisco. But she said she would have to stay home, and anyway, I

[318]

would fly out and be back in six days. We would talk every other day on the telephone. She was planning to go to the airport with me but at the last minute we couldn't find a sitter—it was a night flight —and anyhow it was pouring rain so I left her and took my taxi."

If he spoke of every detail it would take him longer to get to the point, which would be so difficult to tell. I must let him justify his poor state of existence, if he were at last to acknowledge who he was and what he had done. So much about him and his style spoke between his words that I could complete his pictures, as though I were he. Between us both spoke a soul.

Sometimes when you get away from everything, even everything that you really love, there is a charged feeling of freedom and excitement for what may be ahead. There didn't seem anything especially wrong about thinking like that but then it wasn't even thinking, it was just feeling, and you let it feel.

The plane went through the rain and ascended above it, going like cold silk up that high and there was less time between cities way below than ever before. There were those islands of tiny lights in the far darkness. It was great to look down at all the streets crisscrossing and the long roads and think of people. They really were great. They made you think of—this was really funny—they made you think of love.

Going west you took the night right along with you across the United States and it was still dark or almost when you touched down at San Francisco airport. There was fog but not more than you could use to get down and you knew that the Pacific smelled like the *ocean* but not the *Atlantic* ocean. (That was something to put on a postcard to your little boy after you got to the hotel.) Meantime you had all your facts and figures in your head for the meeting at the bank at ten o'clock. Five days of it and the first impression was going to be the important one. It felt great to be ready.

You wondered how California bankers shook hands. Depended on where they went to school and college. Thank God you were so healthy, inside and out. You had a feeling you owed it all to her, and that God or somebody was good to you. Your very health belonged to her because it came from happiness—just the way the children came to you and belonged to you both.

"That's how I was, Father, before."
"Before?"
"Before the recent thing in San Francisco."
"Yes. Yes?"

The meetings went along up there golden, three days of them, and evenings some of the others had you out to dinner, or took you on the town, several couples, and they really knew how to do it, and you talked home to her almost every day. The home weather was better. She said they all went to the park every morning. Billy had a helicopter on a little stick. Maura got out of school at eleven and had her books with her and they walked awhile and then sat down and she would read to them and make up new sentences between the ones in the book. She was better than the book. She wrote poems about the pigeons on the park walks. One morning she recited a poem to a pigeon who just stood there with his head over on one side and listened. Billy got so jealous because everybody was paying attention to the poem and the pigeon that he threw something at the pigeon which then walked rapidly away. Maura called her brother a wretch. You couldn't imagine where she got the word. She was always getting new words. You always had to pretend not to notice.

The third evening in San Francisco at supper after seeing a play you looked around the soft gold-lighted room filled with slow elegant music and people dancing and you saw someone you knew who was still living in San Francisco ever since you were with her during the Korean War when San Francisco was your staging area and with other new officers you had a couple of weeks there before sailing. You knew her in the whole way a man can know a woman, a wartime encounter full of urgency, but now you couldn't quite think of her name. You asked the business wife next to you, who knew her right away, and told you the name was Frances and the rest of it. She was still unmarried. They all loved her—whenever they had a chance to see her, which was not often, as she was so popular and so taken up with everything. You think people sometimes get something across the room even if they aren't looking because just then she turned slowly at her table and looked across and she saw you and you both waved really pleased.

What, said the business wife next to you, do you know Frannie? Oh yes, and she said, Why how marvelous, how long, and then you told about the war, or part of it, anyway, and Yes, said the business wife, Frannie practically ran the whole war singlehanded, and then there was about to be something not nice to be told, but you didn't wait to hear it, for you said Excuse me and went across the room and asked Frances to dance with you.

It wasn't all that long ago, then, after you moved a little way to the music, and how she looked at you. She had made more of it that other time than you had. Actually, you used to wonder if it shouldn't've gone even further and ended in marriage. She always hoped it would. But the war, and pretty young, both of you, and you were spoiled by freedom and success with women, and it didn't. But now the band was making golden sounds like the low light in the supper club. Frances asked and you answered, So you are married? Yes. She saw your ring.

You knew what you should do but you went right on thinking and dancing. It felt innocent and lovely, even if it wasn't both. Those were two other people way back there, during the war; except that they knew all about these two people right here, dancing, now, in the gold sound and light of after midnight in a city a long way from home. You thanked her for the dance and there was a word about meeting again. Why not? You returned to your table.

"I never meant anything to happen. I truly did not."
"No. Ah, no."

The next night you still felt great, after all the day's meetings and the little dinner at somebody's place, where they all made you feel very well about how the meetings had gone, for they had gone your way. The San Franciscans made little messages at each other about you without saying anything, and you were pretty sure you could have any job in San Francisco that you wanted, bring your family right out, have an interesting house like this one hanging on a cliff in Sausalito with the whole Bay before you, and sailboats leaning every weekend toward the Golden Gate Bridge.

She had said if you wanted to take a minute after the dinner party out in Sausalito to run by for a nightcap she would be home. What a lot there was to talk about after so many years and so much life —you, married, and two children, imagine: hard to believe.

It was, though what she meant was, hard for her to accept, though nothing of this was put into words; and how did you feel then, finding out that it had meant so much to her, all that time? Did she mean it? Or was she merely possessive? If she didn't, did it matter, with everything settled at home? And yet, how could you think that someone as—as self-sufficient and knowledgeable, as beautiful, as she, would have held on to some sort of expectancy, as if you meant all that to her ever since, and what could be done about it now, with everything seriously changed, at least for yourself? But if you could remember anything of all that time before, how could

[322]

you help remembering all of it? And what that did to you! So the worms of reason began to move in the dark.

The nightcap was used up telling all she wanted to hear about home, and the children, and how you lived, and who it was you married, and what everybody did, including Whisky, your wire-haired terrier. There was another nightcap and then she telephoned for a taxi.

"I didn't want to leave. You know what that meant."
"Yes."

She made you leave, but if you liked you could take her to dinner the next evening, if you wouldn't be too tired after the last day of meetings. Tired. She laughed because she had never seen you tired. She shivered when you kissed her cheek and you went to the hotel.

Now this part: in the morning before you went to the last board room downtown there was a letter from home. It was thick so you knew there were pictures and poems and X's from the children inside, with a letter from their mother. Then you did something that made you know what you hoped might happen that evening, later. For you said to yourself that you were in a rush to get off to the meeting, so there would not be time to read the letter now, and therefore you put it in your pocket, unopened, and went downtown.

It stayed there all day, and when you went back to change for the evening, it was still unopened. You looked at it, and you felt something begin to burn deep inside you, there was a strange feeling of watching yourself do something you had no clear intention of doing later. What you did not want to do now was to mix the two things—the letter from home and the evening that waited ahead. The fact that you couldn't mix them ought to have been enough to tell you something.

Though at the time it was remarkable how you could go right

ahead knowing all the time what you were going to have it all come to and what you wanted in spite of envelopes that you had to put off opening until tomorrow morning, when you would be up and getting ready to take the ten o'clock flight to New York.

You dined very publicly because Frances lightly said that there was some sort of safety in that. But there was none anywhere, and you both knew it, for if anything her hushed feeling was even stronger than yours and neither of you said anything about it because you did not have to say anything. It was something that put its own extra breath into everything you said about anything *else,* and when she answered it was there too. You felt as though something was stinging you in a way hardly to be felt, all over and under your skin. When you asked her to dance and she refused, you knew it was because you could look at each other better sitting at the table than out there looking across each other's shoulder. When it was time to go, there were various small excuses to wait just a little while yet, as if something might still happen to prevent everything. Nothing did, and you went home with her. You were excited and sad. You stayed till daylight.

"I accuse myself of that sin."
"Yes. That time only?"
"Yes."

Well, daylight, and all of your aspects were real, and one of them would like to keep what you felt right then. Ah. Good. Ah, for you. For her, too, surely? Like some lovely depth of breathing beyond identity. Dear and beautiful, to be joined so with the act of life, beyond thoughts, and to spend in taking, and be lost in the very act of knowing how to find yourself: the eternal paradox of desire. And yet the moment soon came when the vision of the world returned, and there you were, in the very center of it, condemned to

[324]

be who you were, which meant that you again saw yourself through the eyes of others, including those who loved you best and trusted you most. So going through the foggy dawn you hungered for the look of the fresh world, to see common sights, for these would help you to forget who you had been only a little while ago, in the silky silvery darkness of that other embrace.

You made the taxi hurry to the hotel, for there was safety there, you would there meet the self to whom that fat envelope had been sent, which you could now open, to know again the love that would bathe you in safety. The power of that love lay in a certain mystery —that you could betray it, and still want it more than all other things.

It was such a powerful restoration from excitement and sorrow that you once again put off reading it, not for the previous reason, but because the joy of it would be even greater if you made yourself wait just a little longer, until after you had showered, shaved, and ordered breakfast sent up to be laid by the sitting room window where you could read by the fine silver light of the fog rising off the bay. You opened the envelope with joy.

There was a drawing by Maura showing Whisky wearing a pair of spectacles and smoking a pipe, and another by Billy, in wild eccentric scribblings that filled a whole page, with a pair of crossed eyes and a Halloween mouth somewhere to make a face. You kept the letter until last for a number of reasons, one of which you did not care to remember. There were four pages, very clear, upright handwriting on her stiff pale blue stationery with white engraving. "Darling," it began, and everything that followed made that word real, as if nobody else was ever called that. You supposed that someone at her school a few years ago had taught her to make her letters brightly interesting, and now she tried to do so, but with a self-mocking humor that gave all her news a second value—an undertone of happiness so sure of all its parts that she must be playful about these in turn, for fear it wasn't all true. You read it rapidly. Her letter seemed to reach out all about you and take you in its arms, holding you against yourself. Your heart began to beat slowly and heavily at the thought that anything might happen—you could not say "had happened"—to disturb the wonderful balance between the love in the letter and the love held in your heart. Well, the weather was so fine they wouldn't dream of missing a single instant in the park, and so they all went every morning, and were going again tomorrow, and the next day, as long as the sun shone. Billy was now in charge of Whisky—could handle the leash, even crossing Fifth Avenue, and coldly refused to let Maura have it even for a moment. Maura accepted the loss of her old privilege with queenly grace, glancing at her mother to exchange a female smile over the small boy and his scowling pride. Hurry home, as you were booked for dinner on the nineteenth, and the theater on the twenty-second. Everybody was in great health and spirits, longing for you to come, working on a surprise about which nothing could be told but which would take your breath away on your first evening, and the only bore of any sort was that the regular sitter was ill and the substitute ones were impossible to find, and if found, looked shifty, and if not shifty then full of cold-germs. She supposed her duty was to stay home, leaning out of the round-tower window, combing her long golden locks and keeping vigil until you rode toward her out of the wood. Actually, there was nothing to worry about, really, and she was keeping up with her meetings and this evening was dining with Tad and Dolly at the Cosmopolitan Club. New York was so beautiful in the autumn. If you closed your eyes halfway and put your head a little to one side and looked down the long narrow views, you might almost think the blue in the air came from Indian summer haze instead of from gasoline fumes. Weren't you glad you had decided not to move anywhere else after all? Oh, she said, why wouldn't you hurry home! How I love you, she wrote, and isn't it ridiculous (but not really ridiculous, this is only one of my double words, that mean just the opposite), after two children, and your beginning of a heavier jaw and my definitely gray hairs—I found another one this morning which Cartier will put into a locket for you to hang next to your gold key on your neat little Wall Street vest watch chain. Come home, you don't know how empty these rooms are, even with our two little lives making their motes of energy everywhere about. But they don't yet know how to give, they can only take, and we know how to do both, darling, don't we. God keep you. I kiss you. —And there was more of it, and since you hated to think of how it made you feel, you refused to feel. All you wished was that you were already on the plane, pressing your foot against the seat ahead, to make it go faster.

He turned his face away.

"I can't."

"There's no hurry."

"I have to. How can I ever."

Monsignor ticked away in the hall, deliberate as fate. If it would help to have any communion at all with anyone, I would put my hand on his shoulder for a second, but his buried torment bulked so eloquently in all his body, that I must not touch. I waited, I can't think for how long. It didn't matter. The notion occurred to me that a soul has no dimension. Finally,

"If I am ever to—"

And it was in your return to speech, however sorely diffuse, that you resumed your search for meaning as well as pardon. Your plane came home in a late autumn bronze afternoon. As it went into a banking turn over the Sound you saw the city in every glint of the gold sun down over New Jersey. The grand settling of the plane into lower and lower altitude heavied yourself, and it seemed that

[327]

the plane made you feel your heart heavying and settling with desire for all that awaited you—herself, her dark-lashed blue eyes, the children, the famous surprise.

The taxi driver luckily made a record trip from the airport, in spite of heavy traffic. You hoped he wouldn't talk, so you could think ahead. The closer you came to home, the more like yourself you felt, the farther—it was as far as years, those other years, during the war, on the West Coast—it all seemed, and the truer you felt your renewed vows to be. You wondered whether, if a man was just once *enough* of a fool, he would be safe against ever being a fool again. You felt sure of it as the taxi came to your house, and you got out in a hurry, and gave the driver an extra five dollars for his speed and silence, and ran up the steps to the stoop and unlocked the door and went in.

There was nobody downstairs. You threw down your bag and ran up the red carpeted stairs, hauling yourself by the white banister. You called out all their names. At the head of the stairs a strange woman in a nurse's uniform came out of the nursery doorway and put her hand to her lips for silence.

They are sleeping, she said, we'd better not disturb them just yet, and it soon turned out that she meant the children. She took you into your room and shut the door to tell you that at half past eleven that morning, coming from the park, crossing Fifth Avenue, your wife, turning to see if it was safe for the children and the dog, did not notice a cab coming too fast on the last of the amber light, and when she did see it, it was too late to do anything but thrust the children back. The car struck her. They had all the details at the hospital, where she was now. The hospital had sent the children home with the nurse, and here they were, waiting for you to get home. They had waited all afternoon.

But how was she—was she badly—?

The nurse couldn't tell you anything except that as she had left the hospital she knew they would operate within an hour. It was a serious emergency. If he would like to go over to the hospital now? she had another two hours she could stay with the children, but after that, they would have to get someone else, as she went off duty at eight, so if he could be back by then?

Down the hall, behind the nursery door, you heard Whisky making little breaths under the door, and small claw sounds, to get out to see you.

It was nothing you could call a process of thought that got you to the hospital, but it was like returning to consciousness when you reached the seventeenth floor, and her door, and were met by an intern, who kept you out of the room and closed the door after him so he could talk to you.

What he had to say was so final that your uppermost idea at the moment was to show how politely controlled you could be. He was young and not too experienced yet, and he began to sound impatient, wondering what sort of individual you could be who heard with such solicitous amenity that your wife was not expected to live for more than twenty-four hours, if that. But how could he know what struck you with the effect of a double bolt of lightning? One was her death that must be, and the other was the thought, out of your childhood's notion of God, that this was your punishment for being who you were, capable of what you had done.

Even, you kept thinking in silence, even at the very time I was flying home, the thing happened to her.

You waited to be told what to do. The young surgical intern said you could go in for one minute if you felt like it. You would not see much, and that would be too much even so. You nodded and tipped the door open and the nurse inside got a nod from the doctor, so she let you approach the bed. You went on tiptoe as if the faintest pressure of sound or act might kill. You leaned over her. Her head was swathed in bandages that outlined her face. Her eyes were closed. She was as white as the gauze. She was unconscious. Her left hand lay on the upper sheet. You leaned and kissed it with held breath. She did not move, but in a whisper as far and as near as her sound during love, she spoke your name. How could she know you were there if she was unconscious and paralyzed? But she knew. The nurse leaned sharply forward at this event. Then silence again and hardly life. You were asked to go. To go.

The young doctor was gone when you returned to the corridor. Where was he? Could he be found? Who was the surgeon who had operated? Where was there someone who knew what to do, and who would do it, instantly? What was all this defeatist nonsense about not living? Where was anyone? Why were you allowed to live?

But the children were at home. That was why you were allowed to live, even after what you had done to them all. You arranged for a new nurse to go home to stay all night with them. You asked if you could remain at the hospital through the night. What if she —what if, while you were gone from her near presence, the end might come? But it must not come. What was needed was to get things *organized*. It had always worked for you before! Take charge! Have a plan! You spent the night in a wicker chair in the solarium down the hall. Every time a buzzer sounded at the nurses' station, or a door opened releasing far light and a sound of any need, you tiptoed to her door, sick with hope. It was never different there. New nurses came and had to be told who you were and where they could find you if. Their efficiency for which you were grateful seemed also to contain menace. You sat awake until daylight. Someone persuaded you to go downstairs for some coffee. When you returned the head surgeon was present, and he gave you without any suggestion of feeling a report of the nature of the injuries—they were multiple and sure to be fatal—and an account of what had been done in conscientious surgical effort. It was probable

[330]

that there would be little change during the day but it could be expected that toward nightfall the impaired circulatory system would begin to fail. It would then be hours if not minutes until the end would come. He suggested that you would be more helpful at home, with your children.

How ridiculous—but that was a word now to recoil from—how full of idiocy it was that you had a powerful impulse to take the impassive surgeon, who rather resembled a woodchuck with eyeglasses, as if Maura might have drawn him, and tell him what was shredding your heart in secrecy, as if that admission to him might help her to gain some power to defeat death.

But almost without you noticing how, the doctor was gone. You went home. A nurse would come at six to keep the children while you returned for vigil.

"How could I let them know? I had to pick them up and hug them and smile, and tell them their mother was asleep, and that we must all pray for her."

"They saw the accident?"

"Oh, yes. They said they cried when it happened, and then the excitement was so great they had enough to do to watch."

"Did they have any idea—?"

"Not really."

"There is something sweet, something touching, about the misinformation in which small children have to live. —Do you want to continue? Or do you want me to say a few things to you now?"

"Please, let me. Though how. Good God, what kind of man?"

The home nurse had to be relieved, and it was not possible to find another, or a sitter, until tonight. There was no one but yourself to be with the children. You had them all day. It was the most false day of your life, in the sense of pretending. They wanted to do

[331]

their surprise for you, but you said that it would be better to keep it for the time when they could *all* be there, because their mother would surely not want to miss it? But she knows what it is, they said, and you said, Yes, of course she does, but it really would be better this way, and they finally agreed. You had a game of getting breakfast together, and then doing it all up afterwards, and then there was a great clamor set up about going to the park.

The park? How could they ever want to see it again? But they did, and it was promised for after lunch, with Billy leading Whisky, or the other way round, and Maura with her crayons to do some pigeons when it would be time to sit down near the playground, and take a little rest, as always. That is what you did, and Maura asked why you were so funny, and you said, What do you mean, funny? and, while Billy watched you make this exchange, she said, Oh, funny and sort of far away.

It was the first coming to the surface of all the—all the hell, you supposed you had to call it, that was underneath everything in your world now. If you couldn't look straight at your children: that was hell. If you knew what you had done to make that so: that was hell. If she whom you only loved was dying: that was hell. If pigeons in their God-given idiocy were so outside any possible reach of relation to them, who had done nothing and could do nothing but be pigeons: that was hell. Come, you said, not answering your sapphire-eyed child, come on, Maura, and Billy, and Whisky, we're going home.

Protest, the usual convention, but now it made rage come up like vomit to be swallowed just back of your tongue. You started off alone, as if to leave them, then, if they would not obey; and they ran after you all the way to the walk at the avenue. Billy started to cross, tugging Whisky sideways. You had to reach and pull them back. Other people were waiting for the walk light. Billy felt something much more wrong in your touch than merely the angry grasp

[332]

for his safety. He looked up at you warily, but with some familiar propitiatory charm that was deliberate, and it was so like yourself in miniature at your old moments of trying to win your way that you saw yourself in him, your little boy, whom you loved with pride so great it was buried. You could not bear what you saw, his innocence as the vehicle of your loathed likeness, and you struck him. You struck him so hard that your hand stung from it. He fell aside but recovered himself with a small humble scramble. Some woman who saw this act said, That man should be reported. The light changed. You led your family across the street. At the other side you halted and leaned down to Billy. He shrank away. He did not cry. He was white and about to be sick. He was shocked out of himself. Maura looked at you like a grown stranger. In silence you all went home.

How long, then, must you go on compounding your crimes? Oh God, you cried out inside, generalizing your anguish.

You were shaking. You went to get a stiff drink. Why shouldn't you call up Dolly and Tad and beg them to come and help? But there was nobody you knew whom you really wanted to see, except the children, and you went to find them, if you ever could again.

Billy was in your room, lying with his face turned to his mother's pillow. His longing was painful to observe. When you called to him he did not acknowledge you. You sat down and tried to take him up and he was inert, absent, not giving you his eyes or his face. Maura—where was she? You found her in the nursery. She received you politely. Her small exquisite face was composed and pale. She answered you, wanting nothing. She was combing Whisky's knotted fur with exaggerated concentration. Whisky leaped away from her and into your arms, a hero of affection. When you put him down he thought it was a game and danced forward and backward, barking challenges, just as in the old days. Day declined early in late October. Light was needed in the house. If light was needed, that meant the hour of evening had come. It was time to go to the hospital again.

They had sent the new nurse who now rang the doorbell.

"I asked her if she had come from the hospital and if there was any word. She said no, she had not seen the patient. Where were the children? Upstairs, absent, gone from me. I went to the hospital. Until then I had not thought of what anyone must do for her."

"And that was?"

"That was, if they meant what they said, to arrange for the last sacraments."

"Did you?"

"Yes."

"In time?"

"Only just."

He put both hands over his face gently against the edge of the desk. Presently he spoke from there.

"In an hour it was over. They called me. I saw it. Then they had me leave. They had me answer questions and they wrote down information which I signed. I went out to walk around."

Anywhere. About an hour ago you found yourself walking by here. You walked past and then came back and tried the main door. It was locked. You walked on again. Then you noticed the entrance, the steps down to the small areaway and the almost hidden door, and you saw the old brightly polished brass doorbell. It was all built in to the side of the church, a city rectory, and the thing to do was go down the few steps and ring. Someone might come. If nobody did, it was no better than you deserved, regardless of what you might need. But at the thought of what you would have to say, you could not go down the steps and ring. You walked on to Third Avenue and up a block to a corner bar and there you had two drinks of

[334]

Scotch. Your stiff silence kept you alone. Nobody spoke to you, though the place was crowded. Five minutes after the second drink you pushed yourself away from the bar and came back here, and this time you rang. It was a long wait, and with perverse relief you were about to go, feeling excused by circumstances from performing your fearful desire, but just as you were turning away, you saw the light come on, and then the shadow on the frosted glass, and then the open door, and you entered. You walked with a certain air of courage. It was all that was left after hope.

"That's all, Father."

"Yes. You have had dreadful trials."

"I brought them on myself."

"How, do you think?"

"Is this punishment for what I did?"

"I would say no."

"But she is dead."

"If she lived, you would still have known guilt and sorrow."

"Yes, yes, but I would have had a chance to—"

"To forgive yourself."

The idea shamed him. He looked down. I added,

"You must still do so."

"How can I?"

"You can, if God can."

"I don't know how."

"Do you think you are perfect?"

"No."

"Or that you were born to be?"

"No, no."

"Then you must believe in God's mercy. Isn't it what you came here to ask for?"

"I don't know. All I know, if I helped to have her taken away, I don't know what I shall ever do."

"Your guilt is real. Your grief is real. There is no necessary connection between the two. You have confessed. I can absolve you. I wish I could help you further."

So did he. He waited. I could almost see coursing through his shapely, close-cropped head the thoughts of a boy in terror at first hearing of the power of God—probably from some hard-working nun in parochial school who had to maintain the trivial discipline of her classroom by establishing God's wrath and a promise of destruction directly as a result of any fall from grace, and whether this should relate to spitballs in class, or gumchewing in chapel, or impurity anywhere, could cause a lifetime's confusion behind the face of reason.

The sinner's worst suffering was always his sense of solitude—nobody else could possibly understand him, alone in his iniquity. I believed I must somehow find a way to bring the power of feeling back into the shocked man before me. If he might only know what he had lost, he would suffer, but he would not remain frozen in fear.

"You must believe," I said, "that what you have lost is understood by someone else. Now make an act of contrition."

Like a small boy he bent his head and rapidly murmured the words learned as a child and used all through life. I absolved him, and then stood up, and then so did he. For the first time he looked directly at me.

"Why don't I feel it?" he asked. "I know it but I don't feel it. I cannot believe that she is gone. I feel dead, myself. Have I killed us both?"

I was sure he must be made to think of what he had lost at its most dear and immediate—the companion of all his life ahead, now gone, and not the charming friend of a night or two who still lived.

He must feel his grief more than what he believed about himself.
I said,

"Do you read?"

"Read?"

"In college, did you ever read poetry?"

"Oh. Yes, I did. We all had to."

"Yes. Do you remember any?"

"Yes, some. Not much. It's been a long time."

He wondered, looking at time. I said,

"I don't know if you ever read these few lines, but if you did,
they might tell you what someone else lost four centuries ago. This
man's feeling has never changed, ever since he wrote it down. May
I say it to you?" He nodded. "These words, then:

> O *western wind, when wilt thou blow,*
> *That the small rain down can rain?*
> *Christ! that my love were in my arms,*
> *And I in my bed again!"*

He regarded me silently until the words began to fill up his mind
and he could weigh the emptiness of his heavy arms. Then he
brought his hands to his mouth and said,

"Oh, God, that's it, father. Do you know it, too?"

"Like anyone."

"Oh, Christ!"

He turned away. He longed to be alone. His grief broke past the
barriers of his guilt. He began to hulk with it, bent over. The sound
of grief is not lovely. He made sounds like those of illness or rage.
Now he knew.

"You can let yourself out," I told him. "The door will lock after
you. Good night. God keep you."

Leaving him, I envied him for what he mourned in his full
knowledge. *Confiteor.*

[337]

The Peach Stone

As they all knew, the drive would take them about four hours, all the way to Weed, where *she* came from. They knew the way from traveling it so often, first in the old car, and now in the new one; new to them, that is, for they'd bought it second hand, last year, when they were down in Roswell to celebrate their tenth wedding anniversary. They still thought of themselves as a young couple, and *he* certainly did crazy things now and then, and always laughed her out of it when she was cross at the money going where it did, instead of where it ought to go. But there was so much droll orneriness in him when he did things like that that she couldn't stay mad, hadn't the heart, and the harder up they got, the more she loved him, and the little ranch he'd taken her to in the rolling plains just below the mountains.

This was a day in spring, rather hot, and the mountain was that melting blue that reminded you of something you could touch, like a china bowl. Over the sandy brown of the earth there was coming a green shadow. The air struck cool and deep in their breasts. *He* came from Texas, as a boy, and had lived here in New Mexico ever since. The word *home* always gave *her* a picture of unpainted, mouse-brown wooden houses in a little cluster by the rocky edge of the last mountain-step—the town of Weed, where Jodey Powers met and married her ten years ago.

They were heading back that way today.

Jodey was driving, squinting at the light. It never seemed so bright as now, before noon, as they went up the valley. He had a rangy look at the wheel of the light blue Chevvie—a bony man, but still fuzzed over with some look of a cub about him, perhaps the way he moved his limbs, a slight appealing clumsiness, that drew on thoughtless strength. On a rough road, he flopped and swayed at the wheel as if he were on a bony horse that galloped a little sidewise. His skin was red-brown from the sun. He had pale blue eyes, edged with dark lashes. *She* used to say he "turned them on" her, as if they were lights. He was wearing his suit, brown-striped, and a fresh blue shirt, too big at the neck. But he looked well dressed. But he would have looked that way naked, too, for he communicated his physical essence through any covering. It was what spoke out from him to anyone who encountered him. Until Cleotha married him, it had given him a time, all right, he used to reflect.

Next to him in the front seat of the sedan was Buddy, their nine-year-old boy, who turned his head to stare at them both, his father and mother.

She was in back.

On the seat beside her was a wooden box, sandpapered, but not painted. Over it lay a baby's coverlet of pale yellow flannel with cross-stitched flowers down the middle in a band of bright colors. The mother didn't touch the box except when the car lurched or the tires danced over corrugated places in the gravel highway. Then she steadied it, and kept it from creeping on the seat cushions. In the box was coffined the body of their dead child, a two-year-old girl. They were on their way to Weed to bury it there.

In the other corner of the back seat sat Miss Latcher, the teacher.

They rode in silence, and Miss Latcher breathed deeply of the spring day, as they all did, and she kept summoning to her aid the fruits of her learning. She felt this was a time to be intelligent, and not to give way to feelings.

The child was burned to death yesterday, playing behind the adobe chickenhouse at the edge of the arroyo out back, where the fence always caught the tumbleweeds. Yesterday, in a twist of wind, a few sparks from the kitchen chimney fell in the dry tumbleweeds and set them ablaze. Jodey had always meant to clear the weeds out: never seemed to get to it: told Cleotha he'd get to it next Saturday morning, before going down to Roswell: but Saturdays went by, and the wind and the sand drove the weeds into a barrier at the fence, and they would look at it every day without noticing, so habitual had the sight become. And so for many a spring morning, the little girl had played out there, behind the gray stucco house, whose adobe bricks showed through in one or two places.

The car had something loose; they believed it was the left rear fender: it chattered and wrangled over the gravel road.

Last night Cleotha stopped her weeping.

Today something happened; it came over her as they started out of the ranch lane, which curved up toward the highway. She looked as if she were trying to see something beyond the edge of Jodey's head and past the windshield.

Of course, she had sight in her eyes; she could not refuse to look at the world. As the car drove up the valley that morning, she saw in two ways—one, as she remembered the familiar sights of this region where she lived; the other, as if for the first time she were really seeing, and not simply looking. Her heart began to beat faster as they drove. It seemed to knock at her breast as if to come forth and hurry ahead of her along the sunlighted lanes of the life after today. She remembered thinking that her head might be a little giddy, what with the sorrow in her eyes so bright and slowly shining. But it didn't matter what did it. Ready never to look at anyone or anything again, she kept still; and through the window, which had a meandering crack in it like a river on a map, all that she looked upon seemed dear to her. . . .

Jodey could only drive. He watched the road as if he expected it to rise up and smite them all over into the canyon, where the trees twinkled and flashed with bright drops of light on their new varnished leaves. Jodey watched the road and said to himself that if it thought it could turn him over or make him scrape the rocks along the near side of the hill they were going around, if it thought for one minute that he was not master of this car, this road, this journey, why, it was just crazy. The wheels spraying the gravel across the surface of the road traveled on outward from his legs; his muscles were tight and felt tired as if he were running instead of riding. He tried to *think,* but he could not; that is, nothing came about that he would speak to her of, and he believed that she sat there, leaning forward, waiting for him to say something to her.

But this he could not do, and he speeded up a little, and his jaw made hard knots where he bit on his own rage; and he saw a lump of something coming in the road, and it aroused a positive passion in him. He aimed directly for it, and charged it fast, and hit it. The car shuddered and skidded, jolting them. Miss Latcher took a sharp breath inward, and put out her hand to touch someone, but did not reach anyone. Jodey looked for a second into the rear-view mirror above him, expecting something; but his wife was looking out of the window beside her, and if he could believe his eyes, she was smiling, holding her mouth with her fingers pinched up in a little claw.

The blood came up from under his shirt, he turned dark, and a sting came across his eyes.

He couldn't explain why he had done a thing like that to her, as if it were she he was enraged with, instead of himself.

[341]

He wanted to stop the car and get out and go around to the back door on the other side, and open it, and take her hands, bring her out to stand before him in the road, and hang his arms around her until she would be locked upon him. This made a picture that he indulged like a dream, while the car ran on, and he made no change, but drove as before. . . .

The little boy, Buddy, regarded their faces, again, and again, as if to see in their eyes what had happened to them.

He felt the separateness of the three.

He was frightened by their appearance of indifference to each other. His father had a hot and drowsy look, as if he had just come out of bed. There was something in his father's face which made it impossible for Buddy to say anything. He turned around and looked at his mother, but she was gazing out the window, and did not see him; and until she should see him, he had no way of speaking to her, if not with his words, then with his eyes, but if she should happen to look at him, why, he would wait to see what she looked *like,* and if she *did,* why, then he would smile at her, because he loved her, but he would have to know first if she was still his mother, and if everything was all right, and things weren't blown to smithereens—bla-a-ash! wh-o-o-m!—the way the dynamite did when the highway came past their ranch house, and the men worked out there for months, and whole hillsides came down at a time. All summer long, that was, always something to see. The world, the family, he, between his father and mother, had been safe.

He silently begged her to face toward him. There was no security until she should do so.

"Mumma?"

But he said it to himself, and she did not hear him this time, and it seemed intelligent to him to turn around, make a game of it (the way things often were worked out), and face the front, watch the road, delay as long as he possibly could bear to, and *then* turn around again, and *this* time, why, she would probably be looking at him all the time, and it would *be*: it would simply *be*.

So he obediently watched the road, the white gravel ribbon passing under their wheels as steadily as time.

He was a sturdy little boy, and there was a silver nap of child's dust on his face, over his plum-red cheeks. He smelled rather like a raw potato that has just been pared. The sun crowned him with a ring of light on his dark hair. . . .

What Cleotha was afraid to do was break the spell by saying anything or looking at any of them. This was *vision,* it was all she could think; never had anything looked so in all her life; everything made her heart lift, when she had believed this morning, after the night, that it would never lift again. There wasn't anything to compare her grief to. She couldn't think of anything to answer the death of her tiny child with. In her first hours of hardly believing what had happened, she had felt her own flesh and tried to imagine how it would have been if she could have borne the fire instead of the child. But all she got out of that was a longing avowal to herself of how gladly she would have borne it. Jodey had lain beside her, and she clung to his hand until she heard how he breathed off to sleep. Then she had let him go, and had wept at what seemed faithless in him. She had wanted his mind beside her then. It seemed to her that the last degree of her grief was the compassion she had had to bestow upon him while he slept.

But she had found this resource within her, and from that time on, her weeping had stopped.

It was like a wedding of pride and duty within her. There was nothing she could not find within herself, if she had to, now, she believed.

And so this morning, getting on toward noon, as they rode up the valley, climbing all the way, until they would find the road to turn off on, which would take them higher and higher before they dropped down toward Weed on the other side, she welcomed the sights of that dusty trip. Even if she had spoken her vision aloud, it would not have made sense to the others.

Look at that orchard of peach trees, she thought. I never saw such color as this year; the trees are like lamps, with the light coming from within. It must be the sunlight shining from the other side, and, of course, the petals are very thin, like the loveliest silk; so any light that shines upon them will pierce right through them and glow on this side. But they are so bright! When I was a girl at home, up to Weed, I remember we had an orchard of peach trees, but the blossoms were always a deeper pink than down here in the valley.

My! I used to catch them up by the handful, and I believed when I was a girl that if I crushed them and tied them in a handkerchief and carried the handkerchief in my bosom, I would come to smell like peach blossoms and have the same high pink in my face, and the girls I knew said that if I took a peach *stone* and held it *long enough* in my hand, it would *sprout;* and I dreamed of this one time, though, of course, I knew it was nonsense; but that was how children thought and talked in those days—we all used to pretend that *nothing* was impossible, if you simply did it hard enough and long enough.

But nobody wanted to hold a peach stone in their hand until it *sprouted,* to find out, and we used to laugh about it, but I think we believed it. I think I believed it.

It seemed to me, in between my *sensible* thoughts, a thing that any woman could probably do. It seemed to me like a parable in the Bible. I could preach you a sermon about it this day.

I believe I see a tree down there in that next orchard which is dead; it has old black sprigs, and it looks twisted by rheumatism. There is one little shoot of leaves up on the top branch, and that is all. No, it is not dead, it is aged, it can no longer put forth blossoms in a swarm like pink butterflies; but there is that one little swarm of green leaves—it is just about the prettiest thing I've seen all day, and I thank God for it, for if there's anything I love, it is to see something growing. . . .

Miss Latcher had on her cloth gloves now, which she had taken from her blue cloth bag a little while back. The little winds that tracked through the moving car sought her out and chilled her nose, and the tips of her ears, and her long fingers, about which she had several times gone to visit various doctors. They had always told her not to worry, if her fingers seemed cold, and her hands moist. It was just a nervous condition, nothing to take very seriously; a good hand lotion might help the sensation, and in any case, some kind of digital exercise was a good thing—did she perhaps play the piano. It always seemed to her that doctors never *paid any attention* to her.

Her first name was Arleen, and she always considered this a very pretty name, prettier than Cleotha; and she believed that there was such a thing as an *Arleen look,* and if you wanted to know what it was, simply look at her. She had a long face, and pale hair; her skin was white, and her eyes were light blue. She was wonderfully clean, and used no cosmetics. She was a girl from "around here," but she had gone away to college, to study for her career, and what she had known as a child was displaced by what she had heard in classrooms. And she had to admit it: people *here* and *away* were not much alike. The men were different. She couldn't imagine marrying a rancher and "sacrificing" everything she had learned in college.

This poor little thing in the other corner of the car, for instance: she seemed dazed by what had happened to her—all she could do evidently was sit and stare out the window. And that man in front, simply driving, without a word. What did they have? What was their life like? They hardly had good clothes to drive to Roswell in, when they had to go to the doctor, or on some social errand.

But I must not think uncharitably, she reflected, and sat in an attitude of sustained sympathy, with her face composed in Arleenish interest and tact. The assumption of a proper aspect of grief and feeling produced the most curious effect within her, and by her attitude of concern she was suddenly reminded of the thing that always made her feel like weeping, though of course, she never did, but when she stopped and *thought*—

Like that painting at college, in the long hallway leading from the Physical Education lecture hall to the stairway down to the girls' gym: an enormous picture depicting the Agony of the Christian Martyrs, in ancient Rome. There were some days when she simply couldn't look at it; and there were others when she would pause and see those maidens with their tearful faces raised in calm prowess, and in them, she would find herself—they were all Arleens; and after she would leave the picture she would proceed in her imagination to the arena, and there she would know with exquisite sorrow and pain the ordeals of two thousand years ago, instead of those of her own lifetime. She thought of the picture now, and traded its remote sorrows for those of today until she had sincerely forgotten the mother and the father and the little brother of the dead child with whom she was riding up the spring-turning valley, where noon was warming the dust that arose from the graveled highway. It was white dust, and it settled over them in an enriching film, ever so finely. . . .

Jodey Powers had a fantastic scheme that he used to think about for taking and baling tumbleweed and make a salable fuel out of it. First, you'd compress it—probably down at the cotton compress in Roswell—where a loose bale was wheeled in under the great power-drop, and when the Negro at the handle gave her a yank, down came the weight, and packed the bale into a little thing, and then they let the steam exhaust go, and the press sighed once or twice, and just seemed to *lie* there, while the men ran wires through the gratings of the press and tied them tight. Then up came the weight, and out came the bale.

If he did that to enough bales of tumbleweed, he believed he'd get rich. Burn? It burned like a house afire. It had oil in it, somehow, and the thing to do was to get it in shape for use as a fuel. Imagine all the tumbleweed that blew around the state of New Mexico in the fall, and sometimes all winter. In the winter, the weeds were black and brittle. They cracked when they blew against fence posts, and if one lodged there, then another one caught at its thorny lace; and next time it blew, and the sand came trailing, and the tumbleweeds rolled, they'd pile up at the same fence and built out, locked together against the wires. The wind drew through them, and the sand dropped around them. Soon there was a solid-looking but airy bank of tumbleweeds built right to the top of the fence, in a long windward slope; and the next time the wind blew, and the weeds came, they would roll up the little hill of brittle twigs and leap off the other side of the fence, for all the world like horses taking a jump, and go galloping ahead of the wind across the next pasture on the plains, a black and witchy procession.

If there was an arroyo, they gathered there. They backed up in the miniature canyons of dirt-walled watercourses, which were dry except when it rained hard up in the hills. Out behind the house, the arroyo had filled up with tumbleweeds; and in November, when it blew so hard and so cold, but without bringing any snow, some of the tumbleweeds had climbed out and scattered, and a few had tangled at the back fence, looking like rusted barbed wire. Then there came a few more; all winter the bank grew. Many times he'd planned to get out back there and clear them away, just e-e-ease them off away from the fence posts, so's not to catch the wood up, and then set a match to the whole thing, and in five minutes, have it all cleared off. If he did like one thing, it was a neat place.

How Cleotha laughed at him sometimes when he said that,

because she knew that as likely as not he would forget to clear the weeds away. And if he'd said it once he'd said it a thousand times, that he was going to gather up that pile of scrap iron from the front yard, and haul it to Roswell, and sell it—old car parts, and the fenders off a truck that had turned over up on the highway, which he'd salvaged with the aid of the driver.

But the rusting iron was still there, and he had actually come to have a feeling of fondness for it. If someone were to appear one night and silently make off with it, he'd be aroused the next day, and demand to know who had robbed him: for it was dear junk, just through lying around and belonging to him. What was his was part of him, even that heap of fenders that rubbed off on your clothes with a rusty powder, like a caterpillar fur.

But even by thinking hard about all such matters, treading upon the fringe of what had happened yesterday, he was unable to make it all seem long ago, and a matter of custom and even of indifference. There was no getting away from it—if anybody was to blame for the terrible moments of yesterday afternoon, when the wind scattered a few sparks from the chimney of the kitchen stove, why, he was.

Jodey Powers never claimed to himself or anybody else that he was any *better* man than another. But everything he knew and hoped for, every reassurance his body had had from other people, and the children he had begotten, had made him know that he was *as good* a man as any.

And of this knowledge he was now bereft.

If he had been alone in his barrenness, he could have solaced himself with heroic stupidities. He could have produced out of himself abominations, with the amplitude of biblical despair. But he wasn't alone; there they sat, there was Buddy beside him, and Clee in back, even the teacher, Arleen—even to her he owed some return of courage.

[348]

All he could do was drive the damned car, and keep *thinking* about it.

He wished he could think of something to say, or else that Clee would.

But they continued in silence, and he believed that it was one of his making. . . .

The reverie of Arleen Latcher made her almost ill, from the sad, sweet experiences she had entered into with those people so long ago. How wonderful it was to have such a rich life, just looking up things! —And the most wonderful thing of all was that even if they were beautiful, and wore semitransparent garments that fell to the ground in graceful folds, the maidens were all pure. It made her eyes swim to think how innocent they went to their death. Could anything be more beautiful, and reassuring, than this? Far, far better. Far better those hungry lions, than the touch of lustful men. Her breath left her for a moment, and she closed her eyes, and what threatened her with real feeling—the presence of the Powers family in the faded blue sedan climbing through the valley sunlight toward the turnoff that led to the mountain road—was gone. Life's breath on her cheek was not so close. Oh, others had suffered. She could suffer.

"All that pass by clap their hands at thee: they hiss and wag their heads at the daughter of Jerusalem—"

This image made her wince, as if she herself had been hissed and wagged at. Everything she knew made it possible for her to see herself as a proud and threatened virgin of Bible times, which were more real to her than many of the years she had lived through. Yet must not Jerusalem have sat in country like this with its sandy hills, the frosty stars that were so bright at night, the simple Mexicans riding their burros as if to the Holy Gates? We often do not see our very selves, she would reflect, gazing ardently at the unreal creature which the name Arleen brought to life in her mind.

[349]

On her cheeks there had appeared two islands of color, as if she had a fever. What she strove to save by her anguished retreats into the memories of the last days of the Roman Empire was surely crumbling away from her. She said to herself that she must not give way to it, and that she was just wrought up; the fact that she really *didn't* feel anything—in fact, it was a pity that she *couldn't* take that little Mrs Powers in her arms, and comfort her, just *let* her go ahead and cry, and see if it wouldn't probably help some. But Miss Latcher was aware that she felt nothing that related to the Powers family and their trouble.

Anxiously she searched her heart again, and wooed back the sacrifice of the tribe of heavenly Arleens marching so certainly toward the lions. But they did not answer her call to mind, and she folded her cloth-gloved hands and pressed them together, and begged of herself that she might think of some way to comfort Mrs Powers; for if she could do that, it might fill her own empty heart until it became a cup that would run over. . . .

Cleotha knew Buddy wanted her to see him; but though her heart turned toward him, as it always must, no matter what he asked of her, she was this time afraid to do it because if she ever lost the serenity of her sight now she might never recover it this day; and the heaviest trouble was still before her.

So she contented herself with Buddy's look as it reached her from the side of her eye. She glimpsed his head and neck, like a young cat's, the wide bones behind the ears, and the smooth but visible cords of his nape, a sight of him that always made her want to laugh because it was so pathetic. When she caressed him she often fondled those strenuous hollows behind his ears. Heaven only knew, she would think, what went on within the shell of that topknot! She would pray between her words and feelings that those unseen thoughts in the boy's head were ones that would never trouble him. She was often amazed at things in him which she recognized as being like herself; and at those of Buddy's qualities which came from some alien source, she suffered pangs of doubt and fear. He was so young to be a stranger to her!

The car went around the curve that hugged the rocky fall of a hill; and on the other side of it, a green quilt of alfalfa lay sparkling darkly in the light. Beyond that, to the right of the road, the land leveled out, and on a sort of platform of swept earth stood a two-room hut of adobe. It had a few stones cemented against the near corner, to give it strength. Clee had seen it a hundred times—the place where that old man Melendez lived, and where his wife had died a few years ago. He was said to be simple-minded and claimed he was a hundred years old. In the past, riding by here, she had more or less delicately made a point of looking the other way. It often distressed her to think of such a helpless old man, too feeble to do anything but crawl out when the sun was bright and the wall was warm, and sit there, with his milky gaze resting on the hills he had known since he was born, and had never left. Somebody came to feed him once a day, and see if he was clean enough to keep his health. As long as she could remember, there'd been some kind of dog at the house. The old man had sons and grandsons and great-grandsons—you might say a whole orchard of them, sprung from this one tree that was dying, but that still held a handful of green days in its ancient veins.

Before the car had quite gone by, she had seen him. The sun was bright, and the wall must have been warm, warm enough to give his shoulders and back a reflection of the heat which was all he could feel. He sat there on his weathered board bench, his hands on his branch of apple tree that was smooth and shiny from use as a cane. His house door was open, and a deep tunnel of shade lay within the sagged box of the opening. Cleotha leaned forward to see him, as if to look at him were one of her duties today. She saw his jaw moving up and down, not chewing, but just opening and closing. In the wind and flash of the car going by, she could not hear him; but from his closed eyes, and his moving mouth, and the way his head was raised, she wouldn't have been surprised if she had heard him singing. He was singing some thread of song, and it made her smile to imagine what kind of noise it made, a wisp of voice.

She was perplexed by a feeling of joyful fullness in her breast, at the sight of the very same old witless sire from whom in the past she had turned away her eyes out of delicacy and disgust.

The last thing she saw as they went by was his dog, who came around the corner of the house with a caracole. He was a mongrel puppy, partly hound—a comedian by nature. He came prancing outrageously up to the old man's knees, and invited his response, which he did not get. But as if his master were as great a wag as he, he hurled himself backward, pretending to throw himself recklessly into pieces. Everything on him flopped and was flung by his idiotic energy. It was easy to imagine, watching the puppy-fool, that the sunlight had entered him as it had entered the old man. Cleotha was reached by the hilarity of the hound, and when he tripped over himself and plowed the ground with his flapping jowls, she wanted to laugh out loud.

But they were past the place, and she winked back the merriment in her eyes, and she knew that it was something she could never have told the others about. What it stood for, in her, they would come to know in other ways, as she loved them. . . .

Jodey was glad of one thing. He had telephoned from Hondo last night, and everything was to be ready at Weed. They would drive right up the hill to the family burial ground. They wouldn't have to wait for anything. He was glad, too, that the wind wasn't blowing. It always made his heart sink when the wind rose on the plains and began to change the sky with the color of dust.

Yesterday: it was all he could see, however hard he was *thinking* about everything else.

He'd been on his horse, coming back down the pasture that rose up behind the house across the arroyo, nothing particular in mind—except to make a joke with himself about how far along the peaches would get before the frost killed them all, *snap,* in a single night, like that—when he saw the column of smoke rising from the tumbleweeds by the fence. Now who could've lighted them, he reflected, following the black smoke up on its billows into the sky. There was just enough wind idling across the long front of the hill to bend the smoke and trail it away at an angle, toward the blue.

The hillside, the fire, the wind, the column of smoke.

Oh my God! And the next minute he was tearing down the hill as fast as his horse could take him, and the fire—he could see the flames now—the fire was like a bank of yellow rags blowing violently and torn in the air, rag after rag tearing up from the ground. Cleotha was there, and in a moment, so was he, but they were too late. The baby was unconscious. They took her up and hurried to the house, the back way where the screen door was standing open with its spring trailing on the ground. When they got inside where it seemed so dark and cool, they held the child between them, fearing to lay her down. They called for Buddy, but he was still at school up the road, and would not be home until the orange school bus stopped by their mailbox out front at the highway after four o'clock. The fire poured in cracking tumult through the weeds. In ten minutes they were only little airy lifts of ash off the ground. Everything was black. There were three fence posts still afire; the wires were hot. The child was dead. They let her down on their large bed.

He could remember every word Clee had said to him. They were not many, and they shamed him, in his heart, because he couldn't say a thing. He comforted her, and held her while she wept. But if he had spoken then, or now, riding in the car, all he could have talked about was the image of the blowing rags of yellow fire, and blue, blue, plaster blue sky above and beyond the mountains. But he believed that she knew why he seemed so short with her. He hoped earnestly that she knew. He might just be wrong. She might be blaming him, and keeping so still because it was more proper, now, to *be* still than full of reproaches.

But of the future, he was entirely uncertain; and he drove, and came to the turnoff, and they started winding in back among the sandhills that lifted them toward the rocky slopes of the mountains. Up and up they went; the air was so clear and thin that they felt transported, and across the valleys that dropped between the grand shoulders of the pine-haired slopes, the air looked as if it were blue breath from the trees. . . .

Cleotha was blinded by a dazzling light in the distance, ahead of them, on the road.

It was a ball of diamond-brilliant light.

It danced, and shook, and quivered above the road far, far ahead. It seemed to be traveling between the pine trees on either side of the road, and somewhat above the road, and it was like nothing she had ever seen before. It was the most magic and exquisite thing she had ever seen, and wildly, even hopefully as a child is hopeful when there is a chance and a need for something miraculous to happen, she tried to explain it to herself. It could be a star in the daytime, shaking and quivering and traveling ahead of them, as if to lead them. It was their guide. It was shaped like a small cloud, but it was made of shine, and dazzle, and quiver. She held her breath for fear it should vanish, but it did not, and she wondered if the others in the car were smitten with the glory of it as she was.

It was brighter than the sun, whiter; it challenged the daytime, and obscured everything near it by its blaze of flashing and dancing light.

It was almost as if she had approached perfect innocence through her misery, and were enabled to receive portents that might not be visible to anyone else. She closed her eyes for a moment.

But the road curved, and everything traveling on it took the curve too, and the trembling pool of diamond-light ahead lost its liquid splendor, and turned into the tin signs on the back of a huge oil truck which was toiling over the mountain, trailing its links of chain behind.

When Clee looked again, the star above the road was gone. The road and the angle of the sun to the mountaintop and the two cars climbing upward had lost their harmony to produce the miracle. She saw the red oil truck, and simply saw it, and said to herself that the sun might have reflected off the big tin signs on the back of it. But she didn't believe it, for she was not thinking, but rather dreaming; fearful of awakening. . . .

The high climb up this drive always made Miss Latcher's ears pop, and she had discovered once that to swallow often prevented the disagreeable sensation. So she swallowed. Nothing happened to her ears. But she continued to swallow, and feel her ears with her cloth-covered fingers, but what really troubled her now would not be downed, and it came into her mouth as a taste; she felt giddy— that was the altitude, of course—when they got down the other side, she would be all right.

What it was was perfectly clear to her, for that was part of having an education and a trained mind—the processes of thought often went right on once you started them going.

Below the facts of this small family, in the worst trouble it had ever known, lay the fact of envy in Arleen's breast.

It made her head swim to realize this. But she envied them their entanglement with one another, and the dues they paid each other in the humility of the duty they were performing on this ride, to the family burial ground at Weed. Here she sat riding with them, to come along and be of help to them, and she was no help. She was unable to swallow the lump of desire that rose in her throat, for life's uses, even such bitter ones as that of the Powers family today. It had been filling her gradually, all the way over on the trip, this feeling of jealousy and degradation.

Now it choked her and she knew she had tried too hard to put from her the thing that threatened her, which was the touch of life through anybody else. She said to herself that she must keep control of herself.

But Buddy turned around again, just then, slowly, as if he were a young male cat who just happened to be turning around to see what he could see, and he looked at his mother with his large eyes, so like his father's: pale petal-blue, with drops of light like the centers of cats' eyes, and dark lashes. He had a solemn look, when he saw his mother's face, and he prayed her silently to acknowledge him. If she didn't, why, he was still alone. He would never again feel safe about running off to the highway to watch the scrapers work, or the huge Diesel oil tankers go by, or the cars with strange license plates—of which he had already counted thirty-two different kinds, his collection, as he called it. So if she didn't see him, why, what might he find when he came back home at times like those, when he went off for a little while just to play?

They were climbing down the other side of the ridge now. In a few minutes they would be riding into Weed. The sights as they approached were like images of awakening to Cleotha. Her heart began to hurt when she saw them. She recognized the tall iron smokestack of the sawmill. It showed above the trees down on the slope ahead of them. There was a stone house which had been abandoned even when she was a girl at home here, and its windows and doors standing open always seemed to her to depict a face with an expression of dismay. The car dropped farther down—they were making that last long curve of the road to the left—and now the

[356]

town stood visible, with the sunlight resting on so many of the unpainted houses and turning their weathered gray to a dark silver. Surely they must be ready for them, these houses: all had been talked over by now. They could all mention that they knew Cleotha as a little girl.

She lifted her head.

There were claims upon her.

Buddy was looking at her soberly, trying to predict to himself how she would *be*. He was ready to echo with his own small face whatever her face would show him.

Miss Latcher was watching the two of them. Her heart was racing in her breast.

The car slowed up. Now Cleotha could not look out the windows at the wandering earthen street, and the places alongside it. They would have to drive right through town, to the gently rising hill on the other side.

"Mumma?" asked the boy softly.

Cleotha winked both her eyes at him, and smiled, and leaned toward him a trifle.

And then he blushed, his eyes swam with happiness, and he smiled back at her, and his face poured forth such radiance that Miss Latcher took one look at him, and with a choke, burst into tears.

She wept into her hands, her gloves were moistened, her square shoulders rose to her ears, and she was overwhelmed by what the mother had been able to do for the boy. She shook her head and made long gasping sobs. Her sense of betrayal was not lessened by the awareness that she was weeping for herself.

Cleotha leaned across to her, and took her hand, and murmured to her. She comforted her, gently.

"Hush, honey, you'll be all right. Don't you cry, now. Don't you think about us. We're almost there, and it'll soon be over. God knows you were mighty sweet to come along and be with us. Hush, now, Arleen, you'll have Buddy crying too."

But the boy was simply watching the teacher, in whom the person he knew so well every day in school had broken up, leaving an unfamiliar likeness. It was like seeing a reflection in a pond, and then throwing a stone in. The reflection disappeared in ripples of something else.

Arleen could not stop.

The sound of her 'ooping made Jodey furious. He looked into the rear-view mirror and saw his wife patting her and comforting her. Cleotha looked so white and strained that he was frightened, and he said out, without turning around: "Arleen, you cut that out, you shut up, now. I won't have you wearin' down Clee, God damn it, you quit it!"

But this rage, which arose from a sense of justice, made Arleen feel guiltier than ever; and she laid her head against the car window, and her sobs drummed her brow bitterly on the glass.

"Hush," whispered Cleotha, but she could do no more, for they were arriving at the hillside, and the car was coming to a stop. They must awaken from this journey, and come out onto the ground, and begin to toil their way up the yellow hill, where the people were waiting. Over the ground grew yellow grass that was turning to green. It was like velvet, showing dark or light, according to the breeze and the golden afternoon sunlight. It was a generous hill, curving easily and gradually as it rose. Beyond it was only the sky, for the mountains faced it from behind the road. It was called Schoolhouse Hill, and at one time, the whole thing had belonged to Cleotha's father; and even before there was any schoolhouse crowning its noble swell of earth, the departed members of his family had been buried halfway up the gentle climb.

Jodey helped her out of the car, and he tried to talk to her with his holding fingers. He felt her trembling, and she shook her head at him. Then she began to walk up there, slowly. He leaned into the car and took the covered box in his arms, and followed her. Miss Latcher was out of the car on her side, hiding from them, her back turned, while she used her handkerchief and positively clenched herself back into control of her thoughts and sobs. When she saw that they weren't waiting for her, she hurried, and in humility, reached for Buddy's hand to hold it for him as they walked. He let her have it, and he marched, watching his father, whose hair was blowing in the wind and sunshine. From behind, Jodey looked like just a kid. . . .

And now for Cleotha her visions on the journey appeared to have some value, and for a little while longer, when she needed it most, the sense of being in blind communion with life was granted her, at the little graveside where all those kind friends were gathered on the slow slope up of the hill on the summit of which was the school-house of her girlhood.

It was afternoon, and they were all kneeling toward the upward rise, and Judge Crittenden was reading the prayer book.

Everything left them but a sense of their worship, in the present.

And a boy, a late scholar, is coming down the hill from the school, the sunlight edging him; and his wonder at what the people kneeling there are doing is, to Cleotha, the most memorable thing she is to look upon today; for she has resumed the life of her infant daughter, whom they are burying, and on whose behalf, something rejoices in life anyway, as if to ask the mother whether love itself is not ever-living. And she watches the boy come discreetly down the hill, trying to keep away from them, but large-eyed with a hunger *to know* which claims all acts of life, for him, and for those who will be with him later; and his respectful curiosity about those kneeling mourners, the edge of sunlight along him as he walks away from the sun and down the hill, is of all those things she saw and rejoiced

[359]

in, the most beautiful; and at that, her breast is full, with the heaviness of a baby at it, and not for grief alone, but for praise.

"I believe, I believe!" her heart cries out in her, as if she were holding the peach stone of her eager girlhood in her woman's hand.

She puts her face into her hands, and weeps, and they all move closer to her. Familiar as it is, the spirit has had a new discovery. . . .

Jodey then felt that she had returned to them all; and he stopped seeing, and just remembered, what happened yesterday; and his love for his wife was confirmed as something he would never be able to measure for himself or prove to her in words.

PART
FOUR

The Hacienda

Only when things were particularly dull at the Elks' Club did anybody revert to the pastime of making a fool of old Don Elizario. Most of the time he was a shadowy fat old man talking earnestly and beautifully to people in midafternoon corners of the club lounge, an old man unreal enough in the clamor of the growing New Mexico city to be forgotten utterly when they forgot him, or to be remembered, when he was remembered at all, with indulgent patience.

His likeness was familiar to the city, which had spread with the energy of a stain over the flat lands by the river and the high lands of the mesa that lay like a plane of light reaching to the great light of the mountains. On the land where his ancestors had put the graces of Spain, Don Elizario saw the city with its transcontinental railroad and its industries and its traffic lights rise in a fury of ambition and appalling architecture. But in his mind's eye he saw very little of the real town, for he remembered the dusty streets and the dashing buggies and the whispering nights of stir in the summer cottonwoods and his own sense of privilege among women as the first gentleman of the region, a post for which his education irre-

[363]

vocably molded him; a style which he still wore and certain people could see it, as he went walking down the modern streets heavily, his large head with the small brown face and thick furry white hair waggling a trifle in echo of his movements as he walked. He had a huge belly and short, bent legs. His arms were short too, and sometimes he would join his hands across his vest with a ceremonial pomp, and his hands would just meet and clasp each other with a touch, like a doll's hands or a toy animal's paws. He always carried a heavy stick with a silver handle made to represent a naked girl modestly wound around with her own engraved tresses.

Nobody quite knew what he lived on in the room upstairs at the Elks' Club, which he invested with some splendor by his presence. Innocently he assumed that this was an exclusive club, and to live at "his club" made him feel that he was a real Americano. But his son who lived in New York and who sent the old man money was always a little embarrassed to receive those vice-regal letters from his father, on the writing paper of the club, lavishly written, and imprinted with the club emblem and address. The faraway son was made mournful by the lost pride of his family; a loss which he could see, and everyone else; but which old Don Elizario himself could not see, for it never occurred to him soberly that he was the last aristocrat of a lyric race, and that to live as he was living, surrounded by the intolerant and complacent successors of his time, was a tragic thing. The son felt something of this; he sent money; he suffered for the indignities of his father's life, without knowing just what they were. But that they existed he did not doubt. The old man would innocently write in one of his twelve-page letters of Elks' Club paper that he had got drunk again last week; and the son could imagine the bland and baby-like content of the old man drunk, and the shrugs of people who might see him.

On the soiled white plaster walls of the lounge at "the club," with stained pine paneling and beams, the retreating light of afternoon

[364]

made shadows. Don Elizario sat there in a corner every afternoon, having a window to look out of and a spittoon to use and two scratched leather chairs, one to sit in, the other for his feet. From this corner he would address everyone who passed through the room, and he would bow and make a little wave of courtesy with his small fat hands that always twinkled with gesture to accompany his speech. People sometimes didn't answer him, and he would think, "I must learn to speak a little louder," while they went on their ways thinking, "That damned old Mexican is getting to be a nuisance."

But they sometimes had a use for him, when Chicken, the club Negro who acted as steward, clerk, bootblack and janitor, had a new supply of bootleg corn he would sell. They'd see Don Elizario sitting in his corner with a bottle of whiskey and go up and speak to him, meanly thirsting and not listening to his words of charm and invitation. They sat down with him and Chicken shambled over with some glasses in response to Don Elizario's command. The Negro, pouting in the shape of his rolled lips, and forebodingly rolling his yellow-shot eyes, went to the window and closed the dry and sandy velvet draperies with sleazy discretion.

The afternoons always began like that when the old gentleman got drunk.

The other members with him were not always the same; but he knew everybody and welcomed all.

On one afternoon, he had sitting with him a real estate and insurance man and the owner of a laundry. They were in their late thirties, both, and their concerns had to do with making the town more and more removed from what Don Elizario's life had been prepared for. The two younger men viewed him, therefore, as a comedian. Stanched against any values of grace and thoughtless generosity, they enjoyed baiting him, with secret glances at each other. They felt tremendously successful in keeping their mockery secret from the old man; they went to audacious lengths, the more of his whiskey they drank, to tread the edge of open derision; which he never perceived, for simple reasons that would have shamed them forever, had they the timber of his world in their characters.

"Another lichtle drink, my frands," Don Elizario said. They leaned forward and let him pour out his whiskey.

"You're a right busy man, Don Elizario," said the laundryman with a gleam of his eye across his thin nose at the insurance man. "Sittin' here all day and workin' at your likker."

The Don leaned back and rolled a gurgling laugh deep down in his contented throat.

The insurance man said,

"Well, it's a job you can do better than most, Don Elizario, eh? —You just better keep at it, we'd never get anything done in this town if we waited on the earliest settlers, now would we?"

"No, no," said the old man. "My people have no gift for business. They are too fond of life. —Your glass."

He poured the fresh drink with a shrugging apology for his words if they had sounded rude.

A young man came up to the group and they recognized him, and spoke to him. He was a young university Mexican who worked in the First National Bank. He winked at the two businessmen; and to show that he understood the joke, and wanted to be of the jokers, he said,

"Hello, Don Elizario. Are you giving the boys a little family history again?"

The old man looked levelly back at him, and when they saw that his eyes were becoming pink and washy, they realized that he was drunk, though he hadn't shown it before. The three men stared at him, and were filled with the mixed pleasures of embarrassment and scorn. In a pause which made the young Mexican's words linger in the head, they saw Don Elizario put his drunken little hand

[366]

quivering like a brown bird on his fat chest and there tap above his heart. He was lost to them. He was old and full of liquor. His eyes reddened with tears. Oh, good Lord, thought the men, impatiently.

"When I was ten years old, when it was in 1860," said Don Elizario aloud to himself, "I planted a cottonwood tree in the patio of my father's house."

Pictures of that time swam fluidly through his brain, dreams fleetingly borne by the present.

By the Rio Grande the great house stood, a fortress and a palace, built of adobe and cornered with shade in some part of its rambling pattern all day. It was a house risen out of the earth and forever subject to the things that qualified earthly portion . . . rain wearing off the face of walls, the river rising and mingling valley with field in the spring floods, the hardening fire of the sun that dried all things in time to dust. The house was in the shape of two great squares, joined by carved wooden doors in the high courtyard walls. In the courtyards grew trees and lived domestic animals. The rooms within were long and narrow and low, secured by walls eight feet thick against the tempers of Indians and storms. In the rooms were beautiful pieces of furniture from Europe, and each piece was tied to the time of its purchase by some family event. A hundred horses and a thousand cows served the needs of the hacienda. There were twenty families of peons who worked the farm. The house was kept by a dozen maids, and the kitchen had three cooks. The family was large, the mother fattening and growing common in her mind as childbearing and isolation slowly wore down the airs and standards of Mexico City, where she came from. It was a hive, that hacienda. Life sprang in every form from the chocolate-colored river and its marshes, where in the pale filters of sunset crimson, tall herons stood, and the suck and seep of enriching river water was audible. Life sprang from the fields and the river banks, and the animals who had green feed all year. It swelled in the women, the maids and the matron alike, as the sons grew to fertile age and the husband seeded his barony with his own flesh, so that this life might go on forever, as the great river would go on, always new, yet possessing the land by right of a source lost in time and mountains. Even the littlest son in 1860 was given a tree to plant in the patio on his tenth birthday, a little cutting from a cottonwood. There was a party with many children and their parents from haciendas up and down the river. There were music and a dinner that lasted three and a half hours. Five priests were there. They admired especially the silver service, great mirrored platters and forks like tree-roots, with silver knots, and candlesticks a yard high of silver as thick as the wax that dripped and beaded on the candles when the breeze of summer went through the long cool rooms of the endless house.

"In 1865," said Don Elizario in words that were shapeless with the vague feeling of his lips after liquor, "we had a visit from a friend of my pappa, he was a Frenchman."

It was a day in spring when the sky traveled low across the house, the gray burden of a rainy time, for rain had come in thunderstorms early that May as it sometimes did, and the torrent had eaten at the house, and now on the day the Frenchman arrived, he found the house alive with men crawling on the roofs and ladders, plastering the corners and the deep hollows where windows were set. They got the mud from the ground between the house and the river and mixed it with chopped straw and when it was well mixed, they plastered it on the house. It took two days for the repairs, and the Frenchman marveled at this business of picking up your house from the dirt of the river bank. The sun came back and dried the new plaster till it was the color of dusty rawhide. Then they painted the whole face of the house with whitewash, and scrubbed the iron hinges of the blinds and the great doors. The Frenchman was interested to hear that a constant effort had to be made to keep the house in condition. He declared that this was indeed a violent

[368]

country, and that such a large and wealthy family was well-rooted here forever. Certainly, in the gorgeous moods of the river landscape there was great beauty; and once inside the house, the style was all that there was of luxury. To get such riches out of the land! he marveled. There would always be enough for the children. But some of the children were gone already. A son was dead in a fight with knives two years ago at a dance in Santa Fe. Two daughters were married and transferred to another life as completely as if they'd been sold in slavery. A son was traveling in Europe. Another son was in Mexico with cousins in the Government. Another was privately planning to go to St. Louis and enter some business. Elizario was ready to go away from his robust father and his mother who moaned beneath her mustache as each child was torn from her huge old bosom by the needs of the wills she had let into being, only to be so betrayed. She longed for unchanging Heaven.

"The first time they could remember," said Don Elizario, "it never happened before, when the river was in flood, and came up as far as the house. Never before."

They had written him a letter about it. He was away in Washington with a delegation from the Territory of New Mexico. When he got home again, where he had been master since the death of his parents, the only son left there to live, he saw what the flood had done. They told him how during the night the river rose quietly and surrounded the corral and lipped up and up the little slope till it got to the house; and the long wing that was lined toward the river seemed to float there on the brown flood water. The flood took houses and animals with it, children's lives, and broke down groves of willow trees. It came to the tops of saplings in the marshes and rose through the orchards and the fields like some strange rise of the ground itself, overtaking blossom and branch as if to make roots of them. Birds flew low over lost land, crying and drumming in consternation. For days all life was dragged southward and sullied with mud. Looking at the wide sheet of the flood that sailed with slow spiral currents in the fields and roads and groves, people couldn't believe their eyes at the damage. The river-bent wing of the great hacienda was lost to the flood. The water edged and seeped and washed; and the walls began to go. The walls sank down and were taken away crumb by crumb in the current. They were never rebuilt because the family was no longer so numerous or so rich. They closed up the room nearest to the flood-spoiled wing, and walled it off, all this after the waters receded, and somehow the peons were more quickly restored to their comforts and had their rebuilding done faster than the people at the great house. There was so much more to be done at the hacienda itself. There was so much less impulse to do it. The vitality of the family was changed.

"What changed everything, afterwards," mused Don Elizario, blinking and nursing his whiskey glass against his breast, "was the railroad."

They came surveying, first; and he gave them dinner and wine in his house. Later came officials, driving in buckboards from Santa Fe to talk business with him. The deal was closed in Kansas City a few weeks later. They gave him a fortune in American money for his land, right of way for the tracks going down the Rio Grande valley, on the way West. He moved from the country, taking many weeks for the transport of his possessions. It was like an emperor moving his capital. But when he decided to build a house in town, people were proud to have him there, for on his hacienda he had been several hours' drive away. He built a new house, and presently he was married, the richest young man in the place, rich enough to capture and marry the daughter of an army colonel from St. Louis. Everyone made it clear that he was from an old *Spanish* family, one of the oldest names in Europe; a name which had merely paused as an incident of conquest in Mexico, which accounted for the wide prevalence of the name in this part of the world. Nobody could doubt this genealogy when partaking of the complete grace of his and his wife's hospitality. They were lavish. They were respectful mostly of the pleasures of taste. They were happy. The railroad sucked in the town to its purposes, and the town grew. Smoke blackened the cottonwood trees along the tracks. The United States lay to the East, a knowledgeable East now, sending its demands and its money and its kind of life out here. Banks were built. The word investment began to take the place of the word cattle.

"They were all very smart, but they were smart about only one thing," said Don Elizario. "That was how to make money with other people's money."

That was what the following years had shown him, as his own money slackened in its stream, drying away as he grew old, and his son grew up and his wife sickened and died, and his brothers and sisters vanished into that remoteness of disassociation and alien interest which is often more final than death. He knew it was true, and that it was a pity, that he simply wasn't smart enough to hold his money against these newcomers, these exhausting gringos. A gentleman didn't have to be smart about money, this he knew also. They got it all, of course. He saw it go, he watched their operations with a helpless affability, until at the very last when he had a terrible picture of himself as he would be old: penniless, probably ill, perhaps a disgraceful old fool whom people would point at and jeer at privately as a fallen grandee; and the picture was so acute and awful that he made one last scramble of energy and with his remaining money, invested in a sawmill in the mountains, a logging and lumber company which a Scotchman from Pittsburgh called McFalloch—a lean-cheeked, wry man—assured him was the great coming industry of the Southwest. Wood was always needed for building; and building had just started, just barely started here. It was perfectly true; and in a year, the mill was bought by a Santa Fe banker, and McFalloch vanished with all the money from the sale.

[371]

Don Elizario's money too. Now that it was here, he could face it, and he never again had that sad and demeaning vision of himself as a drooling old bore. People were still perfectly charming to him, they would drink with him, and listen to his memories, the ghostly rehearsals of days they could never have known, and that had made his life.

The real estate man was getting drunk also, and he sat with a witless smile on his chipmunk face which gleamed with eyeglasses he had got in college. His friend the laundry-owner had a thin and suspicious face, always wearing a speculative smile of denied inferiority. It was often a necessity of his nature to fix his light blue eyes in a hard stare and make a remark that could remind his listener toward some day of suffering or loss or embarrassment. It was a little enough soul that resorted to such a device in order to know itself as more fortunate than many, powerful in a little way, and so, however meanly, alive.

"Well, Don Elizario," he said, in his soft voice, "there's not much left of your old hacienda these days. Somebody pointed it out to me the other day on the way to Santa Fe. All I could see was a heap of adobe. And some trees. —Right there, where the tracks curve, and go due south for a ways? —That's it. That's the place."

The old man raised his head. His eyes were pink all over and milky with salt. He was really drunk. His mouth slobbered a little bit, and his babbling lips served his words with a dim and aged deliberation. He reached with his bottle in his trembling hand and filled the glasses of his guests. As he did so, gasping and sighing began to rise from his breast, and came presently as sobs from his mouth. Gorgeously, he raised his replenished glass and waved it slightly in an invitation to drink. His heart was warm toward these, his friends. When he was with them, all the old times came back. This man had just spoken of the hacienda. What did he say? What was that:

[372]

"My hacienda . . . oh, yes, where the tracks curve a little and go south. Yes. —Oh, but there is nothing left there. Is that what you said?"

He heaved forward a little in his chair, and his heavy head shaggily waved back and forth, until he looked like a polar bear scenting something, even imagining it, and trying to recognize it.

"Oh, yes, now that is what you said."

At that, the tears broke from his red eyes and flowed to his mouth, where their taste made him realize how sad he was and how drunk. He couldn't speak for a long moment, but he kept the others from speaking by sitting with his mouth open in a circle of desire to speak, and by shuttling his forefinger at them to suspend them and make them wait. At last he clicked his tongue in his throat and words came free, and so much that lay behind them.

"My house way out there on the river.

"Yes, it is gone.

"How many times have rains come and washed it away since I was there? Every rain washed down the walls a little bit. It has washed for years, so many years now.

"Do you know: there is just a little hill there where it was my house. The old trees are still there, they keep growing high. But the house falls lower and it is just dirt like the ground, and it goes back to a little hill, because the rain, and because the wind, when it is dry there is so much dust, it blows away, too. When I was ten years old, I was on my birthday, I planted a tree in the patio."

Old Army

to Stuart Rose

It began when he sent his wife away. The only one clever enough to see this at the time was Mrs Truman. At dinner, she said to her husband, Colonel Truman, that she had a feeling.

"I have a feeling that Jack let Mossie go away because he couldn't stand having a lot of fuss here when he had to retire. Or don't you think?"

Colonel Truman growled his chuckle into his coffee and looked at her over the cup. He admired her when she was being clever, though he always was unable to tell her so. He had a sinister look for times like that, and he treated her to it now. It often made her blurt a little laugh—part of his welcome power over her.

"Do you?" she asked again. "Stop looking like that, Bootie. I asked you something."

"I think you're right, but for the wrong reason. I mean I think Jack sent her off because he wants to do it all by himself, because I think he's the kind who would rather not have anyone to lean on. He's always been like that. I admire him for not wanting it made any easier, even by his wife."

[374]

"I see," said Gertrude Truman. "He doesn't want to seem un-soldierly at such a significant moment in his career. Is that it?"

"You always make the words sound so—so bald. A bald state-ment," he added, with a rush of pleasure at hitting exactly what he meant.

Gertrude, or Trucian, as everyone called her, lifted her eyebrows a trifle and smiled at him sedately. Her lovely black eyes were teasing him; the lids trembled and fell ever so little, blurring her regard. She had pale swarthiness and coal-black hair, dressed severely. People often took her for a Russian lady. It was always more interesting that she acted as American as Hoboken, though always with a light, ironic poise.

"Well, Bootie," she said, getting up from the table, "I am the realist and you are the philosopher; I have always said that."

This was a hilarious description of Colonel Truman, for he was stocky, ruggedly matter-of-fact, with his bald head, shrewd eyes and ink-spot mustache.

He followed her into the living room. The two ancient, fat spaniels and the young, lean, ribby hound began to squirm ecstati-cally on the warm stones of the hearth at his approach. He crouched down and greeted them all, calling them each "my girl." Trucian put her coffee cup down on the round table before the photograph of the man they were talking about. He was a major general, gray-haired and erect on a tall bay mare. Behind him stretched the cream-painted wooden buildings of his command at Fort Riley. The sun bathed everything in the photograph in a whitewash.

Trucian Truman's heart gave a little run as she looked at the picture. General Huntington had been so old and so good a friend to them both. It was hardly conceivable that it was already the year, 1942, the midwinter month, of his inevitable retirement. There was such a brilliant record behind him and so much vigor left in him.

This time They *couldn't,* she thought. She never thought of "They" in terms of actual men, solid persons within familiar uniforms, like her husband.

"After all," she said, "they may decide to keep him. How heavenly!"

But she knew the Army's inflexible laws as well as anyone.

Colonel Truman was reading the firelight. He was sorry. Everybody loved Jack. Mentally, he shook his head at regulations and refusals to make exceptions and what looked like injustices, but you could never be sure. It all added up to Army, and it was his life.

"They may," he said.

But They didn't, of course. It was known on Wednesday morning of that week that Washington had called General Huntington, a long phone call, after completing which the general was alone in his office for about twenty minutes. Then he came out with his mackinaw on—it was bitter cold outdoors in Kansas in December— called his aide, and said he wanted to look around for a little while, which meant making an informal inspection. He and the aide spent the rest of the morning driving around the post in the general's sedan with the white stars on the red plate up front. About lunchtime, they paused at Colonel Truman's quarters on Schofield Circle. The general sent the ADC to the door to ask Colonel Truman to step out for a moment, and he came, bareheaded, and climbed into the sedan with his chief. The ADC stayed up on the porch, with an aide's intuitive tact. He saw the general speak a few words, and Colonel Truman nod, and then both sit in silence. It was perfectly plain to the aide that this was it. General Huntington had heard, and it made the ADC as sorry as he could be. Everybody had been talking about what must happen, all along, and the ADC was prepared, like the rest, to do the right thing. Standing on the cold porch, smoking a cigarette, he saw that he would have to manage a little time off this afternoon to get things started.

Later that day, then, things moved. The general did not stay to lunch with the Trumans, but returned to his own mess, where he mentioned casually that he would be leaving for good, next Monday night. Colonel Truman would take over. After making his announcement, he deliberately switched the conversation, and, with hidden concern, everyone swore later that they had never seen anyone so wonderful as old Jack. He was so cool, so calmly blue-eyed, and his quiet voice warned them all that he would appreciate the minimum in "sentiments."

General Huntington himself, however, did not really feel what he had so long expected until late that day, when he came upon a little crowd of junior officers huddled in the far end of the hall in his headquarters. They were being animatedly discreet, their whispers detonating huskily down the boarded corridor. They were raging with good taste and fellowship and love for their Old Man.

With a pang that actually slowed his step down a moment, he recognized out of his own past the excited plotting of youngsters who were "getting up something" for the occasion of saying farewell to their commanding officer. He had done it himself, years ago, for other officers retiring. When they saw him, they fell apart and, of course, one or two of them blushed as they lined the walls to let him by. He caught a glimpse of a scribbled list and a pencil in the fist of one of them.

He nodded and smiled at them, and went past them down the hallway. His heart ached at their zest and propriety. For the first time, he saw himself as their beloved victim, and he dreaded the dinner that was, he knew, already being phoned about, from one colonel's wife to another. He grimly hoped everyone would remember that an officer may not accept presents. Sometimes a thing got started, and before you knew it, everyone was putting in toward a silver tea service or something. Surely they all knew his views. Perhaps they would think of something that had nothing to do with money. Mossie would love it, whatever it was going to be. He wished she were here, but he hastened to insist to himself that it would not do. Mossie was always too easily touched, like all kind and dependable people. Lord only knew what else the youngsters would think up. He smiled at the way youth got run away with, until the running often became an end in itself. Anyway, he was going to get through this alone. Blaming nobody, he mourned the inflexible rule that dropped an officer from service to his country even in time of peril. Well, all his life he had solved difficulties with action. He now proceeded with order to make his personal arrangements to go.

The best of such was the moment when he went to the stables to find Sergeant Robinson, who had served with him, off and on, for twenty-six years. Recruits always enjoyed discovering that General Huntington and Sergeant Robinson looked like each other—the same ruddy leather for complexion, the same steel-white hair, the same bony smartness of experienced horsemen, mounted or afoot. At the old stables, the sergeant was busy and immaculate. He greeted the general quite as usual, and did not even reveal in his expression that they both had a lump of news to swallow. The general said they would go to see Molly, and they marched down the swept stone floor to Molly's stall. The tall bay mare was gleaming dimly in the winter light that came through the round stone embrasure above them. She coquetted largely and slowly as they approached, gave them her oblique attention, and put up her white velvet nose for the general's fingers.

The general believed in doing things with finality, always had, always would. He told Sergeant Robinson that, when he left, he would be leaving Molly behind, a gift to the sergeant, who would know how to care for her. The sergeant said he would indeed. It was all respectable, almost a kind of comfort. This transaction had dignity. His thoughts shifted back to the eager plotting of the youngsters and the wives and the stewards and the other officers, and he reminded himself that it was always done that way, and let him make the best of it.

There must have been nearly three hundred at the big dinner on Saturday night at the club. They had his flag behind his chair. On the buffet, a huge American eagle in carved ice reared out of a bank of roses, and he made a note to send for the chef and congratulate him later on this achievement. There were toasts and speeches, and music by a quartet of talented enlisted men playing on strings. Just before the baked Alaska, the present was wheeled in, wrapped in a cloud of yellow cellophane with a bow which he recognized as the work of Colonel Clayborne's wife, who always managed things of that sort. Besides, two places away, Mrs Clayborne was leaning and smiling a little specially. Through the cavalry-yellow wrappings the general could see a heavy frame enclosing a decorated scroll, bearing column after column of signatures. He caught the gleam of gold leaf on parchment in the candlelight. Somebody must have gone to Kansas City to get it all done. They brought it to him, and he arose, they all did, while the ADC broke the wrappings, and read aloud the three gold-illuminated words at the head of the scroll: COM-MANDER, FRIEND, CHAMPION.

There followed a paragraph of tribute in the stilted form of Reso-lutions. But to those in the room, at that moment, as the aide read on, the words had the beauty of the Psalms, for the service they did to what is unutterable except when people desire the occasion to be greater than themselves. The ADC turned the frame and its glass toward the general. He was blinded by its flash and could not read the officers' names signed to the Resolutions. But he knew them, every one of them.

He took up his champagne glass and slowly held it toward them all in turn, and nodded, and took a sip, and sat down in silence. His lack of words was more eloquent than many a fluent speaker's best effects. They stood without a word for a moment, greatly moved by his look. Then they burst into a storm of applause and cheers, and some of them had tears going down their cheeks. A waft of peace and gratitude came over them all, as the occasion they had all dreaded so much turned into what they had meant it to be all along, and when they said, "Jack is being simply wonderful," as they had been nervously saying for days, they now meant it with all their hearts.

That was the last big hurdle until the very moment of departure. Nothing was planned for Monday evening because it was understood that Colonel and Mrs Truman would take care of that, and General Huntington was glad that he would go there for dinner with no others present. He and Boot Truman might have a lot to talk over, and if there was a prettier woman, and a more sensible one, in the entire United States Cavalry than Gertrude Truman, the general didn't know who it could be. Monday was busy, anyway, and he would be tired. In the morning, he drove out to see the mechanized elements of the command move out on maneuvers. It was a dark day, for it had snowed all night, and the sky was heavy over the leafless trees. The hills looked as blue and pale as air. Here and there the Kansas dirt, the color of wet bricks, showed through the snow. Yellow weeds stood up along the road. The motored column moving by was wintry in its olive paint, with the big white stars stenciled on the vehicles. Light tanks, scout cars, half-tracks, jeeps, they kept coming and coming. The soldiers' faces were bright red with cold and health. The general saw these men always as cavalrymen, and always would, though there wasn't a horse to be seen. The steel column ground on past him and up over the hill above Fort Riley. He knew they were well-trained. He meant to tell them so at review this afternoon, when they paraded the last time for him. He blinked and looked up. It was beginning to snow again.

By four o'clock the snow had turned to sleet, on a sharp wind that drove off the bluffs. Out of consideration for the men, the general had decided not to turn them out for his last parade. Mrs Truman said he had no doubt been greatly disappointed, but it was so like him to call it off. She said this to her daughter Cynthia, and Second Lieutenant Bobby Drew, sitting with her and the dogs in front of the fire at home, late that Monday afternoon. Mrs Truman said it would have been almost unbearably sad, an occasion like that, and she was more relieved than otherwise.

"Why?" said Cynthia.

It was one of the unfeeling questions such as the girl sometimes asked. She was in her early teens, tall, thin and exquisitely promising. She had her mother's black hair and dark eyes, and pale, glowing skin. Because she was undoubtedly going to be a great beauty, she was troubled by more than the usual adolescent premonitions, and her mother often said, in moments of doting exasperation like this one, that she could cheerfully throttle her.

"Why?" repeated Mrs Truman. "Oh, Cynnie, I could cheerfully throttle you when you act like that!"

Cynthia smiled miserably at the young lieutenant, who was watching her with one eyebrow up. She knew he was only her beau in a comic sense, for, though he was barely over twenty, still, she was barely fifteen. She ached to be exposed before him as such a perverse child now, and watched herself make it all even worse.

"Well, jiskers," she exclaimed, "I don't see anything to make a

[381]

fuss about just because it's wet and they can't have a parade for Uncle Jack. What is everybody making such a fuss over him for?"

Mrs Truman's cheeks darkened and her black eyes flashed. "Because a very distinguished soldier is being retired after a long and honorable career. If you can't see that, why—"

"Well, why are they retiring him at all, then?" countered Cynthia in a loud voice that rang crassly in her own ears.

She saw her mother and Bobby Drew exchange an alien, adult glance of understanding, and it made her wild.

Matters weren't helped for her when her mother said gently, "Because the Army has set an age of retirement for all officers. You know that; you're an Army brat. Officially, they just think your Uncle Jack, as you call him, is too old to go on being a general officer. You ought not to be so unkind. He's been your father's and my best friend for years and years. Someday you'll be very sorry for— And if it's too wet and cold for the review, I meant I was personally glad because I'd've been so moved by it if they had held it that— Oh, good Lord," she finished, shrugging at Bobby, since things that couldn't be explained simply could not be explained if they weren't grasped as a matter of course.

The fire crackled and it was rich and warm in the comfortable room. Bobby Drew had only lately been commissioned at wartime OCS. He loved to call at the Trumans', admired the colonel, adored his wife and spoke of Cynthia as his girl, comically, which both excited and depressed her. He had the hard and shiny ripeness of an apple about him. His eyes and mouth and straight short nose were almost childish, but in the set of his head and the aggressive angle of his shoulders there were hopeful betrayals of the hard man he believed he sheltered within himself. Like his convivial senior officers, he liked to sit with his boots and breeches—of the highest quality—sprawled and spread-legged, and grin at all the pretty women within view. Cynthia, pearly pale, was having one of her agonized moods of "distinction," when she would stare, wide and black eyed, her mouth partly opened to her warm breath, her lovely thin hands poised in mid-air.

Gertrude Truman ironically studied the two young people a moment, and then said, with sensible pleasure in saving Cynthia from her own later embarrassed memories, "Cynnie, close your mouth and put your flippers down."

"Oh, *Mother!*" said the child, and dropped her pose.

Trucian turned to Bobby. "You know, all through the Army they call Jack Huntington The Kingmaker. Did you know that?"

"No. Why, Mrs Truman?"

"Because every officer who ever served as his chief of staff has gone right on up to major general and even beyond."

"Gee! How wonderful! And how rotten. I mean, about seeing him go."

"He's a darling. . . . Bobby Drew, what have you done to your spur straps?" she added suddenly, pointing to the big leather butter-flies over the laces of his field boots. "Take your spurs off this minute and turn the guards right side up."

Bobby glanced down and blushed. "They are upside down," he said, and leaned over and unbuckled the straps.

"The idea!" said Trucian.

Cynthia watched, fascinated.

"Don't you think I'm getting old enough to be a character?" asked Trucian, looking so handsome that Cynthia groaned inwardly at how much her mother knew. "But you can't be a character unless you have things to do. One of the things I shall do from now on is make young lieutenants adjust their spur straps instantly if I see they are on wrong, no matter where we happen to be. You must help me to think up other things to do."

They were all comfortable and friendly again, getting the straps properly arranged. Bobby straightened up, flushed with his effort.

He was delighted at how much you could learn from a pretty and clever older woman in the Army when she was a colonel's wife, or something.

"We've been getting something up, you know, for tonight," he said, "when the general goes to the train."

"Who?" said Trucian, for she was interested in people.

"What?" said Cynthia, who was interested in things.

"All the fellows," he replied. "It's a thing we thought up today."

But he was interrupted by steps on the wooden porch, crunching in the new snow that was freezing outside in the black dusk.

"Golly, I'd better be going," he added, jumping up. "It must be the colonel and General Huntington."

"Stay and have a drink with them," said Trucian. "They must be frozen."

The door of the vestibule opened; they heard the two men come into the hall; Colonel Truman called hello; Trucian went to meet them.

"I'm pretty embarrassed," said Bobby to Cynthia, "staying on this way. Flirt with me, will you, Cynnie, so I'll look nice and busy when they come in?"

"Oh," she moaned, "you make me sick, if that's why you—"

The others came in. The general went to the fireplace and rubbed his hands. He looked tired and abstracted. Trucian brought some highballs from the dining room. She was thinking that, now the moment was approaching, she didn't quite know how to make their old friend feel their love and regret at his going, knowing his hatred of fuss, and she wished now that she'd had eleven more people to dinner, for everybody's sake, but chiefly Jack's.

Bobby, with a general in the room, was lightheaded and afraid he would sit down while the general was still standing, and the fear became a powerful urge to do that very thing.

Colonel Truman bent down and beat fondly upon his dogs, one

[384]

after the other. The spaniels breathed wetly with pleasure, and the hound slapped the polished floor with her long tail.

"Cynnie," said Trucian, "you'd better go up and have at your lessons, darling."

"Oh, do I have to?" she said, and then saw that the distinguished thing to do was to go, simply. Convinced that everything was always going to go wrong all her life, she went stiffly up to General Huntington on the hearth, and put up her cheek for a kiss, which the general gave her, and then she said, "Goodbye, Uncle Jack. I'm sorry they think you're too old to go on being a general officer."

In the drained moment that ensued, she looked at their faces and made a helpless gesture. "Well, I'm sorry," she added, and, by one of her agonies of perversity, she burst into a blurt of shrill laughter and went upstairs.

The colonel scowled and laughed at the same moment, and Trucian gave him a quick little shake of her head. The general looked down at the drink in his hand with pursed lips. Bobby took another deep gulp of his and crashed through with what he afterward honestly thought of as tact. "Sir," he said to Colonel Truman, though with a glance at the general, "today I made my first reprimand." His gray eyes brimmed and sparkled with the zest of this milestone.

"Oh?" said the colonel.

"Yes, sir. One of my sergeants was drilling some recruits, and I heard him bawling at them and abusing them—one man in particular. I called him aside and I gave him the works, sir. That old stuff is out. That's Old Army."

He paused a second, worried that this might not sound so good to the general, who was Old Army himself, of course. But the general was looking at him as if he were somebody else, forty-two years ago, beginning another career.

"Why, colonel," continued Bobby, "that sergeant might have

given some enlisted man an absolute complex against the whole and entire Army. Was his face red when I got through with him! I won't have that sort of thing in my platoon, sir!" He was pink with the justice of his act.

"That's right, that's right," said the colonel, looking into the fire, so he could squint away his amusement.

Trucian watched the general, reading unconscious nostalgia on his face. Absurdly enough, she said to herself, she felt almost like his mother, wanting to comfort him. She heard Lolita, the maid she'd brought from Fort Bliss, crossing the dining room to announce dinner.

She turned quickly to Bobby and said, "Bobby, you'll stay and dine with us, won't you?" And when he began to protest, as they all stood, she went and took his arm. "We'd love to have you. . . . Lolita, another place for Lieutenant Drew, please. . . . Jack, I want you here," she added, indicating the chair on her right at the table. As they sat down, she cocked her head a trifle, listening for Cynthia upstairs. *The poor wretched darling,* she thought, and blinked her beautiful eyes, because the same thought so well covered Cynthia, and Jack, and Bobby, who was certain that he'd stayed too long, and had hot ears as a result.

But she saw, with increasing satisfaction, that keeping Bobby to dinner was a good idea. All through the meal, the general talked to him, between the candles on the table. He started by saying that he couldn't help thinking of the morning in 1901 when, fresh out of West Point, he had reported for duty at Fort Stanton, in the Capitan Mountains, in New Mexico west of Roswell. There the first thing he'd had to do was call the sergeant to attention in the porch of the officers' quarters and ask him to recollect that discipline needn't be ignored just because this was a remote post in a distant territory of the United States. After that, the sergeant had taught him a great deal, he added, smiling.

[386]

"Yes, sir," breathed Bobby; for the stars on the general's shoulders flickered in the candlelight and gave extra wisdom to what he said.

"The Army is still the Army, anywhere," the general went on. "It was so then, and it was so today when I watched the mechanized columns go by me up on the hill. Not a horse in sight. But we're still the cavalry. I can remember my father telling about the early days in Arizona in the Apache country, when they used those heavy old horse-drawn ambulances to carry everything from brides to casualties to cases of Scotch whisky out on the plains. He used to laugh about Captain, afterward General, Gibney, swearing and raging against the fool who invented the horse-drawn ambulance as a cumbersome, impractical piece of impedimenta that only slowed down movements against the Apache. But my father never failed to add the story of how George Gibney made an Apache jail out of an ambulance in his column, keeping fifteen troublemakers under one armed guard while the rest of a platoon was off rounding up Nogales Joe and his brethren. The Apaches had the habit of spitting on their bullets before loading their stolen rifles.

"That was the year my mother came out West as far as the railroad would take her, and then finished the trip by ambulance. My father met her on horseback and rode the last hundred miles with her, trying to prepare her for her new home. She said she didn't care what it was like, if only he would carry her across the threshold when they got there. And when they arrived, they found the adobe hut in ruins, still smoking from the bonfires the Apaches had built inside it, and seven men lying dead around the doorway. Even so, it was the nearest thing to shelter as far as the eye could see, and when my father and some of the men with him had cleared things away a little, he still picked her up and carried her across the charred threshold, because there was American soldier's blood there, not to be stepped in. They did what they could and fixed it up and lived there the next seven months. She often said it was the happiest

[387]

period of her life, because they had to make for themselves what they got. That was in the seventies. They finally returned East and I was born in Canandaigua, New York, where my mother came from. She always said you had to live in Arizona if you ever wanted to really love the trees up and down the streets of Canandaigua."

The lieutenant was frowning with fascination.

When they went back to the living room for their coffee, the general was still talking. He talked about his service in the Philippines and China and Hawaii, and on the Mexican border, and in France. He spoke of many first-name comrades whom the Trumans knew, a few of whom were famous enough for Bobby to nod at. He talked measuredly and yet eloquently of service at Baguio and Stotsenburg and Myer and Bliss, and visits to Benning; a tour of duty in Panama, and those Jap fishing boats, even then; General Wainwright as a major; Lieutenant-Colonel Eisenhower in the Philippines; and that Comptroller General of the United States in Washington who had been the bane of so many officers; the Olympic team on which he had jumped Silk Hat; Paris in 1917 and the Rhine in 1918; Fort Sill in the breathless quiet of a hot summer night, and the comradely sense of membership in a corps whose motives, in personal terms, were clean. He was gentle and dignified. His eyes seemed to make shafts of meaning and persuasion as he looked at Bobby: take this, all of it; it is just as much yours from long ago as what you will go forward to after today.

The fire thudded down in velvety ash. The dogs breathed contented sighs now and then. Bobby was leaning forward, both satiated and hungry with that life he was hearing of.

"Sometimes just hearing about a thing does it," said General Huntington. "One day, when I was a little boy visiting my grandfather at his place up the Hudson River, I went out walking with him and an old friend he had staying with him, Colonel Todd

[388]

Beston. Both of them Civil War officers. We walked through the woods to the top of the cliff overlooking the river.

"I was more interested in a white steamship going down from Albany than in what the two old gentlemen were talking about, until my grandfather, General Huntington, poked me in the back with his cane to make me listen to Colonel Beston. The colonel was telling about that early morning in October, the nineteenth, 1864, when he had been awakened from a sound sleep by an orderly who came to say that General Sheridan wanted him to come at once. Little Phil, the colonel said. They were at Winchester, Virginia. Colonel Beston got up and dressed hurriedly and went back down the street with the orderly to General Sheridan's headquarters, where he found Sheridan drinking coffee and standing with his foot up on a chair while his boot was being wiped off for him. Said the staff was coming in by ones and twos. They all stood around in the breaking day while Sheridan told them the Union Army was being cut to pieces at Cedar Creek, farther south on the Winchester Pike.

"In a few minutes the horses were brought up outside, and the last thing Sheridan did before he put on his cap was cross himself and lean over and turn the lampwick down. Then they all went outside and mounted and rode off through the town. They rode at a fast trot as long as the horses could stand it, and then they walked a ways while Sheridan told them his plans. They could hear the artillery and see the white smoke in the low hills. Said they took up the gallop, and rode like Indians. Sheridan had to take to the fields with his staff, for the roads were blocked with wagons and wounded. They began to meet the retreating troops. Sheridan stood up in his stirrups and signaled to the men with his saber. The sun was coming warm, and Colonel Beston particularly mentioned how the light flashed on the blade of Sheridan's saber. Said he didn't have a particularly big voice, but the men heard him, and began to yell back. A little farther on, he sent Colonel Beston to the left of the line, and another staff officer to the right, and for the next two hours, things were precarious—precarious. But by late morning the tide began to turn, as they say, and they all knew the day was saved, though it was a big job they had to do to finish it off.

"You see, until then, Phil Sheridan had been only a name in a schoolbook poem to me. I remember, as we went back to the house, my grandfather told me that General Sheridan was born in Albany, which made him seem like a neighbor, though I was a little boy and he was dead. Old Army, I suppose. I don't suppose I realized it at the time, but since that day, it all seems neither old nor new, but simply continuous. You see, I heard it from a man who was there himself." General Huntington smiled. "I've been talking a good deal, Gertrude."

She put out her hand to him and he squeezed it.

Upstairs, a door slammed, like a willful reminder.

As if to reply to it, "I am shot," Bobby sprang up and said he had better be going. His face was pink with embarrassment. He wrung the general's hand without the awkward respect that he usually remembered to display toward his seniors.

"Sir, I've never heard anything like it in my life. Goodbye, sir, and I certainly hope we meet again sometime. I'll never forget tonight."

The general nodded and smiled upon him, and let him get out the door. Then he said to the Trumans, "You never know who might turn into somebody, do you?" He stood up and took his own leave. "You'll be at the train?" he asked anxiously. "I don't expect there'll be anybody else but my ADC and one or two others."

"Yes, yes, of course," said Colonel Truman.

"And you, too," the general insisted, turning to Gertrude.

"If you really—" she said.

"Certainly, certainly."

His car was waiting in front, and Bootie put him into it and ran back into the house from the freezing night. The ice was so heavy on the trees that it was cracking the thinnest limbs. When he got inside again by the warm fire, he cocked his head, in family habit, to listen for Trucian and Cynthia. He couldn't hear anything, but knew they were upstairs together. He made himself another drink and sat down to think about things. This ended up as usual in thinking about going duck hunting. He had often noticed that when he thought about hunting, everything else seemed to come clear and be put in its place, no matter how het up he might be inside.

When Trucian came down later, she found him lying back with his eyes closed, but not asleep. "Everything all right?" he asked without moving.

"Poor Cynnie, she couldn't go to sleep. I found her in tears."

"She knows she ought to be spanked."

"Oh, Bootie, you can't spank a child fifteen."

"I didn't mean it."

"I know you didn't."

"Was she crying over Jack?" he asked.

"Or was she crying over Bobby?" she replied.

He looked at her ironically. "Love, not remorse, hey? You would," he said.

Trucian faced up to him. "Well, both, I suppose," she murmured.

"I guess," he said, "there's been a lot of feeling loose around here for the last few days. Cynnie probably felt it, but didn't know what to do with it. . . . I'm going to see what the station says about the train. It'll probably be later than usual." He went out to the spacious white hallway and called the Fort Riley station agent on the phone. He came back in a moment and said the train would get in at one-

[391]

fifty. They had two hours to wait. They were glad they could wait together, in silence and in comfort.

It was the coldest night of the winter. The Trumans were there a little early, in case the general came down ahead of time. Gertrude Truman was unprepared for the sight and sound of what came down the dark road from the post at a quarter of two, and turned to her husband to berate him for not having prepared her. But the colonel was standing at attention, almost as if he were at parade, so she said nothing. Her heart was in her mouth as she looked back up the road.

First she saw the torch fires, advancing down the road through the pitch blackness, but could not understand them until she heard the rumble of the tank treads on the freezing ground. It was an armored escort bringing General Huntington to the train. Every vehicle showed two torches with oily flame and smoke. Leading the column was a half-track mounting a 75-mm. gun. As it drew into the pale cast of light thrown from the ticket office on the white frosty ground, she saw that it carried the general's flag. His car was right behind it. After that came light tanks, scout cars, command cars, jeeps, more half-tracks, a weapons carrier with his luggage, and a rear guard of M-10 tank destroyers. All the vehicles were manned entirely by young officers. The treads, gears, motors, the weight of the armored tonnage on the freezing ground, made a growling music in the bitter, still night.

The ceremonial procession was well-timed, for the eastbound train came in as the escort rolled to a stop by the yellow-and-brown depot. The general got out of his sedan. He was like a man already lost in a great formality. This was no farewell to a family. A bugler in one of the open half-tracks sounded the General's Flourish. In the dark and the random-spilled light from headlights and the station doorway shone the gleaming boots, the gold devices of the caps, the frosty breaths and the general's white face, as he brought his hand up to the salute. The young officers returned his salute together. Lieutenant Drew was among them. With a shiver of emotion, he thought, *I heard it from a man who heard it from a man who was there himself.*

Above them all, quiet and invisible on the widening hill, Fort Riley was asleep. Inconspicuously, Sergeant Robinson took the general's bags to the waiting Pullman. The general walked over to the Trumans, kissed Gertrude on the cheek and shook hands with the colonel, and started to speak, but he shut his lips, walked rapidly to the train and climbed the steps. He did not wait in the doorway, but went right inside the car.

On the platform, the officers stood until the train left. It was too cold and dark to say much. The train began to move away. They watched the green light and the red light on the last car vanish around the curve going east.

Then they all went back up the snow-covered hill to the sleeping fort. It was only four hours until reveille, and Lieutenant Drew was falling asleep on his feet. Even so, he wondered how he could find ways to share with his new platoon in the morning something of what he had listened to that night.

The Head of the House
of Wattleman

Mrs Wattleman was a short, wide woman who had given her life to the theater with no regrets, and only a few reservations. When I knew her, she was entering that era in her life when, with an intimate sense of the nearness of life's baffling meaning, it became necessary to admit that the little daily gaieties of her calling and her household were about to be supplanted by the irascibilities of slowly settling age. My visits to her establishment were, I enjoy believing, a kind of temporal link that might have held together for a few precarious minutes the hull of her past and the rotting anchors of her future. This belief of mine I take from the evidence that attended my various arrivals: I ring the bell, there is a brief speculative silence, I am recognized, I am admitted by Mrs Monk (the suppressed assistant), I clatter down the stairs to the important basement room (catching a terrible glimpse of Mr Wattleman, looking useless in the parlor), I doff my hat and there she is, receiving me with an abrupt courtesy which makes me momentous because she is fussing with her gray hair in my honor.

Then, too, it came out in our first interview that I was more than an employee of a theater: I was a passionate lover of it, and so when I came to Mrs Wattleman for costumes or properties for our productions, it was not as a customer, but as a fellow artist, engaged in a common project with her, who alone, surely, knew what would be correct for my needs.

Would she ordinarily spend any time with the average customer, telling about her trip to Egypt one winter before Mr Wattleman came down "poorly"? Or describe with richness those rare moments she enjoyed in the presence of Madame Modjeska, "who played piphteen nights in this town, all told, and I missed not a phingle one, and how phine she was, piphteen perphormances. . . ." (Mrs Wattleman didn't always wear her teeth, and when her small lips were unsupported by the brazen excellence of her set, she spoke with a muffled labial quality that still could not destroy her bridled emphasis.) No, I am sure she shared her confidences with me alone, of all her customers, most of whom were young people getting clothes for costume parties.

When they came, "Mrs Monk," Mrs Wattleman would say to the woman who had worked for her foɪ twenty years, "one Rob Roy with sporran." I would turn to Mrs Monk to see what would happen, and the customer in question would look indifferent, lest people think he cared anything about dressing up.

"One Rob Roy with sporran, Mrs Wattleman," would come the answer, as Mrs Monk took her way out of the musty little counter room, and went deeply into the amazing jungle of costume racks that undergrew the whole large house. If, on these occasions, I happened to be in one of the back clearings of the ornate thickets, Mrs Monk would converse with me as she slipped her hand and gaze between the coat hangers, looking for her prize.

"Um-hum. She's getting old, she's old, I've been watching it for some time now, she don't know her own mind half the time, I have to take a lot I wouldn't otherwise take if I hadn't been with the

[395]

Wattlemans for so long now, I wonder if them suits is *all* out—no— here's—no it isn't either."

I said nothing, but went on considering how a cloak of the Garter would do for Sir Joseph.

"*Mr* Wattleman came to me only last night, he said Mrs Monk, there were tears in his eyes, he said Mrs Monk, she's asking me what I did with the string from those packages we sent out that came back. Tell her I gave it to you, he said, and I never saw the like in my life the way that grown man cut up, he's sick, of course, and she's enough to—here it is. I always find it after a while, though I can't say this is a good one, we've had better but that's like her, she won't spend a penny any more. I have to repair and stitch on stuff that ought to be thrown out. Well, I haven't worked here for nothing all this time, I know a thing or two, I . . ."

Here, often, or at the later equivalent of this point, a terrifying clairvoyant scream would rise in the outer room, and come threading its way through the musky alleys to us.

"MIRZus Mo-o-NK?"

Mrs Monk would give me a stare that said, "You see?" and nodding her yellow head, go off to the front room, her pinned and streaked black dress cruelly outlining the lumps of flesh that composed her, and that should by every right of mere animalism have been beautiful mature surfaces contributing to a serene womanly entity. So she would go, answering that imperial shriek, and I would wait a decent interval before emerging with my selections. Mrs Wattleman would take them, pass them on to Mrs Monk: "Wrap."

Mrs Monk would accept them, ignoring the exaggerated efficiency of her mistress's instructions, and preserve a social relation with me by smirking as she wound the string about her fingers and endeavored to break it by pulling until her gray knuckles swelled and her shoulder strained upward. It was like Mrs Wattleman, at this

[396]

point, to reach in her apron pocket, withdraw a pair of scissors, lean over with one fast movement, and cut the string, and with it, the poor pretense of her assistant. All the time she would converse with me, the collops under her small chin dancing like a petulant turkey's wattles, her yellowish fat hands with the dim diamonds and the cracked, streaked nails playing across her disordered coiffure; or one hand would lie on the rumpled shelf of her bosom, there to let its fingers restlessly tap and displace the brooch made of gold with designs picked out in black enamel. Her eyes were behind glasses, and her cheeks rose and quivered with her talk. The packages finally wrapped, Mrs Monk handed them: "One cloak of the Garter, Mrs Wattleman."

Taking it, "One cloak of the Garter, Mrs Monk."

"One sir knight sword, Mrs Wattleman."

"One sir knight sword, Mrs Monk."

"Two—no, *three* helmets, Mrs Wattleman."

"Three helmets, Mrs Monk," and a glare.

"And one dozen spearheads, Mrs Wattleman."

"And *one* dozen spearheads, Mrs Monk."

Mrs Monk leaned for a moment on the counter, plucking and rubbing her bared forearm with her hand, and Mrs Wattleman undertook the regal matter of delivering the things to me across the counter. While she was counting them off to me with myself echoing her in the established fashion, Mr Wattleman made a disreputable and tentative appearance in the doorway of the little room.

Immediately there was a suspension of all activities. Mrs Wattleman withdrew her head upon her neck until her shoulders were far ahead of the beetling disapproval in her countenance. Mrs Monk, with a duck of her brass-colored hair, pretended not to notice him. The poor man stood in the doorway, clutching the ragged portière with a gray fist, and making little circles of cordiality with his other hand, greeting me, proving his importance as head of the house of Wattleman with the insistent whimper of his talk.

"Good morning, Mr Wattleman."

Then *she* said, "Mr Wattleman: have what you want and good-bye to you!"

Her tones lacerated him through the thick dirtiness of his vest, and his shriveled heart must have turned over with memories of fifty—piphty—years ago. He released his head in a series of nods that seemed uncontrolled, and indicated me.

"I just came to see Mr . . ."

If he had forgotten my name, still he knew who I was; and it was his place to welcome me. His wife divided her hands between her brooch and her upper lip, fingering both.

I turned to Mr Wattleman. "Well, we've made some good selections this morning, and I think our show will be a success."

He brightened, with a poor effect of emerging at all apertures from his formless clothes. In his exuberant embarrassment, he dropped his cane so that his ravaged limbs were undefended against the impulses of locomotor ataxia. But he recovered the stick, and beaming on me, showed Mrs Wattleman with his other hand that I was a friend of his, and that he was, to the extent of my importance, important.

"We'll come to see it," he said, and then suddenly, "Now I've got to go and do some work."

The idea that he could direct his thinly arteried physique in conscious activity amazed me, but Mrs Wattleman and Mrs Monk nodded with their first approval of him that morning, and the former said, "All right, Mr Wattleman, do your work; do your work, we do ours, he does his, and so you go and do yours." Her voice was shrill like a parrot's, but she was at last tolerant of his unhappy presence.

He nodded several times again, and plucked his watch chain, and

[398]

turned to go up the little steps that led to the respectable parlors of the house. We all watched him leave, and as his last shoe disappeared with wavering aim from the last visible step, we returned to our affairs.

I have said that Mrs Wattleman had given her life to the theater with no regrets and only a few reservations. Her long career as a costumière had satisfied her artful and dramatic desires. But the reservations—one of them was that she never approved of grand opera, and another was that any thing in the nature of an extravaganza or spectacle, like *Ben Hur,* for example, that required extra-brilliant effects, she could not accept. This morning, after Mr Wattleman left us, I learned why she had so often been censorious of the super-attraction, and even of the aspect of the main street after dark, when the electrics blazed and resembled so many fireworks.

I turned and said, "Mr Wattleman must have a great many interests."

She recoiled with a shock of pleasure in this dignification of her abject spouse. Mrs Monk wagged her head with emphasis, and attended to her elbows, smiling her agreement.

"Mr Wattleman, sir," said his wife, "was once the greatest American designer of pyrotechnical difplays!" She leaned and then withdrew in support of this remarkable statement.

"He did the Johnstown Fair!" said Mrs Monk hastily before her mistress could catalogue the first achievement. "The Johnstown Fair," she said, and Mrs Wattleman turned on her with an angry confusion of her collops.

"MIRzuz Mo-nK?" she said, with the fury of a vindictive kite that so often clouded her voice when she addressed her assistant. "You'll leave me to tell this!"

Poor Mrs Monk slid backward and blushed, but the little gleam in her eye assured me that she was glad to have spoken, and that it was

[399]

indeed worth it. For my astonishment at her utterance had been highly satisfactory. I rearranged myself to listen.

"Mr Wattleman, sir," resumed Mrs Wattleman, "was called upon by managers from far and wide to plan the phireworks for all sorts and kinds of special occasions, to say nothing of anniphersaries, national holidays, receptions of distinguished guests, as well as numerous other kinds of ephent."

I recognized the jargon of catalogues.

"He has been called to Syracuse more than once to lend his adphice."

I nodded, wonderingly.

"And," she concluded, "the Republican Phtate Committee has time and again had him to phix the difplays for their elections!"

"And then he lost his health," said Mrs Monk, retiring at once into the back room, to escape for a moment the positive drenching in Mrs Wattleman's anger that she knew would come to punish her for having usurped the second climax of the recital.

"Yes, he lost his health, he broke down, and had piphe operations, and I paid for 'em!" added Mrs Wattleman rapidly, so that the effect was, after all, one of her triumph. "I've kept him ever since. But I knew I'd have to . . ."

"What an excellent career!" I said. "He must be a genuine artist!"

"Well," she said, "if you could only have seen Main Street in nineteen-aught-phour: that's all I say: if you could only have. It was stupendous: oh, pinwheels! red phire! the geysers! and phestoons of Chinese whipphlares—if you could have."

The clock banged the hour in its musty entrails. I found with astonishment that it said an hour slower than my watch, which I regarded.

"Excuse me, am I fast or are you slow?" I asked her.

She spent a rapid smile upon the clock. "We run it always an hour slower here," she said.

[400]

What an establishment! I became more aware than ever of the strange room in which we stood: the desk in the corner, where Mrs Wattleman angrily wrote out her bills, the drawers in that desk, which held curious miscellanies, from which she once had extracted for one of our actors the Order of the Golden Fleece; the glass case filled with wigs on stands, and a whole shelf of carefully deployed false mustaches; the arms and armor in the other corner, bravely shiny under the cobwebs; the long counter with its machines for tying packages—the spool for the thread, the tacked razor blade for cutting the string, and the wrinkled piles of old paper; and the gay lithograph of the River Nile over the doorway, leaning into the room at a confidential angle to recall, eternally, those dizzy days of the trip to Egypt before Mr Wattleman came down poorly, and all that they stood for.

"Well," I said, picking up my packages, "I have to go now. But be sure to remember, Mrs Wattleman, that I want to hear about Modjeska's performance of Hamlet the next time I come, because we may do a Hamlet scene in the dramatic studio. That would be interesting, to know about her . . ."

We both nodded at one another, I with farewell cordialities, she with a rich, assertive pride and promise. Then, assuming my hat and coat and gloves, I again said goodbye to her, because leaving Mrs Wattleman was like leaving a tyrant whom one must propitiate even overmuch, and started up the stairs to the ground floor, where the door was.

I came to the landing, and was ascending the next step, when a striped, odorous curtain hanging against the wall at the turn trembled and came away until I could see that the hand which parted its folds belonged to Mrs Monk.

"Wisss!" she said, superfluously attracting my attention, thrusting out her fat yellow arm to pluck at me.

I turned and took off my hat. "Well, Mrs Monk."

She moved her head in mournful circles which gave a foreboding aspect to the little scene enacted on the landing. She did not quite dare to come out from behind the curtain, which concealed a doorway, and since her mistress was only a few stairs away, she had to be most delicate in her utterances. But as I was about to resume my departure, she began to whisper into my ear with ghostly intensity and silences.

"Mr Wattleman said to me that she was heading for bankruptcy, he said she's been buying clothes and things at a mad rate, and every month she orders a new set of teeth! He says she dresses up in the evenings then, and sits around looking grand. He says she says it's time for her t'enjoy life, she ain't going to make any stints on herself, she says. He just sits there and looks at her, she reading, and wearing them clothes, and a new set of teeth every month—do you know what they cost?"

Before I could answer "No," and hear her awesome estimate, her face faded white about the eyes and I was startled; for a familiar shriek arose from the nether rooms.

"MIRzuz Mo-N-K?" It was like the wild interrogatory cry of some fowl, and as I heard it, I could imagine the bird crouching as it began the noise, then growing and fluffing as it finished, with a stretching of all ligaments and a raising of the head to complete the utterance with all of the force in its powdery body.

The curtain stayed a shocked second, exposing the agonized blank of Mrs Monk's face; then it fell into place as she retreated through the door, to reach her mistress by some back way of that labyrinthine cellar. Whether Mrs Wattleman had heard that rapid whispering on the landing and was determined to halt it, or whether the absence of her assistant made her merely suspicious, I do not know; but the effect of her shriek was startling in any case.

I went on up the stairs, and opened the door, and stepped into the street. There, opposite the doorway, sat Mr Wattleman at the wheel of his automobile. He greeted me with one of his palsied smiles, and contrived with his knotted fingers to fling open the door of the car, inviting me to sit beside him.

"What! will I never be rid of this household," I said to myself, as I hesitated, then entered the car.

"I'll drive you uptown," he said, whereat my heart tumbled and raced in fear; for to be guided through the broiling traffic of the city by the cripple beside me would be a trying adventure. But nothing I could think of was a good excuse. And sooner than I expected, the car was gathering speed, Mr Wattleman's touch on the wheel helpless and tentative. He worked the pedals with spasmodic difficulty, and I was nervous. But not content with trying me with his jerky driving, he began to divide his attention in conversation with me. We went, somehow, up the street and even passed intersections without mishap.

"You know," he said, "I once did very interesting work."

"Yes," I said, "Mrs Wattleman was telling me you made some very remarkable designs in pyrotechnical works."

He turned square upon me, and I had to urge him to watch the street.

"She did, eh?" he said. "She knows nothing about it, she has nothing to say about it. Let me tell you, I know just how things are *there*. I was making a very fine career, I had done some famous pieces. I wish you could have seen my piece of the Battle of Manila Bay, with a portrait of Dewey in red, green, and yellow flares, just seen it, that's all."

I reflected on the unhappy impermanence of such pieces of art as a fine firework, and how both Mr and Mrs Wattleman expressed the earnest regret that I had not seen any of his productions; then I thought that it was the same with an actor's good performance, for it was planned, rehearsed, and finally executed with nothing but memories left, which people might recall with some such phrase as "I wish you could have seen it."

"Well," he continued, "what a fine thing it was. And the Johnstown Fair! And when the Republicans won in nineteen-four I staged them a sky full of sparks, I'll tell you, sir. Yes.

"Well, you see, Mrs Wattleman was always a restless body, and so she was up and off on a trip to Egypt, me along, before I knew what was doing. Yes. Then we came back and b'gad if she didn't start in business. Well, she worked and I worried. That's how it always was. I did the worrying and she did the work, me meanwhile making my own business pay. The upshot of it was I broke down. It was all her fault. She *would* work, she *would* make me worry. She was always a strong-willed woman, Mrs Wattleman; and I was in a hospital for months, with the different things, the surgeons, and so on. My business went Bang!"

"What a shame," I said.

"Oh, yes," he said.

The car was uneasily coursing into the most intricate traffic.

"My work was labor, it was labor all right. I'd come home of nights and collapse in bed; and then the next day, here was a committee to receive about some displays they wanted me to do. Oh, oh!" He shook his head.

It made me wonder why he had to resign his career. The sinister leers of Mrs Monk contained more than her rapid confessions to me. If a man could guide this motorcar through momentary death (so it seemed to me), might he not also be able to sit at a table with his fireworks catalogues and plan a display? The surrender of his career and the commencement of his wife's business were, perhaps, not simultaneous, though so he had suggested to me. And Mrs Wattleman's proud statement that she had kept him—had worked, after his illness, had expected to, even. There was an angry loyalty in her spotted taffeta bosom with its gold brooch on black.

It was enough that he now and then fixed a pretense of activity. "I must go and do some work now." And how that always soothed and stimulated Mrs Wattleman!

He talked; and soon we were at the stage door of my theater. With amazement at my safety, I left him with thanks, and entered, not caring how he drove away.

In one of the dramatic studios there was a rehearsal of the ballet. The ballet girls came out in their pink tunics, knocking the floor with their stiffened shoes, and throwing their little bodies into space with exquisite faith that the floor would be there a second later when they tapped for it with their toes. They were merry, but serious about their jobs. The pianist and the conductor were directing the rehearsal, and the ballet mistress sat on the sidelines, harboring her criticisms for the first intermission.

I sat with the producer.

It was intolerable to consider, as some black fate made me consider then, the simple facts of youth and joy, shadowed by sorrow. The anchors of unsatisfied age held the three of the house of Wattleman to the bottom of the ocean. They were smothered in waving weeds, and they longed for air. These pink-limbed dancers, blowing airy kisses with their little arms, touching an idea of beauty with the directions of their little brains, danced on the caps of the waves, unconcerned with the kelp on the sea floor.

Having looked that morning at the Wattlemans, I could not stay, I could not watch the ballet girls, though the stagy noise of the piano followed me into the corridors when I left, and I knew that tomorrow my sad connection of the old and the young would disappear from my mind, for the sparks leap from a sky rocket, leaving a blackened stick that is insignificant when considered next the glories of the brief fountain of fire in the enchanted heavens.

The Devil in the Desert

to Virginia Rice

One summer morning almost a hundred years ago in the town of Brownsville near the mouth of the Rio Grande on the Gulf of Mexico, Father Pierre Arnoud awoke before dawn in great distress. "Yesterday," he said to himself bitterly, "I should have told him yesterday."

He listened in the dark of his room whose little window was just showing the ghost of day over the Gulf. Yes, he could hear what he dreaded to hear. Deep in the house were sounds of footsteps moving about. Father Pierre could tell where those steps went, and what their maker was doing. Now he was in the study taking up certain printed materials—a breviary, a missal, a handful of ornately printed blanks for baptisms, marriages, and first communions, which could be filled in as occasion required. The footsteps receded toward the refectory, and there a battered leather knapsack soon was being filled with a cheese, two loaves of bread, a little sack of dried meal, a flask of red wine, and a jug of water. Presently, a distant door opened and closed and the footsteps went across the paved garden to the side door of the sacristy in the church, where another leather

[406]

case would be stocked with sacred vessels, holy oils, communion wafers, and a set of vestments made in France of thin silk from Lyon. The sacristy door sounded again, and Father Pierre knew that the next stage of all these preparations for a journey would move out beyond the rectory and the church to the ragged field where in a corral the two priests of the parish kept their horses. There, he knew, Pancho, the eight-year-old gelding who was the color of rusty weeds along the river, was going to be captured after an absurd moment of delicacy and apprehension, saddled, and brought back to the courtyard where the saddlebags and knapsacks were waiting. By then it would be light enough outdoors to see where you were going. It would be time to go.

From the sounds he could hear and the activities he could imagine, Father Pierre knew all over again something of the formidable man who was getting ready to depart. If those footsteps sounded like those of an old man, trotting and tentative, yet there was in them a stubborn force. There was plain contempt for human comfort in the noise he made before dawn when others might be sleeping; he seemed to say that if one man could get up to make all that noise in the name of God then any other should be glad to awaken to it.

Father Pierre knew there was grim joy in the world that morning for his friend and colleague Father Louis Bellefontaine. He knew also that Father Louis tried to control a capacity for anger that could flare as quickly and as madly as a cat's. In the new stone rectory the two men lived harmoniously for the most part. It took much government of their natural temperaments to make this possible, for over everything lay the difficulty that Father Pierre, who was many years the younger, was the pastor; while Father Louis, who had come from France a generation before Father Pierre, was the assistant, and so subject to the orders of his junior. But they made jokes about this, as they did about Father Pierre's education. Father Louis knew only his God, his duties, and what he had learned from hard contests with nature. He knew it was proper for a fine gentleman like Father Pierre to be his superior; and he would wrinkle his old face with shrewd estimate and relish of silken details when Father Pierre was busy with narratives about life at home—which meant France, where one day without doubt the younger priest would be consecrated a bishop. But Father Louis never envied his superior anything, for he knew that in his own work he was a great master—a master of the distance, the heat, the fatigue, the menace of time in slow travel, the harsh vegetation of the brush desert, the ungoverned Indian whose soul was within him but not yet claimed, the fears, hopes, and needs of the Mexican families who lived so widely separated, along the inland course of the Rio Grande. For thirty years Father Louis had ridden, mostly alone, and twice a year, on his journeys up the river.

He always undertook them with a sense not only of duty but of escape. Nowhere else did he feel so close to God as alone in the hard brush country riding to bring comfort, news, and the sacraments to some family in a *jacal* hidden by solitude open to the hot sky. The older he grew, the more Father Louis longed for his escapes from parish authority. The more infirm he became with the years, the stronger was his sense of mission. Father Pierre would see a glow of youth come back over that sun-stung, seamed old face as time drew near for Father Louis to make his plans to go on his ride into the upriver country, which would take him from two to three months. If his eyes were dim with age, not so the vision in his mind, which showed him so much of what people wanted of him, and of what he could bring to them. If his hand now trembled so that he could hardly write down the names and dates on one of his sacramental certificates, he could always joke about it, and assure his families that the deed was recorded in heaven, anyway. If sometimes his heart fluttered like a dusty bird in the cage of his ribs, and made him wonder what was ready to take flight, he could lie down for a few minutes and feel the thing calm itself; and however unworldly he may have been, he always clamped his jaws together with sardonic satisfaction that his time had not yet quite come. He had things to do, and would do them.

Much of this was known to Father Pierre by intuition, and he recalled it as he arose this morning. He hastened, for if he was going to catch Father Louis and say to him what should have been said yesterday, and even long before that, he would have to hurry. Do you suppose it could be, thought Father Pierre, that I am afraid of him? Or am I afraid for my dignity? What if he simply will not listen to me? He has pretended before this to be deaf when he has preferred not to hear me. Or do I not want to see a look of pain in his small, old, blue eyes? Actually, is there not a possibility that what I must tell him will shock him so that it might make him ill?

Father Pierre shrugged angrily at his doubts and tried to answer them reasonably.

Nonsense. After all, a letter from the bishop has approved my decision and given me authority to do what is wise. Why must I heed for a second the individual feelings of anyone, myself included, when a duty is to be done? If I have been a coward for days, in spite of all my prayers for strength and enlightenment on how best to do what needs doing, must I not be doubly strong today?

And yet, as he went downstairs and out to the courtyard where a rosy daylight seemed to emerge from the ochre limestone of the church wall and glow in the very air, Father Pierre was as never before conscious of the difference in years between him and the old man who was at this moment hauling at straps and buckles, with one knee raised against Pancho's belly to brace himself.

It was a picture, as Father Pierre could not help pausing to notice.

The horse was laden, ready and patient. His summer coat was nicely brushed. His bridle was of woven horsehair. His saddle was bulky and tall, with some of the leather worn away so that the wooden forms of horn and cantle showed through. That saddle was chair and pillow, living room and store to Father Louis. To it he had attached many ingenious and cranky accessories, among which there was nowhere any provision for carrying a weapon. Father Louis went unarmed.

The old priest was dressed in a long homespun coat and heavy trousers. On his head was a woven cane hat with a wide brim under which his face, peering around at Father Pierre, looked like a crab apple underneath a shelf. His boots were high, the color of dried clay. Now, in the presence of the younger man, he redoubled his efforts at finishing his preparations. He made extra movements to show how difficult the job was, and he completed them with a little flourish to show how easily he overcame all. His breath went fast, making his voice dry and thin when he spoke.

"Well, Pierre, I am just about off. I hoped I'd see you before I went."

Father Pierre laughed. His heart beat. He said to himself, Now, now, I must tell him now. But he heard himself reply only,

"How did you think anybody could sleep with all your racket?"

"Ha."

It was a dry, indifferent comment. And then Father Louis looked sharply into his superior's eyes. What he saw there made him hurry.

"Well, I have everything. I'll send word back to you, if I meet anybody coming this way."

"Yes. Do. But before you go—"

Father Louis began to slap at his breast pockets with sudden dismay.

"Oh, Pierre, think of it. I nearly forgot my sunglasses, the new ones, you know the pair, which my niece sent to me from Vitry-le-François?"

[410]

"I have seen them, yes. They have green glass and metal rims, I believe?"

"The ones! Would you be a good angel and just get them for me? They must be in my room."

"You'll wait for me?"

"But of course."

"I'll be right back."

How could it be; and yet it was. Father Pierre, at the very point of discharging his sorry duty, was sent off on an errand by his victim. He shook his head. What did he fear so? The acid rage of Father Louis? The years of unspoken submission of the older man to the younger? The human aches that can invade the hearts even of those promised to God? He didn't know. All he could believe was that the unshaven knobbled old man waiting down there by his packed horse, with his hands that trembled on a regular slow beat, and his old blue eyes, was stronger than he. Father Pierre was tall and slender and chiseled in man's noble likeness. His soutane was always clean. His white face and dark eyes could blaze with the Holy Ghost. He had proper respect for authority, but could not now use his own.

Lifting piles of papers, and putting aside apples that had dried up, and mineral specimens blanched by dust, he searched Father Louis's room for the green sunglasses with their oval lenses and tin rims. He smiled at the condition of the room. He did not find the glasses. He returned to the courtyard.

Father Louis was already in his saddle. In his hand he held the sunglasses.

"I found them," he said. "I am sorry you had to go for them. Goodbye, Pierre. Give me your blessing. I must be getting along now."

Through his thin old voice, and his clouded eyes, there spoke a boy who was off to a picnic. Father Pierre's heart sank as he looked

[411]

at him. He knew now that he was not going to tell what it was his duty to tell. Chagrined at his own weakness, and touched by the joy in the face of the impatient old man, he lifted his hand and blessed him with the sign of the cross, to which Father Louis bent his body, leaning forward with the elegance which, no matter what they may be on the ground, men used to the saddle assume the minute they are mounted. Then with a tart smile on his face under the woven cane hat, Father Louis waved grandly to his superior, turned his reins, and at a rapid hilarious walk was taken by his willing horse out of the courtyard and down the road toward the river, where the first light of the sun lapped at the brown ruffled water which came from so far beyond even the country where he was going.

After all these years he had a map in his head. The river came on a long diagonal, so. An old Indian trail went off northwestward at another angle, so. The farther inland, the farther apart they were from one another. There was one kind of country here by the seacoast. Presently it changed to another kind. Finally, in the distance of weeks, where the map would have only faltering scratches of the pen, based on rumor and legend, lay the farthest wilderness of Father Louis's journeys. The natural limits of his endurance were determined by water. His private map had an X for the end of each stage of travel—a settlement, a farm, a creek, a spring, a water hole (and pray it was not dry).

For the first several days, on these journeys, he hardly seemed to have left home. The earth was still low and sandy, and he could read in it how epochs ago the sea itself was here, hauling and grinding the stuff of ocean bottoms where now he rode. The air was moist and little clouds came to be and to vanish almost before his gaze. He could not closely follow the river for it wandered and turned, in some places doubling back upon itself in its last exhausted efforts to reach the sea. And so he followed the Indian trail, leaving it only to go to the isolated river farms in turn.

At such a one he might spend the night, or longer, depending upon what he found. Sometimes death approached in the family, and he gave the last sacraments. Sometimes there were infants to baptize. In the mornings under a tree at roughhewn planks set across a pair of hogsheads he would say Mass and give communion. He listened to the local news from Mexico across the Rio Grande— there was talk of another war between the ranchers of Coahuila and the Mexican troops; it had not rained for a hundred and seventy days; robbers came over the river a while back and killed four men here in Texas and stole some cattle and horses and went back across the river; a child was born in the Bolsón de Mapimí who spoke, quite clearly, at three days old, of a flood that would come but who when further questioned seemed to have lost the power of speech; and so on. Father Louis in his turn told how things were at Brownsville, and farther up the coast at Corpus Christi and Galveston, and across the sea in France, where under the new emperor business was booming, and trade with Mexico was growing, as you could tell by the many ships that came from Marseilles and Le Havre into the Gulf of Mexico. And then after receiving gifts of food from such a family, the rider would leave the river and return to the trail, going northwestward once more.

Days later, though the sky did not cool during the daytime, the quality of the heat changed, and was dry, as the old seacoast plain gave way to a wilderness of rolling country thickly covered with thorny brush. When he encountered it as it wandered, the river bed was rocky, and rock showed through the hard, prickly ground. Everywhere he looked he saw only that endless roll of empty land. Here, near to him, it was speckled with the colors of the olive, both green and ripe, but not with any of the grace he remembered from long ago in Southern France, where the olive trees gave a silver sweetness to the landscape. Farther away in the distance, the land rolls swam in glassy heat. Way off at the horizon there was a stripe of hazy blue where the hot white sky met the earth. Nowhere could he see a mountain, either in Mexico or in Texas.

As he rode, the country tried to hold him back. The thorns of the mesquite dragged at his boots and tore his clothes. Pancho was clever at avoiding most of the hazards, but in places these were so thick that all they could do, man and horse, was to go slowly and stoutly through them. But this was nothing new. Father Louis had persisted before against the thorns and had prevailed.

As for water, there was always too much or too little. Too little when, after years of drought, certain springs he looked forward to would, as he came upon them, reveal only dried white stones. Too much when, in hot spells so violent that they could only be ended with violence, there would be a cloudburst and the heavens would fall almost solid and bring the first water which as it struck the baked earth actually hissed and made cracking sounds until the varnished desert was slaked enough to receive the water in its fissures and let it run. When it ran in such quantity, every finger-like draw became a torrent in which a man and a horse could easily be drowned. If he crossed one in safety, another was waiting to engulf him beyond the next roll. There was no place for shelter. When the rain stopped, the sun came back and dried everything the same day except the running arroyos, which went dry the next day. All too soon there was bitter dust that sparkled in the light and rose with the hot wind. Against it Father Louis tied across his face his great bandanna that came from New Orleans.

And they went on, making a small shadow of horse and man moving slowly yet certainly across that huge empty map where days apart, each from the other, little clusters of human life and need clung to being and shone in Father Louis's mind and purpose like lanterns in the darkness—which usually was the first image he saw of his destination when by his reckoning it was time to reach another of his families.

Was this a hard journey?

Very well, then, it was a hard journey.

But so was the life hard that he found at the end of each stage of his travels. He had seen men grow old and die in his visits here, and their sons with their wives bring new souls to this wilderness in turn. They learned severe lessons in isolation, heat, and the hostility of the animal and vegetable world. Everyone, the child, the grandfather, the husband, the wife, the youth, the horse, the maiden, worked unceasingly against dust, thorn, ignorance, and scarcity from dawn to dark. The great world was but a rumor here, and, by the time it came to the brush deserts, mostly wrong. But a world without limits of dimension dwelt behind the eyes of all those parched, brown people obedient to the natural terms of their lives. It was the world of the human soul, in which the betrayals of impersonal nature could be survived, if only someone came from time to time with the greatest news in all life.

For Father Louis knew in a simple flatness of fact—fact as hard as rock, as mysterious as water, as unrelenting as light—that without God the richest life in the world was more arid than the desert; and with Him the poorest life was after all complete in a harmony that composed all things. To be the agent of such a composition put upon him a duty in the light of which all peril on his journeys became at worst mere inconvenience. Everyone he toiled overland to see needed and deserved that which he, at the moment, under existing circumstances, alone could bring. In a practical way he was still awed by the mystery of his office. And as a human being he could never deny himself the joy it gave him to see in their faces what his coming meant to his people in the harsh wilderness. They knew what he had come through. They were proud to be thought worth such labor and danger.

His mind was active in the solitude through which he crawled day after day mounted on Pancho. One of his favorite fancies was this, that a great triangle existed between God in heaven and any little ranch toward which he rode through the days and himself. It was an always changing triangle, for one of its points was not fixed: his own. As he came nearer and nearer to his goal of the moment, the great hypotenuse between himself and God grew shorter and shorter, until at the last, when he arrived, there was a straight line with all in achieved communion. He smiled over this idea, but he respected it, too; and sometimes he would take a piece of charcoal from a fire and draw a series of pictures of what he meant, explaining it to the people he was visiting, and they would murmur, and nod, and consult each other, and enjoy the notion with him, marveling.

One day at noon on the present journey he knew he should soon see what would look like a long thin blade of cloud shadow far ahead on the earth that slowly quivered with wafts of light like those in wavering mirrors. But it was not a cloud shadow, as he had found out nearly thirty years ago. It was the distant gash of a long canyon whose yellow rock walls were stained with great stripes of slate blue. It came from the north and far away to the south opened into the rocky trough of the Rio Grande. In its bottom were all the signs of a river but running water. Here and there were shallow pools fed by the underground flow which needed storm water to call it flowingly to the surface. Father Louis always paused at such a pool for a bath. There were sores on his body from the catch of thorns through which he rode. Sometimes a needle of the brush would break in his flesh and burrow its way under his skin. For the most part he was unaware of such an affliction, but by its comfort the warm alkaline water of the pool reminded him of the misery he had forgotten to notice. It was usually midafternoon by the time he reached the canyon wall as the sun went lower. The place was like a palace to him, open to the brassy sky. Wrens and hawks came to look at him in their wary turns. To be below the surface of the rolling plain in the canyon was to have for a little while the luxury of privacy, somehow. He bathed, and dozed as he dried, and sat in the shade reading his breviary. He knew when it was just time to gather himself together and resume his ride in order to come by nightfall to the house and the spring of Encarnadino Guerra, where he would spend the night.

This friend was a boy of ten when Father Louis first met him. He was now the father of six children, the husband of a silent, smiling woman named Cipriana, the son of a widowed mother called Doña Luz who on his last visit told Father Louis she would not live to enjoy his next one. He remembered how she sat blinking in the brilliant shade of the desert bowing to him over and over, while a triumph of patience went over her face eroded by time and trouble and work and pain, as she said,

"At night, when everything is quiet, and I am awake and alone, for I cannot sleep much any more, something speaks to me, and tells me to be ready, and not to make any other plans."

She looked at him with hardly any light in her small eyes, and he knew she was right. When he said Mass for them that time, he thought he saw in her face some powerful, direct understanding of the holy sacrifice which during all her pious life had slumbered within her but which at last came clear in her whole, small, withered being.

He wondered whether through any dry, desert-like tenacity she might still be living.

But when he rode up in the arching twilight to the dwelling of the Guerras, almost the first thing they told him after their excited greeting was that Doña Luz had died early in the summer while sitting in the shade on her bench holding her stick of ocotillo wood which her hands had shined so smooth.

In the light of the candle lantern the family looked at him and then at each other. They were shocked by how he had changed since last year. He was stooped and he slowly trembled all the time. He had to peer at them to see them, even though he preserved a smile to make nothing of this. Burned by the wind and sun, his face looked smaller. He breathed shallowly, with his mouth a little open. He seemed to them a very old man, all of a sudden.

It was like a secret they must keep from him.

After their first start, they got busy making his supper. The younger children lost their shyness and came from behind chairs and the edges of the table to see him, and at last to climb upon him. He smelled dry and dusty to them, like the earth.

After supper he held lessons in catechism for the younger children, who tomorrow would receive their first communions. The parents and the two older sons listened also.

After that, there was a little time left for gossip. The family's news was all of the seasons. The priest's was boiled down out of letters and newspapers from France. The Guerras already knew that the earthly love of his life was his native country, which he had not seen for over thirty years, but which still spoke in his darting eyes, his cleverness at description, and in the accent with which he spoke Spanish. They listened respectfully while he made picture after picture in his talk of what he loved and missed; but they could not really see with him either the cool green fields, the ancient stone farmhouses, the lanes of poplar trees, the clear rivers, or the proud old towns, or the towering cathedrals, or the silvery web of his city of Paris sparkling delicately in daytime, glowing in the long dusk with golden lamps and violet distance.

But they were honored simply to have him here, and stared before his marvels, and held their breath for tomorrow, when he would give them sacraments.

In the morning he visited the grave of Doña Luz. Everybody went with him. She was buried a little way off from the adobe house. When he saw how little earth she displaced, he nodded and smiled, as though meeting all over again her modest character which he knew so well. Guerra brought some water in an earthen vessel, not much, but enough. Father Louis took the jug and held it in both hands a moment, and gazed into it. They were all reminded of how precious water was on the earth, how it determined by its presence the very presence of life. Then he blessed it, and they all knew what this meant in terms of their daily struggle. Then, reciting prayers for the dead, he walked around the small mound of the grandmother and sprinkled the holy water upon it, and they knew he was affirming once again a promise made between heaven and earth a long time ago.

After that they returned to the house and he took them one by one and heard them confess their sins, of which as they were contrite he relieved them. Then, at an altar improvised against the wall where the old woman used to sit for so many hours, he said Mass, wearing his embroidered French silks, and using the pewter chalice that came out of his saddlebag. The family knelt on the ground in a straight line facing the altar. The famous triangle of Father Louis was brought into a straight line also. God and mankind were made one. As he recited the words during the offertory, "Oh, God, Who hast established the nature of man in wondrous dignity, and even more wondrously hast renewed it . . ." Father Louis felt behind him the bodily presences of that isolated family, and an almost bitter sense of the dearness of each of their souls humbled him at his altar.

When Mass was over, they returned within the house, where, at the raw table polished by countless unnoticed contacts of all the family, Father Louis sat down to fill in certificates of first communion for the younger children. He had a flask of guizache ink and a German steel pen. Sitting as far back from the documents as he could the better to read, he began to write. A look of disgust came over his face as his trembling hand gave him trouble. Exclaiming impatiently, he put his left hand on his right wrist to add strength and steadiness where they were needed; but this did not help much, and when he was done, he pushed the papers toward the head of the family saying,

"Nobody ever can read my writing except God."

They all took him seriously, prouder than before of their papers.

"But that is enough, isn't it?" he demanded in comic ferocity.

They had a merry breakfast when all talked as though they would not soon again have a chance to talk, which was true; all except Guerra, who was going to speak of something as soon as he had built up enough of his own silence. Finally he was ready.

"Father," he said, leaning back a trifle in his chair, and half closing his eyes to disguise deep feelings, "you won't be going on anywhere else, after us, will you?"

"Oh, yes."

"Where will you go, Father?"

"Why, I plan to ride from here over toward the river—I have a couple of families over there—and I may go as far as the town of San Ygnacio, to see if the priests from Mier are making visits there, as they ought to. Why?"

Guerra put his head on one side and shrugged.

He did not want to say that the old man was exhausted and ought not to go so far in the pitiless country under the searing sun. It would not be polite to say the old man was older than his years, and he must be seventy anyway. He might be misunderstood if he said that everybody reached a time after a life of hard work when he must pause and rest and let stronger people do what needed doing.

It would hardly do to show outright that he thought Father Louis should give up, and stay here, and rest a few weeks, and then perhaps Encarnadino Guerra might leave everything here in the hands of his two strong, quiet boys, and just ride with Father Louis until he saw him safely back in Brownsville.

Father Louis peered close to his younger friend and saw enough of these thoughts to stir him up.

"Eh?" he cried, rapping hard with his knuckles on Guerra's skull, "What goes on in there?" He was sharp and angry. What were they all thinking? That he was a feeble old man? He knew all there was to know about that; but if anything was to be said about it, he, not they, or anyone else, was the one to say it. "Mind your manners, you, boy," he said to Guerra, screwing up his small eyes until all that showed of them were two sharp blue points of light. "Eh? You have opinions, have you? Who told you to think anything! Eh? When I want you to think anything about anybody, I'll tell you. Eh? I got here, didn't I? How many times have I managed to come? And what for! Does anybody tell me to come? Or where to go? Or when? Or why? Then you keep your place, and thank God for your blessings, and for your friends, and understand that it is just as bad to hold an impolite thought as it is to say an impolite thing. Eh?" His whole body shook with the passion he failed to control. "Bad. You'd just better be careful, that's all I have to say, do you hear?"

The family were appalled at this burst of feeling. They sat with downcast eyes, fearing that it would be disrespectful to look upon Father Louis in his rage. But they had little glimpses of his un-shaven face whitened with anger, and they could hear how pulse-shaken his voice was. Guerra was more Indian than anything else, and his countenance became fixed. He leaned back, let his eyelids cut his gaze in half, and took his dressing-down without response. He was not even hurt by it. He knew why it came to him. He knew how much it proved him right in his concern. He admired the flare of spirit in the old man. He was at peace with himself for trying what he had tried.

The youngest child, not understanding what had taken place, now, belatedly, felt the emotion among all the older ones, and turning up her little clay-doll face she burst into wails of misery and fear, bringing her tiny creature-paws to her howling mouth until she resembled the small sculptured masks of earth buried with the dead centuries ago deep in Mexico.

Father Louis roughly took her upon his lap. He bent his bristly face close to hers, cactus and blossom together, and in barely audible murmurs quieted the child, and himself, which took about five minutes.

This act reclaimed them all for each other. Once again the visitor was kind and smiling, and the family without fear.

"And so, goodbye for this time," said Father Louis, putting the child down and standing up. "If you will get my horse for me?"

Guerra spoke to one of the boys, who went to fetch Pancho. They all met him outside. Cipriana brought some tortillas for the saddle-bag. Everyone knelt down to be blessed. The hot sunlight smote them. They had lingered over their breakfast. It was late. Father Louis, mounted and ready, blessed them three times, and then turned and rode off to the south. After a while he looked back. They were still kneeling. The next time he looked back it was hard to see them, for at even a little distance they made the same shadows as the scrubby bushes that grew on the caked earth, and seemed just as eternally rooted there.

He had a bad morning.

The sun seemed hotter to him than before. The savage brush seemed animated with spite as it clawed at his legs going by. Pancho, after a lifetime in the brush country, took it into his head to be terrified of familiar things, and from time to time, without warning, executed a rapid dance step to one side while throwing his head back and rolling his eyes at his rider.

"Hush, you fool!" Father Louis exclaimed at such times. "You fool!"

But he addressed himself as much as he did the horse. For the first few hours of that day's ride, he reviewed many times the loss of his temper at Guerra, and developed a masterly case, closely reasoned, lucid as only a French argument could be, compassionate with a largeness of heart, yet as logical as music in its progression, about why it had been not only natural, but actually necessary to reprove Guerra for having presumed to hold views about him. Reprove? Perhaps actually more of a scolding. Scolding? Thinking it over, possibly even a tongue-lashing. And the knuckles? The furious raps on the head? Still, how else could he be made to understand? But understand what?

It was no good.

As he always did, in the end, he lost the argument with himself. He knew that after hours of exhausting search for conclusions that would excuse him for what he had done, he would at last come to the truth, which was that he had offended God and man through his lifelong besetting sins of pride, self-esteem, and attempted condonement of his own shortcomings; and that there would be nothing left to do but go down upon his knees and admit how wrong he had been and pray to be forgiven and to be granted strength once more to conquer himself.

He began his penance with a resolve not to eat or drink until nightfall.

By midafternoon, the brush grew thicker. Only occasionally did he come to a little clearing between the mesquite bushes, which rose higher than himself mounted on Pancho. In spite of his green sunglasses, the ground sparkled and glared enough to hurt his eyes. He watched for but he could not see the long pale blur which would tell him that another canyon lay ahead which he would follow until it took him finally to the Rio Grande. He kept the sun on his right, for it was declining in the west in the white sky and he was going south. The day was still.

But how was this?

He thought he heard a singing wind, but when he tried to notice whether he could feel the air stirring, or see dust rising ahead of him, there was no sign of wind. He halted Pancho. What did he hear, then? He turned his head. Yes, he could hear something, now far ahead, now here in his very ear. He searched the undulating horizon but he saw nothing except the wavering image of heat where the white sky met the dusty earth.

As he rode on, the singing in the air became louder. It sounded like the voice of the desert heat. He shook his head, resentful of natural conditions that hid behind mystery. And then suddenly he knew, and scornfully he rebuked himself for taking so long about it.

He was riding into a swarm of cicadas, and now he could see the first ones, clinging to the mesquite as they raised their shrieking song of the heat. The farther he rode the louder they became. He bent his head under their stinging assault upon his hearing. There were thousands and millions of them. Blindly they fulfilled their natures in their collective scream of response to the sun and the desert. The very atmosphere seemed to be in flames, and the sound of the stridulating insects added to the illusion.

Father Louis had touched the desert often enough. He had smelled it. He had tasted it when its dust rose on the wind. He had seen it in every state. But never before in so real a sense had he heard it.

He was suddenly exhausted.

In a clearing, a little lake of baked dust a few yards in diameter, he halted and dismounted, tying Pancho to a stout mesquite branch. Disturbed, a cloud of cicadas rose on crackling threads of flight and found another bush. The ringing song rose all about him. He could not even hear the sound of Pancho stamping his foot to shake off flies. He clapped his hands, but made barely a sound against the strident song in the air. He felt removed from himself. All desert natures combined to render him impersonal. Here, humbled not only from within but from without, he could find real contrition. He knelt down to pray.

Sunlight was brilliant in the center of the clearing, a little open room hidden by time, distance, and mesquite clumps. At the west side of it there was lacy shade, cast by tall bushes. But Father Louis rejected it and knelt in the plain sunlight. He bent his head under the beat of his spirit and of the insect scream which seemed to invoke the zenith. He prayed to be forgiven for his miserable anger.

His thoughts came alive in French, the language through which he had first met God.

He was not long now at his contritions, for he knew that prayer was not so often a matter of length as of depth. Much sobered, even saddened, by his intense self-discovery, he arose wearily from his knees and went over to the shade to lie down. He went as deeply as he could into the underboughs of the thorny mesquite. He closed his eyes. At once he felt cooler, just to have the hot light shaded from his sight. Ah, this was delicious, just to lie for a few moments and gather strength to go on for the remaining hours of daylight. He felt how his limbs all went heavy on the earth as he let himself drift off to sleep.

Little coins of light fell over him through the intricate branches. Where he lay, he made solid shadow himself under the mesquite tree. He was as quiet and substantial as a rock. And if he used nature, it in turn used him, without his knowing, for he was asleep.

He did not see, or smell, or feel what came in slow inquiry along the trackless ground, striving forward in orderly, powerful progress, flowing in a dry glitter and advancing through always new and always repeated thrust of form from side to side and yet ahead. It was a diamond-back rattlesnake in search of shade and cool. It came from deep in the scattered brush, and it found the heavy sleeping man under the bushy tree. With what seemed almost conscious caution against awakening the sleeper, the snake drew closer and closer in infinite delicacy, until in the shade of Father Louis's right shoulder it lay heavily at rest, its length doubled back and forth in inert splendor.

The sleepers did not stir for a while; and then Father Louis grew tense in dream, his mouth fell open, and awakening with a jerk he sat up, lost in forgetfulness of where he was or how he came there. He stared at the white sky.

The thick snake at the first quiver of motion beside itself drew instantly into its coil and shook its dozen rattles.

Their dry buzz could not be heard over the general din of the cicadas.

"Ah, yes," sighed Father Louis, as he discovered where he was, and why, and whither he was going. He put his hand to his brow and sank roughly back to the earth to take a few more minutes of rest. The snake struck him in the shoulder and struck him again. Its coils turned dust into liquid light as they lashed. The strikes came like blows made by the thick, powerful arm of a young man.

"What then?" said Father Louis at the sudden stabbing pain and the blows that shook him. He first thought of mesquite thorns on a springy branch; they were long and, as he had often said, sharp as fangs, and their prick could fester if not treated. It occurred to him that this would be troublesome now, as he could hardly reach his own shoulder to wash, cut open the skin, and dig out the thorns if they had broken to stay in the flesh.

But he turned to see the branch that had attacked him, and saw the snake instead.

[426]

The snake was retreating. He could see its eye with its glaring drop of light. His heart began to beat hard. He had a surge of rage. He wanted to kill the snake, and actually rose to one knee and scraped the ground with his hands for something to attack with—a rock, a club of dead wood, anything—but he could find nothing. He sank down again and out of habit in any crisis brought his hands together with crossed thumbs in the attitude of prayer.

"No, no, no anger," he besought of himself with his eyes shut. He had just endured and come through a storm of his own pride, and he must not now create another. He opened his eyes and looked after the snake, and saw where it paused half in, half out of the dappled shade of the next bush.

"Go," he said to it.

What he meant by this came to be more and more clear through calm and struggle in the next hour or so. The snake, as though it heard him, resumed in infinite slowness the gliding flow of its retreat until it was lost to sight among the hot thickets where the insects still sang and sang.

"Yes, go," he repeated bitterly, and was ashamed to discover that he was trembling. It was the humanity in him that shook because death was coming. He fell over upon his face and put his cracked and dusty hands over his eyes. His mouth was open and he took into it the loose acid earth with his breath. His tears ran down his fingers. His heart was pounding rapidly upon the ground. It seemed to shake the earth. It told Father Louis that he was afraid.

"Afraid? Of what?" he thought. "Afraid of death? But I have dealt with it all my life and I have robbed it of its terrors for those who knew how to die. Is death the only victory of life? Or do we have to defeat life in its own terms? That depends. It depends upon whether sin is ever outside oneself, or always within. Yes, this is a very interesting matter."

He made himself lie quietly without thought for a moment. If, perhaps, he conserved his energy, he might by natural vitality, by pure goodness, defeat the murder that had been dealt him by the desert. He forced himself to relax, and promised that in a little while his head would be clearer, his heart would calm itself, and, moving with infinite caution, he would arise, mount his horse, and go slowly, steadily, cleverly, toward the long evening and come to the canyon where there must be a familiar trickle of water. A cool night with much prayer, a stout will, and tomorrow he would go forward and by the end of the day come to friends who would know how to make poultices and feed him and recover him to the use and enjoyment of many more years of duty, work, and acquired merit.

But the poison worked rapidly, and he felt it charging his mind with throbbing pain that confused him. Shining bars went across his vision behind his eyes like spokes of a great wheel. He was dazzled by their power. When he raised his head they took it with them, rolling and rolling until he fell down again upon the ground where his cheek was cut by little pebbles of gypsum. He tried to say,

"Let me not live for vanity, though, Lord."

Questions now became academic, for he went blind in his inner vision, and lay trembling as the terrible message that had been stricken into him traveled the course of his blood and reached him everywhere within.

Tied to his mesquite tree, Pancho stamped and waited.

Presently Father Louis believed that he awoke.

His mind was working sharply and with what seemed to him exquisite new ease and clarity. He saw all his thoughts as in crystal depths of cold fresh water. He knew he was in the mesquite thicket, and what had happened to him, and he possessed this knowledge with an elated purity such as he had always known in the state of grace, after receiving or administering the sacraments. It was more than mere physical well-being. It was a sense of delivery from the ordinary guilt of his own clay, and the exasperating weight of the world. It was the real meaning of communion with all that lay beyond himself. In such a state truth needed no seeking, and no definition. It was here, within, and it was there, without. It was everywhere. When all was known there could be no astonishment.

He was therefore not astonished now when right before him, lying at ease in the light of the sun, was the snake gazing at him with piercing sweetness. He spoke to it.

"I do not hate you. It is enough that I recognize you."

The snake replied, "That is my damnation."

"Yes," said Father Louis, "for when evil is recognized all other powers move together to defeat it."

"And yet they never do defeat it, do they? How do you explain that?"

"Ah. You and I do not see it in quite the same way. You conceive of the possible death of evil as being one, final end after which only goodness will survive."

"I do."

"That is your vanity. For the fact is that evil must be done to death over and over again, with every act of life. One might even say that this repeated act is a very condition for the survival of life itself. For only by acts of growth can more life be made, and if all evil, all acts of death, were ended once and for all, there would be nothing left for the soul to triumph over in repeated acts of growth."

The snake sighed despondently, and said, "Do you not permit me a comparable purpose and privilege? That is, of triumphing repeatedly over all acts of good, that is, of life, until only I remain?"

"I permit you your established role, but I do not admit the possibility of your triumphing repeatedly over all acts of life. I must point out that historically your premise is untenable."

"And yet I have played a part in every human life."

"Oh, admittedly. We are not discussing the fact that your powers exist; only the fact that they have their limits."

The snake smiled.

"This? From you?" it asked with ironic politeness.

"What do you mean, sir?"

"If my powers have their limits, then how is it that I have killed you? What greater power is there than that?"

Father Louis passed his hand across his face to hide his amusement.

"You have betrayed the weakness of your whole position," he replied, "for it appears to be impossible for you to know that the death of matter is of no importance, except to other matter. The materialist can see only destruction as the logical end of his powers. I, and my brothers, and my children, know that beyond matter lies spirit, and that it is there where answers are found, and truths become commonplace, and such efforts as yours, so restless, so ingenious, so full of torturing vanity, are seen for what they really are."

The snake frowned for a moment, but then shook off its irritation, and said, again with politeness, even with a charm and appeal that Father Louis was the first to admit, "Everyone must do that which his nature dictates."

"There again," said Father Louis with assumed gravity, "there is much behind the formation of that nature which you do not take into account."

"Oh, come, after all, I am a snake, I came from snakes, I do a snake's work, how could I behave like anything else but a snake?"

"The outer form is hardly the point. You can assume any form you choose, I believe?"

The snake hesitated before answering. A gleam of admiration went through its expression, and it marveled frankly for a moment at the astuteness of Father Louis.

"I must say, even if we are enemies, you force me to admire and like you," it said.

"Thank you," said Father Louis. "Viewed abstractly, you have great and beautiful qualities of your own."

"Do you really think so?"

"Oh, yes, I do. But I must add that they seem to me less important, in the end, than they do to you."

"You can also be very rude, you know."

"I do not think of it in that way," said Father Louis mildly. "Finally, it doesn't matter how things are said or done, it is what things are said or done. For example, I really believe you can do things far more expertly than I can. But when it comes to what things, there I have you."

The snake looked away, far from pleased.

Father Louis resumed, "I can't assume any form, for example, as you can. I remain always what I am, a man, an old man, a dirty old man when water is scarce or I am busy, an old man full of pride and sin and vanity and all the rest of it; but nobody is ever in doubt about what I mean, or about what I think life means, and with all my mistakes in style and good form, the garden I scratch keeps growing."

"And I?"

"And you, sometimes you are a snake, and sometimes a whisper, and again, a daydream, a lump in the blood, a sweet face, an ambition, a scheme for making money, a task for an army. Sometimes you can even be a man and disarm everyone entirely who cannot see your heart. But someone there is who always sees. Goodness is often performed without the slightest knowledge of its doing. But evil is always known."

"Yes, I think more people know me than the other thing."

"But don't congratulate yourself upon that," said Father Louis, "for it always means one of your uncountable defeats when you are known."

Father Louis saw that the snake would have to grow angry unless the subject were changed. The snake changed it.

"I wonder," it mused, "why I ever came to you today."

Father Louis shrugged.

"Sooner or later, we would have come together," he said.

"Did you expect me?"

"I have been expecting you all my life; though not exactly in this particular guise. You came to me in my sleep, like an evil dream."

"All I wanted was a little comfort. It was so hot, so dry."

Father Louis smiled in delight.

"You see? For comfort, even you have to appeal to the powers of goodness."

The snake habitually wore a scowling smile and now for a moment the smile disappeared leaving only the scowl. Then with an effort it restored the smile, and said,

"Why did you let me go?"

"I had no weapon."

"You could have stamped upon me."

"I do not believe in killing."

"Yet I am your enemy."

"Yes, you are. But I believe there are greater ways to dispose of you than in revenge."

"You do not have much time left, you know. Just think of all the time you would have left if I had not come to you. If you had seen me and killed me first."

"Yes, I have thought of that. But you speak as though time were my property. It is not. How can I count it? Or know how much of it is my share?"

The snake frowned and looked from side to side evasively. Unwillingly, against its own comfort, it asked,

"Who else can decide your share? Where do you get it? What do you refer to?"

The snake began uneasily to bring its coils together. There was anguish in its movement, slow as it was. It seemed to be obeying desire which was hurtful and yet impossible to deny.

"You do not really want to hear," said Father Louis tenderly.

"Oh, yes, I do, tell me," said the snake, with broken breath, already suffering under the answer it demanded.

Father Louis bent over the snake with compassion. There was torture in the creature, as with glittering sweet power it begged Father Louis to answer.

"Very well, my poor sinner," said Father Louis gravely. "I, and all creatures, draw our share of time in this life from God our Father in Heaven."

At these words the snake with the speed of lightning knew convulsion in its dread coils and with mouth wide open and fangs exposed struck again and again at the earth where the dust rose like particles of gold and silver. Father Louis regarded it with pity as its paroxysm of hatred and chagrin spent itself. At last, gasping softly and stretched out in exhaustion, the snake said, sorrowfully,

"And so it was not by my will that you die now?"

"No."

"I was only the means?"

"Only the means."

"Your hour was designated elsewhere?"

Father Louis looked upward. His face was radiant.

"My hour was fixed by our Heavenly Father."

The snake closed its eyes and shuddered reminiscently. Then it said,

"And my hour?"

"You will die in your bodily form by His will."

"You're sure?"

"Yes. But you will live only on earth, no matter what form you assume."

The snake grew pale.

"Oh no."

"Yes," said Father Louis, as his argument drew to its close, "for there can be no evil in Heaven."

The snake lay with its mouth open, its tongue like a little tongue of fire flickering in despair, its eyes staring without sight. It was vanquished, destroyed, made trivial. Father Louis shook his head over it and wished it might not have suffered. Then he felt his brow where the diamondine lucidity of the past quarter of an hour seemed to be clouding over. His skull was cracking under blows that beat and beat there. How could he feel so ill after feeling so well?

"And now you must excuse me," he said, uncertainly, to the snake. "I have things to do, and actually, I do not feel too well, thank you, if you will just go now," and he looked to see if the snake was leaving, but the snake was already gone.

The battering pains in his head brought Father Louis from vision to consciousness.

"Oh, my God, my God," he said devoutly and with much effort, even with modesty, representing his trouble to Him whose suffering he had dwelt upon so deeply in a lifetime.

He looked around.

The air seemed entirely silent. This was because there was a ringing in his head so bewildering that he could no longer hear the myriad insects at their screaming celebration of the heat.

He saw Pancho tied to the tree.

"No, you must not stay with me," he said, and tried to stand up. He could barely stand, for his legs were weak as paralysis crept into them. And so he crawled across the open place among the thickets

[434]

until he could hold to his stirrup, haul himself up, and lean with his head on the saddle for a moment.

"You need not die here, tied to a tree," he said. "Let me get my things, and you may go."

He fumbled with the buckles and straps until he was able to haul the saddle off the horse. It fell to the ground. He worked at the bridle until he had freed it enough to pull it off over Pancho's head. The horsehair bridle hung from the thorny tree and trailed in the dust.

"Huya! Huya!" cried Father Louis, waving his hand at Pancho to make him trot away, as he so often had done after unsaddling the horse at the corral in Brownsville. But Pancho simply stood and regarded him.

"Very well, very well, in your own time, then," he said, and went down to his hands and knees, fondling a pouch on the saddle. Out of it into his hands came the objects he wished to hold once more. Holding them to his breast, he crawled back to his fatal shade across the clearing. The sun was almost down.

"Magnificat anima mea Dominum," he murmured while pain pierced him through and through, "et exultavit spiritus meus in Deo salutari meo," he said without knowing he spoke. But he brought a lifetime of prayer with him to death's door; and in a little while it entered there with him.

Pancho late the next evening finished finding his way through the brush back to the house of Encarnadino Guerra. The family saw that he was without his saddle and bridle. Guerra and his big sons went searching, and though they persevered for days found nothing in that wilderness of repeated clump and glaring shadow and lost sameness. They had to give up. Later that year when surveyors from an expedition of the United States Army came by his place on their way to Brownsville, Guerra told them the news, and asked them to see that it reached the proper authorities, along with the horse Pancho which he hoped they would take with them.

And then one day, eight years afterward, Guerra was on his way to San Ygnacio on the Rio Grande to see his new grandson, born to the household of his oldest boy who now lived there. Coming into a small clearing in the brush, he found quite by accident what he had looked for long ago. There was not much left, for the desert earth and sky were voracious. Coyotes and blowing sand, vultures and beating sunlight and wind had worked with the years on flesh and leather, French silk, parchment and homespun. Reverently Guerra took up the few bones that had not been scattered, and the few hard things that still stayed by them: the pewter chalice, a rosary of small sea shells, three American silver dollars, the pair of green sunglasses, and, from a mesquite tree where it hung now off the ground, the horsehair bridle.

When he could, he made the journey to Brownsville bringing the relics of his old friend with him. He found his way to Father Pierre Arnoud.

"How these things speak to us!" said Father Pierre, after hearing the end of the story that had begun eight years before. He looked at Guerra and saw that this was a man who had lost a dear friend, who would understand anything said to him in the name of Father Louis. He added, "I am leaving soon for France. Do you know where that is?"

"Yes. He used to tell us much about it."

Father Pierre was making ready to obey a summons to return home to receive the dignity of bishop of a French diocese.

"I am going there to assume new work," he said. "These things, this sacrifice," he said, indicating what Guerra had brought, "will help me to do it better."

Guerra nodded.

"We will bury him here in the churchyard," continued Father

Pierre, "and you must be present. As you were his friend, and have served him so well now, I would like to ask your permission to keep this."

He held up the little string of sea shells.

"Yes," said Guerra, accepting with simplicity the power to dispose.

"I wonder how he died," murmured Father Pierre. "Indians? A heart attack?"

"Not Indians."

"Why not?"

"They would not have let the horse go."

"True. What then?"

Guerra made a gesture with his mouth, putting his lips forward as though he would point to a place far from there and long ago. He saw the clearing in the thorny brush again, and he knew its nature, all of it.

"I think I know."

"How could you possibly?"

"He did not die suddenly."

"No?"

"No. He had time to free his horse."

"Ah."

"If he thought he could have saved himself, he would have come with the horse."

"Undoubtedly."

"But he did not come. He stayed. That means he knew there wasn't any use."

"And so?"

"Where I found him was just like the place where it would happen."

"What would happen?"

With his hand Guerra made in the air a slow, sinuous motion from side to side in an unmistakable imitation.

"No!" said Father Pierre. "A snake?"

Guerra nodded.

"I think so," he said.

Father Pierre shuddered at the nature of that fate, and then presently he kindled at the memory of an old weakness and an old strength.

"Do you know? I will tell you something," he said. "Our dear friend was an old man, tired, and ill, when he went on that last journey. For days before he left, I was supposed to tell him that he could not go. I tried, and I tried. But I could not tell him. Even on the last morning. I could not give the order."

Father Pierre put his hand together in emotion.

"What could I have saved him from? From dying at his work? That is how we—all of us—want to die, when our time comes."

He looked earnestly at Guerra, but if he thought he would find the abstract pardon of life there, he was mistaken. Guerra simply looked back at him with the impersonal judgment of the world.

"No, I could not give the order," resumed Father Pierre. "And do you know? I am sure he knew what I had to say. He would not let me say it. He gave the orders. Just to prove it, he even sent me upstairs to find his green sunglasses. I went, and I did not find them. When I came down again, there they were, he had them all the time."

Guerra laughed out loud at the crankiness this recalled, and what it meant. He bent over, took up the pair of green-glass spectacles with their rusted tin rims, and with a gleam of meaning, handed them to Father Pierre.

"Then keep these also," he said.

"Thank you," said the bishop-elect soberly.

The Candy Colonel

THE PRESENT

Colonel Fielding couldn't have been more conventional in his type. He stirred respectful affabilities from young men; and old women his own age felt tenderly toward him, seeing their youth alongside his in a mixture of memory and imagination. He was a tall old man, with a hardy pink face and white mustaches brushed up to his cheeks. He had dash and style, even if he moved slowly and a little fearfully. He wore his hat over one ear, his white hair brushed up against the brim. His eyes were hawk-brown, and his brows over them eagle-white.

He came in the autumn to stay a few weeks in the town, with that desire to look with age upon the places of youth.

The town sat in a little valley that occurred on the plains of New Mexico where several springs broke through the desert crust and made creeks, and nourished trees, and ran narrowly in the general hollow left by some great river movement of a thousand other autumns. To the west were mountains; they could be seen from the town, sometimes snow-white; sometimes hazed with blowing dust; sometimes glazed like china with evening light.

The colonel looked toward them many times a day.

He stayed in a hotel in one of the leafy cross streets of the town, and it was still warm enough to sit on the hotel porch. The cars went past on the pavements; he remembered dusty streets and stepping ponies. The bank down in the next block loomed white and portly; he remembered a slat-front store that included a lawyer's office. Picture shows winked down the street at night. Radios threaded house to house together in the same current of occupation and attention. He remembered distances between one lighted window and another that had seemed far enough to remind him of stars.

For several days he had a modest pride in walking the streets of the town he had helped to make possible, and wondered when somebody would recognize him and call his name. But nobody did. Then he began to ask a few questions at the hotel; but the clerk was a youth who considered his time wasted clerking when he could croon so good; and, hating his town, he knew nothing of it and could say nothing to the colonel about where the old-timers were now, except that they were probably dead and buried, hi-dee-hi!

So the colonel, dressing with his habitual style and dash—brown homespun suit, and tilted hat, chamois gloves and a Malacca stick—got the habit of going more or less regularly to the Court House square and there sitting all morning, watching the hard brisk sunny Main Street river of unconscious life go by, in cars, and traffic signals, and loudspeakers on trucks advertising movies, and at times little Mexican newsboys running along with papers. Nowadays, he heard, they were called Spanish-American, as was only proper.

He felt at peace, but puzzled. How could everything appear so thoughtless, hurrying toward something quite unrelated to where it all began? Had they never heard of the Brady's Mill Massacre? Was Patricio Melendez a memory that belonged only to Colonel Fielding himself? Oh, yes, they forget, they forget; but not while the leaves fall, surely? and the air smites the heart with some pang, like an essence of a man's very own creation?

He was going on to California where it was warm, when winter came.

He had a married daughter there.

He always enjoyed his visits with her, in the breezy luxury of her house; all the new books shining with fresh print stacked and waiting for him; where he could be bossed and pampered and pretend to hate it and yet be furious if they decided for a day or two that he really was a very independent old man.

Why didn't he go on, and arrive there early this year?

He didn't think very articulately; and so he felt very keenly.

All his life the solution for odd feelings had been activity. He had risen in the Army in a very proper line of distinction and respect. Had he had two or three more years, and a little more guileful charm, everybody said he'd have been made a general officer. He didn't care. He said to everybody that he was ready to sit back and look at life now, rather than make it for himself.

One of his mornings in the Court House yard, when he was sitting on a bench and recalling how it used to take two days and nights to reach Fort Banning in the Capitan Mountains by horse-back, he saw standing in front of him several small Mexican children, who were dazzled by his strangeness and the splendor of his clothes, the air of his style, which they would have always perceived more readily than Anglo-American children. They were from four to seven or eight years old. They regarded him through eyes like big black cherries, with some glow of ruddy light inside them. When he leaned a little and said hello to them, they smiled and shied together to make a sort of group statue of Innocence Confronting Age; and he reached in his pocket and brought out a roll of peppermints with holes in their centers, and handed the packet around. In silence the children took the candies, and then he took one; and they faced one another again and grinned generally, getting nowhere, but very content so. The leaves were falling, little shells of gold, abandoned by the faithless summer.

He looked at the bare feet, the smeary faces, the embarrassed stomachs stuck out, the black frosty eyes—exactly like the children of the Mexicans up in the mountains where Fort Banning was in the old days.

Presently he got up and went away.

The next morning they were there again; and he fortunately had some peppermints left, so they had another party. The day after that he came with a bag of candy; and because the town was not a city and everybody crossed the Court House square several times a week, and because the colonel was so unignorably distinguished and the children so dependent upon him now, he became a sort of anonymous celebrity in the life of the town, and children spoke of him as the candy colonel.

One day they brought a little girl with them from Chihauhua, the Mexican settlement east of town on the outskirts, and he said,

"What's *your* name?"

"Mary," she said.

"Not Maria?"

"No, Mary."

"Here's a candy for you."

"Gracias."

"What is your other name?"

"Mary Melendez."

"Melendez?"

"Sí, señor."

She spoke with a trilling purity, a precocious neatness that delighted him, and when she told him her whole name, he felt his heart turn over, and he looked at her closely to behold her pale brown face with its charming wideness at the round cheeks, and her

[442]

little fox-teeth in her exquisite, sharp little mouth; the furrows of softest darkness between her brows, some puzzled and tiny-animal-like modesty which might become pity when she grew up.

He was losing his breath and feeling his hands turning cold where his palms gripped his cane.

He got up and waved goodbye to the children and said to himself, "You are an old fool," and began walking back to the hotel, but he was followed; the memory of that exquisite little face went with him, and the eyes beholding him so doubtfully yet so warmly, moist and pure and he thought darling and pitiable.

When he got home to his room, he lay down.

"Nonsense," he declared alone, "it is just some little digestive upset," for his heart was rubbing along with little velvety tremors on his breast.

So he could neither explain away his agitation nor banish the acute memory of the child Mary Melendez and the curious, cruel, impersonal significance she had; as if a tree long dead should yield a new shoot from a root hidden a whole lifetime.

But he knew, really, now, why he had come back to see the sunny distant land again; and while he knew the hot summer of his twenty-fifth year again in the mountains far west of town, he said to himself:

"It is not uncommon for people to have grandchildren or for generations to go on; the striking likeness and the coincidence of names need not be surprising, either; I suppose it is a fairly common name among these people!"

That night when he slept, he stirred against his memories; his eyes released little streams, though he never knew it. A kind of muscular recollection of deeds long past and desires repudiated gave him no rest. When he awoke he was exhausted, which he would not admit; he went again to his bench under the nostalgic sunlight, and the children came; he could have cursed himself when at the

[443]

sight of the tiny Mary his cheeks began to burn and his heart hurried with its soft stifling rub upon his arching bones. But he took her on his lap and stared through her eyes at the past.

THE PAST

At Fort Banning in the Capitan Mountains seventy miles away and above the town, Lieutenant Fielding had a reputation for hardness and misanthropy which hardly suited his appearance. He was bright-cheeked and black-eyed and of the kind of good looks which his friends had to make fun of lest they admire. He spoke very little, and was barely induced to play cards in the dull long evenings. The commanding officer of the fort, Major Daly, tried to get him loosened up from the beginning, with frontier humor and drinks of whisky, saying that men on duty in a remote New Mexican post like this one, in 1884, had to make their own fun. Nobody but Mexicans lived up and down the little valleys, and a few white families who were busy robbing the natives, or stealing each other's cows, or struggling to set up an honest store or two at some crossroads.

But Richard Fielding stayed to himself, doing his duty well, reading the Philadelphia papers sent from home, writing long letters whose addresses no one ever saw, and finally earning for himself the reputation of a cold fish.

Major Daly used him often on reconnaissance trips into the hills; the Mescalero Apaches in the Ruidoso Valley needed watching.

He was brisk and simple about doing his jobs.

The soldiers thought him inhuman because he had no friends. They remembered once the trouble Major Daly had in getting him to join the other officers on the porch of the post headquarters when a photographer from Roswell wanted to take their picture. He finally stood there leaning against a porch post, half hidden by a band of shadow.

Then they found out that he did have friends.

He liked the Mexican people.

He learned to speak Spanish sooner than his fellow officers.

There was some aroused and avid mess talk about what use he put his new tongue to.

Instinct reconstructed the truth for his comrades after a time. They decided, haphazardly and correctly, that he was "disappointed in love," and was soured on the world and hiding his wounds like a small boy, with sternness and youthful dignity. Major Daly knew some people in Philadelphia, and, now that he thought of it, it seemed to him that he'd heard talk of an engagement broken off between Dick Fielding and Hope Trumbull, shortly before this Western station.

The junior officers sometimes got leave for five days and went down to Roswell because it was the nearest town—a wide dusty, or muddy, street, depending on the weather, with several houses where cultivation reigned and several houses where it did not; and between the two they had themselves all kinds of good times.

Fielding never went along, even when there seemed a chance of running into cattle thieves who ranged along the Pecos and now and then got as far west as the town.

If he didn't want to get drunk and make love and have a fight, then what did he want?

Patricio Melendez was a Mexican farmer who used to bring fresh vegetables to the fort and sell them to the mess officer. He was a mild, heavy man with sad eyebrows and a peacefully composed mouth that laughed or sorrowed with the same expression. He seemed kindly, and resigned to the prices he was paid for his vegetables. He came often. It was a fairly long drive from his little ranch up to the fort; and that summer was especially hot, the sun like a silent locust shelled in gold above the dry mountains, where the brittle pines exhaled so little of their cooling essence. He came in a wonderful old wagon whose wood resembled parched skin, drawn by two stinking mules of saintly character.

Over the driver's seat was a hood of white muslin.

It threw down a gold light.

Patricio's daughter Maria came with him once, and Lieutenant Fielding met them to do the business of the mess officer, who was away.

"Six dollars for the load."

"For that long hot drive? Six?"

"Yes."

"Well, I will take it, but heaven knows that friendship towers over selfishness!"

"Good health has its values, and I am glad to perceive them in you."

They were unloading the wagon during this social and perfectly serious exchange of Spanish saws.

"My health is but a reflection of your own, since it is a pleasure to observe it."

"Ah, well, a good man is like an oak tree, the longer he lives the more useful he becomes."

In other words, Richard in a foreign tongue found expression for himself that was fresh, vital, and unmindful of the bitterness he had come to use among people of his own kind.

The daughter sat in the wagon and beamed at him, puzzled and charmed by his accent in her language.

They gossiped, too.

"How are things down your way?"

"Oh, *señor,* I tell you!"

Melendez shook his head prophetically.

"What?"

"That Brady, some day someone will shoot him."

"Where, at the mill?"

"Yes! . . . You know my cousin? Well, he took his corn to Brady to have it ground; and when he was done, Brady said he would keep half for payment, and hold the other half until my cousin could pay cash and buy back the *first* half. —Great God? He nearly killed Brady right there."

"So what did your cousin do, finally?"

"*Well,* Brady— Well, he went home!"

"Is that all?"

"Yes; only:"

"What:"

"My cousin is a crazy man when he is angry. You will see!"

Maria laughed at this in delight. Richard looked up at her: hot and golden in the sunny shade of the muslin wagon sheet.

He reached and helped her get down.

He saw that they got some lunch.

Later he showed Maria the whole fort, with its long narrow barracks of adobe, cool and sulky dark inside; and the fieldpieces placed on the high ground that saw down the valley where the hills were bluing in afternoon; and the stables of rough stone, more precious stuff than adobe for their animal transport.

She was about as tall as his breast.

"Yes," he said to himself, "at least admit that you feel like all the other fools in the world who are touched by brown eyes looking *up* at them!"

She kept her face turned to his, and her eyes with their brows puckered in earnest attention to his stiff Spanish.

Her lips moved in imitation of his as he spoke, so she could get his words by two senses.

[447]

Patricio took pity on his mules and decided to stay all night at the fort, when Richard asked that he do so.

Richard felt something tumbling and knocking in his breast at this ingenuity, its occasion, and its success.

That night the moon stood above the plains like a specter of the hot summer, and the pines released something of their airy message; it cooled off.

He stood down to Maria and shadowed her like a pine tree himself.

He kissed her; her cheek was so soft and cool and precious that he felt like melting back to childhood. Then her face grew hot under his mouth and another torment arose and in a moment she was scared; he heard her swallowing and trying to speak. He opened his arms; they hunted one another like night creatures, then, like halting people, stood away and walked back down the piny hillside toward the fort, which they'd been away from only since a little after dark.

He was glad most of the others were gone, and that the Melendezes would be on their own way in the morning before the others could possibly get back.

He said goodbye with further elaborate and embarrassment-killing proverbs the next morning.

Maria was tender and showed toward him a sense of secret which he felt to be promising and questioning both. She sat there under the muslin hood; he was reminded of a portrait by Corot in the Trumbull house in Philadelphia: a girl, tawny, goldish, with dark hair, her head bent, her dress plain stuff like this—gray cloth pulled tight over tight roundness—and little tannish hands clasped in mischievous modesty, holding two white wild flowers; and black velvety shadows; and some pulse of fallibility and charm, life, in the whole.

[448]

He jeered at himself as they drove off, for this extravagant comparison; but as they went, he said,

"No matter how superior I feel, there's not much I can do about *this.*"

When his friends returned to the post, they found him somehow harder and crisper than ever. He was stiff as a general's aide; and someone said his mouth looked like a stale old biscuit, pressed together.

They brought back the prints of the picture made by the visiting photographer some time before: and there they were, all of them, with long hair and sideburns, and faint mustaches; tight low collars on their military tunics, which had only the top buttons fastened; tight gray trousers creased at the joints; over all a powdery sort of light, gray powder turning to black shadow away from the sun.

The photograph somehow held the tone of that dead summer, the drive of the heat and the dusty creek beds all through the mountains, the 'dobe walls crumbling under the sifting winds, the exiled soldiers executing their mission in manly duty and manly exasperated indulgence both; men secure and watchful in mountains, in a time of unsettlement and the stir of new life on the plains of New Mexico.

The following week when Maria came back with her father Patricio, with another load of green vegetables, it was she who made the assault this time. She contrived to find Richard and take him alone. The intervening week had enriched itself in her memory like a dream; and she was enraged at herself for being so coy and cool with him before, now wanting by wanton tenderness to make him forgive her.

She was articulate with the sweet touches of her hands and lips and cheeks; her little heart, as he thought of it, must be hurting, for it seemed to be crowded with so much. He was confused and excited and touched with some pity that he tried to forget.

[449]

Some sensual and excruciating weld of passion and death moved the soldier and the girl as it always moved everybody.

Sometimes he remembered Philadelphia and felt indecent about Maria in that ancestral light.

On her part, she had secret little dramas in her mind about running off from her father Patricio and following Richard wherever he went all his life.

Nothing seemed so immediate and forever.

How ready they were!

He strove her against him in his hug, feeling her movement alive and foreign, yet of him: they took each other.

She was hardly a woman; yet committed, glad of it, precocious like the girls of her race in the quick perception of life's duty before which they were fatalistically helpless.

The Melendezes went back that same night; Patricio said he couldn't trust anybody down the valley not to be foolish.

"What do you mean:" asked Richard.

"My cousin wants to get drunk and do something."

"Well?"

"Well, a lot of people think about the same thing, and I don't know:"

"—You don't mean Brady: they wouldn't dare do anything."

"Yes, but Brady has been chewing up the livelihood of Mexicans where I live for years now."

"Yes, I suppose he has been unfair."

"Do you know him?"

"I have seen him once or twice."

"What a face!"

"Perhaps I can ask Major Daly to go over and speak to him. Brady surely doesn't want trouble!"

"He is as bad as my cousin, that Irishman."

"Well, *adios.* —Come back soon."

[450]

"I will. —And the lieutenant must come to our house. Our house is his."

Richard tightened his jaw for a second and glanced at Maria sitting in the wagon. She said nothing, and he felt the flow of her claimant sweetness.

"I shall be happy to come," he said. "A night under a friend's roof is riches for the poor, and simplicity for the rich."

Patricio mooed with cordial pleasure through his calm fixed face. They drove off. Richard watched them as the wagon itched and rasped down the graveled road and released its little kick of dust into the evening gather of light and lucent shadow.

Later he reported his conversation to the commanding officer.

"We'll wait and see," said Major Daly. He squinted at Richard and wished he could figger him out; but concluded that he was a deep one and probably having the quiet laugh on everybody else when he got what he got from the Mexicans, some of whom were mighty pretty.

"You speak pretty good Spanish by now, don't you, Fielding?"

"Yes sir, fair. —I mean for ordinary purposes I can."

"I'll bet you can!"

The major suddenly felt jovial and fatherly and slightly prurient, imagining what the surly and handsome youngster got away with. He offered Richard a drink of whisky, which Richard drank respectfully, without falling into the fond and confidential mood of the successful rake, which Major Daly felt to be the only proper conversational grounds for men to meet upon.

Richard felt when he was alone in his quarters that as soon as she was gone he returned to what he hoped were his senses. It was forlorn comfort: in the meaning that he had rather not return to them, but keep alive instead the other obsession.

He slept lightly, as he always did in the severe and fugitive air of the mountains, which seemed to sustain breath with lightness and to keep the heart trying.

So he heard the horse coming before anyone else and he sat up in the dark to listen hardly.

The hoofs came scrabbling in a gallop up the gravel road toward the fort.

Someone called in the dark.

The guard.

He leaned from his bed and looked through the open door of his room.

The light in the C.O.'s house flipped alive in a match and then caught in the lampwick.

The peace, the nightliness of the mountains shouldering the heaven were put awry by the reawakened concerns of men there.

He could hear a Mexican talking in a high rhythmic rise and fall. Presently the guard came across the parade ground and knocked for Richard.

"Major Daly, sir; he wants to see you."

It was a young Mexican boy who was trying to tell the major something. His hair hung forward and his eyes through it snapped like a mountain cat's.

Richard listened and then explained.

His heart sank but he spoke calmly.

"The Brady trouble has gone right to hell, Major. The boy says a pack of them got drunk all day today and during the afternoon they went to Brady's Mill on the Guadalupe Creek and tried to get at the storehouse to take what they said was their flour and stuff that Brady had taken away from them. But Brady locked up and shot through the window and killed Enrique Melendez, who had the idea in the first place. . . . That's Melendez's cousin, the man who brings our green produce. —The boy says Patricio Melendez sent him up here for help. His cousin is dead, and that ought to end everything; but the people are really stirred up now."

Major Daly was in his nightgown, and some unconscious need to fill the moment properly made him narrow his eyes and stand with one hand spread on its fingertips on the table, a great man deciding.

"How far is it to Brady's?"

"I've ridden down there in five hours."

"H'm."

Silence, in the room. Outside, faint washy noises of wind in night-looming mountains.

"Yes. Lieutenant Fielding, you will march in an hour with four picked squads from B troop and once you arrive at Brady's Mill, attempt to mediate, since you understand Spanish. But your orders are to subdue any trouble, shooting to kill if necessary. I will survey the situation personally if you need me later."

"Yes, sir."

The fort awoke now.

Fires and lamps turned out the night.

By dawn, that came ascending over the far-lying plains, the soldiers were moving down through the chill canyons, in a chorus of working leather, chiming equipment, knocking hoofs, wondering men; when they reached flatter shelves in the valleys, they went at the trot; the sun went on over to morning; the air was still, not even the delicate hang of the great cottonwood leaves was disturbed by any breeze; and at almost eleven o'clock they saw far and standing as if motionless against the pale blue light-wanton sky a column of smoke inclining to the south, tall and mysterious.

"That must be about at Brady's." . . .

So for several miles the smoke was their beacon; then coming down over a yellow baked hillside crawling with acid weed and shifting stone, they could look down upon the Guadalupe Creek. The smoke came from a burning outhouse behind the mill. Nobody was visible outside the mill. The soldiers could not see why. The mill's windows were black and white with shadow and sky.

By noon Fielding had the men dismounted in a grove of cotton-woods along the creek; and he went forward to the mill, which stood whitewashed by sunlight and oddly silent. The creek behind it was shallow and feeble in the dry summer; but still it made enough whisper on its white sand to be heard.

Up a few stone steps, he knocked at the front door of the mill.

Instantly within there were voices, as if they'd been waiting for this very knock.

They spoke in Spanish.

What?

Yes; during the night, they explained, they had seized the mill and the soldiers had better leave them alone; for they came only to get what was theirs, and perhaps a little more besides, if there was any justice in the world!

"Where is Brady?" demanded Fielding through the door which they refused to open.

His answer was a choir of laughter full of the excitement of scandal.

"What have you done with Brady?"

"Go back to your army and we will show you!"

"Listen: I am Lieutenant Fielding of the United States Army. I am sent here to keep the peace and help everybody. —Will you open the door and come out and we will all talk and settle this? I will help everybody. Mr Brady can tell what he thinks and then you can tell what you think. We will be good friends and arrange every-thing."

More yells of laughter, poundings of ecstatic enjoyment on the floor and inner walls, a smashing bottle.

"Then they are all drunk!" said Richard to himself.

He banged on the door again in the name of the Government.

[454]

The mill had a hallway inside that door; then immediately steps, and an upper half story, and then a full story above that; so the first windows were fifteen feet above the ground.

One of the narrow windows to his right in the white stone wall was now pulled open and he saw a bundle stuffing its way through it and beyond in the dark shadow of the room up there above him at a close angle he heard trials of glee and scratchy breathing.

The bundle resisted and was punched and pushed until it fell to the ground. It was Brady, rusty with blood, fat and cold and dead.

The window slammed.

Inside came sounds of riot, the reassurance which the marauders needed now.

Richard coughed down a feeling of sickness.

He went back to the troops.

He announced a siege. The men cherished what he told them. He sent three to bring the body of Brady away from the angle of sunlight where it lay under the blazing wall.

As the soldiers were coming back to the encampment with their burden, they were shot at from the top floor of the mill.

"That's done it," said Richard.

He strove to keep his temper down, but the men didn't; they luxuriated in theirs; by what seemed almost caprice, destruction and rage were turned loose, each in one kind of man opposing itself in another.

They were perhaps three hundred yards from the mill, in the shade; the creek ran by for the horses; men in mottled shades were hard to hit; still, Richard retired the position deeper into the grove; the ground rosebush-covered; even here they could catch the odd break of the packed summer silence every time someone in the mill drunkenly let out a yip or a yell.

It was a remote, almost childish sound.

"What a shame we can't use childish means!" thought Richard.

[455]

Toward midafternoon he moved around the mill to see its vantages. He sent a soldier up the valley for his friend Patricio Melendez who would help as mediator. When his reconnaissance was over, he found the soldier back in camp with word that Patricio was not home; hearing of the Brady's Mill trouble on his return from Fort Banning, last night, he had sent the boy for help from Fort Banning, after which he had come right on to the mill. That's all they knew at his home.

"Who told you all this, his daughter?"

"No, she came on with him. It was his old woman, I guess."

Richard walked out to the clear ground and stopped fifty feet from the mill. He called out:

"Is Patricio Melendez in there?"

There was a busy pause; scrabbling behind the door; then with a curious effect of surprise Patricio's sad and amiable face appeared at the upstairs window, where the coming evening fanned a pale embery light.

"Patricio! We must stop this terrible business!"

Patricio bobbed like a puppet and made sad, charming noises.

He was suddenly as remote in spirit from Dick as he was in space.

He seemed to deplore, vaguely; yet now that his cousin was murdered, so was Brady, and this might be a new way of life.

"Why won't you all come out, Patricio? And go home? —All I want is the man who killed Brady. That's all. Tell them, will you?"

He disappeared from the window for a moment. Then he was back, sadly shaking his head.

"My poor friend," he said to Richard, with great warmth, through his unchanged face.

"What are you talking about?"

"It was a mistake, I see it now, to send for soldiers," said Patricio.

"Everybody in here says they will probably get killed by the soldiers."

"No, what nonsense! Damn it, tell them all I want is the man who killed Brady; the rest of you can go home!"

"I told them that, a minute ago. —They all killed him. So nobody is guilty. Praise God."

It was a heavy hot descent of evening, among the hills. Richard felt the light going. He turned and looked down the long valley, vaguely perceiving the far plains through the low open notch way to the east. Before he could turn back, they shot at him; the bullets ripped alive a little sprite of dust behind him. He turned and stared, and the windows were empty; then he turned and ran back to his camp; the men were charged with prowess now, and ready to burn down the mill and cut up who's inside it.

The night settled dustily.

The mill glowed like a banked furnace through its windows.

There were long silences, dramatized by the listening soldiers as defiant; then there were bursts of sound: sometimes song, sometimes shrieks of childish defiance (except that they were men), and once they heard a sobbing in a different temper—a woman by one of the windows, probably, crying against her hands in hollow sounds that came across the distance like the muttering of the owl.

Richard heard it, and he believed the truth of it, and he felt such pity that he could see right away what the hazards were: it was Maria crying in the mill, there with her father, and the drunken, scared murderers; and the soldiers outside had to go and take those men; there would be a fight; there would be many hurts and perhaps death.

He went all around the mill again while it was dark, alive in the late-cooling valley like something that must prowl else it fall into rage at inactivity. On the creek side the mill wall rose flat and unbroken except for the little door opening above the wheel.

He came close and thought of calling her name, but did not.

But when it was getting light, and the mill stood insecure among dewy mists native to the mountains, he went again to the open ground in front, and called out to them that if they had Maria Melendez and any other women, in there, they must send them out before there was any trouble.

Now Patricio was once more his ally.

Patricio declared that he had never thought of that; poor Maria had no business there if there was going to be trouble. Why not open all the doors, and everybody walk right out?

He was in the window, and he now faced into the room, talking; Richard could only see, not hear. He saw Patricio jerked down out of sight, vague disturbances of darkness within that meant people moving there. He cried out,

"Maria, let me talk to you!" and they slammed the window, but he saw it open again a second later, and there she was, almost white in the rising light; but as he called, they hauled her down and away into the crazy silence of the besieged mill. His heart thumped the bones of his breast. He was certain they'd been rough. What had happened to Patricio?

"We shall take this place forcefully, then!" he called.

No answer.

Another morning, opening over them all; the sky a silvery yellow doming to warm gray. Then the sun, which made them shiver in its early stirring beam through the mist.

Until the full light was upon them, they waited.

Then Richard ordered an advance.

At the edge of the grove they halted to look. Maria was pulled into view at the window, and they indicated her, as if to say, "So long as she is here, we are protected; you surely would not attack while there are women among us!"

Maria was like a dejected doll, handled by her people.

[458]

There was a muffled shot inside the millhouse. Someone opened the front door on the stone stoop and a body was kicked out.

"What happened?" asked a soldier.

"They shot him."

"Who is it?"

"Some Mexican."

"What for?"

"I don't know."

Richard knew.

It was Patricio; for soberness; for law.

There seemed nothing left but a primitive necessity.

He gave his orders, and the men deployed around the mill, and the high terrain took some of them above; some of them went by way of the creek. The people in the mill opened the battle. They fired first. The soldiers answered.

The windows went out.

The door cracked achingly and splintered.

Soldiers came down and others came up, closing in. The high mill windows now without glass showed the dark rooms and the puppet-like men appearing there to shoot and fall away again.

Richard went carefully.

A soldier was killed about nine o'clock.

It shocked the men and reminded them of self-bodies and the sweetness of power there.

They were ready to kill.

Soldiers on high ground shot down through the windows whenever they saw a movement.

Soldiers below the creek watched the mill-wheel door for any crack of presence.

Soldiers with Richard, among the outhouses, crouching in the bright squares of light and shadow, watched so hard in the blinding light that one of them said he saw the body of Patricio Melendez

[459]

moving, there, on the front stoop. Everybody watched for a while; it didn't move again.

Toward noon it was a battle of eyes; waiting; watching; the slightest shift of movement, either in the mill rooms or out on the ground, brought a shot or two. Animals facing each other, each heart beating for the other's fatal false move.

The heat sang with bugs and locusts and the flowing creek. Somehow like an image of song, the heat waved far away down the yellow plains below the mountains.

Richard wondered how he would take the mill.

Perhaps he should send for Daly?

The men were pricked with sweat.

The waiting in the sunny silence became dream-like.

After one o'clock Richard went to the high ground and from there led a little wave of rushes down the hillside, where there were white dusty boulders for cover. They scrambled and slid a few feet at a time, taking up positions of fire when they shouldered against the warm rocks. From here they could see well into the mill rooms, white walls deep in shadow, and the lift of head, poke of muzzle, the sunny inch of finger when one of the Mexicans shot. The shots were so slow in coming now; intuitive signal between the two forces was no longer a thing to be felt, as it was in the early rapid fire. A soldier half stood behind his rock and peered; it was a movement of distraction, and the head and finger and barrel in the mill window did their job before he could crouch again. He fell and cracked himself on the rock and then rolled to the ground, bleeding; and saying,

"Now, Lieutenant, that sure was smart of me, now wasn't it!"

He died.

They took his shirt and pants off him, and filled them with smaller rocks and told their best shot to be ready. Putting aside the white naked dead soldier, they lifted the dummy of dirt and uni-

[460]

form and jumped it across the protective boulder, where it fell and rolled like someone crawling for a moment.

That was long enough.

The window was busy again.

But the shooting soldier shot first, and the figure in the window rose up and then fell back.

Now that was the end of everything.

The silence came back.

The heat was like a covering of glass.

They waited and waited.

Then the soldiers became perversely brave, rising a little to peer, then kneeling, then standing, then walking a few steps with a certain strut; and nothing happened.

"Somebody must be left alive in the mill?"

They would look at one another, and then shrug.

"Maria? If she is the last one? She would let us come in."

He could hardly wait; but because it involved his men, he said that he must wait.

Finally he said that they must wait for him while he went back to the creek among the trees, and there crossed and came up the creek to the farther mill wall, and there pressed himself until he could get around to the front stoop: climb up past the body there; and break his way in. When he waved them to come, they must come.

Twenty minutes later he was alone in the downstairs hall of the mill. The door had been shot at the hinges, had fallen in at his thrust, and been lain in a tragic geometry against the near other wall.

It was dusky in the mill.

There was a smell of wet hair; it was the smell of blood. He could smell the sour gas-burned empty cartridges that littered the stairs and the floor, and as he climbed the stairs he knew that if there was anybody left with a gun he was going to be killed when he turned the shadowy white landing up there; but he went, slowly; the boards talked; his heart was in his mouth; before he knew it, he called,

"Maria! Maria!"

but there was no answer.

At the landing, he did hesitate, a second; then went on; the next steps were fewer; he could see the dark upper hall, and the doors opening off it into the rooms, the tall high narrow rooms with stone walls where it was almost chilly in spite of the hot summer day outside.

They were dead and watching him and mild.

Their guns lay dropped.

Just so had his own two soldiers outside fallen down when they died; and his mind which knew they were all dead, still thought of what their bodies now did as if from their own want and volition; and the dead men lying there seemed to him to be seeking the covering of sleep; wooing the floor to receive them; their spent flesh finding comfort in their own weight at rest.

One, two . . . five, six, he counted in the hall; and went into the near room.

Two more.

One alive? One alive, seeing him, but really seeing him, with eyes that moved, he leaned and was more shocked at the living man than at all the other dead.

The wounded Mexican nodded to him, like a puppet, and put out his tongue which was white.

Richard made a note to send a canteen in here later.

He went to the next room.

The white plastered wall was shadowed and spattered, both in the same color; below it was a broken chair. Clinging to it was a young Mexican, face downward on the floor.

By the window was another, older, and his hand was delicately laid across his eyes.

The rooms were so narrow and tall that he looked up as he went into the next one. Oh, yes, he found the window of this one faced the high ground where the soldiers were. Before him was the last man to shoot. And what was this, behind him? Let him see. If he turned, he would observe.

Oh, yes.

He had seen her from the corner of his eye when he came into the room a moment before.

He knelt down on both knees with his knees spread and his hands on his thighs; sitting on his heels, he felt that he towered above her, who like all the men in that outrageous charnel house, with its vague hollow stench of fury and obscene change, now lay wanting the meager sanctuary of the floor, or the earth, or anywhere she could lie—for it was what forever after she would do, and only that.

He had held her like a rabbit, warm and little in his arms in which she had made warm little struggles to go, and had stayed.

He heard the ringing in his ears now as reminders of the firing of soldiers, under his command; he had killed her; everytime someone moved, a soldier shot.

Now it would not even be inconvenient to imagine her going with him wherever he went.

Nobody knew anything about it.

The tears scratched down his face at this ultimate thought. It was a thought that seemed to cap the humility and the brevity of that love with a certain shame.

What offices now?

Looking around, he saw a coat in the corner and he went for it and brought it and laid it over her. It was moldy with dust, some coat of Brady's? The cloth was almost stiff.

[463]

She was covered from his sight forever.

Then he got up and went to explore the rest of the mill, the dark chamber above the milling room downstairs. It was an attic, empty of any life but that of little creatures who lived on dust and darkness.

The soldiers came at his signal downstairs.

They were disappointed in the flavor of their victory; and so they ranged through the mill loudly, guffawing at what they saw, the ancient rite of fouling the remains of the enemy, an impulse of guilt.

"But I sure thought the' was more of 'em than this!" they said. And,

"Boy, ' tell you, ' way we's firin', wha, nobody coulda stayed alive in here!"

"Boy, haddi, nobody did!"

Laughter.

The lieutenant came after them and saw them poking and marveling and testing, like scavengers, and the sight made him blench with anger; but he held his temper; he went past them, and in the corner room upstairs he took up the covered weight of Maria, and brought it down, outside, and just before darkness fell, he had his troops started on the march back toward Fort Banning, leaving Patricio and his daughter at the Melendezes' from up the valley.

He had left eight soldiers at the mill, on guard.

The battle news had gone abroad; they began to meet people on their march of retreat.

They all spoke of it as a massacre at Brady's Mill. Feeling among the natives was against the Army. The Anglo settlers anxiously cheered the soldiers and swore that life and property needed protecting.

They camped for the night, tired and longing for escape from the ringing valley-held memories of the fighting.

In the morning they marched on, and saw far down the plains the white opulence of the heat above the yellow ground.

Richard wondered if the cattle thieving were still going on.

How excellent! he thought, if it was. We'll all go and hunt them, and kill them.

He was loaded and aching with the ugliest and most hurtful things to do and want.

In the summer of 1884 everybody who knew him said that he was one of the handsomest young men they'd ever seen, and one of the strangest.

THE FUTURE

It was a sense he often had, that he was going to live again; and that life always had richer desires and grander pardons in it than any he could imagine as having existed before his time, or in his own experience.

In 1894 he was married; and it was his wife who always meant grace and comfort to him, and seconded his professional career with the seasonal rightnesses of family life. Through his children he was going to live again; he was going to the future in them. They grew and departed, and he was shocked at how often he forgot them.

Then the future was a long and simple old age with his wife; but it was so ordered that she died and left him a prospect of a fifth of his life, the last one, alone. What had wiving done for her? Something remarkable in the way of supplying a vehicle, so to speak, for the essence of goodness. Her beauty had changed but never vanished. Her modesty had deepened into the recognition of experience as life had used her. All that had only enriched her soul and sweetened her claim on life.

[465]

When she died and left him the future, he knew again that the past never died.

It was like his own body, to wear and exist in; never gone, exacting demands from him. If the past was Maria, in 1884 in a forgotten event of a hot dead summer in a remote Southwestern valley, then the future was surely in the image of his wife? The goodness man always aspires to? The dearest peace of sanction for man's every want and act?

THE PRESENT AGAIN

Colonel Fielding went every morning for the next week to the Court House lawn, and sat among the acrid leaves as they curled to the ground through the Novembering air. Some of the children came each time; but the small Mary did not come back, though he asked for her every time. They told him that she was sick, at home. They were fascinated and enthusiastic, telling him about the doctor coming, and Mary's mother wringing her hands at him as she went to meet him in the broom-swept packed mud yard before the Melendez house in Chihuahua, where everybody's business belonged to the whole tin-canny neighborhood.

"Tshe's sick."

"Is she getting any better?"

"I theenk tshe's go'g to be all *right.*" . . .

He watched the children scratch around among the bitter leaves, their shell-like golden husks; and had his thoughts known as much as his heart, he would have said to himself,

"I am an old man, brooding upon children, the proper task of the aged. And I hunger for the recovery of one of them who is ill because in my mind there is some almost musical harmony between the need for this child to survive and the fact that in the mountains (which I can almost see down the street west of town here) a beautiful child not much older died fifty-one years ago by my agency, in line of duty. And was not that duty the larger one which put us together in life than the one which put us indifferently separate in death?"

CHRONOLOGY OF THE STORIES
IN THIS COLLECTION